THE CRACKLING SEA

GRYPHON INSURRECTION BOOK 6

K. VALE NAGLE

STET PUBLISHING

Cover art and map by Jeff Brown.

Interior artwork by Brenda Lyons.

Interior graphics by Crystal Gafford of Crafty as a Coyote.

Author portrait by Murphy Winter.

Published by STET Publishing, Denver

WWW.STETPUBLISHING.COM

WWW.KVALENAGLE.COM

10 9 8 7 6 5 4 3 2 1

Trade Paperback Edition
ISBN: 1-64392-036-7
ISBN-13: 978-1-64392-036-8

BELAMURIA

ALABASTER
EYRIE

REEVESPORT

CRESTFAL
PALACE

WHITEBEAK

DUCKBILL

ARGENT
HEIGHTS

ABYSSAL NAZE

NIGHTSKY

NEW
EYRIE

ALWREN

JADEBEAK
MOUNTAINS

EMERALD
JUNGLE

FLOW
OUTPO

SUNKEN
EYRIE

STORMTAIL

RAFTW

KING'S
REACH

SUBMERGED
FOREST

BLACKTALON

MOTHFEATHER
EYRIE

BLACKWING
EYRIE

PITOHUI
EYRIE

ASSWORKS

GLACIER
PRIDE

POISONMAW

CRACKLING
SEA EYRIE

REDWOOD VALLEY
EYRIE

KJARR
NESTS

TAIGA

WEALD

STRIX
PLATEAU

KJARR

LUMINAIRE

For Dr. Schofield and Chandra, without whom this book could not have been written.

THE SLEEPING CITY

A young Khalim soared over the fields outside Blacktalon, his dark plumage iridescent in the dying light of day. It had been a good summer for starberries, but the autumn crop of sugar beets would be harvested soon, and that meant days of processing them into a sweet, thick pulp. He'd promised to stay until the last of the fall crops were done, then he was off to the Blackwing Eyrie's university to become a scholar.

From the edge of the forest, another opinicus chirped to get his attention. He nearly missed her grey and black plumage against the rocks nearby. Wendl was a fast flyer, however, and soon caught up to him.

"Hey! Where are you flying to?" she asked.

"The university!" He laughed, the bell-like sound of a red-winged blackbird. "But not for a month yet. I'm just practicing for the flight. I hear the Blackwing Eyrie is several days away."

They landed next to the chill waters of a pond and stretched out on the rocks. The sky was starting to look more orange than blue.

"I went there once to visit family." Wendl's voice was the deep chirp of a poorwill. "It's about two days' flight from Mothfeather. You could break up the trip, visit a different eyrie each day. It'd be fun."

Khalim rifled through his harness pockets and found a few dried nuts and berries to share. Wendl had only moved here in the spring, but they'd become fast friends. There were even rumors of scandal, though that was just because opinici liked to talk. Khalim's heart had always been set on Vilessa. Like all mothfeathers, Wendl was keen on grooming and preening anyone she came across, which was probably where the rumors started.

"Thanks for the food. Tell your family they have the best berries." She gave him a hug, embracing him with her wings as well as her foretalons. "I need to head back. It's the equinox. My family will be looking for me."

"A little longer won't hurt." He knew autumn was a busy time, but it would be even busier once the beets were ready for harvesting. This was their last chance to chat before he left for the big eyrie.

She preened her neck feathers, a sign of anxiety he didn't share.

"Is everything okay?" he asked. They'd spent longer than he expected sunning on the rocks. Night was nearly upon them and, with it, the equinox celebration. He was supposed to meet Vilessa outside her farm soon.

"I'm fine. It's just—" Mid-sentence, Wendl fell over, unconscious.

"Wendl?" he prompted.

No response.

"Wendl, are you... are you okay?" He checked for a pulse. Faint but still there.

He sighed with relief. Not dead, at least. He looked around for any snakes or spiders that could have bitten her. Nothing. Maybe tick paralysis? He wished Vilessa were here. She'd know.

He pulled Wendl's body atop the rock to keep her out of the grass and was about to go for help when a voice called out from behind him.

"She's asleep." The voice had a touch of unhappiness to it.

Khalim leapt around. His fiancée stood by a tree, a scowl on her face.

"I know she's asleep, but I don't know what caused it," he said. "Help me bring her down to the medicine opinicus. If we walk, we can take turns carrying her. Wait, no, you go get help, and I'll carry her."

Vilessa didn't move. "Nothing's *wrong* with her. She's from Mothfeather."

His lack of understanding showed on his face.

"The Sleeping City?" she prompted.

He managed to get under Wendl and lift her. She weighed next to nothing. "I thought it was the Waking City?"

"Only until the equinox. Then it becomes, well, you see what it becomes." She padded over and helped stabilize Wendl.

Khalim finally understood. "They all... hibernate? For how long?"

"All winter. They close up the entire eyrie," Vilessa said. "Only a couple of trashbirds remain to keep it clean and take care of the scarabs."

"Pitohui," he said absentmindedly. By the glare she

gave him, she didn't appreciate the correction. Or Wendl's wing-hug, if Vilessa had been watching from the trees the entire time.

His nares flushed with embarrassment. As much as he enjoyed Wendl's company, she was just a strange new friend he'd made, and he didn't want the actual focus of his affections to feel jealous.

"Sorry, I was running late," he tried. "I didn't realize how the day had gotten away from me. I wanted to say goodbye to all of my friends, so we'll have these last few weeks together with just the two of us."

Now, it was her turn to flush red. Her nares turned the color of the markings on her shoulders. "I wasn't jealous. I just stopped by the pond for a drink and saw it was occupied."

"Well, I'm glad you arrived when you did," he said. "I would've worried myself sick otherwise."

Vilessa took over carrying Wendl for the last part. He'd seen large opinici modeled after birds of prey that could carry three times their weight and fly for short distances, but he could barely keep himself aloft after a hard day's work.

They were both breathing heavily by the time they arrived at Wendl's farm. Inside the main building, seven of her siblings were asleep in their nests. Only her parents were missing.

Finding Wendl's nest was easy. It was laced with cassia and smelled of cinnamon. Khalim and Vilessa tucked her in and went searching. The capybara pond was empty of opinici, though the large rodents were only just starting to settle down. It was risky to keep them this close to the red coast. One big storm could push the algae-laden water inland and kill the herd. In Khalim's opinion, they'd have done better to sell them before they moved here.

He and Vilessa continued their search and found Wendl's mom unconscious in the goliath bird stables.

"It's a good thing the birds were in their pens," his fiancée said. "I heard about a trash—er, *pitohui*—who fell and hit his head. A goliath bird tried to eat him and poisoned itself. Neither of their bodies were found for days."

"Sounds like a gryphon tale," Khalim said, but there was a peck mark on the sleeping opinicus's back foot. Hopefully, it'd heal while she hibernated.

They spread out and searched the grounds for Wendl's dad, flying circles around it. Unfortunately, everywhere there weren't crops there were rocks, and mothfeather plumage was the perfect camouflage.

"Over here!" Vilessa called out. She'd flown in wider and wider circles, hitting the nearby forest.

Wendl's father hung from the canopy. Only the thick vegetation and vines had kept him from falling to the ground.

They got to work untangling him, snipping the vines with their beaks one at a time, then gliding down together with his body. He had some nasty cuts, including one that gave Vilessa a scare as she wiped blood from his eye.

"It's okay," she said at last. "He had his eyes closed when he hit. The scratch is only on his eyelid."

"He's going to wake up with a nasty scar in the spring, but at least he'll wake up." It wasn't lost on Khalim that this was all his fault. If Wendl had made it back in time, her father wouldn't have been out searching for her. Khalim would find some way to make it up to them.

He was lucky Vilessa was an apprentice medicine opinicus. She patched Wendl's father up, then they carried him back to the nests.

"Are they going to be okay here?" Khalim asked. "Will they be safe, I mean? And what about the capys and goliaths?"

His fiancée finished applying an aneda wrap. "I'll check in on them tomorrow, and there are farmtalons staying at the ranch over the winter. They should arrive in the morning. I'll make sure the medicine opinicus in town gives the family a once over."

Khalim nodded. He hated to think he'd caused Wendl harm. But, in retrospect, she'd have been flying when she lost consciousness if he hadn't delayed her. In a roundabout way, he'd saved her life.

Though he doubted her father would see it that way.

Khalim fluttered up to the roof of the ranch with his fiancée. There were cushions and a table. The moth-feathers hadn't had time to put away the food before losing consciousness. They'd probably been too worried about Wendl and had forgotten.

He offered Vilessa a craneberry tart.

She gave him a look like he was a padfoot.

"Oh, come now," he protested. "Nobody else is here to eat them. They'll just attract pigeons. We should eat all we can and put away the rest."

She shook her head but popped the tart into her beak. "Oh! That's really sweet. It's not, well, *tart* at all."

"Well, if it's too much for you..." He tossed two in his beak. They were sweet but good. He thought he tasted orange and apple mixed in with the craneberries.

"No, no, I can handle it." She grabbed the rest and ran, laughing as she flew off the edge of the roof.

When she dropped one, he managed to dive under her and catch it. They flew around the empty ranch, a family of ten hibernating in the cellar, laughing and playing as stars filled the sky.

A chill in the air finally settled them back down on the cushions.

"I'm going to miss the sky here," he said. "And you! I'm going to miss you more than the stars themselves."

She preened craneberry juice from the feathers around his beak. "Well, that's good. I'd hate to think I'm going to spend all that time pining over you while you've run off with some *city* blackwing."

He laughed. "I have eyes only for you. And if you haven't run off with some *country* blackwing by the time I finish my studies, maybe we should make a nest of our own."

"What would the Pigeon Society think of that?" She feigned scandal but intertwined her talons with his. "I promise not to run off with any country or city blackwings."

He squeezed her talons.

"Though if one of those long-eared glacier gryphons comes through town, all bets are off." She winked.

"I suppose we all have our limits." He laughed. "Though I do find myself less inclined to share the last craneberry tart now."

"Well, if you really do have one, I promise to be loyal to the end! Not even death will keep us apart." She used her beak to search his harness pockets, coming up empty. "But if you just lied to me about tarts, I'm going to run off with two glacier gryphons!"

He nodded to the side, pointing his beak at an upside-down bowl on the table. She lifted it, revealing the last two tarts.

She chirped with delight, tossing hers into the air and catching it before giving the last one to him.

"I guess we're stuck with each other, then," he said.

"Mmmm, more like stuck to each other," she replied. "At least until we groom all this sugary filling out of our fur."

KHALIM LEFT his homestead to fly towards the Blackwing Eyrie. After years of study, all that was left was to be granted full scholar status, but the ceremony was held by the reeve's waterfalls. Wendl and Vilessa both saw him off. He'd stayed with Wendl's family until they went into hibernation, then he and Vilessa said their goodbyes privately.

Wendl had begun attending summer courses at Mothfeather Eyrie's university but had returned home to hibernate with her family. She said the feeling of sleeping next to a thousand other opinici creeped her out. She preferred the country.

Khalim and Vilessa had their own nest, but with the new hatchling and him gone most of the year, she traded off spending time with each of their families. Their mothers and siblings enjoyed watching the bundle of fluff when she had to go out and make the rounds. The old medicine opinicus had finally retired, handing her his old practice.

Next year, though, Khalim had promised to come home and live here for a while. Blacktalon had a group of scholars looking into the blood coast. He hoped to find a solution to the red blooms that killed capybaras and caused serious issues in opinici. He just needed a little more clout to get reassigned. He hoped his chick remembered who he was with all this time away.

Ahead, he saw the crater-like shape of the Mothfeather Eyrie. Somewhere in its catacombs slept an entire city. Up above, most of the shops were boarded up, but a nice pitohui couple ran an inn for travelers.

An arch led the way down into the depths. Glyphs had been carved along its edge, and chimes of Crestfall glass glistened and sang in the breeze. While the pitohui were allowed to tend to travelers and handle the scarab infestation, the Blackwing Eyrie kept a small force here to protect the way into the caverns.

Due to sleeping away a third of the year, the mothfeather opinici couldn't afford to make enemies with their closest eyrie neighbors.

Khalim flew on the next morning, continuing his journey east. The largest mountain on the continent loomed to the south, housing the glacier pride, which had finally been permitted membership into the Blackwing Alliance. Forests and farms stretched to the northern shores, where several coastal eyries and another gryphon pride petitioned to join.

He followed the edge of the mountains, crossing them to reach the terraced city and waterfalls of the Blackwing Eyrie. When he landed, he could tell something was amiss. The university's headmaster waited for him in his small quarters.

"Hello, hello!" the blackwing headmaster said, dark

of plume with red on his shoulders. He wore a harness with rubies set into it. Each gem represented another academic accomplishment, with larger gems signifying important contributions to Blackwing Eyrie scholarship. "Congratulations on your pending academic honors. I hear you have your sights set on Blacktalon. Is that right?"

"Yes, Headmaster," Khalim said. "My mate and chick are out that way, along with our family farms and my grandmother's ranch. It would be nice to live near them."

The headmaster nodded sagely, showing off a few greying feathers atop his head in the process. "Ah, yes, your mate is a rural doctor of some sort, is that right? The chick should grow up smart."

"Well, we hope so," Khalim said. "But the important thing is he's happy with whatever he chooses to do. There's a lot of joy to be had growing starberries."

"Juicy things, starberries. A bit sweet for my taste," the headmaster replied. "It's not common for new scholars to be given their choice of posts, especially not one as close to the front lines as Blacktalon. Trouble is brewing, you know."

Khalim's heart fell into his stomach. If he stayed away for years, there was a good chance his mate really would find a glacier gryphon to run off with. And there was no chance of forming a close bond with his child.

"However, I think I can help speed things up for you. I'm nothing if not magnanimous." The headmaster gestured towards an opinicus in a gold and blue harness across the hallway distracted by a mural of Crestfall glass. "Our colleague comes to us from the south. He's in need of an assistant. The research portion will last all winter, but what he really needs is help putting together an expedition for the, shall we say, practical portion of his experiments."

Khalim's first thought at seeing the stranger was of an argent hawk. But when he turned and Khalim could see his face and talons, he realized he was wrong. This was a peregrine falcon with most of the color drained from his plumage, his talons and beak the color of blood.

"Don't stare," the headmaster chided, though the other opinicus remained oblivious that they were talking about him.

Khalim shook his head. "I'm sorry, it's just, shouldn't he be dead? That's bloodbeak, isn't it? I've never seen the disorder progress so far without killing the patient."

Vilessa had told him of a talonful of cases, and they all ended the same way: dead adolescents. There was some sort of pretreatment—effective only on eggs—that had come out of an obscure eyrie in the south, perhaps the same one the stranger hailed from, but it was still expensive. Only families that had already lost one chick to bloodbeak would spend the beads to have their future eggs treated. Every new parent feared the worst, and Khalim and Vilessa were no exception. She checked their son's eyes and talons every month.

"He's the most brilliant alchemist on the continent," the headmaster said. "His elixirs have kept him alive, but they haven't cured him. You're to help him find that cure. If you can do that, you'll be allowed any posting you want."

Khalim stared at the stranger. There was a spark in his bright blue eyes. Hope? Intelligence? Khalim didn't know.

"I'll do it," he said. Vilessa would forgive him anything if it provided a cure to the iron disorder. "A winter of research and a spring and summer of field work?"

The headmaster clasped his shoulder in approval. "Yes, that's right. He'll need help putting together the team. You have your pick of apprentices, whomever you believe is best."

Spring and summer field work, Khalim mused. That worked perfectly with whom he had in mind. "May I bring in some apprentices from Mothfeather University?"

"Of course," the headmaster replied. "Whatever you feel is best. I suppose our sleeping colleagues will be awake by then."

Things were already starting to look up for Khalim.

The headmaster guided Khalim towards the stranger. "Now, would you allow me to introduce Scholar Mally?"

The foreign opinicus bowed his head the slightest amount, taking note of Khalim's travel harness. "I hear you're going to be managing the scholars and apprentices for me. Are you really the best choice?"

Khalim had forgotten to change out of his old apprentice harness, but he didn't let that deter him. "I am. Are you really the best chemist of our age?"

"I'd be dead if I wasn't." Mally grinned and held up his blood-red talons for Khalim to see before turning to the headmaster. "My last apprentice had just the same type of attitude. Good opinicus, extremely loyal and willing to go to impossible and terrible lengths to make my life easier. I appreciate those qualities from my help. This one will do nicely."

"Well then, I'll leave you two to it." The headmaster disappeared into the university.

Mally pulled a tome off the shelf and put it at Khalim's feet. *Nachlass Mal* was scratched onto the cover. "We'll meet tomorrow evening after dinner to begin. You'll find that I'm much more active at night. I need you to have read the book by then. Is that a problem?"

"Not at all." Khalim picked up the hefty tome. *Nachlass Mal* was a strange title. Had Mally named it after himself? The binding said Redwood Valley, but *Nachlass* suggested it had never been published through the university down there.

Khalim had a lot of questions, but they were left unanswered. The promise of getting any post he wanted was too important for him to inquire too closely. And if the headmaster was to be believed, he'd even get to bring his best friend along for the ride. Wendl would be excited to find out what was in store for them.

Wendl screamed at Khalim to take the elixir. The walls were stained with blood. The shivering forms of apprentices, their blackwing feathers molted and dark green starling plumage forcing its way through, whimpered in the corners.

Only he and Wendl were left. She forced a vial of purple salts into his talons. She shouted at him, but the entire world sounded like it came through a waterfall. He couldn't make out her words, only her tone and intent.

He stared down at his black talons. They were soaked red, nearly as red as the Nighthaunt's. The body of a white opinicus blossomed crimson at his feet as blood spread out from the wound on his neck.

Wendl pointed to the starling in the corner, the vats of boiling blood, the last of the purple salts Mally had left behind.

She only stopped her verbal assault when he accepted the vial. She drank and pulled herself into a vat. The smell of cooked fowl filled the room, drowning out the blood for a few moments as it had with the other apprentices. Her kind, brown eyes changed. Her feathers, her beautiful grey and black plumage, floated to the top of the bloody mixture.

Khalim looked down at the body in front of him. There was no going back home now. With Mally's betrayal, all his apprentices would be executed as traitors. No one would believe they were innocent. It was a stigma that would pass on to his mate and son.

There was only one path left for him.

As Wendl looked on in horror, Khalim tore the Seraph King badge off the opinicus at his feet. He took a bite of the cooling flesh and pulled the body into the last vat, downing the elixir between bites.

His young body burned, but he refused to stop. He drank until he threw up. Then he drank again. Only once his feathers had come in white and the chittering of the starlings filled the camp did he pull himself out and flee into the Emerald Jungle, still clutching a badge that read: *Piprik*.

1

THE CRACKLING SEA

In her dreams, a young Satra trembled at the edge of a long, low table. Gryphon blood, the blood of her pride, felt caked on her beak despite her constant grooming. She wiped at it, but the iron smell wouldn't go away. Every room in the Crackling Sea Eyrie smelled like the workshop to her.

She still had the last hints of her adolescent plumage, and the table loomed larger than it had in life. At the other end of it, tossing small fish down his long beak with ease, was Jonas. Not Reeve Jonas, not Reeve's Consort Jonas, not Ranger Lord Jonas—he insisted everyone refer to him only by his first name.

Laying couchant around the table were a dozen opinici, mostly captains. There were two empty spots. One was for the old ranger lord. Word had come that he'd succumbed to his wounds this morning. The other spot was reserved for a captain named Grenkin. He'd lost an eye and nearly a foreleg, but he was stable now.

Satra forced herself to stop whimpering. She looked at the food on the table, careful not to make eye contact with any of the opinici. She couldn't stop thinking about her family and friends, about her father and sisters, about Thenca and Urious.

"You haven't eaten anything." Jonas stared at her.

She flinched. "Thank you, but I ate this morning."

"That's not what Ellore says." He speared another fish on a talon, peeling it off with his beak and tossing it down his gullet. "She says you haven't eaten in days."

Memory in dreams was a fuzzy thing. Satra didn't know if Ellore had been present. If so, Satra hadn't known the blue opinicus's name, hadn't known she was Mignet's mother.

And yet, in the dream, Ellore stood in place of the usual ranger who haunted Satra's memory. Ellore: tall, thin, and rosetted. Was there a touch of silver around her eyes, hinting at what was to come? Her badge looked worn, the veneer showing a darker design underneath.

"Her food bowl hasn't been touched in so long, it's started to mold," Ellore said.

Jonas watched young Satra. The look in his eyes was of concern. Its sincerity either real or practiced. "Satra, you have to eat. I've raised half a dozen children in my years. I know gryphon culture says you're an adult, but I can still see the same rebellion and moodiness within you that my own stepdaughters had as adolescents."

Satra remained silent, judging whether it was safer to respond or better to keep her beak clenched shut.

"You need to eat, or you'll waste away." He tossed a fish towards her with a well-practiced arc, landing it on the edge of the table. "There are a lot of gryphons depending on you."

Satra reached for the fish, paw trembling, but her

stomach turned, and she couldn't stand the thought of eating food given to her by an opinicus.

Jonas watched Satra closely but directed his words to Ellore, "Are the gryphlets doing well?"

"Yes, Jonas." Ellore's voice held a hint of fear in it, too, that Satra hadn't noticed before.

He used a talon to swirl the small bowl where the fish were held. "Have any fledged?"

"No, Jonas. Not yet." Ellore's posture, like many of the rangers, stiffened. Fledging had been the determiner for who kept their wings in the kjarr and bog prides—at least, that's the story he'd told. It was a promise Satra had never trusted.

Jonas, however, had another idea in mind. "Go fetch the eldest."

Ellore bowed her head and went next door.

"Satra, you're my charge," the leader of the Crackling Sea continued. "When I'm done with you and the fledglings, you'll be full members of the eyrie. I will teach you to read. I will teach you to write. I will teach you manners and unlock a safe future for all of you. *But only if you'll let me.* I hope you understand this is for your own good. I've dealt with unruly children before, but I lack the patience of my better years."

Ellore returned, holding a scruffed gryphlet. The kjarr gryphlet's down had darkened, and she would probably be the first to fledge in another year and a half, maybe two.

"Satra, eat your food." His voice wasn't that of a leader but of a concerned parent. This was, most likely, how he'd spoken to his stepchildren, the ones killed by Rybalt Reevesbane.

Satra reached for the fish. She knew something

terrible awaited her if she didn't eat it. But her throat remained true to her morals, closing itself off. Her paw hovered above the food, unable to touch it.

"Toss the gryphlet over the balcony," Jonas said. "And continue tossing them over until Satra eats or we run out of kjarr children."

Disbelief froze Satra in place as the first child was thrown over the ledge. Her father had given her one command: *Protect the gryphlets at all cost.*

She dashed to the edge, slipped over the side. The gryphlet was already a story below her.

The child spread her paws and wings the way she would if she'd fallen off a tree. Gryphlets were resilient, but what awaited her at the end of her descent wasn't solid ground. Rocky spires broke through the Crackling Sea's surface. Sailfin monitors lazed along the shore, chasing prey through the surf.

Satra's mind screamed for her to open her wings to slow her descent. Only her promise to her father kept them closed. She streamlined her body, holding her paws and legs close, and gained on the falling gryphlet.

The skies were cloudy, but the storm curtains had yet to be lowered. She passed by shops, homes, and craftsopinici as she fell. Just when she was certain they'd both hit the water, she grabbed the child with her forepaws and beat her wings.

Despite her best attempts, her back paws and tail were caught by a wave. Sailfins, attracted to her wild flapping, swam towards her. She got just enough lift to catch the ledge of the bottom floor of the eyrie, pulling herself up.

Shadows enveloped the depths of the lower levels. The opinici didn't believe in wasting braziers on gryphons. Yet there was movement in the dark, hundreds of wingtorn writhing in pain and infection.

Satra saw mask markings and, for the briefest moment, thought Urious or Thenca had come to help. Instead, the mask grew long and thick as the wingtorn stepped forwards, and she saw it was another bog gryphon, one who'd often fought with her father.

Black Mask peered out at Satra and the gryphlet. The scars on his back were fresh. Satra wanted to shout at him, to explain she was doing the best she could, wanted to cry, wanted them to say it was okay she still had her wings.

Instead, she scruffed the gryphlet, pushed off with all four paws, and flew upwards. Jonas's threat wasn't idle. Ellore was probably already fetching another gryphlet to toss off the edge if Satra didn't eat her dinner.

Satra awoke to the sound of two egrets fighting over a fish. The sour, salty mist left a bad taste in her mouth. She wandered the eyrie to shake away the memory. Ever since finding Jonas's smell in the old reeve's quarters, she relived her first year at the Crackling Sea in her dreams. He was out there, somewhere. The only question was whether he'd come for the kjarr pride or the Blackwing Eyrie first. Was he more upset at the opinici who had sent assassins to kill his mate and stepchildren or the gryphons who had overthrown his eyrie?

Despite the bright sunlight, a constant shower fell upon the sea. Without lightning to lure the crackling jellies to the surface, the water looked peaceful. On the thought of deadly things that looked serene, Satra turned her attention to the shrine behind her.

Once Jonas's workshop, later the site of Bario's explosive capture and eventual escape, the room Satra sat in now had become a shrine. The stone table where wingtorn had once been tied down had been transformed into an altar. Someone skilled with a chisel had filled the wall behind it with stone renditions of all the wings lost in this room, framed around a pair of gilded wings.

Wings surrounded by wings. The small channels that once carried blood to the ledge and down into the water had been filled in with red metal.

She didn't know if it was in bad taste. The wingtorn had been consulted and, for the most part, approved. Satra was a lone dissenting voice. Since she had her wings, she deferred to Urious and Thenca's judgement.

The old secret passage she'd used to enter the Crackling Sea, the one Bario had destroyed, remained sealed. Merin's pride had left paw prints on the brick to remember their fallen.

She still thought of them as Merin's pride, but after their leader's death, the harpy eagle gryphons had joined the feathermanes. The maned gryphons had been unable to select a successor after the death of Zrim Feathermane and were happy enough to accept Merin's appointed successors, the co-consorts Askel and Triddle, as their new leaders. It was rumored the harpy eagle gryphons and feathermanes had once been a single pride before the Connixation.

The old medicine gryphon, never really accepted as a temporary leader by the other feathermanes, had stepped down, turning her attention to providing treatment for the sick and elderly. *Feathermane* seemed to be a bit of a strange name for a pride now ruled by two gryphons without manes. Askel had suggested the Tailtuft Pride but bowed to Triddle's recommendation they retain the name Feathermane in honor of Zrim.

It's hard to believe the giant, muscular gryphons of those two prides would honor Merin's final words, but the same thing that makes all opinici wary of Askel is what makes the feathermanes love him: He's blown up two eyries.

Satra turned away from the shrine and moved to the ledge, where a circlet and a pair of metal talons awaited her. She padded over and touched the circlet. It was carved of stone and set into the floor. She remembered the design of this particular headwear. A Reeve's Guard captain had tossed it off the edge when he surrendered the eyrie to her. Supposedly, that poor opinicus had gone straight from guarding Reeve Brevin to trying to hold the Crackling Sea Eyrie from the Ashen Weald. She wondered where he was now, if he'd survived the wounds Zeph had given him.

The metal talons next to the circlet belonged to someone she knew even better.

"They're not my actual prosthetics," Grenkin called from below. "The artist took some liberties."

She looked over the edge. One story down, the leader of the Crackling Sea waved up at her.

"I hope you don't mind," she said. "I've been admiring your work while I wait for Soft Paws and Biski to finish their brew."

He flew up to meet her, leaving behind several heron opinici who looked upon the gryphons in their eyrie with distrust. "When a caravan of sand gryphons arrived with a red metal too soft to use for weapons, some of the wingtorn gryphons and sea opinici suggested we put it to use. They want to make sure what happened here isn't forgotten."

Satra nodded. She couldn't imagine a wingtorn forgetting the loss of their wings, but she appreciated Grenkin's attempt to forge the red and blue opinici into a force for good. Part of that meant ensuring they never forgot how easily they were once led astray.

"And how're those efforts going?" she asked.

He led her away from the rain and through the paths to the main balconies and amphitheater. "Overall, pretty well. I've kept an eye on the Jonas loyalists you let go. They act strangely sometimes, but there's nothing I can quite put my talons on. They certainly don't like the gryphons being here, but I think if we give it time, they'll come over to our side."

Keep an eye *out. Put his* talons *on.*

Grenkin had the grim sense of humor of a ranger still. It had just taken her a year to experience it. He only made subtle references to his lost eye and talons around gryphons and opinici he considered friends.

The center of the Crackling Sea Eyrie was open balconies, and Satra was surprised to see a large number of wingtorn walking through the markets and exploring.

"They don't go into the lower levels," Grenkin said. The lower levels were where Jonas had kept the wingtorn here locked up. "Those have all been converted to storage. But Urious insisted all wingtorn know the layout of the city in case they were ever called upon to defend it. We've had the architects adding tunnels, corridors, and ramps to make it more wingtorn-friendly."

Satra and Grenkin made their way through the open market. Most of the vendors seemed reputable, but a splotchy blue one had a display of pink feathers she was selling, claiming they'd come from the leader of the taiga pride when he'd reclaimed the kjarr nesting grounds.

Judging by the number of feathers sold, for that to be true, Younce must molt once a week.

Satra itched just thinking about it. "I don't know how I feel about the deception."

"Not deception, just souvenirs," Grenkin protested. "Everyone wants to feel close to the heroes who saved them. As soon as someone figures out a golden feather paint, I suspect we'll see a lot of crests in your honor among the fledglings."

She sighed. She was grateful for the sounds of happy gryphons and opinici, but the war wasn't over yet. At best, this was a reprieve, and they weren't ready for what the white king or blackwing reeve would throw at them next.

Confirming Grenkin's suspicions, several young bog witches flew by with gold on their crests. It wasn't quite the same shade as Satra's flamecrest, but the paint merchants were getting close.

She shot a disapproving glance at a sandy fisherfolk selling feather dye. The fisherfolk just winked at Satra, then had her taiga assistant spread his wings, revealing several of his primaries had been dyed bright pink.

"A shame they didn't choose to idolize Zeph and turn parrot hunting into the next great trend," the ex-ranger lord commented. "Then our larders would be full."

Satra took the northern path out of the market.

"That could have turned out worse. At least this way, the parrots have a chance of repopulating the weald before the giant salamanders get them all."

Satra and Grenkin reached the butchery, where Soft Paws and Biski were busy overseeing the creation of a paste not meant to be eaten. Instead, this was the mixture Satra would dip her paws in and use to mark the new border with the starlings. An unhappy chef looked on as they got goo over all his cooking pots, and Biski's taiga apprentice seemed to be at his wit's end with her chirped commands.

"Kjarr Satra." Soft Paws bowed. She'd been brought in specifically because the bog witches specialized in marking things with paste, as her skull and flower make-up attested to. "I apologize, but I have been unable to keep Biski clean."

Biski, on the cusp of adulthood when the Redwood Valley Eyrie burned down, had grown an impressive mane in the time since. No amount of paste markings could hide the mismatched gryphon: She had the feathers of a bluejay and spotted orange fur.

"How're your paws doing?" the colorful medicine gryphon asked.

Satra settled on her back paws and rubbed her forepaws together. Part of the mixture required her scent, so the past few days had been spent massaging the glands on her paws.

"Sore," she admitted, "but I'm starting to get feeling back. How long until we're ready? Erlock and Nighteyes said they'd meet us outside New Eyrie tomorrow morning."

The starlings suffered a peculiar quirk of biology called green wing altruism. Rather than altruism in the traditional, selfless sense of the word, it meant they suffered a violent reaction when other gryphons or opinici were around, and they needed to be in constant contact with their pride. That same sense of altruism had kept infected starlings from turning on each other, instead creating the rabid horde that had caused so many problems last year.

Because of the altruism's dangerous influence, messages were traded back and forth via a cave by the Jadebeak Waterfall. The best way to deal with starlings was not to be around them at all. Failing that, however, there were two elixirs one could take. Starlings could temporarily suppress their biology with something Wendl, a sort of nearly-starling opinicus, had concocted.

And it appeared the weald once had a mixture that allowed their kind to speak to starlings without being torn apart, though the free pride scholars were still trying to work out the recipe. Most of the ingredients the old medicine gryphons would have used had burned in the weald fire.

Nighteyes, purple leader of the Nightsky starling pride, was on loan to the Ashen Weald until the new territory glyphs were up. Judging by how ragged she looked having now been away from her pride for months, she was past ready to return home.

"Do you think this'll work?" Grenkin asked. "I can't imagine the starlings we fought at New Eyrie stopping for anything, let alone some decorative paw print."

"I can't speak for the infected, but this has worked against healthy starlings for generations," the bog witch said. "Only when Jun the Kjarr's scent faded did the starlings invade."

Jun's decision to salt the fields and kill wildlife to starve out the Crackling Sea opinici had cost the kjarr pride all their medicine gryphons. His daughter often wondered how many legends and medicines had been lost the day the crones abandoned him.

We're lucky Soft Paws knew how to make the paste. I hate to think what knowledge the old crones took with them to the grave.

Biski tried to groom the mixture out of her plumage without success. She finally wiped her mane on her long-eared apprentice's fluffy grey flank when he wasn't watching. "We'll be done here very soon. You should find something to eat, then head to New Eyrie. You don't want Erlock getting nervous. She forgets to take care of herself when she's anxious."

When did Biski and Erlock grow so close?

Satra said her goodbyes but decided she'd eat at her destination. She rarely strayed so far from the kjarr, and it would be a good opportunity to get to know New Eyrie's inhabitants better.

She set out into the rain-shine but flew a circle before she continued west. The stone domiciles of the Crackling Sea opinici now housed many of their Redwood Valley cousins, turning a section of the cliffs into a dancing tapestry of red and blue neighbors. The areas where the stormcloth barrier could be secured were guarded by teams of fantails and opinici. Wingtorn crawled through the upper levels. And atop the cliffs, set back a bit, was a bazaar of gryphons and opinici trading wares in the rain.

Outside, several taiga gryphons huddled under a tree, their thick coats drenched through. They made a stark contrast with the fluffy sandgrouse gryphons who danced in the rain, soaking it up into their voluminous coats.

There was a lie some of the Jonas loyalists spoke about how, a decade ago, the world was a much better place. They talked about times where food was plentiful, where the university was at its height, about aqueducts, about peace. And, for a select group of opinici, that was true. They'd had it well. Perhaps even for most opinici, life was better before the wars, before the Blackwing Eyrie's first failed invasion.

But back then, gryphons and opinici were neighbors who didn't get along. It was as though several different societies existed in the same space, hostile yet ignorant of each other. There was a lot of heartache and pain that happened during that time and in the wars after, but when Satra looked down at the Ashen Weald and free prides travelling to an eyrie to enjoy themselves, she saw the shape of a better world in the making.

SATRA'S FLIGHT stayed north of the Clover Ranch. Ever since finding the bloodied rags and wingsaw in the reeve-consort chambers at the Crackling Sea, she'd tried to avoid areas that had meant a lot to Jonas. She hadn't known him while his mate, the blue reeve, lived, but she'd often heard his stories while locked up, had been *required* to hear them.

The Clover Ranch was one of Jonas's favorite places. It was where he'd made his fortune as a trader. It was where he'd met the blue reeve, fallen in love, and eventually been made consort. When that happened, he'd given the ranch to all the opinici who'd worked it under him, which presented a new problem.

Those same ranchers, now freed from their cells after Merin's death and the dissolution of his secret cave prison, demanded the ranch back. By all rights, they should have it. But it had been run by wingtorn and reds for months now. It served as the start of a ranger-guarded trade route that stretched from the sea to the Flower to the raftworks to Bogwash.

It was, to put it bluntly, the exact spot where Satra did not want Jonas's most loyal opinici in charge. As much as she didn't approve of Merin's methods for rooting out corruption, she also didn't trust anyone who had served loyally under Jonas for years.

She tried to put politics and leadership from her mind while she flew. The responsibilities were heavy, but individual pride leaders had stepped up to lighten her burden. In another year or two, she could concentrate on the kjarr pride and let the Ashen Weald run itself. Perhaps she would even step down as Kjarr.

Along the seacoast, she passed over several destroyed docks and fishing pavilions. In one section, the sawgrass and salt marsh had a large, snake-like indentation to it where the reeve's pet had crawled out of the water to knock down a watch roost.

At first, she assumed it was an isolated incident. But the farther she flew, the more she realized no building stood on the coast for miles. Something had upset the monster, and it made life hard for the opinici who lived along the sea.

She'd tried to put Grenkin in charge of solving the problem, but he had just laughed and joked he would put out a call for *monster hunters*. Of course, that was exactly what they needed. The catch was the massive serpentine whale loved to hide in swarms of the toxic crackling jellies, making it hard to see from the sky, let alone get close to.

Satra slowed as she approached New Eyrie. The docks here still stood, but it was only a matter of time before the reeve's pet went after something as large a coastal eyrie. As much as it could slither and claw along the ground, she couldn't imagine it scaling the rocky cliffs of the Crackling Sea Eyrie, which meant New Eyrie was in trouble.

She chirped a greeting to the patrol, and two fantails changed course to escort her down.

Satra was surprised at the cheers that greeted her. There was a time—more than one time, in fact—when she would have considered herself the most wanted enemy of this fishing village with eyrie aspirations.

Between the invasions, sea monster, and everything else, most of the civilians had left the village behind for the Crackling Sea Eyrie's cliffs and stormcloth. It had only taken the burning of two eyries, the attack of a horde of starlings, and being kidnapped for use in Mally's experiments to convince them they were better off as members of the Ashen Weald.

In the wake of the last war, New Eyrie had become more of a military outpost. Though the rangers stationed here still did a lot of fishing, as the current feast being offered to her in the Reeve's Nest building attested to.

Mia, Kia's sister and veteran of the conflicts at Sandpiper's Dune and the bog, arrived shortly after to dine, flanked by Henders and a pale parrot opinicus with a red beak and talons.

Satra stood and greeted the newcomer first. His resemblance to both Kia and Mia was obvious, though his white and crimson markings stood out. If she looked closely, she could just see hints of his old blue plumage fading away as his disease progressed. "Olan, I don't think we've met before. I'm glad you were reunited with your sisters."

When Olan bowed, there was a slight tremble in his talons that worried her. While she was grateful to have more opinici return home, especially ones with a newfound sense of Ashen Weald loyalty after being betrayed by the Seraph King, she worried for those Mally had given his iron disorder to. They didn't have access to the same treatments here, and a couple of the sicker opinici had passed away. All anyone seemed to know was Mally had been draining the blood from those he infected, though whether that was meant to help them or further his research, no one knew.

"Thank you for taking us back in." Olan bowed. "And Mia says you had something to do with finding my parents a nice nest across the water? I'm grateful."

"That was all Foultner." Satra looked around. "Where is the infamous ex-poacher?"

"Searching for Blinky." Henders brought out more food than they'd be able to eat. "Our owl friend is supposed to be your bodyguard while you're in the bog, but she's been aloof lately, so we were worried."

Satra laughed, then realized she was in a room of all opinici. "She's found a mate, Henders. Last year at this time, it was all conflict. This year, things are looking up. She probably just found someone she likes."

Henders looked surprised. "But Blinky never spends time with anyone except Foultner and me. Where'd she meet another gryphon? All she does is sleep and snack. Surely, we'd have seen her spending time with someone before now?"

Satra settled in to eat, not bothering to point out that Blinky could have found an opinicus mate. The meal was impressive: spiked knife fish with rimu olives, water with pumpkin leaf, and salted goliath bird. The Redwood Valley opinici had mostly fruit and vegetables. While it would be a kindness and a lie to say the crops grown along the sea weren't salty, it was true they were *less salty* than the previous year. Flooding the fields was working.

While Henders launched into a story about freshwater sharks to Olan, Satra took a moment to check in with Mia.

"How're things going here?" the Kjarr asked. "How're you liking the ranger lord role?"

Mia tossed what she thought was a starberry into her mouth, then made a face that suggested it was actually a rimu olive. "It's uneventful. My main worry is we can't defend this place. It was designed to hold back wingtorn. The walls won't do much against the Seraph King. And if the reeve's pet comes calling, we're going to lose all our fishing rafts even if we manage to kill it."

"What's your plan when the northern eyries show their talons?" Satra kept a tufted ear out for military matters but plans changed daily. The feathermanes and fantails had a proven track record of just flying in and attacking anything that came close. The kjarr and bog prides wanted hit-and-run tactics. The fisherfolk fought best over water from high up. The taiga prides suggested hiding in caves, then coming out to attack only during blizzards.

Perhaps Hoppy and Sponge, the sand gryphon pride leader and his champion, had the most original idea. They weren't big on waiting and defense, so they suggested the Ashen Weald should be running teams of thieves who would sneak into other eyries and steal everything while no one would expect it.

If you eat their food, they can't eat their food. Understand? Hoppy had explained to her on her last trip to the desert.

In the end, the current defensive plan was a combination of all those things.

2

BLACK MASK

"Cut off his wings." The voice was calm, clinical, and disinterested.

Black Mask fought against his restraints. He was still groggy from the jelly toxin. Ahead of him, one of the bog wingtorn was being escorted away. His vision was blurry, so it took his mind a moment to realize that the gryphon was being escorted in one direction while her wings went in another. An opinicus tossed them off the edge of the cliffs into the Crackling Sea.

Several rangers tied him to the altar. He threw up his last meal, carrots and fish guts, and one of the rangers swore and kicked him.

"It's just the medication. There's no need to take it personally." The disinterested voice had returned. A Crackling Sea opinicus with an unusually rounded tip to his beak walked into view. It took Black Mask a moment to recall his name.

Jonas.

The reeve-consort offered Black Mask a bowl of water, but the gryphon refused. He'd bent the knee to

Jun the Kjarr, and then the Crackling Sea opinici, but if he ever got free, he'd never again bow to anyone.

Jonas shrugged and walked away, talking to another opinicus holding a metal instrument that glistened in the light. "Careful to disinfect it thoroughly. We've lost too many kjarr already. We don't have enough medicine to keep them whole."

I'm not kjarr. I'm bog. Black Mask felt something rise within him, a contempt for both the blue opinici and the kjarr pride. He struggled against his bonds, but more rangers came and tightened the bindings.

Jonas sat down on a makeshift throne in the corner of the workshop. He dipped a softened talon into ink, a thin groove cut into it to direct the ink to the tip of his talon, and sketched figures and numbers while he watched Black Mask.

The opinicus holding the metal tool came closer, and Black Mask could see it was a saw. He struggled against the bindings, but the opinicus stretched Black Mask's wings wide and made marks on where to cut.

Black Mask awoke with a scream. It was pitch black, and he was surrounded by the earth. He tried to struggle, but he couldn't move. Someone was holding him down. He could feel her paws pressing against his stomach, pressing against a set of old scars.

Her owl face came into view with three long slashes across it. He shouted again, but she made cooing noises until he realized he was awake.

His paws were sweaty and his breath rapid, but he forced his body to relax.

"You are okay," Blinky repeated. "The sun is up soon. You are in a hunting den overlooking the Heart of the Bog. Can you feel the breeze on your face? The entrance is in front of you. Can you smell the spike palm outside? It is raining softly."

He continued breathing. He made the trek out here every other week to spend a few days with her under the pretense of scouting for starlings.

She licked his tears. "Too much salt. I should not have shared my fish bar with you."

His mind recentered. He wasn't in Jonas's workshop on the Crackling Sea. His wings were long gone. He'd learned to live without them.

"Here, food. I caught a minnow." Blinky dragged a river shark in from next to the spike palm. Her common had improved since they'd first met, but she still insisted on calling all fish minnows. She even said there was one particular minnow she was after in the lowlands, one that had betrayed her on her first trip into the bog.

"Thank you." He took a few bites and felt better. "I'm sorry you have to see me like this. The nightmares are fewer and less often."

She didn't reply. It was a lie he often told, but they'd been together long enough for her to know this was a common occurrence. And if she was still guarding the kjarr nesting grounds at night, she'd probably heard similar outbursts from the wingtorn there.

In a way, he envied Bogwash. It had become a city of bog gryphons without wingtorn until recently, which meant it spent a brief time as a bog city without nightmares. Many of the remaining bog wingtorn felt as he did—Bogwash stood a better chance without them there. And something resentful and vainglorious kept him from bowing to any Kjarr, especially not a Kjarr who had befriended the blue opinici.

Blinky groomed his feathers while he ate. "I did not

hear her say this myself, but Mia says Ellore believed that the rangers have a code. They do not leave behind other rangers. Mia says Ellore tried to help a ranger who was hurt not in body but in his mind. She said rangers do not leave behind the wounded, whether body or soul."

"She was talking about herself." Black Mask knew of Ellore, knew of the rangers from both his days as a rebel and from his brief time in the Ashen Weald when they'd freed him. "Her fur is taiga, and the Crackling Sea Eyrie left her and the other opinici with gryphon fur patterns behind when it abandoned them to the nesting grounds."

Blinky paused the way she did when she searched for the right words. "Something can be about more than one thing. *Leaving behind* can mean many things at the same time. You are wounded. I am not leaving you behind. You are not just wounded. You are also whole. You need to see your new wholeness."

She repeated her message in owlish.

He tried to remember the new words. It was slow going, but he was starting to pick up the basics of the owl pride's old language. "I don't know how to get better. I don't know how to heal from this wound."

She pushed the shark towards him again. "Eat. Talk. Love. It is working for other wingtorn. Forgive."

"I can't forgive." He pushed the shark away and stretched his legs, moving aside the spike palm to see the morning sun. "All of us abandoned here in the forgotten depths of the bog share that in common. It's a burning hate. A wound that needs to be excised."

She watched him, and he could feel her judgement.

He shook his head. "I know, not Satra. I know,

Grenkin is trying to make amends. I don't share the crone's hatred anymore. But without a focus, without a target, I can't let it go. I need something to sink my beak and claws into."

She cleaned her feathers in the misty air. It was a sign she was leaving soon.

"There's still time," he said. "You could find someone new before mating season begins in earnest. I'm never going to be able to go past the Jadebeak River to see your nest and pride. I'm never going to be able to walk among the Ashen Weald."

She looked at him. "I do not need you there to raise an egg. That is what the den mother is for. I do not mind the nightmares. But do not forget there is more to life."

"I'll try." He thought of the Crackling Sea's old reeve-consort, of the saw. "I'd just give anything to have been there when Jonas burned alive, to know he's really dead."

Blinky finished her grooming. "I am late. Satra will pass through here soon. Make sure it is safe."

While the lone surviving crone seethed, Black Mask was the only thing keeping the last of the rebel bog pride together and functional. It was a simple thing to divert their patrols to let Satra and Blinky come through, so long as they were fast.

"Your Kjarr will be safe," he said. "I promise."

Blinky stretched her wings and paws, then did a little wiggle to make sure her feathers and hips were all moving the right way.

He stifled a laugh, knowing she was careful not to do her preparatory dance in front of Foultner or anyone she worked with.

Grooming and wiggling out of the way, Blinky seemed to be in working order and ready to fly back north. She looked him in the eyes, the light catching the scars across her face. "Jonas did not burn in the valley. I have smelled him. He is alive. When I find him, I will send word. If the other wingtorn feel the same, be ready. You will get your chance soon."

She left him, flying north to cross the Jadebeak River on her way to New Eyrie.

Black Mask froze, nonplussed by the revelation, until the morning sun warmed his hide. His thoughts, always so scattered, found a new focus.

Jonas is alive.

The wingtorn's scars were tight from sleeping in a hole in the ground instead of a warm nest. He found a small pouch of supplies in the back of the den and carried them in his beak to a pond. With the occasional drop of water upsetting his reflection, he put ointment on his scars. Even the ones on his back ached, and he regretted not asking for her help with them.

Once that was done, he found the blossom paste. The bog rebels had started mixing blood in, giving it a violet color instead of the light blue they'd once worn. To help compensate for the loss in camouflage, they'd allowed the invasive bee plants to spread, filling their section of the bog with purple flowers to help conceal them.

He dipped his beak and painted his sides. He'd heard the expedition call the markings of his pride *wingtorn flames*, referring to them as bog wisps. It was strange how the same design could look different to two gryphons based on their culture.

He finished filling in all the intricate designs in violet, then waited for the water in the pond to settle.

Where the kjarr pride saw long flames, he saw violet wings.

He climbed a tree and surveyed the Heart of the Bog. In the distance, he caught sight of a sparkle of emerald as several starlings tried to sneak into their territory to steal bog blossoms to treat their infected.

He let out the well-practiced sound of a coastal bird. The exact same sound came from the other side of the sinkhole, echoing across their small hunting grounds.

This was the signal for the last of the rebel bog pride to prowl the cypress forest, closing in on the group of jadebeak starlings from all directions.

3

THE NIGHT SKY

Nighteyes looked down at the orange mixture she'd taken every day for months. It made her head fuzzy and her stomach nauseated until after she'd eaten. She'd been feeling more and more disconnected, and she suspected this elixir was the reason why.

She dipped a claw into the bowl of orange, idly tracing the emblem of the Nightsky Pride in it. Outside, she could hear Erlock talking to a group of gryphons and opinici—Satra's escort. Nighteyes had promised to make sure the territory glyphs were right before going home, but her entire body cried out at the thought of eating the paste even one more time.

The sun came into the strange opinicus tent where she'd made her nest. Opinici didn't care for being rained on. She hadn't really thought of opinici and gryphons as being any different before coming out here. In the Emerald Jungle, the few opinici like Wendl had all adopted starling customs and settled down. But seeing the opinici out here, they had a different culture than their gryphon allies.

"Hey Nighty, you okay in there?" Foultner poked her head into the tent.

It was as though someone had thrown a rock at a swarm of bees inside Nighteyes's brain, like a bog crawler had leapt on her face. Her claws extended on their own, and her beak chattered, anticipating a bite.

She quickly downed the orange mixture. "I need a little longer."

"Sure, no problem." Foultner's eyes were on the starling's extended claws. "Seems like it's taking longer each day to work. You'll be home soon."

Nighteyes was careful not to look outside the tent as the chemicals took effect. The sense of panic was replaced by a feeling of overwhelming loneliness. She hadn't realized until now how much she needed to be around her pride. Not even the faint star pattern on Erlock's feathers helped replenish Nighteyes's need. Erlock may be descended from starlings, but she didn't *smell* like part of the swarm.

Outside the tent came Foultner's voice again, "Blinky! Where've you been? I was looking for you."

"Mating," the owl gryphon replied. "Where is Satra? You did not lose her?"

The nest sparrow opinicus and owl gryphon continued their friendly banter. The most Foultner got out of Blinky was that her mate was a gryphon. Similarly, Foultner continued to hide Satra's location to annoy her owl friend.

Nighteyes's beak stopped chattering. With great force of will, she retracted her claws. She'd hoped to spend this mating season with a stormtail who kept swimming in the rivers around the Nightsky nesting grounds. It was a long way to travel just to annoy her pride. She'd been chasing him off all summer, but she suspected the reason he kept returning was so she'd remember him when autumn came. Had he found someone new? Or was he still swimming the rivers around her pride, waiting for her?

Outside her tent, she heard the arrival of Satra.

"Hey, the great Kjarr finally made it here." Foultner was one of the few opinici who could speak to the Ashen Weald's leader like that. "Stayed at New Eyrie so you didn't have to sleep in the marsh nests, eh? Too good to get pinched on the tail by a crab the size of a coconut? Staying out here builds character."

"You have too much character. It overflows out of your beak." Blinky slow-blinked.

"Henders sent breakfast along for both of you," Satra the Kjarr said. "He thought you might be hungry. Based on how cranky you two are, I don't think you've eaten."

"I had minnow," Blinky said.

"You've gotta eat more than that," Foultner scoffed. "Don't you want to keep your strength up for... What did you say your mate's name is again?"

"Minnow," Blinky repeated.

Foultner shook her head. "There is no gryphon named Minnow."

While they ate outside, Erlock slipped into the tent holding a basket in her thick beak. Her long tail-feathers trailed out of the entrance. "Here darling, you need to eat something with the paste, or you'll just throw it up."

Nighteyes forced herself to eat. Cooked crab was easier than eating raw meat, and Foultner's portrayal of what the Ashen Weald's hideouts in the marsh were like was accurate. Nighteyes had a few crab pinches on her tail and was happy to taste revenge.

She looked over Erlock. The fantail called everyone darling, it was just her way. On the starling side of the Jadebeak Mountains, Nighteyes had thought the fantail anxious and ineffective. There was something about the gryphons with only distant starling heritage that made the pure starlings disregard them, and Nighteyes hated that about herself.

Since spending months here, she'd come to realize that Erlock was both a strong fighter and a capable leader. Her pride looked up to her. The Seraph King's forces she'd fought over the summer had feared her. She was, in some aspects, a better leader than Nighteyes herself.

That thought bothered the violet starling. There was a chance when she returned home, she'd return to the kind of hive-mindedness that all starlings shared. She didn't want that, but she couldn't keep taking Wendl's strange orange mixture. It had worn her down to nothing.

"Thank you for the food, Erlock Chartail." Nighteyes finished up and began her late morning preening with help from the fantail.

Erlock's answer to the prolonged effects of Wendl's elixir had been to talk to the weald medicine gryphons and figure out the elixir Merin's eldest child had used to enter starling lands without triggering green wing altruism—a term Nighteyes had only learned from Erlock herself. That had been a perfect plan until they'd discovered that the key ingredient was yolkbloom, a yellow and white flower that grew on vines in the southern weald—the part of the weald that forest fires had consumed. There was a good chance they'd regrow, but for now, Erlock had ordered everyone to leave the vines alone until they recovered next year.

"Are you okay?" Erlock asked. "You don't seem okay."

Nighteyes took a deep breath. "The sooner I get back to the Emerald Jungle, the sooner I'll be okay. Let's go."

NIGHTEYES SNIFFED the trees along the Jadebeak Mountains northwest of New Eyrie. She was careful to keep them south of the Argent Heights, pausing when she came upon the crossed feather glyph of the silver reeve.

"Here," she told Satra. "I can smell the old Kjarr on this tree."

The current Kjarr sniffed the tree. "I don't smell my father. I don't smell much of anything except broadleaf. I can't even see the glyph."

Nighteyes was sympathetic. "It's there. I can't describe the scent, but I can feel it."

Memories and scents of loved ones faded over time. It was the way of things. She'd replaced her mother as pride leader, and she, too, had taken this journey to replace her mother's territory glyphs.

While Satra's owl and fantail bodyguards kept watch, Nighteyes climbed a spiketrunk to catch a squirrel. The furry rodent had grown bold, assuming that none of the gryphons on the eastern side of the Jadebeak Mountains would be willing to pursue it through the spikes.

She snapped it up with a well-placed paw and

tossed it down to her friends to snack on, then found a thick frond to perch atop. Jun the Kjarr's scent had been more of a primal reaction in some part of her brain, but the argent reeve's scent was clearer, and the Jadebeak glyphs stank like a four-day-old monitor corpse. The Jadebeak Pride had been trying to overcome the faded kjarr scent markers—had, in fact, succeeded in doing so —allowing them to send small hunting groups into the bog.

Satra pulled her paw away, and her scent, mixed with the marking paint, flooded Nighteyes's senses.

"It's good," the starling called down. "It will fade in time, but you should have three years before you need to renew it. Let's head south."

Erlock, Blinky, Satra, and a small force of Ashen Weald rangers and gryphons followed Nighteyes along the edge of the mountains. They stopped several times to take notes on the locations of caves or springs.

Nighteyes found it amusing the bog and weald gryphons still called these hills the Jadebeak Mountains when they didn't know who the Jadebeak Pride was. When had the word traveled east? Had the jadebeaks once traded with the bog pride? She'd have to ask Wendl. The jadebeaks wouldn't answer the questions of a nightsky starling, but Wendl had a way of getting prides to talk about themselves.

The Ashen Weald troop continued south, marking trees every so many miles. At Nighteyes's insistence, Biski and Soft Paws made the paste concentrated. It was good to send a strong signal when renewing territory markers.

"Does the rain weaken the glyphs?" Satra asked. One of her paws was stained with black and gold paste.

The shape of the glyph mattered less than the scent associated with it, and she'd chosen a new design that better matched her own plumage.

Nighteyes sniffed her to make sure the smell was right. "Not much. Otherwise, how could they mark the stormtail nests?"

"Does anything remove it?" Satra shook her paw.

Nighteyes considered. "Bark beetles. They don't usually come so far south, but one year, they chewed up the glyphs between the naze and heights. One of our fledglings almost made it to the plains before we caught her. The gryphons of the abyss and the opinici of the heights don't like to risk coming near each other, so they're sloppy with marking their borders."

One of the rangers was scribbling down everything she said, and Nighteyes realized she should be more careful about what information she shared. Having a friendly border wasn't the same as having an ally. The pridelord had made it clear non-starlings weren't welcome in the jungle.

They resumed their trek-and-mark cycle and neared the Jadebeak Falls when Nighteyes realized something was off.

Or, rather, something was on. The slight buzzing in her head she felt when she was away from other starlings was gone. She was calm and alert for the first time in months.

She breathed a sigh of relief.

"You look like you're feeling better," Erlock said. "Is it being close to home?"

Nighteyes perked her ears up. "In a manner of speaking. There are starlings nearby."

The Ashen Weald rangers readied their nets and talons.

Nighteyes motioned to Blinky with her beak. "Is your eyesight good in the day? Do you see the spiketrunk in the distance? I need to know how close the jadebeaks are to it."

Blinky cooed a reply and crawled through the mesh of cypress and hanging moss to get a closer look. She stopped just before the trees grew thick and pulled down some thorny vines and leaves. She kneaded them to a pulp and mixed in root sap and rolled in it. She looked ridiculous, but her scent had vanished.

While the owl gryphon proved her stealthiness, Nighteyes sniffed the air. She'd lost the scent of the last glyph. The smell of jadebeak, dry mint with a hint of thyme, was overwhelming along here, covering up any whiff of Jun the Kjarr.

A soft cooing noise came back through the cypress trees, and Erlock translated. "Blinky cooed four times, so there're twenty starlings. The delay between the coos means they're far away."

"You speak owlish?" Nighteyes asked.

Erlock shook her head. "Nobody speaks owlish except the owls. You just work out a code of sorts for the bog."

Nighteyes sniffed Satra again. With any luck, she'd function as a movable glyph. If she could mark the spiketrunk, it'd fix this border. Assuming her scent and what it meant had been spread among all the starling prides. Assuming these jadebeaks had been back to their nesting grounds to learn the new scent.

That was a lot of assumptions.

"What's the plan?" Satra asked. "Head back a bit and

find a place to spend the night until they go away, then mark it?"

The buzzing in Nighteyes's brain softened further. The starlings were closer than they had been minutes ago. "No, they're planning to raid the bog. They probably got word the northern glyphs have been secured and want to stockpile pumpkins and blossoms before you close the border down here, too."

Erlock groomed her feathers the way she did before a fight. "We can force our way through them."

"And kill starlings even as we try to renew a kind of peace?" Satra asked. "We'd do better to spend a few days waiting. Let them take what they need and return to the jungle."

"You want to know if your scent is working, right?" Nighteyes asked. "Twenty starlings aren't too many to fight with nets and sea-poison. Send the Kjarr to the tree to mark it. The paste on her paws should protect her until she finishes. Once the glyph is set, the starlings won't be able to cross it. We stay back and see."

Erlock stretched her wings. "I'm coming with her. I'm half starling, they won't attack me."

Nighteyes wasn't so sure. Half-starlings sometimes came to the Emerald Jungle to seek their heritage, but they didn't stay. Nighteyes didn't want to hurt Erlock's feelings, so she instead said, "No, we need to know Satra's scent is strong enough to do this on its own. The owl is watching from nearby if something goes wrong."

Satra put a paw on Erlock's shoulder. "I'm pretty good at running away. This'll be simple. Just stay out of sight so the starlings don't swarm, right?"

"Sure," Erlock grumbled. "Easy."

4

SATRA THE KJARR

S atra dipped her left forepaw into the mixture, then used her other three paws to push off into the air. A flew flaps got her moving in the direction of the spiketrunk. It wasn't lost on her that all the trees she'd marked had been emerald broadleafs or spiketrunks located on the wrong side of the mountains. She'd have to ask Nighteyes if the type of tree was important.

Somewhere below her, Blinky waited in hiding. Satra knew better than to try to locate the owl gryphon. She'd eluded bog witches, infected starlings, and Satra's older sister in the past. Finding her was a fool's errand. Instead, Satra kept her eyes on the starlings.

Blinky's cooing suggested twenty, but Satra saw only five. They were relaxed, grooming their ears and whiskers, chatting amongst themselves. One playfully swatted at another. They were gryphons like any other.

Then the one who'd been swatted saw Satra, and his posture tensed. He flung himself into the air, flying straight at her without any regard for his pridemates. He flew like a flechette towards his target, nearly catching her before she landed and put her paw print on the spiketrunk.

The starling recoiled at the scent. Whether there was some component on the tree, or he just hadn't smelled Satra before getting this close, she didn't know. He let out a loud hiss but stayed back.

His friends joined him, both those she'd seen and others who'd been hidden in the foliage. Satra had nineteen hissing starlings, their eyes following her every move, keeping their distance. She took a step forwards; they took a step back. She moved to the south and found another tree to put a paw print on.

Better safe than sorry.

As best she could tell, they also avoided the second glyph.

Could I walk straight into the Emerald Jungle like this, or are there limits?

She stepped back, letting the glyph on the tree create distance between her and the starlings. The look in their eyes was of violence and loss. She wondered if they'd even remember this when she left.

She continued backing up, assuming Blinky had miscounted. From the rear of the starling pack, however, a face looked up from behind a branch. A starling opinicus, possibly Wendl, pointed to Satra, then at the sun. Satra nodded back. She assumed that meant to come back after dark, though Nighteyes could confirm it.

The starlings were still hissing from their side of the border when Satra disappeared from view. Once she was lost in the brush, Blinky materialized, shaking off an outfit made of moss.

"It is a strange thing to see." The owl gryphon pulled vines from between her paw pads. "They did not have the same reaction when a swamp grouse flew by. It is only gryphons who make them *al-tru-is-tic*."

Satra washed her paw off in a creek. "And opinici. Let's not forget them."

"We will set up camp north of the river." Blinky made a cooing noise to give their allies the all-clear. "We need Black Mask's permission to continue south. It is crone territory."

The sound of a mockingbird echoed through the bog, and Satra found herself feeling introspective. "If there were no other gryphons or opinici on the continent, would their altruism still trigger? Do they even realize it's happening?"

"Questions for the nightsky." Blinky shrugged. "If she wishes to answer them."

DESPITE ERLOCK'S WARNINGS, Nighteyes had crept close enough to witness Satra's exchange with the jadebeaks, though she stayed out of view. Even after the Kjarr had disappeared amongst the palm fronds and cypress, Nighteyes continued watching the other starlings.

What she saw disturbed her.

It took a few minutes after Satra finished putting up her paw prints and slipped away before the jadebeaks shook off whatever had come over them. They wandered back to where they'd been grooming and resumed their activities. The only starling unaffected was Wendl, who watched with a calm that made the whole scene feel even more surreal. She'd obviously gone through this at least a dozen times in the past, and she made no attempt to tell her companions what had just transpired.

Once the jadebeaks settled in, Nighteyes backed into the brush and returned to her Ashen Weald allies. She let the rangers set up camp and cook food. She needed to think on what she'd just seen. Her mind barely processed Blinky leaving to find some fish for dinner or Foultner getting a fire going.

Nighteyes spent hours lost in her thoughts, wondering how many times she'd disappeared into a fog of altruism, when a hooting sound marked the coming arrival of their nighttime guest. A few moments later, Wendl spilled out of the brush and into the camp.

"It's me, it's me!" the starling opinicus chirped. Her ears and fuzzy tail put the gryphons in the camp at ease while her taloned forelegs seemed to confuse rather than reassure the opinici in the camp who were unaware of the existence of opinical starlings. "Erlock, good to see you. Your beak still looks like it could split a log. Lean down so I can hug you. Nighteyes, your pride misses you. I guess there have been some scuffles with the jadebeaks about who owns the berry patch, and there's a stormtail fishing out of the river by your burrow, but your sisters have been keeping everything in order. They look forward to your return."

Nighteyes blinked her starry eyes. While the feeling of needing to be around other starlings was overwhelming, she hadn't put thought into any individual starling —except perhaps a spare thought for certain, stray stormtail. Her sisters hadn't entered her mind since she started taking the orange mixture, and she didn't know how she felt about that.

She cleared her head. She'd be home soon enough,

then this surreal dream would come to an end. "It's good to see you, Wendl. I'm just about ready to return. Let my pride know I'll be back soon, once the glyphs are finished. Tell the young ones I'll bring back new foods."

"Absolutely," Wendl said with a practiced slow blink. She searched through the large pockets of her scholar harness, patched many times since Nighteyes had first met her. "Kjarr Satra, the pridelord congratulates you on your alliance with the sand gryphons. He also sends these as a symbol of your pact with him."

Wendl unpacked a jade statue. Of the strange starling opinici who had come to the Emerald Jungle with her, one with talons instead of forepaws had been assigned to go through the collection of unearthed statues and modify them to resemble starlings. He worked non-stop, night and day, converting the relics of lost jungle eyries into starling treasure.

Whatever the statue had originally been, it was a starling now. A train of feathers, painted the colors of the different prides, hinted it had started as a jade peafowl. The tailfeathers were mostly greens but included Nightsky violet and Stormtail blue.

"Thank your leader for me," Satra said. "I'll make sure his gift is displayed in the kjarr nesting grounds."

"I'm surprised he was willing to part with such a nice statue." Nighteyes examined the piece. The pridelord must have held it in his paws, because it smelled of him—part afternoon thunderstorm, part citrus and spice. His scent calmed the anxiety in her brain but left it in a fog. He had that effect on all the starlings who visited his temple. The feeling was like the sun on a chill day, a full meal after having gone hungry, a nuzzle from a close friend or lover on a bad day.

Wendl stared at her. "How have you been holding up? I don't know of any starling who's been able to stay away from the jungle for so long. Is my mixture still holding true?"

Does Wendl need the mixture to cross the border? Nighteyes wondered. She didn't see any hints of orange on the opinicus's beak.

"No, I cannot stay much longer." The Nightsky Pride leader left it at that. She didn't wish to speak of starling matters in front of non-starlings. Erlock was only part starling. Having seen the way Wendl acted while the jadebeaks experienced their green wing altruism, Nighteyes wondered about her talon-footed friend.

"How are the glyphs holding?" Satra asked. "Can you tell if they're working from your side?"

Wendl nodded. "You're doing great. My friends continued north and didn't find any breaks in the scent. The only thing I'll offer is you should extend your northern borders a bit."

"Oh?" Satra's tail and ears were subdued. It was strange to see her acting like a pride leader after she'd spent the morning teasing Foultner and Blinky.

"I spoke with some of the elders," Wendl explained. "Seems the argent reeve has been putting her glyphs farther south every year since your father stopped marking. You should reclaim at least three glyphs higher."

A little ways off, Blinky dragged a fish her size into the camp, and Foultner got a fire going. They argued over the definition of *minnow*.

Satra cleaned an errant feather. "We were supposed to swing by Bogwash, but if you think it's important, we can head north after we finish with the Heart of the Bog."

"Bogwash is no fun when Soft Paws isn't there." Erlock helped clean the fish. "None of the other bog witches know how to have a good time. And I hear she invited Rorin down, and then went north, leaving Thenca to host him as a guest, which is... not a good situation to walk into."

"It'd be nice to see Thenca and Deracho," Foultner mused from the fire pit. "But the sooner we finish here, the sooner Nighteyes can return home. One last party to send you off, eh?"

Nighteyes nodded, but she was having trouble speaking. The calming presence of the pridelord made the world fade away. It was only after Wendl finished chatting—she was good at that—and Erlock had filled her in on how Piprik and Lei were doing that the starling opinicus insisted Nighteyes walk her back to the border.

"I'd like to see what kind of effect the glyph has on you," she explained. "If you have trouble crossing the border from this side, that's something we want to know."

Who is this 'we' Wendl speaks for?

Nighteyes allowed herself to be led away from the camp.

Once they were out of hearing, Wendl pulled her closer. "Something is going on up in the Argent Heights."

The nightsky starling shook her head a little to clear it, but the smell of citrus seemed lodged in her sinuses. "What do you mean?"

"The pridelord thinks it's nothing," Wendl said.

"He's not concerned. But past the glyphs, there's a lot of activity. We can't tell the Ashen Weald directly, but make sure Satra keeps marking glyphs north until she catches sight of what I mean. Got it?"

Most of Nighteyes wanted to decline the offer. If the pridelord didn't feel the Ashen Weald needed to know about what the Seraph King was up to, it was her duty as a pride leader to obey her lord. Yet perhaps his scent was wearing off or perhaps it was the orange mixture, but she sided with the small part of herself that didn't see any harm in moving a few glyphs.

"Sure, I'll do it," she said. "Can you meet me by the ruins of the old blackwing camp once I'm finished helping Satra? I have some questions for you before I return to my pride grounds."

Wendl nodded. "Would you rather I answer them now?"

"No." Nighteyes was adamant. "It can wait a little longer. But it needs to be before the orange paste wears off."

With that, she turned and left Wendl along the border. Her most important charge was making sure the Kjarr finished marking her territory. Everything else could wait a little longer.

5

BLACK HEART

Black Mask tried to see his pride's new home the way Blinky might—from the sky. It would be a mass of cypress, mangrove, and moss no different from the rest of the bog. Or so his imagination told him. It had been a long time since he'd seen the birds-eye view of anything, and just this simple thought exercise caused twinges in his back muscles.

The perspective from the ground was just as tangled and empty—the few uninfected starlings who made it past the sunken eyrie could wander the area for hours and never locate a single gryphon. In fact, several had, getting ambushed when they grew greedy in their plant-stealing efforts and stayed the night, thinking the bog abandoned.

Yet behind every spike palm was a scavenged turtle burrow housing a pawful of gryphons. Where the cypress could be persuaded to grow together, the few loyal bog witches had roosts. And where the palms created an impenetrable mass of green spikes, the nesting grounds hid.

Whoever was currently out of favor with the crone was left in charge of chewing down the spikes facing inwards. That had gone to Black Mask many times since he returned home. Saving Urious from falling to his death during the Battle for New Eyrie brought about endless punishments, never mind that White Stripe had done the same. For the moment, however, Black Mask was popular. Everyone was curious about the Ashen Weald, and he'd spent more time with them than anyone.

He crawled back home, pausing to listen every hundred gryphon lengths. Near the water, a group of sailfins made chuffing noises as they argued over a kill. Farther inland, he heard the sound of a giant matamata digging a nest. This one's eggs wouldn't hatch until spring, almost two hundred days later. He supposed they should be grateful the turtle was digging a new nest and not trying to reclaim one of the old dens now in use by the pride.

In the distance, wingtorn argued. He knew they were wingtorn because so few of the winged had chosen to stay when Soft Paws sang her siren song of stolen eggs and missing parents. Other than the crone, they had four witches remaining, and he knew each of their voices.

Black Mask let out a starling's chitter to see if the bickering wingtorn noticed, but there was no reply from the ground. Up high, in a cypress roost, a single eye peered out from behind a wing painted with violet flowers. The witch made the soft *oo-awk* of a shore bird, acknowledging she knew what he was up to and wouldn't give the game away.

A single eye meant this was Thistle. Where her

other eye, lost to a spike palm as a gryphlet, had healed shut, a starburst of green paint spread out, covering that side of her face. Like him, she'd decided to stay with the crone, had lost too much to the cause to change course now. Unlike him, she'd never shown any sign of second thoughts.

He crawled closer to the wingtorn den, imitating the meandering path of an infected starling looking for food. He let out another soft chitter to see if the arguing gryphons noticed.

This time, one wingtorn hushed the other. While Black Mask moved around to the side of the palm blocking the turtle den, he saw a de-spined branch get lowered and a beak poke out.

"I don't see anyone," the wingtorn whispered.

Black Mask swatted the beak, sending the wingtorn back inside with a yelp. The bruised wingtorn's friend leapt out to avenge him, seemingly startled *not* to find an army of infected outside.

Thistle cackled from her perch.

"Chitter, chitter," Black Mask drolled. "I could hear you two over the river. If I'd been a pack of starlings, you'd be dead by now."

The other wingtorn came out of his hiding place rubbing his beak. "That's not true. Thistle would have warned us."

The gryphon in question stretched her wings and glided down. "You won't always have a bog witch to protect you. Go check on the prisoners. Tell whoever is watching them to take over your post here."

The admonished wingtorn walked off in a huff, leaving Black Mask alone with the witch. There was something about the paint, the wings, and the way the crone treated her last four disciples that gave them authority well beyond their few years. Take away the skulls and flowers, and no one would listen to a gryphon so young.

"Prisoners?" He was careful to keep his voice casual. If they'd captured members of the Ashen Weald or fisherfolk, things could go poorly for all of them very quickly. Despite his wingtorn brethren's pathetic showing a moment ago, there was no stretch of the south so entrenched. The only way to root out the last of the deep bog pride was to dig it all up or burn it all down.

The fact Satra the Kjarr considered diplomacy and kindness an option showed wisdom their own crone lacked. Satra had found a way to bleed their numbers without sending anyone past the glyph markers. The crone and bog witches may complain about the deserters, but in his heart, Black Mask was glad. Ever since they stepped down this path of war with the Ashen Weald, he hadn't seen a way out that didn't end in burning trees and bloodshed. Now, given enough time, he believed he would witness the collapse of his pride. In fact, if something happened to the crone, he didn't think they'd last a full cycle of the moon.

"Starlings." Thistle paused to clean up the lines on his bog wisp paint before continuing their walk.

Black Mask relaxed. Not Ashen Weald, then.

She led him through the hidden paths towards the tangle of trees that formed the new nests. "Caught 'em coming from the mangroves. I guess they thought our territory ended with the cypress."

"Why bother to keep the jade, er, pests?" He narrowly avoided calling them jadebeaks. He'd have a hard time explaining where he'd learned the names of the starling prides without revealing his owl gryphon mate.

Thistle shrugged. "The crone willed it. She has plans for them."

He kept his beak shut for the rest of the journey. You couldn't reason with a starling. You couldn't even really keep jailors around them. They'd go into a frenzy, biting and clawing at their enclosure until their hearts gave out. The best his pride could do was hide them away, stay out of sight, and bring them food every so often. It felt like a waste—not to mention how hard it was to find food that didn't carry the parasite. If the prisoners became infected, they were no good to anyone.

He walked straight towards a wall of spines, careful to look down so as not to lose an eye. Just when it looked like he was about to become shrike food, he slipped into a tunnel that went under the foliage barrier and into the nesting grounds.

BLACK MASK and Thistle came through the underground passage dirtier but unimpaled. There was little light this deep—illumination would mean that a sharp-eyed gryphon or opinicus might catch sight of them from above. He finished cleaning his fur and neck ruff, then helped Thistle with her wings. She purred a sisterly thanks.

The hidden grove was shaped like a starfish. It was a strange happenstance of how the trees had grown, not a product of bog pride cultivation. Each of the legs of the starfish were different lengths. The thickest *limb* was farthest from the entrance and housed the crone while the smaller limbs were divided among the wingtorn.

The leader of the deep bog pride sat atop her nest mixing violet paste, the same mixture Black Mask was currently painted with. Her nest was adorned with the bones of dead starlings and Crackling Sea opinici. Their skulls hung from branches and decorated the walls. Several had been labeled with the names of her enemies—Urious, Thenca, Satra, Soft Paws. Not even the dead were exempt from her hatred, as names like Jun, Jonas, and Strix exemplified. Whatever the owl gryphon leader had done, she'd never said.

Not that Jonas is actually dead... yet.

In Black Mask's mind, bones made for poor bedding material, but he'd always been hard to impress. He favored the mossy bed he shared with Blinky by the Jadebeak River. It was soft on his back scars.

"Thistle," the bog pride leader crooned. The crone treated all the remaining bog witches like they were her daughters. "How does this moon find you?"

"Well, Bog Mother. Blessed," Thistle added. The witches who had remained all shared the mask-like markings common to bog gryphons—those with kjarr colors had followed Soft Paws's treacherous whispers and fled—so it was possible Thistle really was related to the crone. There was no way of knowing.

These stolen children had been lied to their entire lives, and to Black Mask, the way the crone spoke to them was just one more manipulation. If only they'd been alive to see how she'd treated her own children.

That was something he'd seen firstpaw. "And how is the moon treating you, Bog *Mother*?"

She insisted her only remaining child use her new

title, but he chose where he put the emphasis. She didn't bristle anymore. She'd written him off long ago. If she died, as her only living confirmed relative, he should take over the pride. In truth, if the wingtorn didn't side with him, one of her protégé witches would take over. Unless he could convince them to make amends with their Bogwash sister pride.

Or kill them.

He slow blinked at Thistle, who returned his affection even though she didn't understand where it came from. He was pretty certain she had her heart set on someone else, so he didn't feel bad. He liked Thistle as a friend, but he acted this way mostly to annoy his mother, who wanted to maintain the pretense that he and Thistle were possibly siblings.

"I ache, same as every moon," the crone interrupted. "Thistle, be a sweet fish and fetch more blossom paste, would you?"

The one-eyed witch slipped across the nesting grounds, stopping by the enclosure in the center to play with the gryphlets.

"You stay away from her, Black Mask," the crone commanded.

He stood still. "Of course."

Agreeing with the crone just annoyed her more. "She already has someone."

"I'd never get in the way of true love." He kept his tone neutral. He'd been raised by the old bog den mother. The only time the gryphon who'd hatched him acted motherly was when she needed something.

The crone softened a little. "I can help you find someone. A wingtorn. That would be easiest, yes?"

He suppressed a laugh. The problem with someone

having a strong, singular vision was that it meant everyone around them seemed out of focus. The crone no longer knew what her pride wanted or needed. "I'm fine. I always find someone."

"Do you?" The crone had already gone back to her mixing and kneading. She'd had nearly every tree marked. It was a feeble attempt to hold on to a small stretch of bog, and he saw it for what it was.

"Some of the jungle squirrels came across with the starlings and started chewing on our markers by the mountains," he lied. "Mind if I take some? I'm headed out that way to refresh the glyphs and hunt down the squirrels."

She made a non-committal sound, and when her back was turned, he grabbed some of the paste made by one of her apprentices. It lacked the crone's scent but kept the pride's vibrant coloring, so it should work for Satra's purposes. Most of the glyphs his pride put up weren't scented, as no one here knew that the right scent could keep the starlings away. And since no one went into the mountains to check the glyphs, none of his pride should notice they smelled like the kjarr.

And if they do, they'll just assume it's more Ashen Weald trickery.

He said his goodbyes, practically purring his gratitude to Thistle, and slipped out of the spike palm hideaway. He should have been at the northern deep bog border by now, and Blinky hated when he was late.

6

BLACK VOICE

Satra and Blinky waited atop a lost broadleaf tree marked with the faded paw print of Jun the Kjarr. They'd mark this tree tomorrow, on their way back, rather than give the deep bog gryphons a hint she was here.

Satra scratched at her scalp. For this last stretch of their pilgrimage, Foultner had insisted on coloring Satra's crest black.

There's no sense in making it obvious who you are if someone spots you, the poacher had said. Satra finally caved, and even now, she resisted the urge to groom her head feathers.

"You are *rustling*," Blinky hissed. "Stop it. He will be here soon."

Satra stood as still as her nature allowed. It was another hour in the heat before her ears tingled. Months of sitting in meetings with owl gryphons had given her a second sense for when they were speaking. She couldn't make out the words, couldn't have understood them if she could make them out, but the furred tufts on the ends of her ears tickled.

Blinky's eyes picked up the slight motion. "He does not know how to speak lower than he can hear, so he is loud. I am sorry. I am teaching him as best I can."

Satra hid her surprise. It seemed odd that Blinky would teach anyone owlish, but a rogue wingtorn? That was stranger still.

Blinky opened her mouth, but this time, there was no tickle on Satra's ear tufts. The owl gryphon kept her mouth open a while, and just when Satra thought she could hear something, Blinky said, "Ah, there we go. He heard that one. We may descend."

Satra followed her bodyguard down the tree. Gliding would have been faster, but the sight of something the size of a gryphon flying in this section of the bog was as likely to attract rogue bog gryphons as it was jadebeak starlings.

At the base of the tree was Blinky's contact. Several stolen ranger harnesses in various states of disrepair had been secured around him, and the long, poisonous spines of the spike palm had been woven into them. Nothing would attempt to catch him from above. Violet paint, both skulls and flames, covered his body and armor.

Black Mask nodded slightly. He didn't use her Kjarr title when addressing her. "Pride Leader Satra."

"Black Mask." She didn't know if she should lower her head or not. A Kjarr shouldn't, but she felt the weight of the harm her family had caused the bog gryphons. "Urious sends his regards. He hopes you're well."

The rogue wingtorn froze. "I'm glad he's still alive. We should go. Blinky, I'll return Satra after nightfall."

The owl gryphon did not blink. "I am going with you. I have a disguise."

"We're not using thorn vine to mask our scents anymore," he countered. "The bitter scent will make you stand out."

Blinky held his gaze for several heartbeats before conceding. "Fine. But you should not call her Satra in case anyone overhears you. She needs a new name. Something innocuous."

"Tresh?" Satra ventured.

Blinky tilted her head to the side in disappointment.

"Believe me, we *all* remember that name after last year," he said. "What's another name you'll remember?"

Satra's heart ached when she spoke it, but the words still came out of her beak. "Mignet."

"Fine." He gave her a quick look over. In addition to dyeing her crest, Foultner had insisted Satra not wear her harness or bracers. "Come along, Mignet. We need to hurry."

Blinky returned to her tree post, and Satra followed one of the gryphons responsible for plotting her overthrow as he led her into enemy territory.

Satra had been informed she wasn't to ask Black Mask about the remaining rogue bog pride. She was to let him lead the way and the conversation. Which was difficult, because she really wanted to know how Blinky had saved his life.

In the end, her curiosity didn't make it to the first

marker. "Our mutual owl friend said she saved your life. Just how did she do that?"

He seemed to have anticipated her question. "She took her claws out of my chest and stomach, gave me aneda resin and food, and left me alive."

Satra, well, blinked. With surprise.

In response to her skepticism, he rose. While his back was toxic plant quills, only a couple of straps obscured his stomach and chest. And, true to his story, there did seem to be several scars that matched the pattern of owl paws.

"That's... not what I was expecting," Satra admitted. "Honestly, I assumed she'd saved you from some starlings and you two had fallen in love and were now mated."

"We are," Black Mask said as he led her towards an emerald-leafed tree. "Love is strange, at times. Each season is different, each pride has their own customs."

Satra gave a wide berth to exposed kashow roots covered in leafcutter ants. "I've never tried to murder someone, then asked if they wanted to spend the winter with me."

"That's not what they say about you, *Mignet*," he countered. When he saw her hurt expression, he amended an apology. "I'm sorry. I didn't mean that. There's a bitterness that doesn't leave me so long as I'm in the bog. I can't seem to shake it. I'm the same way with family; it's not just you."

She considered her words. "You can just leave, you know. Come north. Join a free pride if you don't want to be around the Ashen Weald. Find a nice nest with Blinky for the season by the plateau. There are paw paths across the taiga, weald, and plateau now. What's holding you here?"

"I believe if I stay, there's a higher chance things will end peacefully," was all he'd say.

She didn't know how that worked, but she trusted Blinky's judgement. If the owl gryphon saw something in Black Mask, maybe he had his part to play.

They reached the first tree to mark, and he rifled through his armor and pulled out several wrapped leaves. Inside was a paste wet with bog blossom and blood.

She pulled back. "That's not starling blood, is it?"

"No, of course not." He looked unsure. "It smells like sailfin. I figured Soft Paws had made you some in black or gold, but if my pride sees those colors here, they'll know something is up. Violet will blend in. You'll need to press your paw to release your scent. You know how to do that, right?"

She waved a paw at him. "Soft Paws showed me. My feet are still numb, so it'll take a few moments."

"We should have the time." Several minutes later, however, Black Mask changed his assessment. "Mignet, get behind the tree. *Now.*"

She obeyed without question, hiding on the starling side of the wide trunk. To her surprise, he joined her. They climbed high enough to look down, obscured from view by a parasitic palm that had taken root in the broadleaf's branches.

Black Mask whispered to himself in different voices, which Satra tried to identify. An old bog witch, perhaps the crone. He shook his head. A younger, feminine voice with a bog accent. He settled on that one

He climbed up a few more branches, still out of

sight, and shouted down, "You two, why aren't you watching the prisoner?"

Two wingtorn jumped.

"Thistle, is that you?" one asked. "I thought you were guarding the river side."

"I'm running an errand for the crone." The voice coming out of Black Mask must have been convincing, because both wingtorn turned and headed back the way they'd come.

"Sorry," Black Mask's real voice came to her. "I'm supposed to be up north, so I couldn't use my own voice. They're both too afraid of Thistle to confront her about this later."

Satra went back to kneading the red paste. "I see. I didn't realize bog voices worked on bog gryphons."

He shrugged. "Sound is sound. If you aren't expecting to be deceived, you aren't listening for the wrong inflections."

It occurred to her that every word she spoke around him was a word he could take, form, and imitate as his own later. Blinky's warning about conversation may not have been a matter of her hiding her romantic involvement with the enemy. It could have been a subtle warning.

The bog pride's old name, the one her ancestors used before conquering them, translated to *word-thief*. Like bog witch or bog wisp, it was designed to turn the deep bog gryphons into myths and monsters.

Something she'd put a stop to was the kjarr gryphon habit of teaching their children stories of spirits in the bog. From her talks with Thenca and Soft Paws, Satra had come to see them for what they were—propaganda and justifications. Instead, she'd had Ari begin telling stories of infected starlings while she had Nighteyes tell a few stories of healthy starlings to help balance things out.

Black Mask sniffed. "That should be fine. I don't smell the blood as much. You saw the bog glyphs, yes? You need to imitate them."

She wanted to continue leaving her crossed feather glyphs along the border, but as the starlings clearly responded to just the smell, it was only her wounded ego at stake. She followed his guidelines and left a deep bog pride mark with her scent on the tree.

"Does the crone know the old recipe to talk to starlings?" Satra asked. "It just occurred to me that she could have worked out her own deal with the pridelord and saved me the trouble of coming down here."

Black Mask walked and talked. "I don't know what deal the Seraph King or Abyssal Naze struck along their borders, but the agreement here was between the pridelord and the current Kjarr. Had your sister's plan to become the new Kjarr worked, her glyphs would have decorated our border. But your assassins killed her."

Vitra, why didn't you come to me as a sister first? Satra didn't point out that technically, a fisherfolk had killed Vitra. Quess's spear had gone through Satra's sister on its way into Urious, who had only survived thanks to Tresh and Soft Paws' intervention.

None of Satra's siblings had paid her much mind as a fledgling. Nor had her father, really, up until the moment the taiga gryphons had accused her of murder.

"How many more?" Satra asked, changing the subject. The answer didn't reassure her.

"Ten." Black Mask rewrapped the remaining paste

and tucked it away, getting some on his beak. "Come, Mignet. We don't have long."

Mignet rubbed her sore paws. When she had to repeat this in three years, she'd break up the journey. She hadn't known she had scent glands in her paws a month ago, and now that was all anyone wanted to talk about. To do ten more glyphs, she'd have to figure out how to use the glands on her back paws, too.

As if that weren't enough, despite the sunny morning, storm clouds were coming down off the Jadebeak Mountains.

7

THE COAST IS CLEAR

"We need to be careful," Black Mask said. When Satra the Kjarr looked towards his pride's nesting grounds, he took her head in a paw and pushed it the other way, west.

"Starlings?" she asked. "Is the entire eastern border of the Emerald Jungle full of jadebeaks? I should have Nighteyes draw a map before she goes home."

He sniffed the air. "Starlings, yes. Jadebeaks, no. This lot is a deep blue with thick, flat, wide-feathered tails. When the drops of rain obscure the surface of the rivers, they swim through them, invisible."

"I've never heard of such a thing." She cast a suspicious glance at one of the many small streams cascading down from the mountains.

He reconsidered his path. If the river starlings showed up, it would be bad, though their appearance was unlikely. What *was* likely was that his pride would send the bog witches to watch the largest rivers.

Well, not the *largest river,* he amended. *The matamata guard the Jadebeak River for us.*

Would the Kjarr's scent deter the river gryphons? He didn't know. If they remained underwater the entire journey, they wouldn't smell the glyphs. Still, they were usually smart enough to stay away. Unlike the jade-beaks, whose numbers were relentless.

He took the gamble. "Come, into the mountains. We're more likely to be safe where the witches aren't standing vigil."

Satra nodded her assent. If she were afraid of being this deep into the bog, she didn't show it. He remembered her as a fledgling: impulsive, selfish, and timid. After the rumors of murder, she'd hardened, but that only tempered her impulsiveness.

When Foultner approached him in the depths of the Crackling Sea Eyrie and claimed Satra had brought an army to free him, Black Mask laughed. When Satra went on to lead the army against New Eyrie to save more bog gryphons, he'd remained skeptical.

Meeting her as an adult, he felt two very different sets of emotions. When he saw her wings, a bottomless well of resentment swelled up within him. But when he saw her confidence and the risks she'd taken to free him, he felt an accompanying guilt.

He never thought he'd forgive the kjarr pride. But with Blinky's help, his heart had grown enough that he felt bad he'd never be able to let go.

"This way, Mignet," he said. "We don't want anyone stumbling across you before you put up the last few glyphs."

SATRA'S PAWS alternated aching and numbness on her mountain trek. With Black Mask's help, they'd reached the ocean. The ground had given way during one of the summer storms, and she had to glide across a crevice to locate the dead spiketrunk that held her father's faded glyph. She flew back up to where her wingtorn guide hid under a leaf, but there was a problem with the last glyph location.

The final spiketrunk lay on its side in the sand, knocked over by one of the summer hurricanes.

"Do we mark the dead tree on the beach?" Black Mask asked. "It'll probably wash away next year, though."

While the lightning had quieted, the storm didn't show any signs of letting up. It was one of those grey days where the rain was ceaseless. If the bog was anything like her memories of the kjarr, the ocean-side had heavy storms all summer, but the real flooding was from the winter storms coming off the Crackling Sea.

"We could see where the closest starling glyph is and mark a tree next to it. Then get the one on the beach, too, for good measure. We have enough paste." She left him behind to fly up the mountains, careful to stay under the canopy, and sniffed until she located the starling marker. She found a blue glyph in the shape of a fern—a deep, ocean blue, not light like a bog blossom. It was a little jagged and didn't resemble any plant she knew of. It was an interesting change from the green triangle of the jadebeaks.

I suppose this is the river pride Black Mask told me about. What do they call themselves? The thunder fern pride? The electric sproutlings?

She moved to a spiketrunk east of the river pride

markings and chewed off the spines until she had a wide enough area to leave her glyph. Well, the bog glyph—with her scent on it.

Her wingtorn guide had gone to the cliffs to look down at the dead tree. When she joined him, she saw something break the water's surface between them and a small island just offshore.

"What was that?" she asked. "Some kind of whale or dugong?"

Since Kia, Zeph, and Cherine had been so instrumental in rallying the New Eyrie refugees and bringing the sand gryphon pride into the Ashen Weald, Satra had invited them all to spend time with her so she could offer Cherine a full pardon and apology. What she'd learned from having all three in the same room was they mostly argued about plants and animals.

Kia believed, based on the research she'd seen from Mally the Nighthaunt on what animals were not safe for pregnant opinici to eat, that manatees, dugongs, whales, and dolphins must be related to capybaras, squirrels, and bats. Her *aquatic bat* theory of serpentine whales was not one her ex-boyfriend seemed to share. Though his objection was mostly based upon his belief that bats were extinct.

Zeph's contribution had been entirely related to how they tasted and how many beads traders would give you for each.

The sea creatures Satra now saw were mostly submerged. The one closest to shore had blue fins and a pointed head barely visible beneath the water.

She tried to remember what she'd learned about ocean life. *Dugongs have flat tails, sharks have vertical tails... right?*

Except the creatures' tails she was seeing were evenly split between vertical and horizontal. And the more she looked at the blue tails, the more she saw their rudders as feathered and not scaled as she'd initially assumed. In fact, if she squinted, she could see how the river glyph she'd located might not be some sort of blue fern. It could be a heavy gryphon tail lined with thick feathers.

"Your river gryphons are now ocean gryphons," Satra said. "And they're swimming right for your shores."

"They normally come with the rain, but they know we're watching the rivers, so they took the ocean route." Black Mask's eyes widened, and he swore.

"Do you lick Blinky with that beak?" Satra scolded. "How do we put a glyph on the ocean? There's no way."

He wiped water from his eyes. "During the dry times, you can walk out to that island. I see some green trees. There must be another marker."

"Erlock did say something about starlings guarding a winter jungle that was underwater during the summer months. This must be that lot." It made a kind of sense to Satra. "Okay, I'll go mark the glyph. With any luck, they'll be like the jadebeaks and ignore me even as they go into a frenzy."

"I need to warn my pride." Black Mask slipped out of his spiky armor and started down the mountain towards the cypress before turning back. "Once you're done marking the glyph, hide."

She looked at the mountains. "I can probably find a spot in the dead space between the mountain glyph markers."

"No, once my pride knows there are starlings

sneaking across, they'll check the entire border," he said. "Are you okay over water? They won't check the island. I can come fetch you before sun up so we can get you back safely. Blinky will flay me, but there's no getting around it.

Satra had visions of last year, being on the small island between the Crackling Sea Eyrie and the fortress. Rangers were trying to kill her, but Merin crashed down from the sky, crushing them under his weight. They flew off as the water crackled with light and the reeve's pet rose, devouring the hapless opinici.

It was a terror that had never left her. Since Merin's death, it had only grown, and she'd hoped to never be over open water ever again.

"I'll be fine," she lied.

Black Mask launched himself down the mountain so quickly it was like he still had his wings. He caught onto familiar branches and outcroppings, and even in the storm, it only took him seconds to disappear from view.

Satra shook the rain from her wings and got them flightworthy. Her feathers were so waterlogged that the river—*ocean?*—starlings had made it past the island by the time she got there, which presented her with a dilemma.

If she closed the gap now, would she trap the starlings on the bog side? Even in a frenzy, the jadebeaks hadn't crossed the line. Was it a two-way barrier? Just how *did* starlings work?

She left the paste wrapped in its pitcher plant container and massaged her paw while she waited. The island was full of rock crabs who disapproved of her intrusion, though thankfully, none came after her. They were all armor and spikes, and she had no idea how to fend one off.

If the stories were true—and seeing what a rock crab looked like outside of drawings made it seem possible—Tresh had shattered her beak trying to kill one of these as a gryphlet.

Satra's best option was to hide in the tree and watch the shore for a good opportunity to seal the gap. Once the altruism kicked in, there may be no hope for these starlings, but she held onto faith that they'd turn back.

8

THE COAST ISN'T CLEAR

There was a moment on the descent down the mountain where Black Mask was tempted to fling himself over the edge and feel the wind across his body for however long it took the ground to rise and meet him. Even with Blinky, even with the possible reintegration of the bog pride factions, he still had these moments.

They felt like a sign of weakness, and he wondered if the wingtorn in the Ashen Weald still had them, too. He'd never heard it talked about among the bog wingtorn here, but that was the real reason their old prison had been moved to the bottom of the Crackling Sea Eyrie. Every so often, a wingtorn would get a look across her face and fling herself off the ledge and into the misty darkness below.

He thought being free would take away that impulse. Instead, it was still there, a battle every day.

He won today's fight and continued by paw towards the cypress. The mangrove was too thick, too wet, too full of tree crabs to navigate quickly. He needed to reach help before the starlings arrived at the shore.

The southern stretch of their pride lands was new to him. In the old days, the mangroves had marked the end of the bog pride's territory. But as they were forced into a smaller and smaller corner, they'd claimed anything they could. He missed the tangle of trees overhead and ignored the *oo-awk* of a diving petrel until it repeated.

He returned the call, and Thistle looked down from her perch.

"Are you here to watch the prisoners?" she asked. "Your mother must have been more unhappy with you than I thought."

He caught his breath. Green wing altruism— another word Blinky had taught him that he couldn't repeat among his pride mates—was already a strong impulse. But if the prison was near the water and the river gryphons found out the bog pride was holding live starlings captive, there was a chance one might escape and bring it to the attention of the pridelord.

That would require the starlings in question to kill all the bog gryphons so they snapped out of their altruism, but Black Mask wasn't willing to rule that out just yet. And if that happened, they wouldn't need the Ashen Weald or Seraph King to make their pride disappear. He had no faith the glyphs would hold.

"There are river starlings coming!" he shouted to Thistle.

She didn't register the urgency in his voice. "With the rains, it makes sense. My sisters are watching the streams with wingtorn nearby. We'll catch them."

Stop calling them your sisters. You're not related to them or the crone. This is insanity.

"They're coming from the *ocean*," he said. "They're nearly to the shore!"

Thistle immediately leapt off her perch and flew north, sounding the alarm. When the first of the other bog witches returned her call, Thistle turned and caught up to Black Mask on a stretch of sandy beach nestled among the mangroves.

"The wingtorn are never going to make it here in time walking," she said. "They're closer to the Jadebeak Falls than the ocean."

The river starlings looked like a pod of dolphins swimming. There was no doubt now, they were definitely coming to shore. Once they spotted one of the bog gryphons, the frenzy would start.

"There must be twenty of them and two of us," she whispered. "I don't know what to do."

For the first time in as long as he'd known her, she looked her age—young and afraid.

He tried not to stare at the island. Had Satra already placed her glyph? "Thistle, how good are you at flying?"

"I'm okay, I guess." Her answer lacked confidence.

Four winged gryphons and only one old crone to teach them. There was no chance Thistle was *great* at flying, but what about the river starlings? Their bodies were thick. They seemed made for swimming first and foremost.

According to the tales, Turresh the Shark had moved through water like it was air. She'd created new rivers by digging through the earth. She'd lifted a turtle the size of twenty gryphons and tossed it down a waterfall.

The stories were only a quarter truth, but Black Mask had seen Tresh take off out of the water and fly. She was a lot lighter than the starlings looked. There was a chance they either couldn't fly without drying off or just that they were bad at it, maybe even worse than Thistle.

"If they see me, they'll swarm up on land," he told her. "But if you fly out over them, they might chase you back to their territory. Then you can fly high, lose them, and come back."

Her whiskers were straight back, and her ears and tail drooped.

"How close was I to the starlings you're holding prisoner?" he prompted.

"You were ten paces away from the jail." Her tone changed as she spoke. "Oh! That won't be good. Okay, I'll do the best I can."

"If you get into trouble, the rest of the wingtorn should be here by then," he lied. "So just swing back by. But if you do this right, there's a chance no one dies."

There was something defiant and protective in her eye, and a bit of her bog witch training seemed to have returned when she spoke. "If you see me coming back and the starlings are still following me, keep everyone hidden."

"I don't understand." But the moment he spoke the words, he *did* understand, and he hoped it wouldn't come to that. The starlings were a menace, but they could also be used as a weapon.

She performed an abbreviated wing stretch. "I'll lead the starlings to the raftworks, to Bogwash if I have to. Let the Ashen Weald deal with them."

"Please keep yourself safe," was what he said. What

he really meant was more like, *Please don't cause an incident that sends a hundred rangers here to get revenge.*

Her canopy hideaway had done a good job of keeping her feathers dry, and with her stretches complete, she took flight while Black Mask found a hiding spot.

The young bog witch flew over the pack of starlings, but they ignored her and kept swimming to shore. She flew around to do another pass, dropping a pouch of bitter herbs into the water, and this time the starlings poked their heads up to see where the smell had come from. The altruism took hold.

One of the river starlings, his muscular body long and his tail over half its length, leapt out of the water and nearly caught Thistle's tail. He spread his wings, and for a moment Black Mask thought he'd be able to fly. To the wingtorn's relief, the starling fell back into the water.

Thistle gained altitude before the other starlings leapt up after her. They followed her back towards the Emerald Jungle, their heads now above water chittering at Thistle, and Black Mask held his breath as they approached the island. The glyph atop the cliffs seemed to hold, sending them farther offshore as they gave it a wide berth, but they didn't shy away from the island at all.

Looks like Satra waited to put up the glyph. She's bright for a kjarrling.

Another of the bog witches, the male, appeared in the sky, but Black Mask let out a loud cry, and he landed near him. With any luck, it would also make Satra aware that the starlings had passed.

"What's going on?" the new witch asked.

Black Mask motioned to the disappearing shape of Thistle and decided to give her the credit. "Thistle had the idea that the starlings may be too wet to fly, so she's luring them away to buy time for the rest of our pride to regroup."

He didn't add that, hopefully, she'd actually lose them before returning home.

"Smart gryphon," the other witch said. "If they'd hit the shore and found their kin, there could be trouble."

"Very smart," Black Mask acknowledged. *But hopefully not smart enough to check the island and find Satra.*

It took two hours for Thistle to return home, ragged but triumphant. After circling back around, the starlings had hit the new glyphs and stopped their pursuit. She tried to protest that it was Black Mask's idea, but when he denied it, they assumed it was her modesty.

He grabbed the two wingtorn he'd startled out of their den earlier and assigned them to watch the water with him to make sure the starlings didn't return.

He picked these two in particular because he didn't think they'd ask questions if he released them from their duties after midnight and called out for Satra.

UNFORTUNATELY FOR BLACK MASK, right as he dismissed his lazy pridemates, Thistle arrived. The timing was suspicious enough that he commented on it.

"Waiting for me to be alone?" he asked.

She looked flustered. "I, well, yes. I wanted to say thank you. It was your idea. All I did was fly—and fly poorly, at that. My wings are going to ache for a week. Yet the pride is singing my praises, and it feels sweet, but there's still a hint of bitterweed. I wanted to know why you did it."

"I just came up with the idea. You did all the heavy lifting." He looked at Thistle. Her skull paint was gone. Even the thistle-like spiral by her missing eye was absent, most likely lost in the heavy rains. Being cut off from the herbs of the northern bog made it hard to find the necessary plants to make waterproof paint. And, contrary to kjarr rumors, they didn't sleep with their markings on. That was a good way to wake up to a blue or purple mess.

She nuzzled him, and even though he'd done the same to her in public many times, somehow it felt uncomfortable in private.

He stood, pretending he needed to stretch his paws. "I don't think the crone would have approved of it being my idea, anyways."

"She's not as bad as you think," Thistle said.

He tried not to laugh. This young gryphon, her colors not fully matured, was trying to tell him about his own mother.

"Really!" Thistle protested. "She speaks kindly of you. She just only does it when you're not around."

He didn't respond.

"Look, I don't care what the pride leader thinks." Thistle puffed up her feathers. "Black Mask, if you don't have a mate this season, I think you should be mine."

His discomfort intensified. "Wait, what?"

"I know we're not really siblings," she began, but he interrupted her.

"Hold on there, I *do* have a mate this season," he protested. "And don't pout at me. I've seen the way you make eyes at the male bog witch. Why don't you ask him?"

Now they were both flush with embarrassment. "Well, there's three female bog witches and one male. He can choose who he wants."

Black Mask sat back and put a paw on her shoulder, partially to keep her a leg's length away but mostly to show friendly, platonic support. "Thistle, there's only one secret to mating season."

Her eyes got wide, and he reconsidered his choice of words.

"Not mating, *mating season*," he emphasized. "Your bog witch *beau* can choose whomever he wants. You can't control that. The only thing you can control is who you ask. You should ask whoever is right for you. That's the only thing you really have power over, the asking. So don't overthink things. Ask who you honestly want to spend the winter with."

"What if I don't really want to spend the season with anyone?" she asked. "At least, not right now."

He shook some of the sand off and stood. "I think that fits under the one rule. If you don't want to have a mate, you control who you choose. Just don't ask anyone."

Thistle stared at him for a long time before continuing their conversation. "I thought you came back and stayed because you wanted your mother's approval. I don't think that's really why you're here. I think you stayed for the rest of us."

"I came back because I'm an idiot." He offered an open-beaked grin. "I stayed because I don't believe the doomsday rhetoric. I think there's a way we all end up okay, and I'm going to stick with it until I find out what that is."

Thistle curled up next to him and put a wing over his scars. "I'm glad you're here. Some days, I think you're the only one of us who isn't crazy, myself included."

He didn't necessarily agree with that. He was, at this moment, housing their sworn enemy on an island nearby. "In the old days, the den mother would have figured all that out for you. About asking or not asking. Advice. Flying. Growing up. Ours just didn't survive the rangers."

"Everyone asks you for advice. I guess that makes you the den mother," Thistle said. "Oh den mother, whom should I pick as a mate? Is it a pretty boy bog witch?"

He rolled his eyes.

"Or perhaps a pretty girl bog witch," she continued to muse. "She's so small and compact, I wouldn't need to expand my nest."

"As your den mother," he said, "I'm advising you not to pick a mate based on their size and portability."

"But she has such pretty wings!" She spoke the words and realized her mistake. She pulled away, taking her wings off his scars, which ached with the sudden influx of cool air. "I'm so sorry."

"It's okay." He didn't feel okay, but mistakes happened, and that was life.

She stammered another apology, but he took advantage of the awkwardness to ask a favor.

"Look, I was supposed to meet my mate tonight," he said. "We're keeping our relationship a secret since things are tense. Would you mind watching the water for me? I'd hate to let her down. She had her heart set on walking through the mountains in the moonlight with me."

"Oh, sure, of course!" Thistle chirped. "I'm so sorry, I didn't realize I was keeping you."

"You're not," he explained. "I'd be stuck here all night if not for you. You'd be doing me a really big favor."

She nodded. "Go with my blessing! Stay out all night, if you'd like. I'll get one of the wingtorn guarding the prisoners to take over when I go to bed."

He started to walk away when she spoke again.

"Black Mask?"

"Yes?" He forced his body not to tense.

"Thank you for being here." She hesitated a moment. "And if you really want to impress your mate, grab some of the flowering blood vine. The flowers are dark, but they glow pink under direct moonlight. If you hide the flowers in your harness, you can bring them out when there's a break in the clouds. I'm sure your mate will swoon."

He chirped his thanks, then slipped towards the mountains and began his ascent. When he was nearly to the cliffs, he sang the birdsong of a golden-crowned kinglet until Satra got the hint and left her island hideaway to fly across the water to the mountains.

9

THE JOURNEY HOME

"**Y**ou told her you were meeting your lover?" Satra said, incredulous. "Are you *trying* to get me murdered by owls?"

Black Mask laughed. "If I were trying to get you killed, I'd have told everyone where you were hiding. Good job waiting on putting up the last glyph, by the way. I saw the starlings try to swim back a few times, but even in the ocean, they couldn't pass it."

"But you actually brought the blood vines, though," she pressed.

He *tsk*ed. "They're not for you. If I show up late and *don't* have a gift for Blinky, I'm the one who's going to end up dead. You know how she loves flowers."

Satra had no idea that Blinky liked flowers. That felt like a parrotface or feathermane kind of thing. She'd seen several young medicine gryphons fill their bushy manes with blooms. Autumn was a strange time for the weald prides.

"Well, I hope Blinky doesn't murder you," Satra said. "I'm grateful for all the help you've given. I don't know how we'd have finished these final glyphs without you."

There was one more glyph waiting at the base of the tree Blinky was guarding, but that was more of a precaution than a necessity.

"I didn't do it for you," he snapped, but his surliness seemed to be a reflex. "If I hadn't brought you here, you'd have had to send soldiers to fight to the marked trees. And there'd always be a chance the crone would remove the glyphs after you left. This way, nobody had to die."

"Not even the starlings," Satra added.

He considered her. "I'm tired of fighting starlings. Infected, healthy, aquatic—I'd love to go the rest of my life without seeing another one. But if I have to see starlings, I'd rather they be behind an invisible wall. Because as tired as I am of fighting starlings, I'm even more tired of being forced to kill them when their altruism kicks in."

"You should leave," she reiterated her advice from the evening before. "Be with Blinky. Leave this behind. You're not the rebelling type. Your heart is too soft."

The words surprised both of them. For Satra, she remembered the tall sawgrass south of New Eyrie, where she'd been forced out of the sky. The grass had parted, revealing Black Mask and White Stripe. Their beaks had clicked with anticipation. It was a scene that often replayed in her nightmares. She'd been sure she would die until Urious stumbled upon them.

Black Mask used a claw to hold one of the vines wrapped around his harness to the light. He'd reclaimed his armor from the mountains before starting their walk home. "The bog witch who gave me this is named Thistle. This year, maybe last, was the first time she was old enough to find a mate. She's scared. She'd rather be alone than risk trusting anyone.

"She's nice, but she can't fly well. She lost an eye, not to a starling or a ranger, just to a careless mishap around a palm. Because she doesn't have any choice except to live in a grove of thorns and spines. Her back and sides have tiny red bruises where their venom pokes her.

"Thistle is a sweet gryphon. She's terrible with medicines, can barely handle an aneda bandage. She can't remember the stories. In any other world, she'd be happy. But she's trapped as one of the last four witches. The crone is never going to let her go."

Satra stared at him.

He let the flower settle back down among his spines. "There are wingtorn who don't want to fight. I hear them crying in their sleep. There's a shared nightmare we all have, a nightmare of Jonas. We've never forgotten what it felt like to fly, and we're never going to move past that while the crone preys upon our hatred.

"But I think one day she'll pass away. Or one day we'll find a way to... excise the wound. And when that happens, there's hope for the wingtorn. I think Thistle will be able to put down her skeletal paint, find a mate she likes, and be happy.

"So I'm going to stick around and wait for that day."

Satra continued watching him while he walked. She didn't know why he'd told her all that. Perhaps because she was the most powerful gryphon other than the starling pridelord, and her empathy may decide what happened to the last of the bog rebels. Maybe he'd come to forgive her, or maybe he'd been tempted by her offer to leave it behind and needed to remind himself of why he stayed.

IT WAS MIDMORNING by the time Satra and Black Mask returned to the edge of the deep bog territory. Blinky was livid, and it took all Satra's pleading to keep her from shouting at Black Mask.

Shouting, for an owl gryphon, sounded more like angry cooing. But whatever she was saying in owlish was getting the intended reaction from her mate.

Satra was grateful he was wearing armor. "Blinky, it's okay! Nobody could have predicted aquatic starlings would attack. We got all the markers except this last one. Here, see? I'm putting up the glyph. We're done. It's all fine."

"Fine is when you say something and do it on time." Blinky glared at Satra. "Fine is not when you are half a day late."

"Didn't you bring some, well, gifts for Blinky?" Satra hinted to Black Mask.

"Oh!" He used his beak to undo the opinicus clasp, letting his armor fall, and carefully picked the blood vine and associated flowers out of the palm spines and offered them to Blinky.

The flowers had glowed pink in last night's full moon, but they were dull brown in the morning sun. Satra thought of how one of those foliage-adorned feathermanes would look with a mane full of them in moonlight. They'd be a sight to see.

Of course, when Black Mask had said *Blinky loves flowers*, Satra had taken that to mean Blinky liked how pretty and fragrant they were. Hence, she was surprised when Blinky shoved the flowers into her mouth and ate them.

"Tasty," the owl gryphon said. "Not as good as minnow, but a good treat. You are forgiven."

She groomed a few of Black Mask's feathers, then guided Satra north to rejoin their camp. The Kjarr looked back helplessly at Black Mask, who laughed. Apparently, he'd had to appease Blinky's anger in the past.

Mating season makes fools of us all, Satra mused.

DESPITE SATRA'S self-assurances that she was done, she'd forgotten Wendl's suggestion they head north and reclaim some old borders. To Satra's surprise, it was Nighteyes who insisted.

"Wendl made it sound important." The violet starling's beak chattered a little, which put the Ashen Weald rangers on edge. The difference between a chattering starling and a chittering starling was the difference between a pumpkin and a New Eyrie carrot. Both were orange, but one was helpful and the other deadly.

Satra sighed. She wanted to go to New Eyrie, settle in with some friends, eat good food, and give Nighteyes a going away party. She didn't want to spend another night sleeping in the woods.

Thankfully for everyone else, being the Kjarr didn't mean doing what she wanted. It meant she did what was best for the Ashen Weald. "Okay, let's do it. Erlock, would you mind letting Mia and Henders know that we'll be a few more days?"

Erlock shot Nighteyes a glance that made Satra wonder what had gone on between them. Based on how haggard the starling was starting to look, Satra wondered why Nighteyes had pushed about the glyphs at all. If anything, she looked like she wanted to skip the party and go straight home.

While Erlock used her impressive flying skills to notify New Eyrie, the rest of them flew north, checking on the previous glyphs as they went. It was also a good opportunity for the rangers to test their maps. Some glyphs were easy to locate again thanks to nearby streams, waterfalls, or interesting rock formations. Others were invisible except to scent, something their map couldn't replicate.

Nor, it turned out, could the opinici's nares detect the glyphs no matter how well the gryphons explained what they smelled like. In retrospect, this helped Satra understand why the sand gryphon culture was so impenetrable to the Crestfall opinici. The hidden paths through the desert changed monthly, and they were always marked by olfactory rather than auditory or visual means. A society under a society, much like the underbough and weald prides had been to the late Reeve Brevin and her northern quarter sycophants.

"We'll have to bring a gryphon with us if we check on the glyphs." One of the rangers made a note on her map. "Which of the gryphon prides has the best sense of smell?"

Satra realized this same ranger had been assigned to guard her on all her outings and wondered if she was the one Grenkin suggested had a crush on Satra.

"Maybe the taiga gryphons?" Foultner offered.

"When everything is frozen, they're the only ones who seem to still be able to smell out frost chickens."

"I think that is only when it is cold." Blinky refused to wear harness pockets, so Foultner had agreed to carry the blood vine for her. What this really meant was that every so often Blinky would dig through her friend's pockets to eat another flower.

The ranger who kept looking at Satra gestured to the markers on the map. "We've seen how powerful scent is for starlings. Maybe it's your lot, Pride Leader Nighteyes? That doesn't help us Ashen Weald, though, I suppose."

Satra felt a pang of guilt. It was easy to forget Nighteyes led a pride across the mountains. Seeing her alone for months—her being the only purple starling they'd ever come across—made it hard to imagine her with a pride. Considering how numerous the starlings were, the Nightsky Pride could be huge.

Nighteyes shook her head, lost in thought again, before responding. "I don't think so. Everyone else perks up before me when we near food. I don't even find the glyphs first. It's more like a birdsong that plays in the background. You know how the overall tone changes when a predator enters the woods? Well, I can't pick out individual birds or scents, but I get a feeling based on the area I'm in. Wendl's elixirs suppress most of it, so it's more like the rumble of a distant storm now."

The ranger continued speculating until Erlock caught up with them several hours later as they reached the northernmost markers. "Henders is disappointed. He had big plans."

Foultner rolled her eyes. "Don't let him fool you. He's miserable if dinner goes according to plan. What he really loves is when things go wrong. He thrives on challenge."

"Like when he tried to cook crabs, but I snuck out and ate them all earlier in the day," Blinky said.

"Wait, that was you?" Foultner asked. "Henders didn't catch those crabs, I did!"

Blinky blinked but did not comment further.

Satra sighed. She'd just gotten feeling back in her paws, and now there were three more markers. They packed their things and continued north, searching for more faded glyphs.

VIOLET NIGHT, STARRY SKY

Despite protests that her sense of smell wasn't better than any other gryphon's, the leader of the Nightsky Pride felt a wave of calm rush over her. They were on the northeastern border of the Emerald Jungle's markers, and she detected a familiar scent on the trees this far north—her own.

Erlock, too, smelled it and tracked down several violet stars with a paw print. "I never noticed, but you smell a little like starberries. A few steps in this direction and you're back home, Nighty."

"This is where I'll cross so I don't anger the jade-beaks or stormtails." Nighteyes was polite enough not to say that what she really needed was several days to get the scent of kjarr gryphon and sea opinicus out of her feathers and fur before she came across more starlings. She also wanted time for the haze of Wendl's medicines to leave her system.

Satra found the Argent Heights' glyph and added her own farther up the same tree.

The effect on Nighteyes was strange. To her eyes,

she was looking at the dull hills of the Jadebeak Mountains stretching north, surrounded by trees and sawgrass meadows. But in the back of her brain, she felt something. Not a scent. Not a wall. It was like a promise she had to honor. The pridelord's promise. With two glyphs, the boundary was even stronger, and she could feel the effect of being on the wrong side of the border more intensely.

"We could quietly cut out Silver's marker." Foultner pulled a Crackling Sea barnacle scraper from her harness. "She'd be none the wiser, and we could claim this area for the Ashen Weald."

"Sawgrass, saltwater marsh, sand, and ruins?" Satra asked. "No thanks. We'll leave this to the padfeet. And, I suppose, the Padfoot Pride, if they want it. Where would you even build a nest here? It's so flat."

It never ceased to amaze Nighteyes that a pride of gryphons had named themselves after the term for a prideless, eyrieless, often-criminalized opinicus or gryphon: a padfoot. A heron and sailfin fought in the distance, a testament to the dangers of keeping a nest on the ground. The refugees from New Eyrie had spoken of ruins halfway to Whitebeak, perhaps the remnants of an eyrie that hadn't been able to sustain itself on lizard eggs and crab claws.

"Just one more." Satra massaged her paws. "Assuming the pattern of lost Emerald Jungle foliage continues, I think I can just spot it atop the ridge. Everyone's welcome to wait here. This should be fast."

Blinky and Foultner were already splayed out on some rocks next to a pond, taking a much-needed rest after several grueling days of backtracking north. The rangers busied themselves making snacks—fish paste spread on flattened stripes of seaweed. That just left Erlock and Nighteyes to look after Satra.

"You two can stay if you want," the Kjarr offered. "Really, we haven't seen anyone since we parted ways with Black Mask."

Nighteyes thought of Wendl's warning. There was something up here she wanted Satra to see. And if it was dangerous, they'd want Erlock.

"I'd like to check my glyph to see how the scent has faded," the starling said. "And I'd like to see if Erlock's ancestry allows her to find my glyph without help."

Erlock shrugged. She was always up for a challenge. "Sure thing."

While Satra's prediction about the lost emerald broadleaf being her final mark was correct, Nighteyes didn't give Erlock any hints, sending her to fly over the hills searching. To Nighteyes's chagrin, her fantail friend didn't find anything out of the ordinary except for a family of squirrels.

Satra's patience was short. "Let's head back. I'm not spending another evening out here."

Nighteyes joined Erlock, pretending to search. She drew it out as long as she could before even Erlock's patience ran out.

"Really?" the fantail said. "You locate a hundred of these things across a mountain range, but then when it comes to this last one, the one between me and my dinner, you're bumbling around like a squirrel that forgot which hole it buried its nuts in?"

Nighteyes sighed and pushed back the leaf showing her glyph. She was just about willing to write off Wendl's warning when the sun glinted off something. "Do you see that?"

Her instincts were to head down and hide in the foliage. Erlock's, however, sent her shooting north into the sky to investigate, and Nighteyes was pulled along with her.

Past the thinning sawgrass, armored shapes marched in a row. Nighteyes's first thoughts were of impossibly large wingtorn. Only her time around the Ashen Weald had taught her the outline of their goliath birds, gargantuan cousins of the cassowaries she hunted back home.

"Why armor a goliath bird?" Nighteyes asked Erlock. "What good would that do against a gryphon in the air?"

The birds were led to a makeshift stable with a small corral resembling the ones the ranch used to keep sailfins away. The construction was new. Several white opinici worked on other buildings, and a black peacock stood atop a tower in the middle of the outpost.

The peafowl opinicus's train was spread, showing off the dyed red eye-like markings from a cobra's hood. A similar banner hung down from his perch.

"Trained goliaths would be effective against wingtorn." Erlock's expression was grim. Light glinted off several small, hawk-like opinici in the sky. "There's the argent reeve's scouts. We need to leave before they spot us. Hurry!"

Nighteyes felt a stronger calling, something primordial deep in her brain. She needed to get back to warn her pride. She couldn't help the Ashen Weald directly, but if the Seraph King's forces could be lured past the markers, her pride would be compelled to attack them.

"This way!" Erlock ordered, but Nighteyes wouldn't be moved.

"I need to locate my pride. We can help you!" she hissed. "I just need to get to them. The enemy is so close to the border..."

The fantail swore. "The pridelord won't let you. Once the elixir wears off, you're going to be as dangerous to the Ashen Weald as you are to the Seraph King's forces. Come back!"

Too late, Nighteyes realized she'd left the last of the orange elixir at the camp. Well, it was no matter, Wendl could make more for her. All Night needed to do was get across, connect with her pride, and bring them here. If Wendl could provide more medicine, she could even lead her army across the border.

She flew home, leaving Erlock behind. The sawgrass disappeared. Then the Jadebeak Mountains passed beneath her. The dilapidated remains of Wendl and Piprik's original expedition.

Then something happened. She stopped to clean herself in the first large river, rinsing all the non-starling smell out of her fur and feathers. Once she was relatively certain she wouldn't be attacked on sight—well, on smell—she went back to the ruins to meet Wendl. She needed to tell her companion to make more orange elixir.

Her mind was abuzz with plans, friendships, concerns, and worry when she hit the glade outside the old abandoned research camp. Yet when she stepped one paw into it, her mind turned as blank as the sky during a cloudy night, and she fell to her stomach.

"Welcome home, Nighteyes." The voice was both calm and deadly, like a lullaby sung by a serpent. A single starling stood where Wendl should be.

Nighteyes's vision told her this was just another starling. Her vision told her this couldn't be the pridelord because he only moved as part of the swarm.

Yet it was him. The section of her brain that held and processed scent and sound knew it. She lost all free will, becoming an observer in her mind.

"Wendl was worried about you." The pridelord circled her prone body, and she could feel the trails of citrus he left in his wake. "She was worried one of the other prides would attack you. So I came here alone to keep you safe. I keep all my flock safe."

Nighteyes found herself nodding. She had memories of what it felt like to be around the pridelord, knew she'd had to come every spring to report to him, but she couldn't remember what happened when they were alone. Would she forget this experience, too? Or was Wendl's alchemy allowing her an awareness she had previously lacked?

"What has you fleeing so quickly, my child? What is it you needed to do?" He settled in front of her. In the distance, beyond hearing, she saw the jungle shift. The trees were full of starlings, all frozen in time, all mindless; Jadebeak, Stormtail, and Newmoon Pride gryphons grouped together, differences forgotten.

But no Nightsky Pride. Did he worry they would feel some sense of loyalty to me?

Where moments before, she couldn't open her beak, now she couldn't keep it shut. Against her silent cries, she could hear herself answering his questions.

"The argent reeve is leading an army against the Ashen Weald," her beak said. "We saw her setting up a supply line. I need to gather my pride, take the suppressor, and come to Erlock's aid. I can help them."

The pridelord's countenance didn't change nor did

his ears or tail twitch, but the starlings in the distance beat their wings in irritation. "I'm disappointed in you. We made a pact not to cross the border. You promised that once you returned, you would honor their glyphs. Would you have broken the promise you made in my stead?"

Even in this state, she wanted to lie. Yet her beak betrayed her again. "Yes, pridelord. I would have done it."

The pridelord turned away from Nighteyes. "Your alchemy works too well, Wendl."

"Yes, pridelord." The voice, clearly Wendl's, came from off to the side, but Nighteyes couldn't get her head to look in that direction. Only when the pridelord turned his beak did hers respond out of instinct.

"You can make more later if we need it?" he asked.

"Yes, of course." Wendl's head didn't move with the pridelord's. Nighteyes could see her friend looking to the side, adjusting herself to be more comfortable—all the things Nighteyes wanted to do herself but was unable to.

Yet the pridelord seemed unaware that Wendl wasn't under his sway. "Then destroy your current stockpile."

"As you wish." Wendl relaxed when the pridelord moved his focus back to Nighteyes. Even as Nighteyes felt her vision move with the lead starling's, she caught sight of Wendl looking away.

Are all the starling opinici resistant to the pridelord? Are they like weaver ants or cuckoos, parasites within our borders?

The pridelord turned back to her. "You will not take the Nightsky Pride across the border. Nor will you cross it yourself. You will return home and be happy to do so.

Your pride needs you. The world outside our border doesn't. We're safe here. No army in the world would dare attack us. We're beyond reproach, unassailable."

Has he always talked like an opinicus? Why don't I remember what he sounds like?

"You'll forget all this. Then you'll come see me in twelve days. You'll stay away from our border with the Ashen Weald, but you won't know why you're doing it. You will feel unsafe near them. When the moon is empty, come to me at my temple."

Will I forget this? I feel like I'm losing my mind.

The pridelord walked past her. The jungle came alive, and hundreds of starlings hopped down from their perches and followed mindlessly behind him.

He was almost out of earshot when he seemed to think of one more thing. "There's a stormtail who wishes to be your mate. He's waiting for you in the river outside your nest. There are already too many cross-pride couplings this year. You will tell him no."

The pridelord took flight, and his flock rose with him, the entire jungle forming itself into a murmuration that cut through the sky like a river through the mountains. Nighteyes desperately tried to remember what she'd been told, but when the pridelord's scent faded, her mind shut off, and she collapsed.

11

TWIN RIVERS, THICK TAIL

Nighteyes awoke in the ruins. The headache that had been her constant companion while taking Wendl's elixir was gone. Her mind felt clear and crisp.

She looked down at the legbands that had once housed Wendl's alchemical concoctions, but they were all empty. She'd had at least one left, hadn't she? No, she'd left it at her camp with the gifts she'd intended to bring home. She'd been flying with Erlock and Satra when all the sudden—

Oh, all of the sudden she'd gone home. She was getting headaches, so she didn't think she'd appreciate the party. Satra must have suggested it. That was very nice of her.

Nighteyes sniffed her wings. They still smelled faintly of kjarr gryphon and sea opinicus, but she thought she'd be safe. Thankfully, she'd remembered to clean herself before napping, even if she didn't remember doing so.

She flew through the Emerald Jungle. This north-eastern section was a dead zone. She owned it, but only until a new pride was formed to take it over. She could smell starlings on the wind. Perhaps the pridelord had sent someone to check on it. The New Moon Pride currently owned some abandoned ruins near the temple, but they were growing fairly large. Perhaps they would be her new neighbors.

She felt an ache inside of her but pushed it down. *It's okay. I miss Erlock and Foultner and Blinky. That's natural. When the yolkbloom bounces back from the weald fires, they can use the Merinkin's elixir to come visit us. It'll be fine.*

And she felt fine. Better than fine. She could smell citrus in the air and a hint of spice. She was home, and that felt great.

She ducked under the canopy into the darkness of the jungle. Up top, spears of light slipped through the cracks. White flowers bloomed above her, creating an illusion of stars. It was common for the younger members of her pride to fly up and create their own constellations by rearranging the vines. At the V-shape where two rivers met, she saw her nesting grounds and landed.

Dozens of grey, downy gryphlets bounded out of their den to leap on top of her. Her sisters chirped their greetings, preening away the last of the bog scent and making her smell like part of the Nightsky again.

She took it all in with joy, spending hours with her loved ones. It was so good to be back. She missed being around other starlings. Everything was as it should be.

When it was time to tuck the gryphlets into their nests, she took a break to check on her den. Several of the purple and gold jungle squirrels had chewed their way in and wrecked it. Her sisters had attempted to straighten it back up, but they'd added fragrant vines she could do without. She gathered some in her beak and turned to leave her small den when she saw a shadow blocking the entrance.

"Wendl?" She dropped the vines to ask.

The starling opinicus offered an open-beak smile. "Nighteyes! How are you? I thought you were coming back *tomorrow*, so I wasn't there waiting for you. Is everything okay?"

There was a slight buzzing in Nighteyes's brain as she said, "Oh, no problem. I must have told you the wrong evening. I got most of the scent off, so it looks like we were worrying for nothing. Thank you so much for your help."

Wendl wrapped her talons around Nighteyes in a hug. "I'm glad you made it back safe and sound. We have a lot to catch up on tomorrow, but I'll let you get to sleep. If you need anything, I'll be around, okay?"

"Wendl, did..." Nighteyes began, but she couldn't remember what she was going to say next. "Did everything go okay while I was gone?"

Wendl's eyes held a clarity that never left them. "Like what? Are you worried someone is going to challenge you for leadership of the pride? No, you're fine. Everyone loves you and missed you. You're safe here. You're completely safe."

The starling opinicus, the only green in her pride, turned and exited the den, leaving Nighteyes alone with her thoughts. Strangely, despite her months of absence and adventures, her mind was at ease. The smell of citrus, somehow ripe despite it being out of season, calmed her like the incense the weald's medicine gryphons used on bee hives. She'd never felt more relaxed.

She'd just started to doze when a loud splash sounded from outside. She rubbed sleep from her eyes and padded out of her den. Despite their proximity to the two rivers, the hill her nest was on stayed relatively dry, giving her a nice, recessed burrow lined with leaves and flowers.

As she neared the river closest to her den, she saw a thick, feathered tail splash down, stunning a fish.

The stormtail, longer than most gryphons and lower to the ground, picked it up in his beak and crawled up the riverbank. "Hello! I've missed you. Without you here, there was nobody to chase me off and tell me to return to the ocean."

Her headache returned, but she always had a headache when someone tried to be charming, so she thought nothing of it. "Well, I'm back now, so you can clear out. Go home to your own nest."

He shook his coat, spraying her with water. "Won't you keep me company while I dry off? I can't swim all the way home. There are too many waterfalls. I need to dry my feathers first."

"I think you can handle that on your own." She turned to go when a fish landed at her feet.

"You look so hungry," he purred. "What if I give you my fish?"

She sniffed at the fish, pretending to consider it. "I think you mean *my* fish, don't you? This is Nightsky territory."

"We could argue all night over whose fish it is," his tail wagged as he talked, "but you look hungry, so you should eat it."

She sighed. She *was* hungry, and it had been months since she'd eaten anything tasty. "A few nibbles, but you'd better dry yourself quickly."

"Of course, of course!" The long stormtail preened and groomed. He stretched his thick tail and shook it a few times. Where the weald gryphons often had furry, featherless tails and the Crackling Sea opinici had tails like birds, the stormtails had a mixture of both to help them swim. A long, muscular tail the way most gryphons had, but with feathers on either side, giving it a shark- or dolphin-like appearance, based on the individual's pattern.

In the case of this particular stormtail, his tail was flat, letting him slam it down to stun unsuspecting fish.

Once he was dry, and she was done eating, he approached her, getting down on his stomach with his tailfeathers spread, "Nighteyes, I know sometimes we fight, but I value how smart and kind you are. Some hunters are content to try to be the best, but I've seen the time you put in helping the rest of your pride. You're never jealous when they succeed, and I can't tell you how much that impresses me."

The buzzing returned like a sound behind her eyes, a swarm of mosquitoes on a hot, rainy day.

"I can offer you friendship and love, from now until the eggs are laid, if we want them," he continued. "Though I'm not really here for eggs. I just want a chance to get to know you better. To hunt and catch fish together. To stay here at your pride grounds and meet your friends, though I think they may have had enough of me these past few months while I waited for you!"

The buzzing grew louder. Her paws itched.

"And if you say no, I'll happily leave and return

home to the winter jungle, content to have let you know how much I respect you."

It sounded like the insects were inside her skull now.

"What do you say? Will you be my mate this season?"

His feathered tail drooped a little when she didn't answer him. Instead, as though held by bog magic, she turned and walked back up to her den. She stepped inside, disappearing from his sight.

He sighed audibly. Even after months of waiting, he must have known it could lead to rejection. He sniffed at the remains of the whiskerfish, but she'd cleaned all the meat off it.

He turned to the river to sleep when her voice came from the entrance of her den.

"So, are you coming inside, or do I have to drag you in like a fish?"

12

THE FIRST SIGN OF MANY

"Evacuate everyone who isn't military," Satra commanded the moment she landed at New Eyrie. "Get them to the Crackling Sea Eyrie. Tell Pride Leader Grenkin to prepare for a siege—extra tunnels for the wingtorn are a priority. They have goliaths, so we'll need a spiked pit."

She told everyone of Erlock's discovery and issued a dozen orders before she realized she was probably stepping on Mia's toes.

The ranger lord waited for the Kjarr to run out of breath, then stepped in. "Take Kjarr Satra to safety. Not to the same place as Grenkin. They're both targets for the Seraph King's assassins. Force the white opinici to split their forces."

"No, I'm staying." When Satra spoke those words, she expected Foultner and Blinky to have her back. Unfortunately, both of them had been charged with *guarding* her back, so they were already dragging her out. "Wait, wait, okay. I want to hear what the plan is before I go. There will be a lot of questions."

Mia turned from Satra to a cardinal wingtorn, one of Urious's top commanders. "Find an engineer and adjust the walls. We're no longer concerned with sailfins. I want the kinds of spikes that'll keep an armored goliath bird at bay but will let you and your kin slip in and out unimpeded. When you're done with that, find some hideaways north of the city by dry land and fresh water. Anywhere a stupid scout might land to drink."

The wingtorn turned and dashed off.

"Who saw the army?" Mia asked. "I need intelligence."

Satra stepped forwards. "Nighteyes and Erlock. Nighteyes returned to the jungle. Erlock—wait, where is Erlock?"

"She went back to scout more," Foultner said. "I thought she'd have caught up to us by now."

"By the depths, weald gryphons are hard to deal with," the ranger lord swore. "Don't you realize your prides will fight harder and with better precision if you're still alive?"

A wingtorn started to go on about bravery and leading by example, but Mia cut her off. "Henders! Grab all the fantail gryphs and peregrine opies and get me Erlock Chartail. Foultner, Satra's heard enough, get her to safety. Blinky, you've been in the swamp, yes?"

Blinky half-blinked.

"It was rhetorical, no need to answer." Mia's tone went from Redwood Valley educated to ranger grunt the more she spoke. "The best and brightest have been working on wingtorn armor that should withstand flechettes. They built it at the raftworks and sent it north. I need you to find out where the caravan is at and get those wingtorn and that armor here yesterday. Check the kjarr nesting grounds first. Understand?"

Blinky disappeared, nearly pushing Olan out of the way.

Kia's brother dipped a talon in red ink and started scratching off watch towers from the map. "The reeve's pet has chewed through all these over the last month. We're going to have to trust patrols and wingtorn hideaways."

"You should evacuate," Satra said as Foultner pulled her away. "This isn't the most defensible position. Nobody has held New Eyrie from a siege."

Mia and Olan both looked up, but it was Olan who spoke. "My sister could hold this city against the reeve's pet itself if it surfaces. A bunch of opinici don't stand a chance."

"I don't think it'll come to that, Olan," Mia said dryly. "Only the blue royal family could control the pet, and they're all dead. I don't intend to hold New Eyrie at *all* costs. But they're expecting a wooden opinicus outpost that's accessible by ground and burns easily. I'm offering them a fireproof, entrenched, flechette-resistant target, and every time they make a wrong assumption about our capabilities, I'm going to make them pay for it in blood. We'll leave when we're indefensible and not a moment before."

Satra bit her tongue. Military matters weren't her department, but now that the enemy was nigh, she hated the thought of running away.

If the Seraph King really was intent on taking a stronghold in the south, it would be the Crackling Sea Eyrie. If she left now, she could start evacuating the non-military to the weald. Younce had opened up a few rediscovered taiga nests. Askel and Triddle had mapped the hot springs and fresh drinking water along the mountains. It shouldn't take much to turn them into shelters.

Only once she'd figured out how to be helpful did she let Foultner drag her away.

ERLOCK CHARTAIL, once Erlock Fantail, had done the smart thing and informed her camp about the Seraph King's army to the north. Then she'd done the stupid thing and slipped away to learn more.

She'd correctly guessed that if she flew high enough, they'd mistake her for a small bird flying low rather than a large gryphon higher up. Her ruse lasted long enough for her to get a general idea of how far back the supply lines went and who was spearheading the efforts.

She flew over the army, all the way back to the desert ruins the New Eyrie refugees had spoken of. They were no longer abandoned. They served as a crossroads for two sets of supply caravans, one coming from Whitebeak and the other coming from the Argent Heights. Their numbers appeared without end.

Yet, seen as a collage from above, this wasn't the composition she expected from the Alabaster Eyrie's forces. Crestfall's flamingos guarded the goliath birds. Hoppy claimed the palace in the desert was empty, and no one was sure where the pink reeve was holed up. A contingent of Reevesport peacocks, their feathers dyed black, carried snake banners. There were an alarming number of Crackling Sea opinici—it seemed she owed

Merin an apology, he'd been right about the number of Jonas loyalists.

Speaking of Jonas, an opinicus with metal armor resembling a twisted octopus stood at the center of the main camp. Erlock made the mistake of trying to fly low enough to see if Satra and Grenkin's suspicions were correct about the ex-leader of the Crackling Sea Eyrie, but she was only able to confirm the burn marks before she recognized another leader who caught sight of her in return.

Reeve Silver of the Argent Heights sounded the alarm, and several of her guards rushed after Erlock.

The fantail changed direction, making a break for the south. She flew high, but a glint of armor warned her of a scout above she'd missed. She had two choices. She could try to gain altitude, keeping him from diving at her, or— Well, the flash of light as he tucked his wings and limbs in told her it was too late for that option.

She twisted back, diving towards Silver's guards coming up from below. She managed to catch two of them unawares. They were used to chasing fleeing targets, not being charged, and Erlock shredded through both sets of wings before the other four scattered.

Their fifth, high sky scout realized too late he couldn't reach Erlock without going through his friends. He slowed down, trying to avoid a midair collision with another guard.

All it took from Erlock was one well-timed bump to send them into each other.

She returned to fleeing as they regrouped. The

smartest silver hawks were gaining altitude. The dumbest lay dead on the ground below her.

Never too old to have fun, she mused as more opinici took to the air to give chase.

SEVERAL SCRAPES and lost feathers later brought Erlock to the marshes north of New Eyrie. She caught a flash of red up ahead and dove, catching one of the last four silver hawks on her way down.

Three left.

She could do this. They were fast but small and not exceptionally experienced at fighting gryphons. And if they weren't experienced at fighting gryphons, they *really* wouldn't be experienced at fighting wingtorn.

Two dove at her. One had poor form and didn't slow down, so when he missed, he got a face full of saltwater and sawgrass, along with at least one broken limb. Several sailfins waddled over to enjoy the free food.

Down to two.

Erlock passed over crushed watch tower after crushed watch tower, a reminder of the danger lurking in the sea to her left.

Another argent hawk harassed Erlock, not quite diving at her but flying just above the fantail and trying to force her to land. Obviously, the hawk had never run through a field of grasshoppers as a chick. Or, if she had, she didn't make the necessary parallel to her immediate survival.

She flapped at Erlock one more time, then seemed to notice the red and brown fuzzy shapes below the reeds. She squawked and pulled away, but a dozen wingtorn leapt up, and one caught her out of the air.

Erlock backbeat her wings, landing outside the entrance of New Eyrie, and crawled through one of the holes the wingtorn used to get in and out of the city—it emptied into Reeve's Nest, saving her precious moments.

She'd barely made it to the other side when Mia and Henders greeted her. Henders offered water and started treating her small wounds.

Mia began by asking questions, though not the ones on logistics and supply chains Erlock had been expecting. "Did you see the Seraph King, Hi-Kun, Mally, Silver, or any other high-ranking targets?"

Erlock caught her breath. "The argent reeve is there. No sign of the others."

"Your compatriots said you only saw flamingos, herons, and argent hawks on your first fly-by," the ranger lord continued. "Does that hold true?"

"Yes, with a few white-plumed builders and a couple of peacocks." Erlock paused to snap up some fish bars. Her body craved the salt. "The peacocks were dyed black. They held banners of their tail feathers. Is that Reevesport?"

"No idea." Mia chewed on a talon while she thought. "I don't like this. When Reeve Silver visited here last, she said the Alabaster Eyrie's forces were like a golden sunrise that struck fear into their enemies. Hi-kun is a walking advertisement for the glory of the Seraph King. Mally strikes fear into everyone who grew up on stories of him as a chick."

"Reeve Silver—" Henders began, but the ranger lord interrupted him.

"Is expendable," Mia finished. "I want to know where the rest of their army is located. Are they dealing with blackwings? Are they going after our sand gryphon allies?"

The fantail pride leader considered her options. Her pride had settled back into the burned sections of the weald as it recovered. It would be hard to rouse them to fight. She needed to figure out if the free prides would give support.

There were dozens of large things going through her mind and twice as many small things, so she was grateful when Henders asked the question that eluded both her and Mia.

"But wouldn't it be stupid to attack the blackwings and us at the same time?" he asked. "Isn't it better to wipe one of us out, then the other?"

"Yes." Mia pulled out her map, trying to make sense of it.

Erlock looked over her shoulder. With the Palace of Fire and Ice shattered and the sand gryphons disrupting caravans attempting to cross the wastes, both the blackwing reeve and the Seraph King had returned to ignoring the desert. After guiding Rybalt to the palace, Hoppy and Sponge had removed all supplies and markers so the blackwings wouldn't find their way back again.

"I still don't get it," the fantail leader said at last. "If it's an invasion, they're taking a lot of unnecessary risks. And if it's not an invasion, I don't know what they're after. Unless they just wanted to get our attention, in which case, they succeeded."

Erlock, Mia, and Henders settled back into the old

Reeve's Nest building, where one wall was dedicated to maps with figures and glyphs next to them.

Henders hopped with excitement when he saw the glyphs next to Bogwash and the raftworks. "Rorin and the fisherfolk! We should call them all up here. Now that the bog is nearly empty of starlings, they could reach us before the fantails and feathermanes make it over from the weald."

When one of the rangers started to move towards the door, Mia countermanded Henders's order. "No, not yet. As far as we know, the Seraph King doesn't have the kinds of ships that would let him navigate the tough currents south of the Emerald Jungle. At least, not in numbers large enough to fight all of us. But I'm not willing to take anything for granted yet. If they do have ships, I want Rorin right where he is."

She scribbled down a set of instructions, mostly about upping spear production and authorizing Rorin to command the rangers if necessary, then handed it to Erlock. "You take the order south."

"Like parrotscat I will," Chartail said. "You need as many fantails as possible up here. You're not getting me out of the danger zone that easily."

"You're the fastest flyer not currently patrolling outside." Mia sealed the order. "All of my peregrines are in the air."

"I can do it." Henders raised his talons to volunteer. Everyone turned and looked at him, having forgotten he was also a falcon. "Erlock can vouch for me. We went on the bog expedition together."

Mia turned to Erlock, but the fantail pride leader shrugged.

"We *walked* through the bog," she said to Henders.

"I'm not sure I've actually seen you fly."

He looked hurt. "We did the kjarr obstacle course together when the fledglings returned home."

Mia was skeptical.

Nothing stirred in Erlock's memory, but she had a job to do, so she slapped the orders into Henders's pocket. "That's right, you were an amazing flyer, practically a fantail in your own right. Go get those orders down to Rorin as fast as you can. And after that, stop by the Flower outpost and make sure they sent the wing-torn armor. If they haven't, escort it up here personally. You're doing the Ashen Weald proud."

As the overeager ex-Reeve's Guard rushed outside, Mia and Erlock went after him, watching him leap into the air and fly away.

"He's not bad, eh?" Erlock said. "Got his wings out and flapped them without hurting himself."

Mia shook her head. "Something's not right here. I can hold New Eyrie against anything except a force of nature for a few days, but I'm worried."

Erlock thought back to the flattened watch towers all along the coast. It was said the reeve's pet obeyed only the royal family, and that it had gone mad with grief after Jonas's death. Erlock hadn't believed Grenkin and Satra's story of finding Jonas's bloody wrappings in the royal chambers of the Crackling Sea last spring, but her eyes didn't lie.

She'd definitely seen a good number of blue herons amongst the enemy's ranks, and then a spoonbill who had both burn marks and swirled metal armor. She wasn't given to superstition, but if there was a chance it was really him.

"About that whole *force of nature* thing..." she began.

13

THE MISSING CRANES

Turresh the Shark stalked the sandstone buildings of Sandpiper's Dune in search of her sister-in-law. Tresh, Quess, and Bruen had flown over from Luminaire to trade and been separated. Quess and Bruen went off to sell Quess's masks and carvings while Tresh found herself serving as the impromptu village elder.

"Tresh, Tresh!" Carru shouted from the top of Naya's house. "We need your help over here."

This was the third time she'd been called away. She'd hoped to get back to her island home before midday to feed her pet salamander, but she supposed she could spare some time for an old friend.

"Heya, Carru," she started to say before the wind off the dunes kicked up again.

"Sorry, sorry," he said as though the weather were under his control. He spread his large, harpy eagle wings to block the wind. "It's been pretty dry, so the dunes are on the move."

"So I see." Since her last visit, another row of nests

had been buried. "How are you doing? Rorin said you went north to spend time with your brothers. That must be hard."

Small talk wasn't her strong point. She cared for her friends, was invested in their well-being, but she liked having a problem that could be solved through action. She grew uncomfortable in any social situation that required her to sit and talk. She preferred large gatherings where food was involved so she could let others chat while she ate, napped, and swam.

She cast a reflexive glance in the direction of the ocean and was embarrassed Carru caught her.

"Brothers and sisters. I have a lot more siblings than when I left. Anyways, I'm okay," he said before rephrasing, "Well, I'll *be* okay. Here's the thing, though. My father wanted me to find my older brother. He disappeared into the Emerald Jungle."

Tresh kept her face unreadable. There was little good that came from the starlings' home.

Carru continued. "I'd like to speak to Erlock Chartail, but I can't get the fantails to even tell me where she's staying. I thought maybe my old pride could help, but Askel and Triddle are almost always up north helping the sand gryphons. I don't mind going that far, but it seems like everyone is cagey about their pride leaders' location since Reeve Rybalt's attacks last spring. Is there anything you can do? You're friends with Erlock, right? Or could Younce make it happen?"

"Younce is very busy right now." Tresh winced as she spoke. Everyone had been asking about Younce since gryphons and opinici started pairing up for autumn and winter. She didn't like fisherfolk prying into her personal affairs. "I knew Erlock briefly, but we were not close. I do not think she would do me a favor."

Carru groaned.

Tresh rolled her eyes. "However, there is one gryphon who knows Askel and Triddle and might do a favor for you. Have you asked Zeph?"

"I don't know." Carru puffed up a little.

Tresh had never been able to figure out what Carru had against Zeph—or Younce, for that matter. There seemed to be something about weald and taiga gryphons that encouraged friendly rivalry.

"It is your call," she said. "I am sure Beeflight would love to help."

While Zeph's epithets were more ominous north of the shore—particularly for parrots or reeves—the fisherfolk had named him after his infamous flight to bring hives down to repopulate the bees after the fire.

Fisherfolk often took great feats as challenges, hoping to outdo each other. The number of giant salamanders flown from Luminaire to the shore attested to their competitive nature. When it came to flying bees from the northern weald down to the dunes, however, everyone was willing to let Zeph have the win.

Carru shrugged. "What do I have to lose? If he's not there, maybe Hatzel will help out. I didn't want to fly all the way north to Poisonmaw, but I'm out of options."

He said his goodbyes and headed off, leaving Tresh to continue searching the markets for her sister-in-law and Bruen. She answered a few more questions on her way. While she'd long given up the role of Crane's Nest ruler when the refugees had fallen apart and either fled to islands or joined Swan's Rest, there was currently a dearth of leadership on the shore. Naya was guiding a trade caravan to Snowfall and planned to meet Orlea there, and Rorin had gone west to Bogwash. That left Tresh as the closest thing anyone had to a leader.

"That will be fine, take what you need," she told two sandy tern opinici who wanted to borrow nets to go fishing.

"You will have to ask Dusty," she told a third gryphon. He wanted a break from the shore and was looking for another settlement. Hoarfrost was always looking for fisherfolk willing to brave the cold heights. Thanks to Askel and Triddle, they'd even figured out a way to heat the caverns all year long.

Tresh heard splashing from the shore and Bruen shouting that the water was cold, followed by Quess's laughter. Tresh had just caught up to them when one final fisherfolk called for her attention.

Above the water, one of the taiga islanders looked frozen in the sky. When the heavy winds subsided, he glided down to her. She didn't know the islanders by sight. Historically, they'd dealt directly with Sandpiper's Dune, ignoring both Swan's Rest and Luminaire.

"Turresh," the islander said. With the scarring on her beak, he didn't need her to confirm, but she nodded anyways so he'd continue. "Something has happened to the Crane's Nest refugees."

Quess and Bruen looked up. They were both a large part of why the ex-inhabitants of Crane's Nest had left in the first place. When Quess advocated for finding peace with the Ashen Weald, that had been the last straw for them. They'd called the fisherfolk on the shore traitors and left for the deep ocean. Not even Tresh knew where they'd gone.

Though it seemed this fisherfolk did.

"What is your name?" she asked.

The islander's plumage was taiga white, complete with stripes that held the black and grey of Younce's rosettes, but he didn't resemble a gyrfalcon. Instead, he had the thick beak and long, feathered tail of a fantail. His head had yet to lose its fluff, and only the tips of his ears were visible.

"Cielle. It's a family name." When he spoke, there was the tinny sound of a songbird in his voice. "We met over the Blue-eyed Festival, when Younce invited us north."

"I remember," though she only half did. When Younce had found out there were taiga gryphons living as fisherfolk on islands deep in the sea, she'd humored him by passing along his invitation to the Blue-eyed Festival, not expecting the islanders to make the trip. She was as surprised as he was when they showed up.

Since then, there was a little tension between the lost taiga pride and the shore. Most of the nests being excavated along the mountain by Younce's gryphons were from prides long lost or forgotten—Hoarfrost and Snowfeather, for instance. The fisherfolk islanders were partially composed of the remains of the Williwaw Pride who had fled the Connixation. Naya and Younce had converted their old nesting grounds into an observation post to watch for starlings crossing the taiga, but it was still unclear if the Williwaw gryphons might want it back. No one was willing to keep it from them, but everyone wanted to know if more starlings showed up.

For as much as we call them the Williwaw Pride, I do not even know if they still think of themselves that way. Perhaps Younce and Naya worry over nothing. While Tresh had never gone that deep into the ocean, it was her understanding that Cielle's home included a variety of gryphon prides and opinicus refugees who had fled the world-altering blizzard so long ago.

Cielle took a moment to groom several feathers back into place while she asked Bruen to fetch some water and food for their guest.

"I have not seen the inhabitants of Crane's Nest since they fled." They'd called Tresh several names, none pleasant, when she brought rangers with her back from the bog. "How have they been doing?"

"Terrible," Cielle replied. "Loss is hard. They found some islands between our home and Ashfoot Isle, figuring no one would go out that way by accident. I try to make it a point to stop in and visit them once a month when I fly to the dunes, but this time, their homes were empty."

"If those islands are remote, did they leave to find a new home?" Quess suggested. "A *new* new home. Maybe the waters around them were running low on fish."

Cielle rifled through his pockets with his beak and pulled out a braid that ended with several fledgling feathers. "Their belongings were all in their nests, and these were still hanging up. They would not have left without them."

Tresh looked to Quess. Everyone who had lost a child had made a similar braid. Even Quess's temporary home on Luminaire had braids hanging from them.

"What if they just... gave up?" Quess asked. "What if it was too much?"

Tresh examined the braid, felt the texture through her paw pads. Several of the feathers were black petrel, the others were white crane. At least two dead children. "They would not. There is another answer."

Quess looked unsure. "Hate only lasts so long. In its place comes despondency more often than acceptance."

Bruen arrived with water and food, which the islander scarfed down. The flight from the deep ocean to the dunes couldn't be done in a day. Still, Cielle had Williwaw fur and fantail feathers—both had been considered the best flyers of all the gryphon prides. He was probably a force to be reckoned with in the air. Maybe he *had* made it in one go.

"Were there claw marks? Was this a serpentine whale?" Tresh asked him. She refused to entertain her sister-in-law's theory. Individuals may give up, but an entire village?

Cielle shook his head. "Nothing like that. No blood, no sign of a struggle."

"Quess, tell Rorin and Naya about this when they get back." Tresh put the braid into a harness pocket. "I am going to Swan's Rest. There are several fisherfolk there who once lived at Crane's Nest. They may know where their kin are."

Cielle looked up. "I'm going with you."

"No." Tresh didn't need an islander spooking them. She'd grown up at Crane's Nest. She knew how to speak to them.

"Please," he begged. "They were my friends. I need to make sure they're okay. If not for their sake, then for the safety of the islands nearby. And if you need to get word back to the dunes quickly, I can fly faster than you."

She thought back to Blinky's help in the swamp. "Fine. I am going to see if anyone is at the old Crane's Nest ruins. You go ahead to Swan's Rest and wait for me there."

"Tresh, be careful." Bruen saw she was going to open her beak and amended his statement. "Look, I know you're capable on your own, but just... watch out, okay? This isn't the bog. Fisherfolk don't just disappear."

Didn't they? Or, at least, hadn't they in the past? Even ignoring the bog tales of island cities that vanished in the night and ghost ships, Crane's Nest really had been wiped from the map. She never faulted anyone for being afraid of the ocean.

Still, she'd grown up with most of the missing refugees. She owed it to them to make sure they were okay.

Cielle finished his meal. "I'm ready."

Bruen's words stuck with Tresh.

"Evacuate Luminaire," she said at last, surprising both Quess and Bruen. "Until we know what happened, I want everyone on the shore. The dunes or Swan's Rest, either is fine. But I want everyone off the island."

With that, she gathered her Williwaw tagalong and headed east. The ocean was too large for her to search, but if she had any way of narrowing it down, she was certain she could locate the missing.

TRESH FLEW along the coast with Cielle in tow. The rocky shore, the redwoods, the occasional *skraarking* of ground parrots snacking on rimu olives—she'd grown comfortable here. Had the wingtorn not come, she'd have spent her life catching fish. Maybe even settled down with another fisherfolk and had chicks or gryphlets.

When the redwoods gave way to bamboo groves,

Cielle got excited. "I didn't know you had bamboo here. I thought it was an island thing."

"There is just the one patch around the bambooworks." She was annoyed at how effortlessly the islander flew and felt noisy beside him. She took solace in the fact that, with his thick taiga coat, their roles would be reversed in the water. "Perhaps the bamboo came from your island to shore."

As they neared the river delta that once housed Crane's Nest, she saw another invasive species—one of the giant salamanders from Luminaire was chasing a ground parrot. The flightless bird disappeared into the brush, causing the salamander to huff and crawl back to the water.

Most of the huts and nests had been cleared away by a mix of weather and fisherfolk, but a single memorial remained. A fire was lit nearby, and an old petrel fisherfolk tended to it.

"Go on ahead," she told Cielle. "I will catch up."

She slowed her flight, touching down outside the city limits. She didn't know why she didn't land by the shrine, but it felt wrong somehow. She crawled over several boulders—it'd been a game when she grew up to drag boulders to mark the edge of the city as it grew —and chirped a greeting at the fisherfolk sitting by the fire.

The elder didn't reply or acknowledge her. He continued tending the flames while she settled down across from him and inspected the shrine.

A large rock with one side worn flat had been rolled to the center of town.

No, this wouldn't be the center. This is where the nests were located.

A latticework of driftwood had been secured to the stone, resembling a spider's web. Braids with feathers in them hung from the wood. She reached into her harness and pulled out the braid Cielle had brought her. She stood on her back legs and tried to tie it to the wood, but her paws didn't have the dexterity. Opening doors in ranger outposts was one thing, tying was something else. Even braiding was difficult—her family had tried to turn her into a basket weaver several times, but her broken beak lacked the dexterity.

The elder stood, revealing his opinicus forelegs. He took the braid from her and tied it among several others.

"These aren't your nieces and nephews' feathers, Turresh." His voice was cold and dry. It brought to mind the wind across the rocks along the beach.

She sat back down. "No, they are from one of the refugees who fled to the islands. I came to ask you about them."

His talons lingered over a braid in the style that Quess preferred. Woven into the design were black and brown petrel feathers and a single patch of white down. Tresh looked away.

The elder drank from a bowl. His chest feathers glistened with water when he spoke. "You want to know what island they're hiding on. Well, I won't tell you."

"You do not believe I am part of Crane's Nest anymore?" Her feathers bristled. Before meeting Rorin, she'd been considered a lost cause by her village elders, and she still held ill will towards them. They'd considered her a problem that needed fixing. What she'd really needed were friends, not to become some greyfeather's pet project.

The elder looked at her. "I consider you as much a part of my village as anyone else. But *they* see you and Quess differently, and they don't want you there."

"I know where their island *was*." She let the words hang, though they weren't strictly true. All she knew was they were near where the Williwaw Pride had settled. "One of the Williwaw islanders went to visit and found the nests abandoned. The braids were left alongside the other belongings."

Here she paused. She didn't know how to pose the next question. Finally, she just came out and asked, "Is it possible they all killed themselves? They were never able to handle their grief. There is no sign of whale attack."

The elder's eyes showed disappointment. "No, they would never do anything like that. Life is too precious now. If anything, they would have risked their lives to try to avenge the dead."

"Are you certain?" She'd seen grief do strange things. She had a vision of Quess holding a fishing spear that had gone through Vitra and into Urious, her eyes silver, her words like ice.

"Yes," he replied. "They had children with them."

Tresh searched his features. He seemed to be clear-eyed and in possession of his wits. "I was not aware any had survived."

"None did." He chewed on a salty fish bar. "They're a new generation."

"I see." She looked away. Most gryphons and opinici from small fisherfolk villages or prides were happy to repopulate their numbers. The taiga pride in particular seemed obsessed with returning to their pre-Connixation population now that so many old nesting grounds had been unearthed.

Tresh didn't hold that against them. Not exactly. She just couldn't imagine anyone wanting to bring new life into the world as it was now. She saw hints of it when Swan's Rest fisherfolk visited Sandpiper's Dune. The way they looked at the fledglings there like they might shatter into eggshell fragments at any moment.

Children were precious and fragile, and she couldn't be around them without having small panic attacks. It was one reason she didn't visit Snowfall Mountain anymore.

One reason.

She missed Younce and spared a moment for him. Was he still searching the mountains, trying to reconnect to the Williwaw Pride? Over the winter, he'd gathered their stories and had an opinicus paint them onto the walls of Snowfeather, Hoarfrost, and Williwaw so they wouldn't be forgotten. The last time she'd seen him, he was surrounded by fledglings who had dyed their feathers pink, much to the chagrin of their parents, and he was telling them about the taiga prides of old.

The elder stared at her.

"Where would they go?" She shook herself out of her thoughts of Younce. "I will not go there myself out of respect for their feelings about me, but I will tell the islander to check."

"Candles on the water," he said at last. "There's an old ceremony for those lost at sea. It's that time of year. Have your islander friend look for lights."

"I will." She turned to leave. Perhaps the other ex-

Crane's Nest refugees who had joined Swan's Rest would have better information.

The elder wasn't done yet. "I'm sorry about your brother's family."

She froze. She knew what he meant—her nieces and nephews, her mom and dad—but it sounded like he was excluding both her and Quess from the word *family*. She remembered the shapes of the bodies on the shore as the blue glow from the bioluminescent shrimp swarmed them.

What Tresh really heard was, *I'm sorry you don't honor your brother's family.*

She looked at the braids and feathers hanging from their latticework, then flew across the delta to meet up with Cielle.

THE OCEAN and the shore had little memory of those who lived upon them. Sand and water were in constant motion. It was, to Tresh, almost more surprising that Crane's Nest hadn't yet disappeared than it was that Swan's Rest was beginning to look like its old self.

Several large fire pits emitted black smoke against the bright sky. The market where Tresh and Quess used to go to sell their wares was open again. Most of the buildings had been rebuilt in their original locations. There were only two changes from the old days. Well, two changes and an addition.

First, where the nests had been was no longer the hatchery. Fisherfolk all felt strongly about death. Instead, a blood-soaked bamboo spear was stuck in the ground where the eggs had once been.

It was a strange feeling, knowing the story behind the spear. In a way, this was holy ground to the wingtorn —a sacred shrine they'd never be permitted to see— because buried with the bones of the chicks he was responsible for killing was the body of Jun the Kjarr. They'd waited to bury the children until the blue lights had released their souls. They played in the star ocean. Only their skeletons remained.

Jun hadn't been given fisherfolk death rites. He'd been buried with his flesh and soul. Rorin's spear still pinned his body into the earth.

I wonder what the wingtorn would think if they knew.

The kjarr and weald gryphons worried about the dead haunting the living. They feared bog wisps and cave monsters. But the fisherfolk and bog pride felt differently. Instead, it was the living who haunted the dead. The bloody bamboo spear testified to that.

The nests' relocation and the hatchery's transformation into a kind of soul prison for Jun the Kjarr were the *changes* to Swan's Rest, but there was also the *addition*. Some of the families from Crane's Nest had moved here instead of fleeing to the islands. They'd learned to forgive, or at least, had come to peace with the treaties Rorin had made with Satra.

Tresh made her way to the new homes, knowing she'd be unwelcome but unable to let go of this thread. Thankfully, Cielle had already broken the ice and was asking questions.

He padded over to catch her up. "Everything here points away from them being overcome by their grief. In fact, it sounds like they were going the opposite way. They were going to petition Naya and Rorin to have their island made into an official fisherfolk settlement.

They were hoping to open up trade back with the main-land and serve as a halfway point between here and my pride. They'd... not moved on, precisely, but were allowing life to continue, I suppose?"

She shook her head. "So where are they? That many fisherfolk do not just disappear."

Nearby, shucking clams at one of the bonfires, a haggard crane looked up. "Disappear? Are you looking into the missing?"

She came over, and it took a few minutes for Tresh to realize they weren't talking about the same fisherfolk.

"Start from the top," Turresh said. "What is going on here?"

The crane invited them to sit around the fire. "We've had six deep-sea fishing rafts disappear in the last few days. There's been no word from any of them. Just this morning, one of them washed up on shore."

The raft in question was propped up against a rock. While it looked a little worse for wear, it lacked claw marks.

"There goes my serpentine whale theory," Cielle said.

Tresh wasn't ready to strike sea monster off the list just yet. "Perhaps it was a crowncrest sea serpent and caught them off guard? Or a swarm of white-bellied sea snakes?"

The crane shook her head. "Every deep-sea raft team has a mix of cranes and petrels, gryphons and opinici. Someone is always watching the water and the sky."

"Even if one set was caught off guard, it's weird that it happened to two, right?" Cielle offered.

Tresh was still thinking. Some ocean life could be

crafty. She'd seen serpentine whales catch unsuspecting manatees and toss them back and forth through the air. The sea could be a cruel place. Wildlife sometimes acted... well, *possessed*, for lack of a better word.

"If it is the same thing, it is moving." She started drawing in the sand. "It hit the islanders here, then came northeast to find the waters off Swan's Rest. Have the other rafts had trouble or reported anything strange in those waters?"

One of the elders looked up from putting fish on spits to cook. "Just those two were fishing offshore. The rest of our fleet went north."

Tresh looked north, seeing only weald. Then northeast, where the ocean and cliffs of the Redwood Valley met. "Is that not fantail, owl, or parrotface coast?"

"They don't use it the same way," the first crane offered. "They think of their territory as land, not water. In exchange for a percentage of the catch, we're welcome to fish there as much as we'd like."

Tresh had spent as much time around the mainlanders as any fisherfolk she knew, and it would never have occurred to her that they didn't think of the ocean coast as part of their hunting territory. They were certainly precious about their freshwater rivers and lakes.

Cielle used a claw to extend the line from the islands to Swan's Rest and up the coast. "If there is a sea creature doing the killings, it could be headed there next. We should warn them."

She nodded and turned to the crane and elder. "We will check on your fleet and tell them to return home until we know what is going on. May Cielle and I get some supplies for the flight? I did not bring any beads with me, but I can repay you once I return."

The elder laughed. "If Rorin were here, he'd tell you to take what you want. You've done enough for us."

She thanked the local fisherfolk for the supplies and warned them to set watches on the shallows. Not all sea monsters stayed in the water. Some of them, like her, were just as comfortable on land.

14

THE STRIX PLATEAU

Tresh led Cielle along the coast, staying over the water so she didn't lose time asking permission from the fantails who controlled this portion of the weald. In a general sense, things were going well as the weald regrew: the rimu trees had their mast, and the ground parrots laid a lot of eggs. There was just one small point of contention between them.

The giant salamanders who'd escaped their pen along the river delta had begun to take over. All the small prey animals had returned, but the weald monitors were still concentrated in the northern part of the valley. As a result, salamanders larger than gryphons now controlled the southern half of Glacial Run.

Tresh stopped off briefly at the Strix Plateau to check in with the owls. While Blinky wasn't there, the rest of her pride had heard about Tresh's efforts in the bog. They gave her and Cielle their blessing to check the coast and confirmed the fisherfolk's story.

The weald owls assumed everyone was either on the side of Strix's sons or his only daughter. By helping

Blinky, one of the Ashen Weald owls, they placed Tresh as friendly to their cause, even though she wasn't sure that was true. She'd just only met the one owl gryphon on her adventures, and the two had saved each other's lives several times.

Cielle was fascinated by the plateau itself. The cliffs were spider-webbed by ropes and bridges to allow the wingtorn access. There were enough nests and facilities for hundreds of gryphons, including the stands where court was held, yet the plateau only had twenty permanent inhabitants.

During the fires, this plateau held the entire Ashen Weald.

"It's so empty," Cielle commented. "I think I'd be lonely here. Why all the wasted space, though? Were the owl gryphons wiped out by the wingtorn the way Crane's Nest was?"

Tresh escorted him away from the owl's sensitive hearing before she answered. "The opposite, really. Their leader died in the eyrie fire, and their pride split in two. Strix's daughter, Ninox, took half the pride north, staking a claim to the Snowfeather Highlands. The others stayed behind and joined the Ashen Weald, led by Strix's sons."

Even though the ocean side of the Redwood Valley was full of cliffs and rocks, Tresh couldn't help but express her surprise that none of the Ashen Weald had tried fishing here. It was a blind spot Kia and Zeph also shared. Maybe Tresh should see if anyone at Swan's Rest was willing to get something going.

There were a few islands offshore from here up through the Parrotface Pride's territory. Since they were already on their way north, she decided to stop off and see if any of the islands had fresh water. The ones closest to the Strix Plateau were just large enough to support a few lost redwoods and some birds who'd been willing to make the flight to avoid predators.

These could work.

She didn't have time to check the next set because she caught a glimpse of a raft along the island's rocky shore. She swooped down to investigate.

"No obvious claw marks." Cielle perched on a boulder and stretched his neck down to examine the bamboo craft. "Is this the other fisherfolk raft that went missing... or are we looking at new victims here?"

Tresh dipped a paw into the surf but was afraid to go into the water and check the underside. It was possible they weren't dealing with a massive serpentine whale but something small, like an algae bloom or jelly swarm. She didn't want to stick her head into that.

It also looked like someone had beached this raft, not that it had been abandoned and drifted here. The current should have taken it the other way.

"The bamboo is telling," Tresh said. "We will ask some of the local fisherfolk when we find them. They will have mapped the currents here before they started fishing. Let us make sure they are okay before we do anything else."

She did a quick fly-through the island to be certain there were no other signs of fisherfolk, then continued north.

TRESH AND CIELLE flew parallel to the Redwood Valley Eyrie along the coast until they caught sight of a craft with living occupants.

Unfortunately, these weren't the missing Swan's Rest fisherfolk.

"Into the water!" Tresh ordered Cielle, practically dragging him beneath the waves. Off in the distance, next to an island with a lake, were three ships. Not rafts like the fisherfolk and Crackling Sea opinici liked to make but genuine ships with massive sails.

Tresh didn't get a good look at the opinici piloting them. Instead, she and Cielle just got a glimpse before Tresh forced her taiga islander companion into the water.

"I'm soaked through," he whined once the boats disappeared from view.

Having spent last mating season with Younce, she was sympathetic to taiga fur's ability to absorb saltwater, but they still had a job to do. "Be thankful you still have your summer coat."

She helped push him to the nearest island so he could groom himself dry while she refilled on freshwater, which she splashed over herself to rinse off the salt. As an islander, he was more adept than his taiga ancestors at handling ocean water, though it didn't look like he did a lot of swimming.

"What're you thinking?" Cielle asked after a few minutes of silence. "Do you know who they are?"

She did not. "I thought they must be Blackwing Eyrie boats at first. But there are too few to invade. And they are not headed south. They are headed the other way."

Cielle must have spent most of his supply runs to

the shore gossiping because he was better informed than most islanders about what was going on in the world. "You think they're the Seraph King's forces, planning a sneak attack on the Blackwing Eyrie? Maybe they're going to assassinate him while Rybalt Reevesbane is busy elsewhere!"

"With just three ships?" She was skeptical. One of the craft was large enough to hold some real military forces, what was usually called a dreadnaught in the stories, but the other two were small. From what little she understood of the Blackwing Eyrie from Piprik, it was the third most fortified city on the continent—after the Alabaster Eyrie and wherever the starlings' pridelord made his nest.

No, this was something different. Ships of that size would be able to take a single gryphon pride without much effort, but they'd never stand against several. And while the Ashen Weald and free prides may have their differences, the pressure from the Blackwing Eyrie and Alabaster Eyrie meant that none of the native southern prides would stand for outside aggression.

In the water drifted another raft of the type often used by Swan's Rest fisherfolk. Like the others, it was empty. There was no sign of its previous occupants, no sign of a struggle.

"If they took the Swan's Rest fishers hostage, we need to chase them," Cielle said. "We should go rescue them now!"

Tresh's tail twitched back and forth in irritation. Without Piprik's whale pheromone, she didn't know how to destroy a craft that large. And she didn't know how to get any prisoners off it safely if their feathers were clipped. What she really needed was more information from a pride who should be watching this side of the mountains.

"No," she said at last. "We will seek out the Strix Pride. We need help to do this."

Cielle shook the last of the water out of his tailfeathers. "Great! Do you know how to contact them?"

She stared at the endless mountains north of the Redwood Valley and shrugged. "We fly towards Poisonmaw. With any luck, Ninox's kin will notice us and chirp a greeting."

LUCK WAS NOT on Tresh's side. In her mind, the northern mountains were full of thousands of black-and-red owl gryphons watching the movement of every squirrel or bug who stepped foot into their territory.

Practically speaking, however, she knew there were only about forty or fifty in the Strix Pride, and they were likely watching the northern border, not the middle of their territory.

She and Cielle not only crossed the entire Owlfeather Highlands unprovoked, they hadn't even see another gryphon until Xavi chirped a greeting up at them near Poisonmaw.

"Tresh!" the magpie, Hatzel's second-in-command, shouted from a tree. "I didn't know you were coming to visit. I owe you for the hospitality you showed me at Luminaire. Come, come, let me find you some nice parrots. Oh! You need to meet Pink Paw. She'll want to thank you for saving me. And a taiga gryphon, is it? Are you with Younce's expedition? He's talking with Hatzel and Ninox right now. I'll get you settled in with your pridemates."

Tresh froze at Younce's name and had to be nudged along by Cielle. The nice thing about having a lovers' quarrel with a taiga gryphon who lived on Snowfall Mountain and led the largest surviving taiga pride was that he couldn't just fly down to the shore to talk to her. She had as much privacy as she wanted to sulk without seeing his bright green eyes and pretty rosettes and soft fur and huggable tail.

The fact that not only was she about to come beak-to-beak with Younce for the first time since spring but that *she* was here invading *his* space unannounced only made it worse. Was he still mad at her? Was she mad at him?

Or, even worse, were they not mad at each other at all? She'd wanted to talk to Younce after he'd already chosen a different mate for the season. To talk as friends and figure out what she wanted without the pressure of mating season.

While those were the thoughts that went through her mind, her heart ached a little at the idea he might have found someone else after their season ended with an argument. She hadn't wanted to hurt him. She'd just spent one too many nights listening to him talk to the gryphlets about how the taiga pride would be great again, about learning their heritage, about opening up new nesting grounds.

She... didn't want any of that. She both didn't want to care for a gryphlet and didn't want the knowledge that the taiga den mother was caring for her gryphlet without her. She hated the thought that she and Younce would have an egg together and he'd raise it and be an excellent father and he'd never care for her.

Of course, shouting at him and running south to the shore may have caused him not to care about me anyways.

She didn't discuss the number of relationships she'd had before Younce, but in truth, she hadn't been invested enough in any of them to spend an entire mating season with one other gryphon or opinicus.

Usually gryphons. Opinici are clingy.

Cielle and Xavi chatted back and forth, filling the silence with talk of parrots and sugar frogs. Cielle promised that if Xavi could get twenty plump parrots to Sandpiper's Dune, he'd make sure there were the same number of ashfin salmon waiting there for the magpie.

"Deal!" Xavi said. "Zeph'll be excited to eat a new type of fish. After he came back from the shore, it's all he talks about."

Where several redwoods formed a circle, a small building had been constructed to serve as Hatzel's home. Tresh could hear her talking to Younce and Ninox in there. There was a slight tone of disagreement, but not in a foreboding sense. It sounded more like Hatzel thought Younce was wasting his time. Occasionally, she'd hear the sounds of a female copper hawk —*Pink Paw?*—or Ninox chime in about security.

Tresh was so worried about stumbling over her words when Younce came out that it was an immense relief when the taiga pride leader exited Hatzel's den, saw Tresh, and tripped over his own tail.

"Hey there, Blue Eyes," she said, trying to sound smooth. She only ever called him Blue Eyes when it was summer, and his eyes were green.

Is that smooth or dorky? Why do I care how I sound? It

has been half a year since we were mates. He probably does not even remember me.

"Tresh!" he squeaked. "I didn't know you were up here. I'm so sorry, I didn't mean to intrude. Hatzel, you should have told me."

The last saberbeak, more like the last adult saberbeak judging by the beak-fanged gryphlets hopping all over Xavi and chirping at him, Hatzel looked unimpressed by Tresh and Younce's relationship.

"I didn't know that'd be a problem," she said. "Or that they were coming. What can we do for the fisherfolk?"

Ninox watched the proceedings with curiosity. When Tresh explained they were actually here for the Strix Pride, the owl gryphon's ears twitched a bit.

"I do not believe we have met." Ninox stood quietly while Tresh explained about the missing Crane's Nest refugees, the missing Swan's Rest fishing rafts, and the strange translucent sails on the boats offshore. "I did not think to watch the water. Who would attack mountains by boat? We would see them long before they arrived at the valley."

Hatzel chirped for Xavi and Pink Paw to come over. "I don't know boats. I don't know any gryphon who does. The Crackling Sea opinici seem to be limited to rafts. Do any of the Redwood Valley scholars know?"

To Tresh's confusion, everyone except her and Cielle looked to Ninox to answer that question.

Even more surprising, Ninox had an answer. "Not that I have seen. I will ask them."

"I know someone who would be able to tell us if they're Blackwing Eyrie or not." Younce finally found his voice. "I'm going up to visit the glacier pride and hear about how they survived the Connixation and what stories they tell of those times that we don't know. You can come with me as my guest. I'm sure a simple question about a boat won't be a bother."

Tresh tried to look at his face, but their eyes kept meeting. Had his beak always been that pretty shade of grey? She tried to say something nice, but only mean words came out. "Unless they are a blackwing scouting force we just discovered, in which case, Iony is just going to murder us all and hide the bodies."

Younce's tail swished when he talked, knocking over a saberbeak gryphlet who was trying to bite it. Unlike everyone she'd met except Rorin, he didn't stare at her scars. "I don't think he'd invite us up there for story time if there was a chance we'd stumble across a hidden Blackwing Eyrie plot. Also, I don't think the glacier pride is as, well, loyal to the Blackwing Eyrie as they are to the pitohui reeve. If you feel unsafe, I can go and ask before I leave. I'll say I saw the boats on my way up."

"If there's danger, you'll need me to protect you." Rolling the words together made her beak ache. She'd never felt a need to impress him last year, why did she suddenly feel self-conscious? "Go pack your things."

"Of course! We leave tomorrow. You're both welcome to join us, you and your... Is that your mate?" He gestured to Cielle. "Well, you're both more than welcome."

"He is not my mate." She forced herself to speak in a way that didn't make her beak hurt. "He is a gift to you."

"Oh?" Younce and Cielle both said.

She nodded. "He is here to answer all follow-up questions you have for the Williwaw Pride after the Blue-eyed Festival. You remember Cielle, yes?"

Cielle looked surprised, but she shot him a look to remind him that he was only here because she'd agreed to let him tag along. Right now, she was depending on him to keep Younce occupied. As the two taiga gryphons from different prides walked away, a saberbeak gryphlet hanging from one of their tails, Tresh could hear her old mate asking if the islander was related to *the* Tielle or Cici from the Connixation myth.

"Younce is not as stupid as many taiga gryphons." Ninox's tone suggested that she thought this was a helpful comment. "The eggs you two would have together would be somewhat smart. And they would swim in cold water, I think. That would be very useful."

"Nox, I don't think she's looking for advice," Hatzel said.

The owl gryphon looked from the saberbeak to the fisherfolk and continued. "I would be willing to take any of your eggs. You would not need to raise them. I am willing to accept eggs from relatively smart gryphons."

"I do not want a family—to have *or* give away." Tresh didn't have the heart to explain about Crane's Nest and burying her nieces and nephews. She didn't feel like she should have to justify her choices to anyone. Maybe Younce, if he'd asked, but she'd never given him the opportunity.

The Strix Pride's leader looked to Hatzel for support. "If you lay fewer than three eggs, it is easy, yes? Your pride is also small, Hatzel. So few saberbeaks. Tell Tresh to have eggs with Younce."

Hatzel, older than both of them, just stared Ninox right in her owl eyes and said, "I killed a fifteen-foot monitor with fangs the size of my femur today. I'm going to find a hot springs to soak in. I'm not offering either of you relationship advice."

Ninox watched the saberbeak wander far enough away to get clearance to fly. "I do not think she meant that. If you reconsider, send the eggs north with one of Naya's caravans. While you and Younce go north to visit the glacier gryphons, I will ask the scholars about the boat you saw."

"Much obliged." Tresh pushed down the irritation she felt at receiving unsolicited commentary on her love life from someone who wasn't Quess long enough to remember her manners. "It was good to meet you, Ninox. While I do not speak for any of the villages, I would like to invite you and your children to the shore to learn to swim once they have fledged. It is a useful skill."

The owl gryphon nodded her head a little. Her ears moved in a friendly manner one beat behind what Tresh would normally expect. "I accept your offer to teach my gryphlets and chick how to swim. I will send them to you once Sound of Snow has fledged."

"Wait, I did not mean *I* would teach them—" But Tresh was too slow, and Ninox had already flown off.

Once the owl pride leader had cleared the nesting area, several more Strix Pride appeared from the trees to join her.

Tresh went to find something to eat, remembering Xavi's promise of ground parrot. She asked Pink Paw if they had a spare nest. Tresh didn't want the awkwardness of spending the evening with the taiga gryphons.

15

THE FROZEN CROWN

The next day, Tresh finished her morning grooming, repacked her harness, and went to find her islander and ex-mate. There was a pawful of taiga gryphons sleeping in a pile. The only way she could be sure Cielle was among them was that she saw one feathered tail sticking out of the fluff.

Younce was on his back with all four paws straight in the air. He'd always been a strange sleeper. His tail swished back and forth, and occasionally he'd twitch a paw.

It was hard not to laugh or poke his foot. She thought back to her trips to the taiga to visit him in autumn. She'd left from Snowfall to go into the bog to search for Quess. The night before, Tresh had heard Thenca and Younce arguing about whether or not to tell her Urious had led the raids on Crane's Nest.

Tresh had snuck out, believing that Younce would have to either hide the identity of her brother's killer from her or break a promise to Thenca. In the times since then, she wished she'd given him the benefit of the doubt. It wasn't why she'd stopped going to visit him, but her old decisions weighed upon her now.

Enough. I have more important things to worry about than pretty taiga gryphons.

She poked Younce lightly and said it was time to get up.

"You know where to get breakfast, Tresh," he mumbled without waking. "Fetch some sugar frogs, and we'll go visit the hot springs to spend some time together."

Sleepy Younce was the worst Younce for her aching heart, so she kicked his tail up and over his paws and into his face, where his reflexes took over, and he bit his own tail with a *homph.*

Then he began coughing and rolled upright again. "What happened?"

"You were dreaming of a snake, then bit your own tail," she told him. "It is time to head north. There are missing fisherfolk in danger."

He shook his head and scratched at a rounded ear. "Missing fisherfolk?"

It occurred to her that she'd been so enamored with Younce, she'd forgotten to tell him *why* they were searching for ships. Once she filled him in on what was at stake, he roused the other taiga gryphons—there turned out to be three who weren't Cielle or Younce once the pile of taiga fur split apart—and got them into the air.

"I'm sorry; I didn't realize," he said once they were aloft. "We could've left last night and slept at the northern border, then crossed with first light."

He'd picked up that she was angry but hadn't figured out that her anger was directed at herself for forgetting. She was too embarrassed to say anything and a little upset that she felt flustered by him now. She'd never been flustered with him in the past, not at the battle for Sandpiper's Dune nor their entire time mated.

A Strix owl hooted from below, indicating the taiga gryphons were leaving the Owlfeather Highlands and entering the no-gryphon zone between Ninox and the glacier pride.

Cielle and the other taiga gryphons gave Tresh and Younce their space. The islander seemed content to brag about how his lineage included both the fantails who fled the Connixation and the Williwaw Pride, meaning he had all the fastest flying gryphons in his family tree.

With his white coat and grey-black flank patterns, she'd thought he looked the same as all the Snowfall taiga gryphons when she'd met him at Sandpiper's Dune. Seeing him next to them now, the contrast was clear. Cielle's ears, where they poked up from his fluffy head, were pointed, and he didn't have rosettes, exactly. His pattern was the black and grey of rosettes, yet stretched long, like thick stripes.

Was that how the Williwaw Pride had always looked? Or was it a result of being on a volcanic island with fantails and opinici for a hundred years? Piprik would know.

Khalim, she corrected herself. She and Rorin had moved his hut from Luminaire to an island farther out. Officially, he was teaching the fledglings on Ashfoot Isle. Unofficially, it was just too hard to keep him from blowing up assassins when he lived along the shore.

Tresh looked back at Younce and tried to break the

ice. "How have you been? Are you still finding new taiga nests?"

"I am!" His voice picked up a little. "We've restored Williwaw, Hoarfrost, and Owlfeather. We even found a few smaller outposts. Looks like they were made by family units who wanted to live outside of the main caverns, but a couple are large enough I think they were on the cusp of becoming new prides if the Connixation hadn't come along. I even got Zeph and his friends to map the southern caves for me while they look for cave gryphons."

She thought of the way he enjoyed showing the taiga fledglings their heritage and pushed down her envy. "I am glad. Your gryphlets may yet see the taiga pride restored to their pre-Connixation glory."

His eyes narrowed, and she realized she'd said too much. He was starting to figure out why she'd disappeared on him.

"Not my gryphlets," he said. "The pride's gryphlets. Tresh, is—"

A cry for help silenced his questions. Tresh suddenly realized no glacier gryphons had greeted them when they'd entered their territory.

It was hard to see what was happening. The glacier pride's home was the largest peak along the mountain range that housed the Redwood Valley, Poisonmaw, Owlfeather Highlands, taiga, and, at the very northern tip of the range, the fabled terraces of the Blackwing Eyrie.

Yet from the glacier peak to the sea, smoke rose into the air. Owl screeches met with the loud cries of white-tailed kites. The loudest sounds were coming from the summit itself, but Tresh's eyes were drawn to the water.

Along a narrow strip, the largest of the crafts she'd been chasing was anchored with a long plank connecting it to shore. An icy mist rose from the ship. Offshore, the two smaller ships were anchored. Small, but well-armored opinici flew in formation against the mountain, like glistening javelins loosed from the Seraph King's quiver. Wave after wave came from the ships. Where they encountered the glacier pride, a red mist hung in the cloudy skies.

Three very specific things caught Tresh's eye before Younce's rallying cry urged them into a sprint for the peak. Atop the dreadnaught sat an opinicus in more gold armor than she'd ever seen. He wore a spiked crown, and in his countenance, she saw the crowned emblem of the Alabaster Eyrie badge Khalim had taken off Piprik.

Curled up next to the Seraph King like a snake poised to strike was Mally the Nighthaunt in all his red-taloned glory. Several guards kept a close watch on the Nighthaunt, though from their poise, it was difficult to know whether their orders were to keep him safe or keep him from escaping.

Lastly, and only when a cloud blocked the sunlight, she saw an opinicus in blinding silver armor leading the attack. If Lei and Piprik's stories were to be believed, this was Hi-kun, commander of the Seraph King's armies.

There was no way five taiga gryphons and a fisher-folk were going to be able to save anyone from this.

The glacier pride was in trouble.

YOUNCE REACHED the peak moments before Hi-kun's forces arrived. The glacier gryphons, while confused about the arrival of these long-lost taiga cousins, let them pass without challenge.

The glacier pride's home was a mix of grey rocks and permafrost. A hollowed-out section of the mountain had chunks of ice-like quartz sticking up. Fifty gryphlets cowered in nests around the peak.

On the edge, atop an outcropping, stood Iony. His face and wings resembled a grey owl, except with long ears and a nub for a tail. He shouted down at Hi-kun. "My great grandmother flies faster than you, and she's dead! Come up here and face me so I can piss on your corpse."

The long-eared gryphon turned and saw Younce. He blinked a few times before he remembered they were coming. "Trounce? Bounce?"

"Younce," Tresh offered.

Iony nodded. "Right. Look, I appreciate you not turning tail and running, but we're outnumbered and screwed right now. If I survive this, we can play story time or whatever you came up here for."

Cielle stepped forwards. "We can help hold them off until your blackwing allies arrive. Reeve Rybalt Reevesbane is always two steps behind you in the tales, pride leader."

"Bleeding tales," Iony grumbled. "There's no backup. We heard the Seraph King used the stormcloth he stole from the Ashen Weald to build some fancy boats. Thing is, we assumed he was coming up the blood coast. There's an army of blackwings, mothfeathers, and pitohui waiting at Blacktalon to ambush them. We were sent home because of a storm. Bloody tide."

More cries came from farther down. The den mother was still rounding up the glacier gryphlets, whose ears seemed even longer relative to their body than the adults.

Iony took a good look at Cielle's stripes. "Well, aren't you something right out of a cave painting. Hoarfrost, are you? What'd they do, defrost you out of the ice?"

"Williwaw, pride leader," Cielle said. "And fisherfolk. Why did they stop here? Aren't they trying to assassinate the blackwing reeve?"

Tresh's eyes hadn't left the boats. "Not with only three ships."

Younce looked down and thought he saw glacier pride prisoners being led inside. If the Seraph King was taking prisoners, he could guess where Tresh was going to search for the missing fisherfolk.

"The shark's right." Iony had finally noticed the scars on Tresh's beak and put two and two together. "There's only one thing they want more than the blackwing reeve."

"A seraph," Tresh said. "You and Rybalt burned the one I found in the swamp."

"Seem to recall it was some fisherfolk and Ashen Weald who did the burning," Iony countered.

Tresh considered him. "The tales say the Seraph King already has one."

He pointed her beak at Mally the Nighthaunt. "It was rotten and didn't take."

While Iony and Tresh talked, Younce examined the glacier nests. A rounded wall served as the central focus. With the morning light coming from the east, the ice lit up, revealing a six-winged shape frozen inside.

He'd heard Tresh talk about the *opinithing* in the

swamp, but he hadn't imagined it like this. It was vibrant, a rainbow of colors and wings. Its forelegs and back legs, while still appearing functional for walking, were also wings. The tail was both gryphon and opinicus, feathered and agile. "This is what they're here for?"

"Aye," the glacier gryphon said.

Tresh turned back. "That... is not how I imagined the mummy looked in life."

"They won't stop 'til they get it," Iony continued. "So you two'd better get out of here."

The den mother in the background shouted that there were gryphlets missing who had been near the shore.

Iony swore. "Last chance. They're nearly here."

"I'm not leaving while taiga gryphlets are at risk." Younce commanded his gryphons to start evacuating the young. "Tell your pride to grab as many as they can. Fly them to the border and drop them off. Ninox's kin will find them and take them to Poisonmaw."

Iony's eyes narrowed. Younce knew he was making calculations about accepting help from the Ashen Weald and free prides. Down below, more of his gryphons had been subdued. He looked back at the fledglings and gryphlets, the den mother and her assistants, and gave the order.

"Fledglings, you know how to glide. Go south until you see strange, scary owls," Iony commanded. "Everyone up here, grab a gryphlet and fly."

The evacuation began, but Iony wasn't done.

He looked at Tresh, Cielle, and Younce. "There were gryphlets missing near the shore. You three find them, and then make your escape. I'm going to bloody Hikun's beak."

"If you survive, you can pick up your gryphlets at Poisonmaw." Younce wasn't sure if the glacier pride leader had heard him. Iony was already on a collision course with The Metalworks.

Younce looked back up at the seraph, incandescent in the morning light. Three ships had circumvented a continent to get here. They wouldn't leave without their prize, but he wouldn't leave without finding those three lost taiga gryphlets.

"Come on!" he shouted, then dove off the mountain and glided around to search the shore.

16

LOST AND FOUND

Overhead, long-eared gryphons and brightly armored opinici clashed. In the alpine forests below, Tresh wove through the pine and aneda. While Iony guarded the nests and seraph atop the mountain, there were smaller villages on the way down and a goliath bird path. Melting snow covered the trees even as they approached sea level. The mixture of brown bark and white frost let Tresh hide just as well as Cielle and Younce.

A fishing village of opinicus construction lurked just off the main path. It had been wrecked, searched, and abandoned by the Seraph King's forces. If she were looking to hide, it's where she'd have gone, so she crouched low and crawled through the underbrush to the first building.

Blackwing architecture, if that's what this was, favored a blocky, cyclopean style she hadn't seen before. The glacier dens above were round with pointed roofs, but the fishing buildings were square with slits and eaves to drive snowmelt away from the base.

Tresh lifted a back paw to let Younce know to stay along the trees. Two glacier gryphons chased an opinicus into an ambush, turning from predator to prey. To her surprise, the white opinici subdued the glacier gryphons and transported them to the large ship.

They are taking prisoners. That is good for the missing fisherfolk.

At least, it was relatively good. It meant they were still alive—for now. Perched atop the mast, the Nighthaunt let out a preternatural cry that resonated through her bones.

She shivered at the fate that awaited the glacier gryphons and fisherfolk who disappeared into the dreadnaught's hold.

But not for the blackwing opinici who'd been in charge of the port. Their corpses littered the cobblestone streets. Some of the supposedly domesticated goliath birds had broken out of their stalls and fed upon the dead.

She decided she'd look into the stables later and pulled herself into the largest building. There was some sort of system that allowed a fire to be placed inside while the smoke exited the roof. Across the room were nests built along the ceiling. Heat rose, so it made sense that's where they'd want to sleep.

The back of the building was separated by a wall and a door. She took a few moments to practice twisting her paw into the right shape, then opened it. The smell of fresh mint hit her nares, intoxicating her.

If I were a gryphlet, I would hide with the gryph mint.

The warehouse was large enough to fit perhaps three dozen gryphons, but instead, half of it was full of crates. They were stacked to the ceiling, suggesting that at other times, the port filled its warehouses.

She went to the mint first, finding that someone had broken the crate open, but there was no indication of the missing gryphlets. She climbed the boxes, looking for any sign of habitation. She saw scratch marks. They looked like gryphon claws but could also have been some sort of large squirrel.

Capybara, she reminded herself. *They are called capybaras.*

As best she could tell, however, there was no way through the boxes. She pushed against a few, but the ones she tested were solid. She reached for one of the ones up top, but it was lighter than the lower ones and tumbled down on top of her. Spices of a type she'd never experienced filled the room, sending her into a sneezing fit. She rushed back to the door to escape into the taiga forest lest someone heard her sneezing, but she caught the tiniest, softest sneeze from behind the wall of crates and stopped.

Would the Seraph King's forces hide here? That makes no sense.

"I am Turresh of Swan's Rest," she called out. "I am here on behalf of Iony to help evacuate any gryphlets or wounded. They are outside searching now. If you are friendly, please let me know. I do not mean harm."

No response, but after a moment, another sneeze. She retested the crates around the sneeze and saw one wasn't supporting the weight of the crates above it. It was just heavy. She pulled without luck. She braced herself above it, pulling with all her might, and it shifted a little.

Oh, it had been set into the ground so it wouldn't slide.

Clearly, someone did not want this one crate being jostled around. Now that it was out of its groove, she managed to work it free.

The crate jingled like it was full of metal beads, and a small bug ran out.

Tresh leapt into the air with a yelp and beat her wings to get away from it. She wasn't afraid of bugs. Insects were potentially food. This one, however, was a bright teal scarab, and she'd learned what that meant.

Pitohui.

An opinicus pulled herself out of the hole where the crate had been. Several more scarabs rushed past her. She wore a dark, cheap cloth over her body. Only her beak stuck out.

When she saw Tresh was airborne, the pitohui threw off the cloth, revealing bright orange and black plumage underneath.

Tresh landed across the room from the opinicus and her beetles. "The scarab startled me. I mean no harm. I will return your crate so you are not found."

A stylized scarab glyph matching the bug that was wandering the warehouse floor had been stamped on the crate. Where the light from the fire in the other room spilled through the door and into the pitohui's hideaway, Tresh saw another dozen crates bearing the same mark.

They jingled, though. Are they all full of metal beads? Why put currency in with the bugs?

The pitohui stared at Tresh's whale-hide harness, flippers, and shark tooth necklace. "You're some sort of fisherfolk? What port do you hail from?"

"Swan's Rest." Tresh wasn't sure it counted as a port,

but they did occasionally have traders come down from the northeast by boat.

The pitohui groomed some toxin-laden oil into her feathers. "I've dined in all seven ports and never heard of a *Swan's Rest.*"

"I grew up at Crane's Nest before it was destroyed," Tresh added, "along the coast of the Redwood Valley Eyrie."

The pitohui seemed unsure, but there was some recognition at the term Redwood Valley. When the scarab scurried back towards the hideaway, she caught it in her beak and swallowed it.

Tresh needed to keep searching before the battle was over and the Seraph King's forces swung back to check the buildings. "I did not mean to disturb you. There are three gryphlets missing. I must evacuate them before it is too late. I will leave you to your hiding."

The pitohui considered Tresh's offer before whistling. All three gryphlets, wearing dark brown trashbird sacks, crawled out from the hideaway. "They are safe. The clothing was to keep the scarabs off. Take them and go."

"I can get you out, too." Tresh helped guide the mint-addled gryphlets to the front door.

The pitohui didn't follow, instead backing into the wall of boxes and pulling the crate after her. "I promised the reeve no one will find these crates. Reeve Rybalt watch over you."

I would much prefer he did not. Tresh swished her tail to cover up the box lines in the dust and guided the lost gryphlets to the forest where Cielle and Younce waited.

While Younce helped calm them—an easy task after all the mint they'd consumed—Tresh climbed a tree and watched the dreadnaught. The cries of Iony and Hi-kun echoed down. It wouldn't be long now.

A shout came from the docks as a prisoner tried to escape. She saw the white wings and worried it was just an alabaster opinicus, but then the black and red designs of a crane fisherfolk appeared before he was pulled back in.

That decided it. She climbed down to tell Younce her plan.

"Three gryphons carrying three gryphlets should be easy enough." Younce picked up the closest mint-addled gryphlet, which was starting to doze off.

"Three gryphlets to one gryphon." Tresh had Cielle locate a larger sack and poked a few breathing holes into it, then put the gryphlets together. If they were anything like fisherfolk or Snowfall gryphlets, they were used to being in a pile of fluff and feathers together.

"What?" Younce looked confused.

Tresh turned to Cielle first. "The missing fisherfolk are on the boat. We traced its route. We know it did not come from the north. You are always bragging about Williwaw and fantail flying. If you hurry, you can get word to Rorin at Bogwash in time for him to get out to sea and intercept the ship on its way home and save everyone."

"What about you?" the islander asked.

She looked out at the dreadnaught. "I will cling to the bottom of the ship in case an opportunity arises to slow it down."

Younce's tail twitched anxiously. "I don't think, I mean, you, it's..." he began several sentences but didn't finish them. "I know you'll be careful and smart. I look forward to seeing you again."

"Stop wasting time," she shouted at Cielle.

He spooked and flew off, fast as a falcon. A few of the Seraph King's forces saw him fly past and gave chase, but he was already past the mountain and out of view.

She nuzzled Younce once it was just them and the sleeping gryphlets. "I am sorry we did not talk in the spring. Come down to Luminaire when this is over. We will spend time catching up."

He nodded in a way that was neither a promise nor discouragement, beat his wings, and finally got some lift. He wasn't a weak gryphon, but had there been one more gryphlet, he'd be out of luck. As it was, Tresh was grateful Ninox's scouts would already be coming north after the initial gryphlets arrived from the glacier den mothers.

The petrel fisherfolk stalked past the goliath birds, their shaggy coats stained with blood. They were full on carrion, wandering into the woods to find shelter, and paid her little mind.

She found an alcove before the coastal ice and slowly groomed oil into her feathers. If she soaked through on the voyage, she might freeze to death or drown. This was going to be tricky.

Only once she was as oily as possible did she slip past the ice and into the water, swimming under the ship. The nice thing about kings and reeves is they liked to travel in style. She found space in one of the gold-plated, open-beaked adornments along the side of the vessel and curled up.

17

THE METALWORKS

Mally the Nighthaunt waited until the all-clear to leave his post. His bodyguards followed behind. While the Seraph King had once been content to let Mally roam free, the incident in the swamp coupled with the palace explosion and the cave gryphons had changed his mind. Now, the Nighthaunt found himself on a very short leash. He was too valuable to lose until the ascension was complete.

He let out a screech. The way his bodyguards looked at him suggested they thought he was trying to intimidate the last of the glacier gryphons. It was a silly, stupid interpretation. He wanted to be sure the glacier pride had really been beaten before he left his perch.

Waves of sound echoed back to him. The only movement that wasn't the Seraph King's forces was something splashing on the surface of the water, before diving down, possibly a thresher shark feeding upon the dead. Despite his recommendations to the king that blackwing bodies could be useful, Hi-kun had ordered all pitohui and blackwings killed. Only the glacier pride was taken prisoner, and only because they'd need someone to test the blood on first before risking the king.

Alchemical supplies were critically low, something Mally had to deal with every day now. He'd done all he could to slow down the progression of his iron disorder, but the pain was constant. His old assistant, Khalim-disguised-as-Piprik, had stolen the purple salts from his workshop even as the Blackwing Eyrie blew up the palace. Mally couldn't reset his biology until they had more.

Of course, the pools where the salts were taken from had been poisoned. He didn't know if that had been Khalim or Rybalt. Both had it out for Mally. All that was left of the salts were in his old workshop on the Abyssal Naze, and the Seraph King didn't want to try to retake it until it was time.

The Nighthaunt looked up at the frozen, iridescent seraph in the ice.

It's time.

He let out a different cry, and several pale, red-taloned shapes pulled themselves from the ship's hold and flew up after him with blackwater and saltpeter. His acolytes, the ones he'd kept alive despite their shared disorder, were loyal in a way the king's soldiers never would be.

The bitter scent of aneda greeted his nares, released when falling gryphons broke tree branches on their way down. Once the army abandoned the mountain, it would be swarmed by feral goliath birds looking for easy meals.

At the pridegrounds, moisture hung in the air, rainbow droplets diffusing the morning light. The

Nighthaunt let out another call, feeling the vibrations echo back to him. The humidity slowed their flow, and the world felt thick around him, but the shapes returned were all ice. No gryphons were hiding atop the glacier pride's peak.

He stood before the frozen seraph and stretched tall, placing his talons against the ice, and let out a final cry.

Some of the Alabaster Eyrie forces backed away, afraid to be too close to the Nighthaunt. Hi-Kun ordered several of them to take the last of the glacier prisoners down to the boats, giving Mally time alone with his prize.

The ice was hard and thick. He could feel the faintest of cracks when he screamed at it, but there shouldn't be any problems. He measured out a margin of error and began scratching figures into the ice with his red talons.

His acolytes pulled out their equipment. If they were nervous under the watchful gaze of Hi-Kun, they didn't show it. Instead, they began using the blackwater and tools to extract the seraph. It wouldn't be easy getting it down the mountain, but even if some of the glacier gryphons had escaped north to go for help, it would take at least a day for more blackwings to arrive.

The hold of the ship was as cold as they could reasonably make it with the goal of keeping the seraph on ice until it arrived at Duckbill, across the entire continent. Sawdust, fragments of icebergs harvested along the way, and a lot of insulation should keep it safe.

Knowing the Seraph King, he'd want someone to paint a picture of the seraph before they extracted it and pulled out as much blood as they could.

While his assistants worked tirelessly, Mally allowed his bodyguards to usher him away from the flames and closer to Hi-Kun.

"Astounding," the commander said. "The Blackwing Eyrie's reeve must have known we'd come for it, but he left the glacier gryphons to fend for themselves."

Mally stretched his long body, an opposite foreleg and hind leg each time. His tail twitched at the thought of being stuck on a ship for the return trip. "My spies showed our enemy boats being built at Reevesport, and they moved all their forces up north. They assumed the currents and starlings would keep anyone from coming south. It was a simple mistake."

The trip past the Emerald Jungle had been dangerous. A few test runs with craft lacking stormcloth sails had ended in failure. Only the cloth stolen from the bog had allowed them to create a ship that was fast enough to slip past the starlings but large enough to hold an army. And even then, they'd riled up some blue, swimming starlings along the last stretch of it.

While his scouts circled the mountain, Hi-kun's eyes looked south. "Even so, there was no garrison here at all. The only opinici we caught were here for lumber or fish. I can't help but feel like this is a trap. The Reevesbane is known for his fondness of the glacier pride. None of our scouts have seen the Mothfeather or Motmot forces for weeks now. I wish the king hadn't insisted upon coming."

If Mally was motivated by his survival, the king was motivated by his legacy. In general, to Mally's black eyes, the more important a reeve became, the more likely they were to hide in their spires and let their commanders and scholars go out into the field on their behalf.

The only reeves he saw on the front lines were the ones from small, backwater eyries. The king, however, had transcended his pampered reeve status with the object of his glory in sight.

One of the acolytes misjudged the amount of blackwater needed and lit himself on fire with a scream. Several nearby alabaster opinici splashed him with water and smothered him with blankets.

"I don't suppose your magical salts heal burn wounds," Hi-kun quipped.

Mally thought back to the wounds he'd received over the years from allies and enemies alike. His pinky talon, once severed but now regrown three transformations later, twitched with sympathy pains. "The blue reeve seems to think they will. If he's successful, I suppose we'll find out."

18

POINTY EARS, FEATHERED TAIL

Cielle flew through the northern mountains, passing over Younce and the Snowfall Pride as they evacuated the glacier gryphlets to Poisonmaw with the help of some Strix owls. One of them cawed something up to Cielle, but he was flying too high to hear. He had a mission.

The farthest north any of the Williwaw Pride had come, not that they really thought of themselves as the Williwaw Pride or even a gryphon pride anymore, was Snowfall. With Younce's constant invitations, a few had finally decided to travel across the ocean last winter and see the Snowfall pridegrounds and check on Williwaw on their way home.

Home, in this case, meant a volcanic island full of shipwrecks and capybaras. The ships were massive, larger even than the Seraph King's flagship, and were stamped with a six-winged emblem. To Cielle's knowledge, there were no remaining seraphs frozen into the ice, but he didn't want word of the ships getting out. His trips to Sandpiper's Dune were as much about gathering information through gossip as trade, and the emblem's resemblance to Tresh's *opinithing* worried them. Especially after finding out someone had sent armed forces to try to acquire it from the bog. His fellow islanders had begun scraping the design off the wrecks just to be safe.

Once upon a time, he'd thought living on an island kept him safe from harm. Really, that was a feeling passed down from the original Williwaw, Fantail, and Redwood Valley refugees who'd fled the Connixation. What had shaken his faith was the disappearance of the Crane's Nest settlement. If an island could just vanish overnight, none of them were safe.

Poisonmaw gave way to the remains of Crater Lake as he continued his flight southwest. He considered swinging by the Crackling Sea Eyrie, but he felt uncomfortable showing up there unannounced. Instead, he veered south, aiming at Snowfall.

The first indication that something was wrong came in the form of caravans coming to and from the eyrie to the taiga. Except they weren't—coming to *and* from, that is. They were all evacuating. The only gryphons and opinici heading to the eyrie were in the air. They flew at a much lower altitude, so he couldn't stop to chat, but something was definitely wrong.

His mind went through a hundred possibilities, sending his heart into a panic. He calmed himself. Bogwash was a long ways off, and he'd need all his energy to reach it. He could stop at Snowfall and find out what was happening while he filled up on water and fish bars.

The tallest peak in the southern taiga grew steadily larger, and Cielle began his descent. In the open common area, a small council had gathered and was beginning to direct gryphons and opinici in all directions.

Cielle caught sight of Naya and didn't waste any time, weaving between the messengers to land in the crowd.

"Naya!" he shouted. "I forgot you were headed up this way. I thought you were at Bogwash with Rorin."

Naya was flanked by Deracho and Orlea. It was a strange council. She looked confused by his arrival. "Cielle? What are you doing this far north?"

He caught them up on everything—the missing Crane's Nest refugees, the stormcloth fleet, the glacier pride, the seraph, the Seraph King, Mally, and what Tresh had commanded him to do.

Deracho shifted his attention to the islander when he mentioned Younce. "We need to send someone to fetch him home. He's the one who should be making these decisions, not me. I just came back with Naya to check on some lost traders."

Cielle gulped down water, forcing himself to stay calm. "You need to send whoever you can south. There's still time to intercept the ship."

"We can't," Orlea explained. He was tangentially aware of who she was, the leader of the underbough opinici, because her traders frequented the dunes. "New Eyrie is already under attack. Everyone is either evacuating the Crackling Sea or preparing to reinforce New Eyrie."

"It's just a distraction." Cielle spoke between bites. "It has to be. They don't want the Ashen Weald to notice them sailing through their territorial waters to make off with the seraph and hostages."

Orlea disagreed. "It's not so simple. Even without the Alabaster Eyrie's opinici, the forces outside New Eyrie are large enough to do a lot of damage. We can't risk it. Not over a frozen opinicus."

"It's the fisherfolk and glacier pride prisoners I'm worried about." Cielle forced his hackles down. He wouldn't get his way with anger, and he may end up alienating any help they could offer.

Deracho hooted something to another snowy owl gryphon, who went into the caverns to fetch supplies. While he looked pensive, he didn't add to the conversation.

It was Naya who broke the silence. "If Tresh and Younce aren't mistaken, this is an opportunity to strike at the king himself. Even if our claws miss his crown, Mally and Hi-Kun are tempting targets."

"Are we assassins, then?" Orlea asked. "No better than Rybalt?"

"No, saving the fisherfolk is our priority, but the Ashen Weald might be more willing to help if they know the king is there." Naya shivered at the high-altitude winds.

Somewhere in Cielle's flight south, the skies had grown cloudy. "I need to get back in the sky, or I'll be stuck here. Where am I headed?"

After several minutes of debate about wind currents, water currents, storms, and armies, there was only one thing they could do.

"The winds and currents are in the king's favor," Naya explained. "Even if you notify the Crackling Sea, even if they send help, they aren't going to move an army to Bogwash in time."

Deracho shook off a few errant snowflakes. "I'll head south and pick up whoever I can from Hoarfrost. We'll do what we can, but I don't think we'll make it before the ships."

"Tell Rorin he's on his own." Orlea stuffed several salted fish bars into Cielle's harness. "The Ashen Weald has probably ordered the Flower's rangers north, but if we're lucky, Bogwash and the raftworks still have guards."

Cielle finished his last feather check and groomed some fur down. His coat never wanted to stay put when he was nervous. "Younce told me to pick up an army. I didn't think it'd be just me."

Naya settled onto her back legs and reached up with both paws, a very opinicus thing to do. She used them to warm his beak while she looked into his eyes. "If you tell Rorin there are fisherfolk in trouble, he has a way of making things work. I know islanders are used to fending for themselves, but Bogwash is full of gryphons and opinici who will help out. Fly strong and have a little faith."

Cielle crouched down, and when the next gust came, he used all four legs to launch himself into the air. The more time Rorin had to prepare, the better things would go. Cielle would do his best.

THE FLIGHT from Snowfall to the bog shore was long, and despite his bragging, Cielle needed to stop and rest. Flying from the islands to the dunes to Swan's Rest to the glacier peak had taken its toll. For long journeys, he usually bulked up and rested a few days along the way. Even on his monthly trip to Sandpiper's Dune, he stayed over a few days to recover before returning home.

Before he left the mountains, he passed by taiga gryphons opening up outposts and moving supplies in. Over the bog, he caught sight of several fantails far below him, their long tails resembling his own.

Unfortunately, when his body ran out of energy, there was no one around to help him.

He dozed off. Between half-closed lids, the ground rose to meet him. A burst of adrenaline brought his mind into focus just in time to keep him from crashing, but he flew through a tangle of moss and thorn vine before landing beak-first in a river.

The brisk mountain runoff jerked him awake. He struggled to get to the surface, coughing up water. He fought the current, but it was too strong. He twisted around, trying to right himself, but still crashed into his first boulder with an *oomph*.

He clawed at the rock, getting two pawfuls of moss for his trouble.

Part of him wanted to let the current continue to take him on his way, but the frigid water was seeping through the layers of his fur, and his flailing had attracted the attention of sailfins hiding in the pools and runoff. Their tall, red-tipped sails wove through the reeds, giving away their locations.

The swift current soaked him more thoroughly than even the ocean ever had, and he could feel the weight of his fur pulling him under. He took a deep breath, then submerged.

Beneath the surface, he could make out two large

sailfins chasing him, their tails swishing back and forth as they wove through the water. Ahead, he saw what he was looking for: a tree that had collapsed into the river.

He reached out, catching plants, branches, and boulders to slow himself down. All the while, the sailfins were gaining.

When the current sent him into the fallen tree, he was still moving too fast. His breath escaped in a burst of bubbles, but his instincts were strong. He reflexively dug his claws into the rotting trunk, pulling away a section of the bark with his forepaws but catching hold with his back. A little wrangling and a desperate curl of his tail around a branch, and he managed to find purchase and crawl up the tree and out of the water.

Cielle was a wet, heavy mess, and the monitors pursuing him weren't going to give him the time he needed to get dry.

Can monitors climb trees? Not the big ones, right?

The nearest tree was devoid of low climbing branches. He tried to pull himself up its trunk, but the added water weight made it a fool's errand. He could hear the splash of the monitors leaving the river and settled upon an old cypress with some lower, broken limbs that made climbing easier. For good measure, he kicked off a couple of extra branches in case they could climb.

Down below, the two red sailfins chuffed at their escaped meal. It must have been a lean summer because their anger didn't seem proportional to his escape.

"What're you so mad about?" he shouted down at them. "Once I dry off, I'll be back in the sky and away from this place. Go back to the river. Find a capybara to eat."

Is there a safe place to sleep around here? I'm so tired.

While the water in his fur was the more pressing issue if he didn't want the branch to collapse under his weight, instinct had him drying out his flight feathers first. He preened through them to the sound of strange birds hiding in the same tree.

At least, he assumed they were birds. The more he listened, the more the chirping had a strange sound to it. Something squeakier than a normal bird.

He finished with his wings and was wringing out his tail when he made eye contact with one of the strange *birds* in the tree. While it appeared true the adult monitors couldn't climb trees, there was a baby sailfin with big eyes on the same branch as Cielle.

It chirped angrily.

"Whoa, hey there, friend," he said.

As the baby sailfin moved closer to Cielle, its parents leapt up and snapped at the wet fisherfolk's long, feathered tail. Whenever the baby chirped, the sound was echoed by another twenty on the branches above him.

While the disproportionately large eyes gave the baby sailfins a cute appearance, it wasn't lost on the taiga gryphon that their teeth didn't look any less sharp for being new. One might not be a problem. Two might not be a problem. But the whole tree had erupted into monitor song.

When the first baby leapt down and latched onto his thick, wet coat, Cielle plucked it off with his beak and tossed it down to its parents like it wasn't a big deal. When five more fell upon him from above, his cool demeanor lasted until one latched onto his ear, then he let out a loud cry and beat his wings to try to fly.

His waterlogged fur kept him from gaining any height, and his perch gave out under his flailing, sending him and a dozen baby monitors plummeting to the ground below.

The branch distracted one of the parents, and Cielle's tail distracted the other. He managed to hit the ground running, but it cost him a few of his tailfeathers.

He dashed, or at least sloshed, up an incline, weaving between the cypress and hanging moss. He didn't know where he was going, but anywhere had to be better than here. The sound of angry chuffing followed him as he ran.

He knew better than to run wildly through any wooded area. He'd heard that goliath birds sometimes came down from the aneda forests to hunt in the kjarr, and they were attracted to the sounds of frightened prey.

The thing was, he didn't know what he *should* be doing. He needed to get off the ground, but the cypress trees were too light for him to climb and perch in with his added water weight. So when he broke through a wall of moss and found a twenty-foot steep incline, he climbed like his life depended upon it.

Unfortunately, the higher he climbed, the less stable the soil was, giving way as he clawed at it with his large paws. Below him, he watched the two sailfins prepare to leap after him and dug his claws into the thickest roots he could find.

One parent missed, but the other caught a mouthful of tailfeathers, causing Cielle to shout a mixture of fantail, taiga, and fisherfolk profanity. Even if he dried out, his flight would be labored without those feathers.

He desperately tried to find purchase to get atop the wall of dirt and roots, but the leaves on the ledge had begun rustling. He thought he caught a glimpse of something feathery.

With my luck, I'm leaving the monitor nest for the goliath den.

He closed his eyes and prayed, but the whimpering of one of the sailfins down below caused him to open one eye to see what was going on. The monitors looked afraid.

He wasn't sure how large a goliath would have to be to frighten such a large sailfin, but when he looked back up the incline, the sight that greeted him wasn't a goliath bird.

Orange, reptilian eyes larger than a fledgling stared out from the brush. A mouth of bright green teeth that could swallow him whole filled his vision. It appeared that a light blue monitor, no, the god of all monitors, had been attracted to his running. He couldn't believe how massive it was.

When it roared, the sound was unlike anything he'd ever heard. It was a mixture of deep-sea monster, giant monitor, and wounded goliath bird. It came from several directions at once.

His paws lost their strength, and he let go, tumbling down the hill. Thankfully, the sailfins had already fled, abandoning him to his fate.

He stared up at the giant reptile's face, and... it broke apart.

The mouth split into four parts. Four *wingtorn*, who started laughing when they saw the expression on his face. The 'eyes' closed their wings and climbed down from the trees. The cheeks shifted to reveal they were the wings of bog witches.

A female wingtorn, masked, lightly armored, and bushy of tail, looked down at him. "I'm Thenca. Looks like you've had a hell of a time. Shouldn't a taiga gryphon know better than to come through the bog alone?"

When the giant face had finished disassembling, there were fifteen gryphons in total. Thenca leapt down to check on him, but the other wingtorn stayed up top.

It took Cielle a moment to get his brain working again and two more for his beak. "I'm fisherfolk, an islander. I brought word from Tresh for Rorin. I need to get to Bogwash."

Thenca sized him up, nuzzling his shredded tail and sea-leather harness before shouting up to the bog witches accompanying her. "Pumpkin, get down here and stop his bleeding. Petal, give your medicine bag to someone else. You're going to have to carry his message for him. We're probably going to have to walk him the rest of the way."

A witch with orange and green paint fluttered down. One of his wings had formed the eye, but his face and other wing were decorated with pumpkin designs. While he had the skeletal pattern on his undersides, green pumpkin leaves and a few yellow, star-like blossoms were woven between the bones.

This bog witch, presumably Pumpkin, started by putting a sticky paste on the bite on Cielle's ear. The other witch, Petal, stared at him while he recounted his tale, attent to every word. When he finished, she flew southwest.

Thenca's face was unreadable, but her ears were up, listening for some sound that never came. "When Deracho didn't come right back, I thought something might be wrong. Bogwash is a city of bog witches, healers. I don't know how you expect them to stop soldiers, let alone a boat."

Cielle winced as Pumpkin inspected his tail. Several other bog witches groomed him dry, and a wingtorn padded out of the wilderness with a beakful of Cielle's lost tailfeathers.

"Healers seem pretty useful to me," the taiga gryphon said.

Thenca's ear twitched. "I find healers are only a boon after you've won a fight. If you're dead, they're a lot less useful."

In the distance, a heron cry tickled at Cielle's good ear. The sound was repeated with precision by a hidden gryphon in the bog to the south. The message echoed a few more times before reaching Thenca, who repeated it, then added her own birdsong, sending it echoing back through the hidden chain.

"Rorin's going to want to question you," she said. "Rangers are on their way from the Flower to lift you the rest of the way. You got lucky, they were just about to leave, it sounds like. If we get you dry and someone guides you, do you have enough strength to stay airborne?

His pride as a Williwaw wanted to say yes, but he'd already crashed once, and pride was overrated. "Probably not. I need food and rest. I've been flying for days now."

Thenca sent a new message, then translated for him.

"They'll bring a fishing net to carry you in. Rest now as best you can."

He wanted to protest that he couldn't sleep, but after the bog witches filled him with salty rations and pumpkin tincture, he started to doze even as some rangers arrived to wrap him in a net.

This must be what it feels like to be a fish.

19

WINGTEARER

The short flight from the overlook to the shore sent Jonas into a coughing fit. There was a time in his youth where he'd once flown around the entire Crackling Sea over the course of a week as part of his honeymoon celebration. Now, his smoke-scarred lungs refused him even short flights.

All around, his allies clashed with the Ashen Weald. Armored goliath birds chased down wingtorn. Argent hawks harried fantails and ex-Redwood Valley military. Crestfall's flamingos fought side-by-side with Reevesport's peacocks. They'd laughed at the Crackling Sea Eyrie struggling to battle the kjarr pride, but now they were learning how vicious gryphons could be. A cardinal wingtorn, perhaps one who'd suffered at the talons of the Redwood Valley's peacock leader, seemed particularly hellbent on bringing down each Reevesport standard-bearer.

"We don't have time for sightseeing." Silver had traded in her grey, leather armor for something in brown that didn't draw attention to herself. She refused to let Jonas out of her sight, but she had a target on her back after her last two incursions with the Ashen Weald.

Jonas brought out a glass bottle filled with red oil. He plunged a talon into the cork and pulled it out but froze as the scent hit him. Inside, oil held his mate's blood and scent, scraped off his death bed. Jonas couldn't bring himself to just pour it in the water.

One of the wingtorn atop the ramparts noticed them by the shore and let out a cry that echoed across the battlefield.

Silver had no time for his delay. "You told the king there was no cost too high to get your revenge on the blackwings. It's just blood. Do it before the wingtorn recognize you."

Just blood. It was a silly phrase, all things considered. If the Alabaster Eyrie's religious were to be believed, blood had transformed seraphs to opinici, opinici to gryphons.

"What did the king promise you?" he asked the argent reeve. "What was your price?"

Silver took her eyes off the cardinal wingtorn to glare at Jonas. "I'm not like you. Revenge is cheap. I made my bargain to save lives."

The alarm from the lookout reached the cardinal wingtorn. She let out a cry, one Jonas had heard screamed at him the few times they'd escaped their cells and been tossed off the cliffs.

Wing-tearer.

Every wingtorn turned and began pushing towards the shore.

Jonas's bodyguards shifted nervously. Silver slipped

her metal talons over her real ones, swearing at him again.

"Opinicus lives are cheap," Jonas scolded her. "Whatever you think your reason is, *reeve*, you're right here on the front lines with me now."

He poured the bottle into the water, letting the current take it out to sea. The oil was designed to hold the scent and diffuse.

As young lovers, Jonas and his mate had spent hours playing on the beach with the serpentine whale, then just a pup. They'd quickly discovered that their pet went into a frenzy when the blue reeve cut himself. The whale became protective, guarding the reeve and attacking anyone who tried to come near, even maiming a medicine opinicus once.

Silver grabbed Jonas's harness and pulled him into the air as the wingtorn converged on the beach. They screamed up at him.

Wingtearer. Monster. And those were the nicer names. They cursed him to the depths and swore they'd tear off his wings—and other body parts.

He looked down. Not at the wingtorn, frenzied like starlings, but at the water off the coast of New Eyrie.

The sea swelled as the reeve's pet barreled towards shore and crashed into the docks.

"Abandon the eyrie." Mia's words fell on disbelieving ears. The reeve's pet had taken out the raftworks, docks, and a large chunk of the northern walls in the process.

Foultner was the first to speak up. "You told Erlock

we'd hold the eyrie until the last moment. Make them pay for it."

"We did." Mia looked out at a line of charging goliath birds splashing through the marsh towards the break in the walls. "This is the last moment. Tell everyone to fall back. Wingtorn should head for the bog, then cut east. The grasslands won't be safe from flechettes. Everyone else should regroup at Clover Ranch and proceed to the Crackling Sea Eyrie."

Foultner was nonplussed. Like Mia, she'd probably expected New Eyrie to last past the first attack. Only the sound of the reeve's pet crawling onto land snapped the underbough opinicus out of her stupor. She'd seen the strange shadow that wove through the jelly swarms under the water but seeing it on land showed just how large a beast it had become.

"You heard the ranger lord!" Foultner shouted. "Let them deal with the sea monster. Someone tell the fantails to watch for anyone carrying flechettes. Protect the wingtorn but get out of here!"

Olan came in through the main entrance. Mia had given him orders that, should it come to it, he was to fill the main structures with bundles of dry straw. He did so now while she rolled up the maps and stuffed them in her harness pocket.

All of the civilians had left days ago. Any important supplies were gone, minus a bit of food. This wasn't the kind of place that would withstand a siege, so there was no reason for more than that. The buildings themselves weren't valuable, but a screen of smoke—combined with the addition of the sea monster—should buy the wingtorn the time they needed.

20

CARDINALS AND BLUE JAYS

Twenty feet above the ground, a red wingtorn nicknamed Cardinal—Card for short—clung to the back of a white-tailed kite. Her opponent kicked back with his only free foot, catching her in the face. When he lashed out a second time, she caught his paw, digging her claws in.

One of the fantails shouted a warning, and she let go right as another of the armored opinici dove through the space she'd occupied a moment ago. He turned to swipe at her, but she latched onto his armor—with a better grip than she'd had on his friend—and climbed up him to get at his throat before he could call for help.

They both plummeted, the northern shore of New Eyrie rushing up to meet them. Card disengaged, pushing against the opinicus and spreading out her paws to distribute her weight evenly. The opinicus did nothing to soften his fall. Perhaps he thought gravity would be a better death than bleeding out. The wingtorn, however, had spent a lot of time practicing her falling and knew what to do.

She was as relaxed as a warm, well-fed gryphlet. Her body was less tense than when she stayed up drinking brews with the bog witches. Even more important than being able to jump high was being able to land.

The red wingtorn hit the ground, expecting mud or sand, and instead discovered one of the hidden tunnels Urious had filled with dry, fragrant reeds to conceal its entrance. It had been stuffed full, and only her impact revealed its location.

She tumbled into the hole, muddy and full of crabs, and hopped back on her feet to check that everything was there.

Beak, ears, paws, tail. Everything.

Almost everything—the long scars on her back where her wings had once been brushed the ceiling, and the damp sent a shiver down her spine. She turned to head through the path into town when a loud *thud* collapsed the tunnel and nearly buried her in muck.

Was that saltpeter? I didn't hear an explosion.

She burrowed out of the tunnel and up onto the northern shore, rolling in a tidal pool to get the mud off. Light glinted off pink glass, and a one-eyed Crestfall opinicus was leading a pack of trained goliaths towards New Eyrie's walls.

Card turned to flee and found herself beak-to-flipper with the reeve's pet. The serpentine whale had flopped down atop of the raftworks, collapsing it and the tunnel beneath it. The creature's face resembled a snake, but its teeth were all monitor. Its long body wound into the sea, leaving her to wonder at its length.

The monster propped itself up on two clawed flippers taller than the fishing huts crushed beneath them, reminding Card of the leaves of a cactus, complete with thorny edges. The creature's eye tracked the fighting over the eyrie. It reared back, then a stream of water knocked a dozen flyers out of the sky.

An opinicus hanging onto the remains of New Eyrie's gates above her swore, and the wingtorn tensed reflexively, ready to pounce—but it was only Foultner.

"Hey, what was your name again?" Foultner asked. While Card wasn't familiar with who Foultner was, she was friendly with Satra and Urious, both of whom thought highly of the Redwood Valley opinicus. As best Card had gathered from Urious, Foultner had been instrumental in the freeing the wingtorn prisoners.

She'd also earned Blinky's trust, a difficult feat not many had repeated.

"Call me Cardinal," the wingtorn answered. As far as nicknames went, it wasn't a bad one, at least among the wingtorn where cardinal markings were extremely rare. Over the years, there'd been times when she'd resented having markings more common to opinici.

There was one strange side effect to her plumage, however. As the Redwood Valley opinici slowly adjusted to Ashen Weald life, many members of the underbough felt more comfortable around her than her pridemates. Between her flair for dramatic leaps and her ability to get opinici to listen to her, she'd been a natural choice to serve as Urious's second-in-command.

It was a position that often required spending long hours talking to her counterpart in the weald camp, a harpy eagle gryphon she'd nicknamed Blue Jay. There were no harpy eagles in the kjarr, so every blue bird was called a jay.

He was supposed to be handling the evacuation at the city gates. She thought back to the tunnel that had nearly collapsed on top of her. *I need to make sure he's okay. The reeve's pet changes things.*

The serpentine whale thrashed around, slithering deeper into the city and reducing several fishing rafts to their individual components. Wood and bindings drifted in the water, alongside the bodies of dead gryphons and opinici.

First, get yourself okay, then *check on Blue Jay,* she amended.

"I don't suppose I can get a ride?" Cardinal called up to Foultner.

The opinicus shook her head. "Sorry, I don't have the wing strength. Those goliath birds are getting pretty close. I think you're going to have to swim for it."

The wingtorn looked out at the water. As far as she knew, it was the flippers and mouth of the serpentine whale that made it dangerous. She'd probably be safer around the back half.

The whale isn't the only dangerous thing in the water, however.

Without lightning, there was no way to know if the jelly swarm was drifting just off the coast. Every so often, the sails of aquatic monitors broke the surface. At the moment, the lizards were content to feed upon the dead and wounded—like the armored opinicus she'd dropped from the sky—but they were just as happy to go after any gryphons that went for a swim.

"Get to the other side and look for a blue weald gryphon," she ordered Foultner. "He'll know what we're supposed to be doing."

The poacher shook her head, clearly uneasy leaving a wingtorn behind. The splashing sound of armored goliath birds grew louder, but Cardinal remained unmoving. She wasn't about to swim with monitors and jellies, and the scales of the whale looked too sharp to climb, but she had an idea.

A goliath bird honed-in on her and let out a loud *mronk!*

The serpentine whale rose on its flippers again, aiming at a flock of flamingos, and Cardinal dashed underneath it, goliath in pursuit.

The ground beneath the monster was muddy, but there were stretches of broken rafts and buildings that gave Card traction. She did her best to hop from one to the other, but when she was halfway under the beast, she ran out of traction-heavy targets and took a flying leap for the other side.

The beast finished spraying the air with its deadly streams and collapsed, crushing three goliath birds under its bulk. Cardinal wasn't quite across, but a wave of mud pushed her past its far flipper and into the southern wall of New Eyrie. To the north, armored goliaths scrambled through the town, trying to root out anyone hiding in the buildings or any of the wingtorn's hidden tunnels.

For all the damage the northern walls had sustained, the southern walls were, unfortunately, intact. The last thing she wanted was to get pulled off trying to climb them covered in mud. The fantails had begun their retreat, and the king's forces were attempting to hold the skies.

Not the smartest birds, Cardinal thought as the reeve's pet snapped a peacock out of the air with a crunch.

The walls of New Eyrie extended deep into the water, but she didn't see any choice. She'd have to risk it.

The red wingtorn crawled through the mud, flattening herself when the reeve's pet switched from knocking opinici out of the air and rooted around the mud to find ones to eat, until she hit the edge of the water.

Cardinal needed to swim about twenty feet out to where the spikes atop the wall thinned, then she could climb up and slip between the wooden stakes. She'd certainly managed to get over them once before when sieging the city. Escaping would be easier.

Or so she hoped. The sailfins were still snout-deep in the dead.

Her eyes on the monitors, she slipped a paw into the water. Now that goliath birds weren't running at her, she seemed to recall an Ashen Weald ranger saying that sailfins weren't immune to the jellies' toxins, so as long as the sailfins were moving, the swarm must be far away.

Cardinal lowered herself into the sea, careful not to splash. Little crayfish nipped at her toes, minnows fled in all directions, but the sailfins were content with their grim feast. The reeve's pet shifted, churning up the mud and pushing her against the wall. She managed to grab a spike with her paws to keep from being impaled upon it and waited for the waves to stop. She couldn't see more than a few inches down, and she prayed she didn't step on a crab or anything worse.

The water level was up to her chest, and the spike-adorned southern wall had yet to end. In fact, it looked taller now that she was partially submerged. Her breathing quickened as she imagined all sorts of strange things lurking beneath the surface. She was no longer walking, she was paddling. Without a sense of how deep the water was, she couldn't tell if a sailfin was submerged and swimming straight for her.

The sea farther from shore looked clearer. Of course, it was also full of sailfins, and she wasn't a fast enough swimmer to get out of their way.

The top of her body was caked with mud from her slide beneath the whale, and while she hoped that made her harder to spot, it was also crawling with bugs. At least, in her imagination it was, and she was torn between a growing sense that she needed to submerge herself and wash the mud off and an inability to take her eyes off the toothy predators.

The water was colder than she expected. Was that good or bad? She couldn't remember. She'd learned to swim in the rivers of the kjarr nesting grounds, which were kept free of predators and never had to deal with jellies.

Something leapt out of the water next to her with a splash. She contained a cry of fear, thankful it was only a large fish. When she turned her eyes back to the sailfins, they were all hyper-focused on where the fish had splashed.

Then they looked past the fish's ripples and noticed her for the first time.

Cardinal swore and swam towards the edge of the wall. She was almost to where it dropped off into the water, where she could crawl over the spikes.

If the sailfins were surprised that a meal was swimming *towards* them, they didn't show it. The largest monitors had already secured their meals and stayed put, eating. But a small monitor was still big enough to eat Cardinal, and they were all wriggling through the water in her direction.

She pulled herself over the wall, leaving a nasty gash along her stomach and nearly losing her tail to a small sailfin, then turned back to shore.

As awkward as they were on land, the sailfins glided through the water like fish, and several were already on this side of the wall. She couldn't do anything except swim and hope for the best, so she swam like her life depended on it.

Swam *because* her life depended on it.

She was nearly to shore when she heard a splash behind her, and this time, she was sure it wasn't a fish. She resisted the urge to look back as long as she could, but when she turned around, a monitor longer than Merin had nearly caught up to her.

It opened its mouth wide, and she got a good look at its teeth. Unlike most monitors, sailfins didn't exactly resemble lizards or snakes. *Monitor* was an old gryphon word that could mean several things, but it hinted at a bitey head, size enough to be dangerous to gryphons, claws, and a tail. The giant salamanders filling the weald were *monitors* by that definition.

Not that sailfins looking different from monitor lizards meant much to Cardinal in her current predicament. A sailfin certainly fit the conventional definition: big enough to eat a gryphon.

A screech came from overhead, and Urious's old poacher friend flew down scratching at the monitor to take its attention off Cardinal.

"Go, swim!" Foultner shouted. She wrapped some rope around the sailfin's spines and was in the air again, trying to hold it back.

Cardinal didn't need any encouragement. She paddled as fast as she could, her head just above the waves. Another sail stuck out of the water, but an alabaster opinicus and a fantail gryphon, too busy attacking each other to remain airborne, crashed into the sea nearby and drew it away.

The red wingtorn had just set paw to dry ground—well, muddy ground—when Foultner landed next to her. "Thanks for the help."

"We're not safe yet." Foultner's eyes were on the sky, where the Ashen Weald was retreating. Any flamingos or peacocks ambitious enough to try to follow them were picked out of the air by Erlock's fantail skirmishers, but the same reeve's pet that had cost them New Eyrie was also helping buy them time to escape. It would twist back to the sea and fill up every so often, then streams of water would fill the skies around the city.

"You should head to the Crackling Sea Eyrie." Cardinal cleaned herself off as best she could, then followed the southern wall, searching for any remaining stragglers.

Foultner stayed. Cardinal didn't know her well enough to speculate on whether that was heroics or if she was just afraid to be in the air with the whale around.

"Fine," the red wingtorn said. "Stick with me. I need to see if everyone's evacuated, then I'm getting out of here."

Please be gone, Jay, she prayed. But she already knew he'd be outside the gates. She just hoped he'd still be alive when she found him.

CARDINAL AND FOULTNER had just hit the main gates, the ones domesticated goliath birds had once used to take goods to the lumber mill, ranch, or off to the eyries in the east, when Cardinal spotted who she was looking for.

"Jay!" she shouted to a large harpy eagle gryphon. Despite her nickname for him, his long beak turned down at the end like an icicle. She didn't know if he was one of Merin's offspring or not, but he was certainly large enough to be.

He guarded the last tunnel out of the city with several wingtorn. "Hey Card, Foult. Watch the pit of spikes south of here. They dug it in a hurry, so it's not marked with the usual signs. Once you get across, stick to the tall grass and look for the parrotfaces. They'll guide you the rest of the way."

"What about you?" Cardinal preened a few of his facial feathers back into place. "I just came through the city. They've got goliaths going through the tunnels. I don't think there are any wingtorn left."

He started to respond, but then one of his wingtorn escort by the tunnel shouted that someone was coming through. Except this wasn't a wingtorn.

A large goliath bird, a metal helmet allowing it to shovel dirt out of the way, squeezed through the tunnel with a loud *mronk* and tossed the closest wingtorn into the air.

Foultner swore and flew out of its reach. Jay rose on his back paws, spreading his wings wide. He was a wall of blue feathers, paws bigger than her head, and a ferocious beak. For a brief moment, she couldn't imagine a more impressive display.

Then the goliath bird pulled itself out of the hole

and reared up to its full height, well over nine feet. A metal helmet protected its eyes, and its spiked harness dissuaded anyone from trying to attack it from the front.

Jay's courage faltered, and he let out a ferocious screech that also served to warn the wingtorn to make a run for it. Jay and Card had a plan for dealing with goliath birds, but that plan involved her keeping the bird's attention while he squashed it from above. The air above them was still full of streams of water from the whale, and Cardinal didn't think she could hold the bird's attention for more than a second before becoming a snack.

The harpy eagle gryphon held his own as best he could, dodging its beak and massive talons. He was fast for his size, which he often attributed to having to hunt in the congested forest of the weald. He wasn't winning this battle, though, not without help.

Cardinal had no better plan than the one they'd come up with, so she swapped the roles. She didn't have his wingspan, didn't have a wingspan at all, but she was fleet of paw. When the goliath bird came close to the gates, she flung herself at a spot where the wooden spikes had been shaken loose by the fighting, caught hold, then flung herself at the back of the creature's neck. She bit down as hard as she could, but it was like chewing old leather—all gristle with a bitter taste. She barely drew blood.

She changed her strategy, digging her claws in as deep as they would go—not deep enough to stop it from dislodging her if it started bucking, but she trusted Jay to hold its attention a little longer—and turned her beak to the fasteners and straps holding its metal helmet on.

Opinici were very proud of their knots and buckles. And sure, Card admired the metalworks' ability to produce such things. But they weren't *that* fancy. With the right bites, a few tugs, some more gnawing, and a hearty application of her claws, she managed to snap something important, and the goliath bird's mask went flying off.

Jay seized the moment and slashed at its face, leaving several long gashes.

For feral goliath birds, this was the moment where they decided their prey wasn't worth the effort and fled into the icy mountains.

Cardinal and Jay got their first taste of how a trained war goliath responded to being slashed in the face, and it wasn't with fear.

It was with *rage.*

There was something cute about the way domesticated goliath birds made their *mronk* noise to get the attention of opinici at the ranch. As much as Cardinal had a deep fear of being trampled, she could admit that much. But the sound the goliath made now was not cute. It was terrifying. It sounded like something the Nighthaunt might make.

Jay turned and fled, the cute tuft of his tail leaping up and down as he made for the pit of spikes. Card couldn't do anything but hang on for dear life. She was stuck. The goliath bird's gait was too strong for her to leap off, but if it got any worse, she might go flying in a random direction.

Though her vision was jarred by the bird, she could see a break in the grass up ahead and spikes poking up. Jay took a bite on the flank, then he leapt into the air, beating his wings to avoid the spikes.

The goliath bird leapt after him. It spread its tiny wings, beating them futilely. Cardinal felt like she was flying again.

Then gravity took hold.

"Let go!" Foultner's voice came from above.

The red wingtorn released her claws and closed her eyes. When she felt small talons grabbing hold of her harness, she instinctively latched on, sending her claws into the opinicus.

Foultner swore, and they plummeted towards the spikes. Something tore against Card's side, and she was afraid to open her eyes and look at the damage. She was hyperventilating when a much larger gryphon caught both of them.

The dry, dusty scent of Jay enveloped her. She relaxed and let herself be pulled up before being dropped on the other side of the spiked trench.

The tall sawgrass hid them from view. She hated the stuff—it had taken her a year to learn to walk through it without cutting her paws—but all her focus was on the gash along her side now.

Jay shouted for help. The brush parted and a parrot-face appeared. His eyes were ringed with starberry-violet markings, and he took stock of the situation, then vanished into the underbrush.

Foultner had been flung deeper into the grass, and she followed the sound of Jay's voice, one wing held at an awkward angle. When the parrotface returned with a medicine opinicus, the poacher helped hold the wound closed while he worked.

"Shhh," Foultner calmed Card, who hadn't realized she'd been whimpering. "A few of the goliaths are heading to the beach to get around the pit. We don't want to attract notice."

The red wingtorn tried not to think about her wound. Her mind was racing from the adrenaline, and the pain was hidden behind a cloud—for now. She expected the strange pinch of leafcutters to hold the wound closed, but when she looked at the medicine opinicus, he was sewing her up like she was a saddle.

Foultner had to hold her down. "Hey, you're okay. This is just like the bog gryphons do, except better, okay? I used to be a poacher, and he sewed me up a dozen times. There'll be a scar, but they just build character, right?"

She didn't respond. She had a lot of scars she'd rather not have, but Foultner was right: Cardinal didn't really care about one more scar, so long as she lived.

Jay stood over her, keeping watch. She reached out instinctively, and he moved his paw closer so she could squeeze it. She was starting to feel the pain now and winced whenever the medicine opinicus stuck a needle into her.

A *mronk* came from the north, along the beach.

"This'll hold." The medicine opinicus pulled the string taut and snapped it with his beak. "We'll have to patch her up better at the Clover Ranch. Can you walk?"

Cardinal started to move, but Jay stopped her.

"I can carry her. Put her between my wings." He knelt, and several parrotfaces materialized from the grasses to help lift Card on top of him. She cried out once before they got her situated.

"Thank you," she said to Foultner, who was helping secure her in place.

The poacher scoffed. "Thank your big friend here.

The two of us were going into those spikes. I can't believe he got us both across."

"Is your wing okay?" The red wingtorn looked at the opinicus's wing, which wasn't folded against her body.

"Just a sprain," Foultner reassured her. "I'll get it looked at when we're safe and away from the fighting. Looks like you and I are going to get to spend a few days at the ranch. I used to work there you know. I know where they hide the best nesting material. I'll make sure you're taken care of."

Cardinal tried to look back, but all she could see was grass and harpy eagle feathers. *Will the king's forces give us a few days? Nothing separates them from the ranch except grass and a trench of spikes they already know about.*

The parrotfaces, normally full of *skraarks* and *booms*, remained silent. She caught the gaze of the one with violet markings around his eyes and blinked her thanks to him. He returned the gesture, then the sounds of fighting broke out nearby, and he disappeared into the tall grass to assist the wounded.

21

BOGWASH

R orin sat outside a hut and sharpened spears. An unexpected bonus to his visit was that he'd convinced the lumber mill at the raftworks to begin producing spears out of new types of lumber. Several rafts had already been filled with weapons, ready to sail east to Sandpiper's Dune on his order.

Of course, now it seemed Tresh wanted him to use the spears for another purpose, to save the Crane's Nest refugees.

I wish I'd brought more sentries with me. A couple of the rangers had taken to learning how to throw, but for the most part, the blue herons were strictly net-and-talon fighters, using their long beaks as spears when necessary. Unfortunately, they couldn't throw their beak from thirty feet above their enemies, which was why *they'd* lost the battle for Sandpiper's Dune a year ago.

A commotion came from the nests, and Rorin could hear *her* voice long before she reached him. While the bog witches and even rangers were happy to reopen trade with the fisherfolk, there was one gryphon here who had made her hostility known from the first day.

Thenca.

The feeling was mutual. The last time they'd met, Rorin had impaled her friend, Jun the Kjarr, upon a spear. Thenca had rallied the wingtorn into a retreat but not before they'd wrecked the city and most of the eggs. There was a lot of hate on both sides now—Rorin would argue that the fisherfolk's was much more justified, but on an academic level, he knew the wingtorn had been acting to save their children.

His invitation had come from Soft Paws, who had either been unaware of the bad blood or, more likely, had decided it was time to put it behind them. Since she'd invited them both here, and then gone north to help the Ashen Weald, Rorin suspected the latter.

Thenca finished barking orders and padded over to Rorin and the opinici. A few cold storms had triggered shedding and molting in the bog gryphons, turning their coats a much darker color. Her mask markings and tail stripes didn't stand out as much.

"Den mother," Rorin acknowledged. He'd heard the bog witches calling her that. He still thought of her as a warrior. With Soft Paws north, the bog gryphons deferred to her. "We've gathered as many weapons as we could find and sent stockpiles to the outlying isles."

He hoped deferring to her would diffuse any hostilities until the Crane's Nest refugees could be rescued. So far, it seemed to be working. The raftworks rangers were inclined to follow his lead since he was an opinicus, and if this were Sandpiper's Dune or Swan's Rest, he'd have taken command. He was a guest here in the bog, however.

Thenca took a deep breath. Talking to him always seemed to be an effort. "Your islander friend just woke up, and I'd like you there while I ask him some questions. Did you find anyone who knew boats?"

Boats and *ships* and *rafts* were a distinction lost on most of the fisherfolk and rangers, who had inherited all three words from northern eyries long ago, but luck was on their side.

A black crane opinicus stood along the shallow outflow from the raftworks. His back paws were on dry land, but one foreleg was in the water while the other held a spear. He formed a kind of umbrella with his wings, shading the water. When fish sought the safety of the darkness, he ran them through with his spear and gulped them down.

Naya's brother had discovered him shipwrecked on an island and brought him to Sandpiper's Dune, where he'd claimed to be a shipwright from Alwren in his former life.

The black crane jerked his wings back and stabbed down, pulling back a fishing spear with two elvers—baby eels—impaled upon it. "Oh, Thenca, you're back. Rorin filled me in. I didn't work with much stormcloth, but I'd say they'll cross south of us tomorrow midday at the earliest. Maybe not until the evening."

He slid the elvers into a bait bucket.

Rorin frowned. The diving petrels with him had been hesitant to swim in the muddy, brackish water of the mangrove coast. Once you moved out from the safety of the root system, several large predators used the low visibility to hunt. The local witches also said that a year with a lot of elvers meant a year with a lot of adult eels off the coast. Some with strange teeth in the back of their throats, some larger than an adult opinicus.

"Any ideas for how to slow them down?" Thenca asked the black crane. "If they're moving that quickly, it's going to be hard to keep up."

The shipwright shrugged. "I'd say burn or slash the sails, but stormcloth is notoriously hard to burn without an oil of some sort, and wooden spears aren't going to do much against even thin stormcloth."

"Urious chewed through some of it at the Crackling Sea," Thenca added. "Said it took hours."

Rorin worried this was a fool's errand. "Can we slash the ropes holding up the sails? What we really need is saltpeter."

Thenca whistled something back to huts and waited for a response. "Orlea only just agreed to re-open the flameworks. None of her new engineers seem to know how to get it going. We've recovered a few caches here and there, but Satra ordered them to the Crackling Sea. It'll be a while before we can blow up any more eyries."

"Thankfully," muttered the local ranger captain. Opinici didn't appreciate having their eyries burned down. Despite his tone and youth, the ranger seemed to get along well with Thenca, and he'd come over with a peace offering of sorts. "Here's the sharpest blades we have. I got this one off a blackwing last time they sieged the eyrie."

The shipwright took the blade and held it in his talons. He lifted it up to the light, showing off the swirled design in the grey metal. "They'll have a backup of some sort, but if you can get me on the ship, I can slow it down."

Rorin tied another cluster of spears and handed them

to a ranger. "Start moving the rafts out to the nearby islands but try to conceal them in case they have scouts. Let's go see if our islander friend has anything useful to tell us about how the king's flagship is put together."

CIELLE LICKED a paw and wiped at his eyes. His body ached, and he suspected he had a day's worth of grooming ahead of him before he looked presentable.

He opened his eyes and was greeted with the carved pumpkin face of a bog witch, the other gryphon's beak almost touching his. Two small paws were pressed on Cielle's chest—not enough to restrain him but still enough to discourage him from moving.

"Do not twitch your tail. We are still fixing it." Pumpkin removed his paws, allowing Cielle to look around.

The taiga gryphon was on his back, which wasn't his favorite way to sleep. His wings had been spread out, and a bog witch hovered over each. One had an imping needle in her beak, another was lightly holding his wing down.

Cielle shook a hind paw a little to get the feeling back in it. His thick coat had been cleaned, but the bog gryphons hadn't used enough saliva, and he was feeling fluffy.

Stretching out of the small hut and into the walkways of Bogwash, several more witches were tending to his tail. By the looks of things, few of his broken feathers had been suitable for imping, and his previously snow-white tail was now a blend of dark greens and browns. He tilted his head to the side and looked to Pumpkin.

"The Feathermane Pride donated tailfeathers last winter in case Erlock was found," Pumpkin explained. "She'd molted by the time she returned, so we put them to use on your tail."

Cielle twisted his head to try to get a look at his wings. "What about my flight feathers?"

With his wings spread, someone had gone in with ash and labeled his feathers with small glyphs. Where new feathers were imped in, they were pink and also marked with more bog glyphs.

"We did not have any in white," Pumpkin apologized. "But there is a merchant's caravan at the raftworks, and she had hundreds of pink Younce feathers for sale, so we were able to go through her supply and locate the ones you were missing."

While his vanity had taken a bit of a hit, Cielle was more concerned with helping Tresh. "Can I fly?"

The witch straddling his tail looked up from inspecting a dark green feather. Based on the flowering vine pattern woven around her skeletal markings, this was Petal. "We fixed your wings last night. They're probably flightworthy, but I wouldn't try anything fancy. We stitched up your baby sailfin bites, too, so you should be healthy. Don't do anything too wild with that ear 'til it heals."

"Then why am I still on my back?" Cielle asked.

"Oh." Petal moved away from his tail and chirped at the witches by his wings to move. "We grew up with wingtorn, so we're new to feather imping. We've been practicing, though! We're just not used to working on a live gryphon yet. Dead birds are not so picky about how you set them down."

Cielle wasn't sure how to take that.

"Oh, we didn't forget you were alive the entire time!" Pumpkin nuzzled encouragingly, leaving orange paint on Cielle's white fur. "I watched to make sure you still took breath in. You continued breathing the entire time. You have a very pretty beak."

Petal nodded. "It was very exciting to work on someone still living from a different pride. Or... village? Marine eyrie? Island?"

"Mainlanders probably say village, but island is fine." Cielle allowed the bog witches to help get him upside-right. His paws tingled a little at the change in blood flow, and his wings were cramped, but he felt good.

The bog gryphons knew how to nuzzle and socially groom each other without disrupting their impressive markings, but Cielle had never dealt with feather paint before. By the time he was done thanking everyone, he had orange, blue, and grey paint on his coat—a fine match for his pink flight feathers and the green and brown on his tail.

He stepped into the light and was greeted by Rorin and Thenca.

Cielle ate while Thenca and Rorin argued over how to best take down the king's flagship, only stopping to answer questions or chime in with new information. His body greedily accepted everything placed before him.

Pumpkin pushed a bowl of water in front of Cielle's beak. It smelled of orange and lemon and had a slight tang when he lapped at it. The rangers offered cooked crab. There was a saying among fisherfolk: there's only one spice, and it's called salt. There was no saltworks on this coast, so the rangers had made do with a spice he'd never experienced before but made his mouth burn. The bog glyph for it was an exploding beak.

"Oh!" The burning in his mouth reminded him of another piece of information. "They must have used something to get the seraph out of the ice so fast. Maybe fire? Oil?"

The shipwright nodded. "We'll bring some flint and tinder fungus and keep our eyes open when we free the prisoners. They won't be able to give chase if they're putting out the flames."

Cielle recognized the dark-plumed crane from Sandpiper's Dune. Cielle's parents had been at the center of a debate on whether or not to allow the shipwright to visit and explore the shipwrecks around their island. One of his moms wanted to know whom the ships had belonged to and what had brought them so far south. If there was an undiscovered eyrie in the ocean, it was better to know. His other mom thought that if word got out, stormcloth hunters would come calling.

"You need wingtorn on the rafts to help out," Thenca argued with Rorin. "Once we're below decks, we're on even footing. This isn't like Sandpiper's Dune, where it was all open beach and water."

Rorin scratched at the feathers under his chin. "How many wingtorn can swim? We're hoping the white opinici will be more invested in getting the king and seraph to safety, but if they toss anchor and fight, they're going to destroy our rafts first. That'll leave all the wing-torn abandoned on the small islands, most of which don't have fresh water."

"A couple of the new harnesses float." Thenca's eyes showed determination, but there was something else to them that Cielle couldn't quite place.

Anger? Shame? He'd been around the remnants of Crane's Nest enough to know how they felt about wing-torn, but he'd never heard the wingtorn's side of the story.

He looked down to ask Pumpkin a question, and the bog witch blinked slowly at him.

"We can use those on the wounded." Rorin sketched a map in a box of sand with an idle talon. There were glyphs marking sharks near the coast and a line for serpentine whale migration, but between the islands where they planned to make their stand was only a question mark.

Thenca stood. "They're designed for wingtorn: they cover our scars and won't fit over wings. If it comes down to it, we can swim ropes out to the wounded. You don't have enough opinici as is. You're going to need all the help you can get."

Rorin grunted, a sound that reverberated in his long throat. "Fine. Everyone with a harness can come. Let's get the last of the rafts out."

Rorin and the rangers departed, leaving behind the shipwright and the bog pride. The black heron reached for the map and changed Rorin's question mark into the long shape of an eel before making his exit.

Thenca slumped down now that the opinici were

gone. "I wish Deracho and Naya were here. It takes all my patience not to snap at Rorin."

Not Soft Paws? She was the leader. Did Thenca have not trust the young witch to serve that role?

"He means well. If you're hunting something over water, there are few better fisherfolk to have by your side. Besides, he'd move star and sea to save Tresh." Cielle finished washing his beak.

Pumpkin was curled up next to him, purring.

Thenca stood and swatted the bog witch out the door. "Stop fawning and get your herbs ready."

Pumpkin made a grumpy sound but obeyed.

"Sorry about that," she apologized. "They weren't well-socialized as gryphlets, and you know how gryphons get during this time of year. I think they've forgotten you're a fisherfolk and not a taiga gryphon."

Cielle stood and stretched his paws, giving his brain time to realize what *time of the year* she was referring to. "I'm a bit of both. We're proud of our Williwaw heritage out in The Wrecks. No real mating season to speak of, though. Just whenever it gets too cold to sleep alone."

He looked out at the orange bog witch. Pumpkin seemed kind enough. He obviously had some medicine gryphon training. Would he fly out to The Wrecks and spend the winter with Cielle? Or would Cielle be expected to spend the winter here in the bog?

Questions for another time.

CIELLE AND THENCA SLIPPED OUTSIDE. A weak mist sat over the city of Bogwash. Every nest had a hut over it, and the layout was gryphon friendly. Unlike fisherfolk huts, there was little bamboo on the mangrove coast. Each walkway dipped down in the center, guiding rainwater towards the field or river.

A blue jay sat atop the roof of the common area, and when it chirped, the nearby bog witches chirped back. It felt more like a nesting ground than a fisherfolk village to Cielle, but there were fish and strips of meat hanging from each home and the long dock. A goliath bird stables had been constructed on the west side of town, the section closest to the road.

White-throated swifts, small pointy birds, appeared every time a goliath wandered through the brush and stirred up insects. Every so often a swift would clip the larger birds, leading to an angry exchange before the goliath went back to searching for lizards and snakes to eat.

Thenca led Cielle to the docks. The wind coming in off the ocean was cold and wet, a nice reminder of his home. To the west, just visible, was the raftworks. Several of Rorin's sentries were showing the rangers how to throw a spear.

Cielle paused to watch, spreading his wings to feel the air pass over each feather. "What can I do? I have no idea how to fight. I'm just an islander."

"Do you know how to hunt?" Thenca asked, waiting for his nod. "It's the same thing, but your prey is smarter. What do you hunt on your island?"

"Salamanders, goliath birds, beaked whales," he replied. "Capybaras, but they're so tame I wouldn't call that hunting. I usually leave sharks and serpentine whales to the opinici since they have spears. Nothing that can fly. The deep-sea albatrosses have learned to avoid The Wrecks."

She sat on her haunches and tapped a claw on his long beak a few times. Then she took one of his oversized taiga paws and pushed on the pads until his claws came out. "Beak and claws seem to work just fine. Williwaw and fantails are supposed to be natural flyers. Give those imped feathers a test, let's see what you can do in the air."

Pumpkin, Petal, and the other bog witches who had saved him watched from atop the stables.

Cielle crouched, his muscles still aching from the days of flight, and pushed off into the air. After the dry heights of the taiga, the ocean's mist felt like home. He stayed low to the water in case his new feathers fell out.

When the winds picked up, he spread his tailfeathers and froze in place until they passed, holding steady out over the bay. The ocean water was dark, but he could see a school of fish fleeing from a young serpentine whale, too small to venture into the deep ocean yet. The aquatic predator was chasing his prey towards the surface, giving them nowhere to flee.

Cielle's instincts kicked in, and he pulled his wings close, diving down to get ahead of the school. Even after eating everything the rangers and witches had put before him, he was still ravenous. He couldn't make out the individual shapes of the fish but guessed from the way they moved that they could be flying fish, perhaps.

They were small, but they'd stay in the air a while, giving him time to grab a few. There were two ways to hunt flying fish about to surface. He could either try to match their speed, flying just above the surface, and use his paws and beak to grab, or he could get ahead of them and swoop back, capturing as many as he could hold while they flung themselves away from the whale and into his outstretched wings and paws.

Flying fish this close to shore should be pretty small, and his appetite was big, so he decided to put his wings to the test. He flapped harder, ignoring the ache, and put some space between him and his second lunch. He looped back, diving down as the first fish breached and spread his wings.

That was when he realized that the whale and fish had been much deeper than he'd originally anticipated. Now that they were at the surface and his wings were spread to catch them, he saw an eighty-pound tarpon springing out of the water and straight into his chest, the open jaws of a serpentine whale lunging up behind it.

His tired mind snapped into focus, ordering his wings and tail into evasive maneuvers. He twisted around, latching onto the fish with all four paws and letting it change the direction of his momentum.

The whale's jaws were closing in on both of them, but Cielle had two advantages the fish didn't: wings and a long, feathered tail. He beat his wings and used his tail to steer the fish, getting it out of the way of the toothy maw just in time.

He was no osprey, and his muscles protested the effort, but he managed to keep the fish airborne long enough to drop it off at the docks and collapse next to Thenca.

CIELLE CAUGHT his breath on the wooden planks. With a single whistle, Thenca summoned the bog witches down from the stables to inspect his imped feathers for damage. Several goliath birds also perked up at the sight of fish.

"That was quite the display. How do you feel?" she asked.

"Exhausted," he admitted. "I didn't realize the water got so deep so close to shore. I was expecting much smaller fish."

Pumpkin lifted one of the taiga gryphon's wings to check the feathers. "The petrel fisherfolk have been afraid to swim around here. I guess their shores are sandy or rocky, no mangroves. I'd love to see the weald coast someday."

When a voice came from behind him, Cielle jumped, dislodging Pumpkin. He was so busy panting and holding still for inspection that he hadn't heard Rorin land.

"You may get your chance," the ruler of Swan's Rest said. "If things go wrong tomorrow or if Satra can't hold the Crackling Sea, you may have to evacuate. You're all welcome to come with me east."

Thenca's hackles rose. "We're not *all* welcome east. And Bogwash is our home. We can disappear into a dozen burrows and hideaways and let the infection eat away at the Alabaster Eyrie's numbers if they try to root us out."

Rorin was startled by the rebuke, but Cielle thought back to the redspine monitors that had chased him and to the witches' comment that some wildlife was still infected. In a sense, the same parasite that had unleashed starling hordes upon New Eyrie and Hoarfrost now served as a shield for the kjarr and bog gryphons who seemed immune to it.

"We took care of Urious when he arrived at Sandpiper's Dune last year." Rorin, already a tall opinicus, towered over the bog gryphons with his long, crane neck. "He came back to you safe and sound."

Thenca hopped on a crate of dried fish to look Rorin in the eye. "Urious came back bandaged up because Quess put a spear through his shoulder. He looked beaten within an inch of his life."

Rorin started to speak, a rumbling like a great bell coming from his throat, but Thenca cut him short. "And the moment just *one* wingtorn stepped foot on your sandy shore, *all* of Crane's Nest fled south into the islands, where they were then kidnapped. So even if your offer is heartfelt, I'm not sure we'd be safe there."

"I can't speak for the dunes, but I rule Swan's Rest, and no fisherfolk there would question me," Rorin said. "I will always err on the side of showing empathy and kindness to strangers."

Cielle thought of the spear sticking out of Jun's grave and wondered if that were true. There was a lot of anger simmering just below the surface of Swan's Rest. If he were a wingtorn evacuated there, he'd make his way north into Ashen Weald territory at the first opportunity.

Several wingtorn and witches peeked out from their huts. Thenca's voice projected when she was angry. It had a hint of kjarr accent to it, as though she were borrowing her tone from an old friend. "You are *one* opinicus, Rorin, and you are *one* bad day from becoming shark food. You can't hold a village together against hate through force of will alone. You have to let them be angry to move through it. That's why Crane's

Nest left. You didn't take their hate seriously, you told them it was wrong."

"But they hated *you*." Rorin gestured to the wingtorn with a wing.

"Good," Thenca spat. "They *should* hate us. They've earned that right, and we've earned their hate. Things don't heal overnight. They take time, and even then, they often leave behind painful scars."

Cielle leaned back to rest a paw on the tarpon he'd caught but ended up putting a paw on Pumpkin's head instead. When he looked down, the fish was long gone. While everyone's attention was on the fight on the docks, one of the goliath birds had dragged it halfway back to the stables.

Thenca leapt from one crate to another, addressing the city. "And you know what? I do feel bad about Crane's Nest. I feel terrible about it. The guilt haunts me. But *you*, Rorin, *you* can't ban us from coming within fifty miles of your shore, and then hop on a raft and shack up at our nesting grounds. You're an unwelcome guest here, and Soft Paws was too polite to say anything, but I have no such qualms.

"Maybe the rangers feel differently, but there aren't enough of them left to help you rescue your friends. You need witches and, most likely, wingtorn. So stop acting like you're in charge. You're not. You don't command any gryphon here, and if you want something, you can ask instead of order like any normal guest."

Cielle had been here less than a day, but it felt like an overreaction. Still, looking around Bogwash, he saw a lot of wingtorn nodding along. In fact, once the shouting started, the streets had filled with them. He'd heard of Bogwash as a city of witches. Even the wingtorn who had rejoined the bog pride wore paint in their fur in intricate designs.

Rorin did not appear to be a fisherfolk who was used to being shouted at. To his credit, he didn't become defensive. He seemed to weigh the words as he looked out at the crowd. The sentries behind him were indignant, but the rangers were serene. Cielle imagined they'd heard worse and had time to make amends since joining the Ashen Weald.

"You're right, of course," the giant crane said. "I hadn't considered the effect I'd have on the wingtorn. Last time I was here, this city was fifteen witches huddled into four reed huts. I apologize for my poor manners and will bow to Thenca's wishes regarding how we get our fisherfolk off the boats."

"Great," Thenca began. "So here's what we're going to do…"

22

SHARKBEAK

A good fisherfolk kept a supply of salted fish bars on them at all times. Tresh was beginning to think she was, at best, a mediocre fisherfolk and wished she'd packed more to eat.

And drinking water. I did not expect to be over the ocean for so long.

If not for an unexpected storm, she'd have had to abandon her hiding spot days before now. While the opinicus sailors hid from the downpour, Tresh drank until she couldn't drink any more, then tried to preen the salt stains from her face. She found herself thirsty again the next day, but luck was on her side. In the early morning hours, she saw a slither of sea snakes rising to the surface.

Despite living most of their lives in the ocean, sea snakes needed freshwater to survive. In the wake of some storms, a film of freshwater floated above the ocean's saltwater. No fisherfolk Tresh knew could tell which storms caused it, but they all knew that if the surface was full of snakes, there must be freshwater.

Tresh waited until Hi-kun was addressing the troops, then dove down from her hiding place on the ship, sipping on the wing and grabbing a few snakes to snack on. They weren't her favorite, but everything sounded tasty after a few days of fish bars.

Since the Alabaster Eyrie opinici were watching the shore for signs of pursuit, Tresh stayed hidden among the golden-beaked ornaments on the ocean side of the ship. The two smaller craft escorting the king's vessel remained on the shore side, waiting to intercept any attackers from the bog. Islands familiar from the sky appeared strange from this far down, but the dreadnaught's lookout was particularly loud, and she announced each new landmark as they passed.

"The crane folk cities are past us now!" she shouted one day. Soon, the "Redwood Mountains" followed.

It took Tresh a bit of guessing, but she assumed this meant they'd moved past the taiga and were sailing off the coast of the bog. She was starting to worry they'd made it past Bogwash. If they reached the Emerald Jungle, she'd have a hard decision to make: Stay with the ship as it returned to a part of the world she knew nothing about, or try to make her escape, abandoning the Crane's Nest and glacier pride refugees to their fate.

The ship continued its course, giving a wide berth to the bog.

I need to decide soon.

THE *OO-AWK, oo-awk* of a coastal petrel woke Tresh from her slumber. It was a sound that had haunted her since her expedition into the bog. If Piprik were to be believed, she looked the way she did because her ancestors had fed upon petrels, but she found their cry unnerving. To her, that would always be the sound of hunting wingtorn, of Vitra stalking the bog expedition through the mists.

Tresh looked out from her hiding spot but didn't see the bird making the noise. That didn't mean anything— the petrel could be diving off the other side of the ship —but her heart beat faster.

Down in the water, no bird shapes darted beneath the waves, but she did see clumps of sweet-weed, a type of freshwater aquatic plant she'd eaten a few times in the bog. It was unusual to see it this deep in the ocean, but floodwaters washed out strange things.

Tresh's ears perked up as she saw the first definitive sign that something was afoot. The shells woven into the weeds were from Crane's Nest, their colors offering her a warning of what was to come.

While Quess was famous for her wood carvings, most petrel fisherfolk were known for weaving reeds. It was common for each village to have a pattern of beads woven into the reeds, symbolizing the land and water around the village. The colors below—their browns, greys, and light greens—were Crane's Nest. But the beads' pattern showed *villages* situated on three islands. The first of which also had a freshwater lake.

Tresh looked out from the golden, ornamented beak on the side of the ship. True to the beads, she could see two of the three islands ahead of them. The echoing cry of *oo-awk* came from the closest.

She fetched Biski's sharpening stone, a gift after

Tresh had nearly shattered her beak pulling an infected starling off Urious, and gave her foreclaws a final pass. Her beak ached with memories of past battles, and she rifled through her harness until she located one of Quess's wooden masks.

Quess had made Tresh many masks over the years, most of which had been lost in the waters around Luminaire during Tresh's rebellious phase. They were intricate affairs, carved with a loving care to resemble both shark and gryphon. Some were ceremonial, most were decorative, and Tresh's main complaint was how hard they were to secure as a gryphon. The leather straps they used were intended for an opinicus.

This mask was different. Biski, Piprik, and even Soft Paws had agreed that Tresh couldn't risk biting things. This mask tied around her beak, holding it shut and keeping it safe. It wasn't a decorative cover meant to be worn during a festival; it was only meant to be worn when Tresh needed to kill.

More of Quess's carvings, sometimes large beads, were woven into Tresh's harness. Each was a memory— Tresh's brother and his kids played on their own beads, another showed Tresh's favorite salamander, and one had been carved with pretty rosettes.

Not all the beads were happy memories. An opinicus caught in a shark's jaws memorialized the battle for Swan's Rest. A serpentine whale swallowing a raft served the same role for Sandpiper's Dune. A lone petrel, surrounded by pupil-less, melting eyes for the bog.

Tresh did not normally wear any wooden adornments to her harness, but Quess had spent the summer working her feelings into her carvings, and Tresh didn't want to let down her sister-in-law. She'd also expected the journey to the dunes to be a day trip and had not adjusted her outfit or expectations even after she followed Cielle east to investigate the disappearances.

A lookout shouted, "Fresh water ahoy!" and the dreadnaught slowed. The temptation of refilling the rain barrels before the Emerald Jungle was too much to pass up. Tresh finished securing the mask with her paws a moment before she heard someone unlatching the portholes and opening them.

She didn't know what Rorin's plan was, and she didn't wish to tip off the white opinici too soon, but she wanted inside the ship before the chaos began. She knew from past experience, namely the city of rafts she'd sunk off the dune coast, that she could fit inside most portholes. What she didn't know was—

Her thoughts were interrupted by the sound of the nearest one unlatching. She climbed onto the golden ornaments, steadying her paws atop the giant, metal forehead. When an alabaster opinicus poked his head and chest out of the opening, Tresh reached up and stuck her claws between the gaps in his harness and into his chest, and then pulled with all her might.

Much like a startled pheasant, the opinicus went into shock and died before he realized what had happened, which was all for the better considering the state of his wings once Tresh got him through the port- hole and stashed in her previous hiding spot.

She couldn't preen the blood out of her feathers with the mask binding her beak, but she managed to stick her tongue out far enough to lick a paw and groom some of the white feathers off her chest. She waited to see if anyone sounded the alarm, but the sailors were too excited about water to notice one missing opinicus.

She pushed the porthole open and slipped inside the Alabaster Eyrie's flagship.

23

THE VOICE OF THE SEA

Thenca shook a muddy paw, and then let out another *oo-awk*. With enough of a lead time, with enough digging and some relocated shrubbery, the bog pride had managed to create several burrows around this island's freshwater lake. Unfortunately, there was no way to keep the burrows dry, and she could feel something crawly squirming against her paw pads.

She pushed aside a visceral feeling, instead concentrating on the small break in the foliage that gave her a good view of the opinici outside. She didn't see any sign of Tresh, though Thenca had been assured by some of the witches that Tresh had learned the *oo-awk* call in the bog.

The Alabaster Eyrie's sailors filled barrels with freshwater, but there was no sign of how they were going to get them back on the vessel. It took two opinici to fly the empty barrels off the ship, and for the moment, they were leaving the filled ones along the lake shore.

If Cielle's memory was correct—and after days of

flying and a soak in the Kjarr River, Thenca didn't entirely trust it—there'd been an opening on the side of the ship and a ramp. She had time. The more opinici that left the ship, the better their chances of getting inside and finding the hostages.

Crane's Nest hostages. Glacier pride hostages. Not groups Thenca thought she'd find herself trying to save. She didn't entirely approve of Soft Paws's close ties to the fisherfolk. While the witches had a unique history, some of the bog pride's wingtorn had destroyed fisherfolk villages.

An image flashed through her head: Jun leaping out of the canopy of a redwood tree to pull Rorin from the air, the clash of talon and claw, and just when Thenca felt sure Jun would win, finding his impaled body on the beach while a bloodied Rorin flew away.

Rorin is not the enemy today, she reminded herself. What she felt wasn't anger at him, not really. It was shame and a longing for the days when she could curl up around a dead goliath bird with Jun and her brother and argue for hours about nothing.

One of the waiting gryphons splashed in the mud, and Thenca silenced him. She'd had to hush the winged bog gryphons several times this morning.

The gryphon, a wingtorn and not one of the young bog witches like she'd assumed, moved closer to her. When he turned his head, she recognized his markings if not his name. One side of his body had thin scars across it, earned from their first war with the Crackling Sea. The leafcutter stitches had let the wounds close with minimal scarring, but whatever the medicine gryphons had used to treat his wounds turned the feathers around them white, breaking up his cream and brown markings.

"Den mother," he whispered, "I hate to bring it up, but we're risking a lot to save some fisherfolk who would be happy to see us dead. I get standing up to Rorin, but... why *not* let him and his sentries take care of it? Why risk our pride?"

Thenca let the den mother title slide. The young witches had taken to calling her that even against her protests that she wasn't staying, and the wingtorn had picked up on it. She didn't have to ask if this wingtorn had been at the shore. She didn't think anyone who had would question why they owed something to the Crane's Nest refugees.

Several more wingtorn and a few of the bog witches came close to hear her answer. She pointed at Pumpkin.

"You were there when Vitra died, weren't you?" She waited for the witch to nod. "Did you go back to the Heart of the Bog, or did you go with Soft Paws?"

"I went back," he said.

She already knew the answer. He'd shown up at Bogwash days later with six other bog pride in tow. "Why?"

His carved pumpkin markings made it hard to read his expressions, but his voice was reserved as though he were holding back strong emotions. "I saw what they did to the prisoners, letting them eat infected food, and I saw how sick they became. I'd heard stories of what the kjarr pride had done, rumors of the Ashen Weald, but I hadn't met them. But there was a moment where I looked at what we were doing and knew it was wrong."

Here he paused for a moment. "When Quess killed

Vitra, I had to make a choice. Two, really. I could keep fighting, but none of us wanted that anymore. So my real decision was whether to leave that moment or go and try to find my friends who I knew also wanted to leave. I went back."

"Even though you knew most of the bog gryphons back at the Heart might kill you for a traitor," Thenca said.

He nodded.

"I could tell you that prides stick together, that we act as one." She turned back to the wingtorn who had asked the original question. "You know that's a lie. Gryphons a season older than me saw the bog pride become kjarr and split off again. Prides are always evolving, improving.

"Both good prides and bad prides do that. But for the good prides, it's about doing the right thing. A pride whose only goal is survival will probably survive. A pride that gets caught up in dogma or vanity or conquest will burn itself out. But those aren't really the prides I want to live in.

"I want to live in a pride that learns from its mistakes. We killed a lot of fisherfolk—adults, fledglings, chicks, and gryphlets. We did that so our own gryphlets would survive. We were presented with an impossible choice, or so I thought.

"I don't believe in impossible choices anymore. I don't think any gryphon can justify evil by saying it stops someone else from being evil. I think that's a lie that's easy to swallow when we feel powerless.

"I can't go back and fix things. I don't think the Crane's Nest fisherfolk are ever going to see us as anything except child murderers. But I'd like to do the right thing anyways because I think that's important.

"When you ask yourself: what makes a pride great? The answer isn't a feathered mane, a fluffy tail, fancy flying, or hunting skills. It's caring about the other prides around you. You want to know what pride won the last war?"

Several gryphons nodded yes. They probably expected her to talk about Urious, Satra, or Foultner. Maybe Merin.

She didn't list any of those. "The Parrotface Pride. They found the antidote to Impir's poison and saved New Eyrie. They kept the fantails and feathermanes fed when the weald burnt down. They took in refugees from three different eyries.

"The bog pride has a history of being both oppressor and oppressed, victimizer and victim. How we're seen going forwards is going to be determined not by a sea of bloody wings, not by stolen eggs, not by the machinations of Vitra—it's going to be determined by who we decide to help.

"I need to help these refugees. My soul requires it. None of the rest of you needed to come, but you still did. Why? I think it's because you've grown tired. Not of the fighting, not of the war. I think you're tired of doing terrible things in the name of the greater good.

"So here's what I'm offering you. There are gryphons who dislike you for being bog. There are gryphons who need your help. They're the same gryphons—and opinici!—locked up inside that ship. The decision you make now is what type of pride you want to be. It's a decision we're all making individually, but it adds up. Any more questions?"

The muddy wingtorn shook his head. Pumpkin puffed up a little.

"Good," Thenca said. "Now look lively, it's just about time."

One of the smaller ships sailed past the dreadnaught, landing at the island where Rorin's sentries lay in wait. The last ship was out of view.

After her speech, her pride was ready for a fight. Every gryphon ear twitched. Tails swished back and forth in the muck, waiting for the sign. Officially, it was the *mronk* of a goliath bird that was supposed to start the invasion. That had been the only sound the raftworks rangers could pull off a decent imitation of. But when an alabaster opinici startled a swamp grouse, and it shrieked bloody murder, the bog pride sprang into action.

Thenca swore and did her best *mronk* to warn the others as the wingtorn sprang upon the unsuspecting sailors.

THE ASHEN WEALD RANGERS, weapons laced with jelly toxin, went after the smaller boats while Rorin took his sentries high into the air. They needed to be above the enemy forces during the battle.

Lei and Pip had been keen to talk about their adventures north of the sea, bringing back tales of how the white opinici fought. The Seraph King's forces were vast and diverse, but with their white plumage and black eye markings, this group looked similar to the ones Lei had seen at Whitebeak. And those opinici possessed something Rorin needed to be wary of: flechettes.

Turning a little metal into a deadly weapon was a surprising trick he felt certain the Ashen Weald would try to duplicate. Already, they had the sand gryphons scouring the sites of old battles and digging up what they could find—both to use against their enemies but also because wingtorn paws would be particularly vulnerable to them on the ground.

Yet the small, weighted points weren't a precision weapon. They required some setup time and planning to deploy, so while the rangers fought on the small boats, Rorin and his sentries caught a thermal and sought the view from above.

The glint of the sun off metal caught his eye. The Alabaster Eyrie lookout in the crow's nest, a white and black woodpecker with a red crest, was filling a bag with bits of metal and handing it off to soldiers, who began their own aerial ascent.

Rorin's command resonated in the cool morning air. His sentries spread out, each marking an enemy with the flechettes.

When the first alabaster soldier shifted his wings to leave his soar and fly over the wingtorn, Rorin didn't give him an opportunity to leave the sky around the ship. His weapon caught the opinicus right between his wings, the spear making a metal *thud* when it pierced through his body and hit his breastplate.

An open bag slipped from the woodpecker's dead talons. Like a sun shower, the air sparkled as the flechettes' shape caused them to right themselves and spin. Many of the projectiles embedded themselves harmlessly into the wooden hull of the ship. Enough of the others hit their mark, based on the screams coming from wounded sailors.

Rorin wasn't alone in his success. With the skies temporarily cleared out, he ordered his sentries to peel back and work on the smaller ships while he went after the opinicus doling out the flechettes. The ivory-billed woodpecker let out a cry like a small trumpet, but no one came to his aid. He grabbed his bag of metal spikes and prepared to lift off when Rorin's first spear hit the wood pillar next to his head.

The woodpecker ducked just as the second spear caught him in the side, pinning him to the mast. Before Rorin could land the third spear, the woodpecker reared back, used his impressive beak to snap the spear in two, and fled into the sky. Rorin tried to catch him in a dive, but the opinicus twisted midair, grabbing Rorin's talons: two spirals of red, black, and white colliding.

Even with his forelegs engaged, Rorin had one final spear—his long, crane beak. The woodpecker ducked out of the way, and Rorin's beak lanced him in the shoulder. The Seraph King's soldier reached up with both talons and grabbed Rorin's beak, then reared his own head back.

Visions of his javelin shattering when the woodpecker freed himself from the mast flashed through Rorin's mind, and with one nimble movement he slipped his gutting knife out of its sheath and slashed up with it, more for protection than offense.

The woodpecker's beak shattered the flint knife, sending pieces in all directions. Before his opponent could recover, Rorin kicked him in the stomach and disengaged, putting some distance between him and that killer beak.

With a twist, the adversary righted himself and reached for his deadly pouch. Down below, the wing-torn had just reached the surprised sailors by the watering hole and were tearing through them on their run for the dreadnaught.

Rorin let out his haunting cry, and from the clouds above, a comet appeared—or, at least, what once would have been a comet with an icy tail trailing behind. In actuality, Cielle looked more like a rainbow with so many borrowed feathers keeping him flightworthy.

The Williwaw gryphon's dive caught the woodpecker in the back, killing him in one blow, but also releasing his grip on the bag of flechettes and spilling some of them into the air above the wingtorn. Cielle pulled his wings in again, catching the bag with a back paw and using his large forepaws to try to capture the spinning death spikes before they righted themselves.

Rorin flew down after him, but several flechettes slipped by. Fortune was on the side of the bog gryphons, and none were hit, though several cast angry glances at the sky.

Cielle beat his wings to match pace with Rorin and held out bloody paws. "I caught as many as I could."

Why are the costs of war so often paid for with the blood of young fisherfolk?

"You did well." Rorin grabbed the bag from Cielle's back paw, then pulled the flechettes out of his paw pads. In the distance, several bog witches were being chased through the skies by soldiers. While bog witches had more hunter and warrior training than the medicine gryphons of the Feathermane Pride, their skill set worked best under the cover of mangrove swamp.

"Go help our allies," Rorin ordered Cielle. He hadn't missed the orange beak-kiss shape on the gryphon's cheek or the worried glances in the direction of Pumpkin. "They're not used to fighting in the air."

As Cielle flew off, Rorin looked down at the bloody flechettes. The bag was overflowing with them. The trouble was they worked best before the chaos began, which was why he'd struck quickly. He couldn't use them on the sailors on the island without hitting the wingtorn.

Below him, in the deep water between the three islands, a splash caught his attention. The bodies of the dead sailors were being pulled under, and Rorin wasn't sure what was causing it. The sound was too small for a serpentine whale, and most sharks wouldn't take an opinicus in one bite.

Thenca's shouts filled the air. A large goliath bird in a tattered harness was being scared to the far side of the island so the wingtorn didn't have to kill it. Rorin scanned the flagship with his eyes, revealing the corpse of a sailor hanging out of an ornamented opinicus beak.

Tresh is still alive. That's good news.

Atop the ship, a gold-and-alabaster seal opened, and an armored opinicus led a small contingent of woodpeckers to the surface. If Piprik's intelligence was correct, this was the one they called The Metalworks.

Hi-kun issued a command, and the side of the ship opened up, revealing a small army of soldiers.

Below, the wingtorn had finished scaring off the goliath bird and were charging the ship. Rorin tore open the bag of flechettes and flung it at the Alabaster Eyrie forces.

THE SIDE of the ship opened up, and a rain of metal cut through the first line of soldiers like sharpened claws through fat eel flesh.

Thenca caught a flash of polished armor in the sunlight atop the dreadnaught that denoted the leader of this expedition. She redoubled her pace, slipping between the bodies of dead sailors, and flung herself into the air, straight at Rorin the Hunter.

The fisherfolk's eyes grew wide, Thenca's reflection in them mirroring that of Jun not so long ago. Unlike her mentor and friend, she wasn't thinking of murder. Instead, she screamed, "Up, up, up!" and hoped Rorin got the message.

He did, catching her out of the air and tossing her atop the ship and into a flock of startled opinici. Sailors and soldiers alike were cut down by her claws and beak. With the nets and rigging, with the boxes and chaos, their wings only got in the way. Thenca slipped between them without a thought, slashing and biting.

The lone dissenter against chaos was the opinicus dressed in more metal than seemed appropriate for a sea voyage. His helmet, his armor, resisted her strikes. Behind him, woodpeckers in significantly less armor guarded an ornamented door engraved with a six-winged emblem: the Seraph King's chamber. Several moved to the entrance to the ship's hold, sealing it shut with some sort of metal lock.

Javelins hit the deck behind her, impaling three sailors sneaking up from below, and Rorin joined her.

"Hi-kun, the Metalworks." Rorin's deep voice echoed against the metal armor, rumbling back to them. Thenca felt the sound moving through her bones, remembered how the screams from the depths of the Crackling Sea Eyrie used to do the same.

Most of what she'd done in the last year had been hunting. The last time she'd raised her claws to other opinici or gryphons, excluding rabid starlings, had been at Crane's Nest: killing Rorin's kin, watching Tresh drown her allies. Before that, Thenca had waged a long war against the Crackling Sea rangers who now sieged the smaller ships across the water.

Still, it came back to her quickly. The same killer instincts Urious frequently made use of also lived inside his sister. They'd hatched from the same egg. While Rorin and Hi-kun bantered like legends out of a tale, Thenca's mind calculated the best way to rescue the prisoners.

Hi-kun stood straighter. His left foreleg rose slightly, ready to strike out with his metal talons. "Rorin the Hunter. I'd ask why you're here, but my hold is full of fisherfolk. I'd ask how you found out, but I really don't care. Flee now if you aren't prepared to die. The Might of the Seraph King has never lost a fight to a full-fledged eyrie, and it most certainly will not lose to gryphon-mating, eel-sucking fisherfolk."

The honor guard of imperial woodpeckers stood at attention, their backs to the sealed doors. Thenca whispered each of Hi-kun's words under her breath, repeating them again and again, listening for his accent and inflections. She and Urious used to do this for hours at a time, building up a cast of voices in their head. In her weaker moments, when Deracho was at Williwaw, and she was trapped atop Snowfall, she'd find a cave with an echo and listen to her own voice, trying to adjust it, trying to imitate the happiness of tone that had once come to her effortlessly before she'd lost her wings.

The Metalworks finished another speech on the impressiveness of the Alabaster Eyrie, filling out the last of the vowel sounds and pronunciations she needed. On her twentieth repetition, she captured his voice.

"We should leave to find the hostages," she whispered so only Rorin could hear. "We don't need to fight him."

Rorin's eyes were on Hi-kun, but his talons counted the spears in his quiver. The fancy ones had been spent in the air, but a few bamboo javelins remained. "No, a commander is most deadly when he's leading his troops. The longer we keep him busy, the better. I'm just worried about being outnumbered. The beaks on those woodpeckers can split skulls and shatter weapons."

Thenca scanned the faces of the royal guard. Their eyes were unreadable. Their fur and feathers were a mix of black and white—only their crests were red. A few shifted back and forth, looking from Hi-kun to the dead bodies littering the top of the ship.

They're nervous. Good.

Only two of the guards, the ones by the Seraph King's seal, showed signs of resolve. Judging by how the ornaments on their armor matched the door, she was going to assume they had orders not to leave their post, which was perfect for her needs. She looked around, spotting several tall crates tied down at the other end of the ship. While they presented a problem by blocking view of some of the doors, they also provided an opportunity.

"Shut him up and lure him behind the crates,"

Thenca said. "Do that, and I can take care of the guards."

To his credit, Rorin didn't question her. Instead, he reared back, throwing his first spear at The Metalworks. His weapon plinked harmlessly off the metal, but it forced Hi-kun to close the distance lest future spears find the gaps in his armor.

Thenca harassed him from behind, slashing at the buckles holding the outfit together, swiping a tailfeather trophy, and earning herself a talon to the chest for her efforts.

Despite the leather on her armor, despite the padding, the tips of his talons reached her flesh, and she cried out. The pain was intense, but she didn't let up.

Hi-kun's eyes widened in surprise as she didn't pull back but instead pushed forwards, forcing him to beat a hasty retreat as her claws snapped one of the leather straps holding his helmet on.

Rorin's beak kept Hi-kun from getting too close, and the fisherfolk leader slashed out with the sharp point of a bamboo spear, aiming for The Metalworks's neck. When Hi-kun used his metal talons to deflect it, Rorin twisted the spear, slamming the blunt end against his opponent's throat.

Hi-kun gagged but kept himself defended. This was the opening Thenca had been looking for, and she leapt atop one of the crates. The woodpeckers remained at their posts. She ducked back down, practiced her words once, then shouted out in his stolen voice.

"You four by the door!" came Hi-kun's voice from behind the boxes. "You need to secure the precious cargo from our escort. And you there, did I order you to lock that door? The Nighthaunt will be up at any moment. Unlock it and go find him!"

Not my best imitation, but it should work.

The real Hi-kun tried to issue new orders, but his wounded voice came out in a whisper. He glared at Thenca, then launched himself off the side of the ship and into the air.

"You go find the refugees," Rorin ordered. "I'll take care of this one."

"Will do," she returned with Hi-kun's voice. Rorin was gone before she could repeat herself *as* herself, so she looked out to confirm that the door into the ship's hold was open, then made a dash for it.

24

ECHOLOCATION

Tresh fought her way through the ship, going claw-to-talon against several sailors and guards before reaching a level devoid of opinici. She crawled through the corridors, her belly nearly scraping the floor, her eyes and ears on high alert.

Above, she could hear the sounds of metal and spears thudding against the top of the ship. Below, she heard some shouting, and it seemed like most of the forces were headed in that direction. But here in the middle, on this particular level, there was no sound, just endless stacked boxes and a single door across from the stairwell where she'd come in.

She wasn't sure what to think of that. She suspected they'd never leave the refugees unguarded, not if they were still alive. There was the possibility that they'd killed the refugees, kept their bodies as some sort of experiment. As much as she hoped that wasn't the case, she needed confirmation.

Lamps lined the corridor, encased in glass. Six-winged ornaments filled the space between them.

She'd always thought of ships as being practical things, not displays of wealth. This was more like a floating eyrie.

She reached the door and placed her ear against it. No sounds came from the other side, but she jerked back when her ear ached from the cold. She retracted her claws and forced them into the strange shape needed to open opinicus doors, unlatched but didn't open the door, and took a deep breath.

She burst through, startling a dozen armored opinici. Even more alarming, she startled a familiar shape from the attack on the glacier pride. Curled around a stack of books—literally curled like a snake— Mally the Nighthaunt unwound himself and looked up at her wooden mask with amusement. The cool mist hanging in the air framed his serpentine silhouette. The arctic temperatures emanated from stacks of ice on top of sawdust and hay that helped protect the frozen seraph in its icy prison.

Its feathers shone like oil on water in the lamplight. Tresh took a wager that the guards had been ordered to protect the seraph at all costs, and she swatted one of the lamps off the wall.

The fixture holding it in place was secure, but broken glass, oil, and fire splashed across the guards and ignited the edge of the hay. Tresh didn't wait around to see what happened next; she slammed the door behind her and pulled down a few of the crates to slow pursuit.

She was nearly through to the stairwell to go down to the next level when she noticed one of the lamps was loose in its fixture. She worked it off the wall and latched it onto her harness. The heat was uncomfortable, but the look of panic in the eyes of Mally's guards had suggested the ship wasn't fireproof.

THE SMELL of the stolen lamp was strange, and to Tresh that meant *not fishy*. She'd heard rumors the Redwood Eyrie's northern quarter once had lamps that didn't require fish oil, but she hadn't come across them herself. And the few lanterns made at Sandpiper's Dune were created by immigrants from the Crackling Sea who were used to working with fish.

While Bario's famed braziers were supposed to be scentless, this was something different. There was a deep, earthy scent to the oil. It smelled like a warm gryphon on a sunny day, sweating in the heat. She couldn't explain why that particular smell made her uncomfortable, but it did.

She was forced to duck behind crates or open doors a few times to avoid packs of running sailors on her way down, but she followed their direction and found the ship's hold, a massive room with a pen full of restrained prisoners. The large cargo doors were open, allowing opinici out, but the ramps hadn't been extended or had been pulled back.

They must be worried about wingtorn. A silly thought, as they were so far out in the ocean. A silly thought, as no one had less incentive to save Crane's Nest survivors than wingtorn.

That level of preparation was worrying, but it gave Tresh an idea.

With every guard's attention on what was going on outside, Tresh slipped through the empty boxes, supplies, and racks of weapons and armor until she reached the pen of refugees.

Feathers littered the ground. Each fisherfolk and gryphon had their forelegs tied up, then the rope tied to the next refugee in line. They were corralled like capybaras or goliath birds at a ranch, and their pen went all the way to the open cargo doors, where only a a tight grip on their neighbors kept them from falling out.

There were guards at the cargo doors, so she came at the pen from the other side. A familiar sight was awaiting her there.

Iony—bloody, missing some feathers, clearly unhappy, but alive—looked up at her. "The motmot gryphons bury their dead in masks. Are you a sea spirit, come to take me away? My wounds are not yet so deep. Tell the ocean of stars it needs more than one small gryphon to take my soul. If you want me, return with your legions, and let us see which comes out the better."

"You mainlanders like to hear yourselves speak." It was too much trouble to remove and re-secure her mask, so Tresh trusted her voice to identify her. "The Williwaw fisherfolk reached the bog in time. We are staging a rescue. How many of you can fly?"

"Sharkbeak?" The leader of the glacier pride chuckled, a gruff, brief sound, then spread his wings to show the gaps where several primaries had been removed. "None of us. They like to toss us overboard if we cause trouble, food for the sharks, and flight would interfere with their sport. Unless you can carry us out of here, there's no point rescuing us into the toothy maw of the ocean."

Tresh took a moment to see that when he said *toothy maw*, he was staring at the shark pattern on her mask.

"We are near three islands. It will be an easy matter to swim to them. There are dead opinici in the water, so swim quickly, but I believe it is safe."

She clawed at Iony's bonds without progress before realizing there was a better way to handle things. She sought out one of the elders of Crane's Nest and worked on his bonds instead. He glared at her, knowing who was behind the mask, but once his talons were free, she turned so her pouch faced him.

"I have one of Quess's old fishing knives. Take it and liberate the rest," Tresh ordered. "You will be free in no time."

Just as she thought she'd be able to free all of the refugees before anyone noticed, the stairwell door opened and a long, lithe shape snaked through it. Black eyes stared into the ship's hold, and a pale, bloody beak let out a scream that alerted the soldiers outside that something was happening.

As the sound reflected off Tresh, Mally the Nighthaunt's focus snapped to her. "The little shark from the glacier bay was a gryphon. How fascinating."

Can he recognize how my feathers sound or is he just speculating?

He must have stopped for reinforcements, because there were at least twenty armored guards behind him, many more than would have fit in the frozen seraph's room. Thus far, Tresh only had one tied-up-yet-loquacious glacier gryphon, beaten within an inch of his life, and an elderly fisherfolk with a gutting knife at her side.

She'd never expected to see the Nighthaunt up close. His body, now uncurled and free of its bookish perch, was far too long to be any gryphon or opinicus Tresh had known. She'd heard the rumors that he'd become part seraph himself, but the ice made it hard to see how long the frozen seraph was, and the desiccated swamp seraph had curled in around itself. Perhaps this was just a mutation gone wrong.

She'd been told his body was mostly white, but that was no longer true. As his disease progressed, the red from his talons and beak had spread across his face, forelegs, back legs, and even his split tail. More than half of his wings were now tinted with iron, resembling dried blood. His eyes and long whiskers gave him an otherworldly feel, like something dredged out of a deep trench or frozen in a forgotten cave—much like the two seraphs she'd seen.

Memories of the mummified seraph came back to her, and she almost expected the strange parasites to flood out of his beak when he opened it. It was like watching a capybara speak, a monitor sing. It just felt wrong.

Several industrious, climbing wingtorn crested the cargo entrance, and the soldiers outside the ship fought valiantly, but they were evenly matched. When the soldiers saw Mally's reinforcements, they stopped worrying about Tresh and went to help fight the wing-torn outside.

"The refugees mean nothing to you. Why not let them go?" Tresh asked, more to buy time than anything else. She had no way of knowing how many fisherfolk Cielle had rallied. For now, time was on her side.

Or so she thought—her hopes were quickly dashed when a cry of "hoist anchors!" started the dreadnaught moving again, and a new panic rose within her. Was the ship leaving because the fisherfolk had been fought off?

Or were they leaving because the Seraph King's forces were losing?

Mally's eyes never left her when he spoke. "I'm somewhat of a collector. The gryphons have spread across this land, mutated, evolved, devolved, re-evolved, survived. I can't discount the possibility that somewhere out there is a small pride of penguin gryphons who have developed an immunity to what ails me. And so I *pick up* gryphons here and there, *pick them apart*, and see how they work. It's not personal, I assure you."

It did not, in fact, assure Tresh. She was trying to figure out her best course of action when a strange voice came from the corridor behind Mally. It was confident, commanding, and appeared to be the only voice the guards listened to over the Nighthaunt.

"The gryphons have breached the seal to the king's chambers! Everyone, up top, now!" the voice shouted.

The guards didn't hesitate. They turned and abandoned Mally and Tresh. The moment they were out of view, she charged the Nighthaunt, slashing at him with her sharpened claws.

Mally was nimble for one so old and sick. He moved in a way she'd never seen before, clasping onto crates and netting with both his front and back legs, using his long tail like a whip to knock her out of the air.

She charged a second time, feigning a bite she was incapable of performing, and raked his chest with her claws before an ear-splitting scream sent her scrambling. His echolocation doubled as a weapon, and she'd been unprepared for it.

Out the opening, she saw the ship pulling away from the island. Once they were too deep, it wouldn't be safe in the water for the refugees. She needed to work fast.

Mally screeched again, forcing Tresh to put her paws over her ears. Her mask had a slight wooden covering, more like decorative ear-guards, but they helped blunt the sound a little. The Nighthaunt reared up, preparing to strike, when the same commanding voice called out from the stairwell.

"Mally! The seraph is under attack!"

"Don't you have a *king* to worry about, Hi-kun?" Mally hissed. Yet when he turned around, it wasn't Hi-kun who waited for him, but a lone wingtorn in tattered leather armor.

Thenca crouched down, her ringed tail thrashing behind her, and switched to her own voice. "I've killed a lot of snakes in my days, but never one that spoke. I wonder what sound you make when you die."

Mally screeched at her, but she'd already braced herself. She screeched back, a fair imitation. The sound wasn't as piercing, but it echoed off the walls the same way his did.

The effect was immediate. The sense of calm, the sense of knowing where everyone and everything was, disappeared from Mally, and for the first time, he was disoriented.

He pulled his tail back to lash it against Thenca, but Tresh caught it, using her claws to hang on. While she kept the tail at bay, Thenca slashed again and again, biting and screeching at him, throwing off his echolocation.

Mally thrashed, hissed, and bit. And, to his credit, he was a formidable foe. Just when Tresh thought she had the upper paw, he leapt backwards, using his four strange talons to pull himself along the netting atop the hold ceiling, and landed on the Crane's Nest elder. Before the fisherfolk could react, Mally was already holding his talons against the old opinicus's throat.

No, not just *against* his throat. The talons had drawn blood, blood which Mally lapped up like an overheated squirrel. Even as he drank his prey, he stared Tresh in the eyes, not making his threat verbal.

Once he figured out she'd imitated Hi-kun, he stopped speaking aloud. This is Piprik's mentor, the one who taught him?

Somewhere in the scuffle, Tresh's stolen lamp had fallen off her harness and rolled next to the stairwell. When Mally took his eyes off her to glare at Thenca, who had started hissing at him like a snake, Tresh pounced on the lamp and held it up.

The heat burned her paws, but she refused to let go. Some of the oil had leaked out the bottom, trailing around the corner. There it stopped, but Mally couldn't see that from the other side of the hold.

"Nighthaunt," Tresh whispered. His attention snapped to her. "Let go of my elder. You do not need him, you said so yourself. But you *do* need the seraph, and when I left the room, I left behind me a line of oil. If I throw down this lamp, your king's prize becomes a tasty, cooked meal."

Mally's eyes narrowed. She couldn't tell if he bought into her bluff or not, but the ship was moving, and she didn't have much time. The refugees and glacier pride captives weren't just bound by talon and paw, they were also tied to each other. It would be difficult to free them from the water before they drowned.

The Nighthaunt made up his mind. He opened his

bloody beak as if to speak, then looked at Thenca and closed it again. He nodded to Tresh, but he slashed the elder and pushed him overboard. Then Mally tossed one of the tied-up fisherfolk after, and the rope pulled the rest of them in one at a time.

Tresh threw her lamp into the stairwell, more to get his attention than anything else, and dove after the fisherfolk from her home village.

Iony, last in line, managed one word of profanity before he was pulled out of the opening.

25

CHUM

Rorin panted, staring down at his opponent. They were covered in each other's blood. Rorin's white wing feathers were as red as his chest feathers. His opponent would need to clean Rorin's blood off before it rusted his fancy outfit.

A single trickle of red dripped from the end of Rorin's beak. Their fight had taken them to the southernmost ship, its sails hanging loose courtesy of the fisherfolk shipwright. Rangers and Alabaster Eyrie opinici played out their own fatal dances in the skies above.

"You fight like the abyss itself," Hi-kun coughed, his voice still raw from taking a blunt spear-edge to the throat. Despite his metallic appearance, Rorin's beak had slipped between the links in his armor a dozen times.

Rorin rose from his crouch, an act that hurt more than he cared to admit, and pulled two spears out of dead crew members. "The ocean is an unforgiving place. Those who hold back get swallowed up by its depths."

Hi-kun laughed, a coarse sound. "The fisherfolk on our shores are fragile, grown soft on the fat of the empire. Your associations with gryphons have made you feral."

"I've seen your eyrie civilization, and I'm not much for it." Rorin threw one of his javelins. Its arc betrayed his lack of strength, and Hi-kun's poor parry spoke to his weakness.

Their fight, for all its spectacular aerobatics, marksmanship, and flash, had run its course. Whichever of them received reinforcements next would claim victory, and Rorin's side began the day outnumbered. Even now, he saw two rangers pull their wounded out of the water and back to shore while the glint of silver armor suggested Hi-kun's allies would soon be upon him.

Better to die fighting, I suppose.

He wiped his bloody talons on his flank, finding a clean spot to dirty, and prepared his final assault when a horn sounded from the dreadnaught. Rather, the resounding sound of a woodpecker hitting the mast loudly several times, followed by a trumpeting cry.

Hi-kun's armored allies above changed course, returning to the flagship. The sailors from the ship with tattered sails evacuated to the sister escort craft, which pulled away from its island.

The Metalworks's posture shifted, relaxing a little. "Until next time, I suppose."

Rorin let his opponent go. Hi-kun's labored flight would normally have made him a good target, but the fisherfolk's talons still shook from the woodpecker's earlier blow.

From below deck, a black crane peeked out from the safety of the shadows. "Is it over? Did we win?"

Rorin laughed, a sound that seemed to worry the shipwright. "Let's go find out!"

The leader of Swan's Rest climbed the mast, then leapt—perhaps stumbled—into a glide. Down below, the water was chummed with the bodies of opinici. The surprise attack had served Bogwash's allies well: most of the bodies resembled white-tailed kites or woodpeckers, not fisherfolk cranes or Crackling Sea herons.

Had the fight gone on any longer, that would not be the case.

Something in the water was feeding on the bodies, and the rangers were already struggling to get their wounded on land before they were pulled under.

The dreadnaught moved past Rorin, and a spiteful woodpecker, hoping to land a parting blow, was pulled out of the air by Cielle. Her deadly flechettes hit the water harmlessly. The Williwaw gryphon, perhaps as tired of death as Rorin, flung the sailor at the fleeing dreadnaught where one of the Alabaster Eyrie opinici caught her and saw to her wounds.

As the fisherfolk leader's glide brought him to the east-most island, the black crane caught up to him. Below, Rorin saw that the water here was full of fisherfolk and glacier gryphons struggling to keep their beaks above the surface. Thenca and the talonful of wingtorn with buoyant harnesses pulled survivors to shore, but they were a tangle of rope.

"Fetch the rangers," Rorin ordered the shipwright. "Tell them to bring their sharpest knives and start cutting the prisoners loose of their bonds before they drown!"

At the farthest point from shore, at the end of the chain, Rorin flew down to help an ornery, long-eared glacier gryphon who struggled with something under the water. He'd managed to work his forepaws loose somehow, but they were clasped around a slippery shape below him.

"Bloody depths, if it isn't the great fish hunter himself," Iony grumbled. "Mind lending me one of those big talons of yours?"

Rorin remembered the trick the shipwright had used on the shore to see beneath the surface and made an umbrella shape with his wings to shade the water from above. Beneath the waves, a thick, serpentine shape writhed in Iony's grip.

Rorin's first thought was sea snake, but none he knew of were so thick. Even the crowncrest sea serpent had been a kind of impossibly long fish, not a true snake. His second thought was a baby serpentine whale, but there were no fins, and what little he could see of the face didn't look right.

When it clicked, it clicked because he remembered the rangers at Bogwash saying the elvers were especially plentiful. Baby eels often migrated long distances, but many lived their adult lives at sea.

And an unusually large number of baby eels means an unusually large number of adult *eels.*

The lithe shape sprang out of the water, its strange double-jaws coming dangerously close to taking a bite out of him.

Rorin returned the favor, spearing the eel through the neck. Iony caught the slippery creature's neck in his beak, and Rorin started pulling the rest of it out of the water to find its end. The eel, from head to tail, was nearly twelve feet long.

Iony said something obscene, but the exact words

were muffled by the creature in his mouth. Rorin hurried to cut Iony loose, but already he could see that their problems were greater than a single eel. In the deep rift between the three islands, the water was alive with slithering shapes coming up from the depths. His only consolation was they were going for the dead Alabaster Eyrie opinici directly above them first, giving the fisherfolk and rangers a little extra time.

The bonds on Iony's back paws snapped, just leaving the rope connecting him to the next glacier gryphon, who was unconscious. Someone had propped a small, floating barrel under her head to keep it above water.

When Rorin started cutting the pride leader loose, Iony interrupted his work. "No, leave me attached to this one. I'll drag her to shore. Go cut the fisherfolk young'uns loose first."

By the time Rorin got the next gryphon free, Thenca was gryph-paddling out to pick them up. The rangers soon joined in, flying the chicks and gryphlets to shore before liberating the rest to start swimming.

Thenca turned to say something to Rorin and caught sight of the strange shapes pulling dead bodies under. "What in the bog are those?!"

"Eels," Rorin explained. "Longer than I am tall. We need to hurry."

Something touched Rorin's leg, and he let out a high-pitched sound and spread his wings to try to catch sight of the eel to spear it before it took off his toes.

Instead, he saw a wooden, sharky face staring up at him. He didn't know if Tresh was grinning under the mask, but its toothy face did that work for her. In the water beneath them, he could see the bodies of a dozen eels she'd killed. He was alarmed to discover how close he'd come to becoming dinner.

"I hate swimming," Rorin grumbled. "Too many weird things under the water."

Cielle, gliding overhead, shouted back with, "You chose a strange profession, then, Rorin the Hunter."

Hunter. Hunting. He had an idea if they could hunt down the goliath birds.

"Cielle!" he shouted at the Williwaw gryphon. "Whatever happened to the goliath bird that was stranded on the shore? Can you grab some rangers with nets and toss it in the water to distract the eels?"

Cielle had just started nodding when Rorin had a better thought.

Nets! The rafts still have their fishing nets.

"Wait, new plan!" he shouted. "The goliath bird gets to live. Tell Thenca to clump anyone still tied up in a group. Have the rangers get the biggest fishing net they can find and bring it here. We'll have Tresh swim it under them, then the wingtorn and flying rangers can work together to pull everyone closer to shore!"

Cielle squawked a reply, his voice more the cry of a fantail than the dry sound of a Snowfall taiga gryphon and flew off to make it happen.

Rorin, once again remembering how much he hated swimming and dreading the feel of more saltwater on his wounds, went under the water and let out a cry to get Tresh's attention.

A gryphon tapped him from behind, and he surfaced to see Tresh there staring at him.

"Do not make that sound. It offends the eels," she said.

He laughed, a few drops of blood flying from the end of his long beak.

She *tsked* him. "You should also not bleed."

"I was so worried about you," he began, but he was cut off by the arrival of the sort of large fishing net favored by Crackling Sea inhabitants.

Tresh understood at once what was required of her. She ordered Rorin out of the water lest he upset more eels, and she pulled the net under the remaining tied-up fisherfolk and glacier gryphons, handing the underside to the wingtorn with floating harnesses.

While the wingtorn swam, the rangers and bog witches grabbed the top side of the net and flew, slowly moving the mass of survivors closer to shore. Once they were out of the dark water, Rorin's sentries patrolled the clear shallows for slithering shapes while the last of the rope bonds were cut free.

It was a harrowing afternoon on top of a dire morning, but Rorin was pleasantly surprised when Thenca finally shouted up to him that everyone was safe.

The wounded, the survivors. The Crane's Nest fisherfolk, the Swan's Rest sentries, the lone islander from The Wrecks. The Crackling Sea rangers, the bog pride. All drank, washed, chatted, and celebrated their victory on the small island.

"How do we get everyone home?" Cielle asked. A bog witch with smudged orange face paint cleaned his wounds and cooed over him. "Do we go one raft at a time?"

Already, some of the eels had invaded the shallows and were making short strikes on land to try to catch the unwary. The rafts, normally a formidable sight, seemed flimsy next to such large creatures.

The black crane fisherfolk looked up from where he was talking with the rangers. "Actually, I propose we take a different ride home."

Rorin looked out at the other islands. While the abandoned craft's sails were partially detached, they were still draped across the bow of the Alabaster Eyrie ship.

"Think you can fix it up?" he asked.

The black crane scoffed. "I wouldn't be much of a shipwright if I couldn't. These raft-wranglers haven't handled a real ship before, but I think I can turn them into sailors, at least enough to hoist the anchor and bring her around to load up everyone."

"We'll, uh, come back for the rafts when things are calmer," the ranger captain said. Whatever such a young captain thought he was going to experience on the southern shore, clearly this wasn't it. He'd probably expected running the raftworks to involve a lot of fishing and napping. If Rorin had to guess, he'd be resigning his post at the next opportunity.

A dark shape rose out of the lake, startling both wingtorn and rangers with its terrifying visage.

"My mask is stuck," the lake monster said. "Can you fix it? I need to preen the rest of the salt out of my feathers."

Rorin laughed, a sound echoed by the abandoned goliath bird hiding on the other side of the island, and helped Tresh free herself. "You'll have to tell us your story. We only got bits of it from Cielle."

"No," Tresh said. "Food first. Story later. I have been at sea for days."

While the shipwright took the rangers to repair the sails, Rorin's sentries began pulling eels from the water.

The normal recipes for eel required much smaller subjects, but Rorin reckoned they could find a way to cook eel steaks over a fire.

Iony, looking uncharacteristically abashed, approached the fisherfolk with a bowed head. "I'm not one for apologies or thanks, but I suppose you two deserve both. Thanks for the saving, apologies for that time we tried to murder one of you at Luminaire."

Tresh stared at him. The shark-faced visage carved into the wooden mask was somehow less intimidating than her actual face when she was hungry. "You blew up my island. You could have killed my favorite salamander."

"Whoa, whoa there, shark-lass," Iony countered. "*Piprik* blew up the island. I don't deal in explosives. Bad for the complexion."

Rorin smirked. "The Palace of Fire and Ice exploded. Shattered into a million pieces last time you were there, so I hear."

"Bad business that." Iony scratched at one of his long ears, dislodging sand. "Was just out there on vacation. I told Rybalt we should stop in, try the shrimp. Strange coincidence, that explosion."

Both Rorin and Tresh rolled their eyes. Rybalt and Iony's reputation was now well-known even among the fisherfolk, courtesy of Piprik and Lei's tales. The fake salt traders had told everyone about the various adventures from Crestfall Eyrie down to Ashfoot Isle, minus a few key details to protect identities.

"Tresh, Cielle, I hate bother you two," Iony began, putting his pretenses away. "What happened to the gryphlets and fledglings you evacuated from my home?"

"I do not know. We split up, and I went into the

warehouses." Tresh paused, and Rorin knew there was more to the story. "I pulled out three gryphlets, and we all split up. Younce took them to Poisonmaw, I believe."

"Blasted Poisonmaw," Iony grumbled.

Cielle, who had been helping Pumpkin re-apply his paint, rejoined the conversation. "I went to Snowfall, then here. I'm sorry, I didn't see what happened to your gryphlets. I assume they're safe. Last I heard, Deracho and Naya said New Eyrie was the front line. They were evacuating the Crackling Sea Eyrie just in case."

The phrase *front line* elicited murmurs from the ex-hostages, Iony included.

"The Seraph King attacked other places?" Tresh asked. "Why? They got their seraph."

Rorin shook his head. "We'll catch you up on the ride to shore. First things first, let's get everyone fed. You're all safe now."

While some of the sentries and bog witches calmed at his words, many survivors had seen too much war to trust so easily. Battles in the north would spill south; they always did. The question for everyone involved was what to do about it.

The rangers here had been ordered to stay south and guard the raftworks, not an easy decision to follow when their home was under siege. The bog wingtorn could sit this one out. None of them held any love for the Crackling Sea. Somehow, Rorin thought Thenca may feel differently, particularly as part of the Ashen Weald.

The fisherfolk had been neutral and forgotten for too long, but the same forces sieging the north had taken Crane's Nest prisoner. Hi-kun's words came back to Rorin: *Until next time.*

There would be a next time. Rorin was certain of it. He couldn't force the other fisherfolk to go north with him, but Tresh would join him.

"Rorin," Tresh said. "As soon as he is able to fly long distances, we need to send Cielle to Sandpiper's Dune. You heard Piprik's stories of the reeve's pet. We need Naya and Orlea's weapon."

Rorin's hackles raised. The rangers near them looked interested, both upon hearing of the reeve's pet and that the fisherfolk had a weapon.

"That's Naya's call. Or Gressle's. Or even Orlea's," Rorin said. "We shouldn't make it for them."

Tresh shook her head. "Now is the time. I know they would agree. I will make this decision if you cannot. No one is there to disagree."

The ranger captain looked up. "I'm sorry, but you have a secret weapon you developed to kill the reeve's pet with?"

Rorin and Tresh shared a look, but he was the one who spoke out. "No, this was something they developed with a different enemy in mind."

The Crackling Sea opinicus shook his head. "Who's that?"

Tresh stood on her back paws to look up at the heron face. "It was originally intended for fighting rangers."

Rorin weighed his options, but he knew she was right. Naya and Orlea's friendship had started down the path of finding out why the weald fires had started, but it had quickly transformed into figuring out how to prevent them in the future. With Naya's access to the ocean and Orlea's access to the trade routes, combined with Gressle's knowledge of the Crackling Sea, they'd stumbled across an interesting solution.

A solution that would work as well against the troublesome reeve's pet as it would have against the rangers, had things with the Ashen Weald soured.

Rorin sighed. "Cielle, rest today and tonight, but tomorrow I need you to fly to Sandpiper's Dune. Find Gressle and tell her we need her."

"And every petrel fisherfolk you can," Tresh added. "Find Quess first, have her rally them. But make sure they all come ready for war."

"Just the petrels?" the ranger captain asked. When Tresh nodded, he looked even more confused. "Well, I suppose we'll take any help we can get."

26

ROAST EEL

Tresh napped on the ride back to Bogwash, waving away fisherfolk and bog gryphons who wanted her attention. There were a certain number of bog pride who saw her as some sort of heroic monster after her part in the expedition, but most were young bog witches who wanted to know how Quess was doing.

It got so bad, Tresh finally put the scary mask back on and found a spot below decks—not an easy task as the ship was filled beyond capacity—so no one could tell if she were awake or not. Still, they left her alone long enough for her to catch up on sleep.

Those who had stayed behind to guard Bogwash were alarmed at the sight of an Alabaster Eyrie ship coming straight towards them, and a small war band flew out to meet the craft until Rorin appeared to reassure them they weren't under attack. Tresh watched the exchange groggily from above deck, awoken from her slumber by the shouting but still wanting to save her energy as best she could. She needed to recover if she was going north with Rorin.

In addition to the entire village of Crane's Nest and every adult member of the glacier pride fitting onto the ship, the nets from the rafts had been filled with dead eels and secured to the sides of the hull. When cut into steaks, the eels turned out to be surprisingly tasty, a combination of whitefish and salmon. At least, once Tresh got past the oily, rubbery texture of the skin, there was a flaky center. Their arrival in Bogwash precipitated one of the most unusual celebrations she had ever been a part of.

Fisherfolk, as the name suggested, loved to eat fish. She'd spent many long nights on the dune shore or at Luminaire eating and talking with friends, swimming, and napping. Whale, tarpon, salmon, clams, crabs—there were many tasty things to eat.

What the bog gryphons brought to the party were liquids—both a variety of sauces to put on the eel and distilled drinking water flavored with mint, citrus, or pumpkin. Stolen, repurposed barrels were rolled out from where the bog witches had been hiding them from their raftworks neighbors, marked with all kinds of interesting glyphs. Tresh lapped at a bowl of mint, only realizing it wasn't just any mint, it was gryphmint, when she got a bit tipsy.

"Slow down there, Sharky," Thenca said. "The witches snack on mint like it's candy, and their tolerance for it is formidable. Let's get you something to eat before it goes to your head."

Tresh allowed herself to be led to the fire pit where Rorin and his sentries did most of the cooking while blue heron opinici sang songs or played musical instruments Tresh had never heard before.

She nibbled at a few spits, tasting the sauces. Some

were too strong. They hid the taste of the eel. Others were too fruity, they tasted like something an opinicus would eat. She finally settled on one that let her taste the meat.

"What is this made of?" she asked Thenca.

The wingtorn shook her head. "Bog cooking isn't like Henders and Quess sharing recipes. Every witch has had medical training, so nothing here is going to kill you. But I promise you, you aren't going to enjoy the flavors if you know where they come from. They're... creative with their ingredients."

Tresh now had more questions than when she started, but she saw Rorin laughing and joking with Petal, who wanted to over-sauce everything to the point of turning it into soup, and Tresh decided she'd take a night off from thinking and just relax.

She'd just found a place far enough from the cooking fires to feel cool and was asking Thenca about how Urious was doing when Cielle and Pumpkin stumbled over. She'd seen that look of young love many times, had experienced it herself once or twice, and anticipated what was coming. Cielle was an adult, albeit a young one, but she'd been responsible for pulling him into the world north of the shore. She waited until Pumpkin went off to get more to drink before she broached the subject.

"Cielle, were your parents..." she tried to think of how to phrase the question, "opinical or gryphonic in their relationships?"

He didn't understand where she was going. "My moms have been together since before I was born. That's... opinical? Do they do something different on the shore?"

"Ah." Thenca caught on. "For gryphons, courtship is... brief. For non-fisherfolk gryphons, I mean. I don't want you to get your heart broken, but the relationship lasts until around when eggs are normally laid, then it's over and you part ways."

"We are not saying you should not be with Pumpkin," Tresh hastened to add. "Just that you should know it will not last past spring."

Cielle thought it over. "Your parents were opinici, weren't they? Did you ever enter into an opinicus relationship?"

"No," Tresh said. She didn't really want to talk about her relationships, but she also didn't want to see some poor fisherfolk get his heart broken. She'd been with opinicus fisherfolk, but she'd always put a stop to it at the end of the season, leading to hurt feelings on both sides. "Mating for life is a long promise, even if opinicus relationships do not often last so long. I did not want that. I make no promises I am not sure I can keep. And I do not expect that from others."

"But Thenca and Deracho have been together forever, right?" Cielle asked.

Thenca nodded. "Some gryphons get back together season after season. It just works that way. But that's a heavy burden to put on someone you just met. Not to dissuade you, either, but you should assume you're going back to the islands come spring if you decide to stay here."

Cielle blinked. "I like the bog, don't get me wrong, but I've asked Pumpkin to come out with me to The Wrecks for the winter. I heard the shipwright talking about where they were going to hide a ship like that, and I think the answer is home. Nobody would look for an intact ship there. And that way, Pumpkin wouldn't have to fly all the way out there."

Thenca and Tresh shared a look.

"Bog and kjarr gryphons aren't allowed south of Glacial Run," Thenca said. "It's a promise we made with Rorin, Naya, and Tresh, back when she led the Crane's Nest fisherfolk."

Cielle's feathers rose, making his tail look like a fluffy eel. "But we're south of Glacial Run now. Bogwash is."

"On the weald side," Tresh explained. "Here in the bog and kjarr, anywhere is fine. But on the other side, it is different."

Cielle was clearly spoiling for a fight, as much a lightweight to gryphmint as Tresh herself was, but Pumpkin arrived back with the Crane's Nest elder in tow.

The old petrel opinicus, ever perceptive, looked from Cielle to the wingtorn and correctly guessed what was going on. "Pumpkin came to ask my permission to go south. Den Mother Thenca, you killed my grandchildren. We will never be friends. But the shore is no longer my home. So long as Rorin and Naya allow it, Crane's Nest no longer asks you to remain north of the river, only north of Luminaire."

Thenca bowed her head. "Thank you, elder. For my part, I have long wished to see Hoarfrost, where my mate spends so much of his time."

"I think you will find it a hard trek by paw, but if you wish to make it, do not allow me to stand in your way any longer." The elder turned to leave, but Pumpkin opened his beak to speak.

"Wait, please," the witch said. "I wish to go south of the shore, as far south as the islanders have settlements. What about me?"

The old fisherfolk looked back. Being in the presence of Tresh and Thenca clearly pained him. "The punishment is for wingtorn only. Their children are not held accountable for their crimes, nor their children's children. You may go wherever you're welcome."

Tresh waited until the Crane's Nest elder was out of sight to speak. He hadn't spoken or even looked at her. She and Quess arriving at Sandpiper's Dune on a stolen raft full of wingtorn, bog gryphons, and rangers had been a moment that made pariahs of both of them. "That is not a turn of events I would have expected."

"Me neither," Thenca said. "Just last year, Younce was looking to split Hoarfrost off into its own pride again, and he offered Deracho the pride leader position. Deracho turned it down because I wouldn't be allowed there."

Tresh didn't know what to say but felt compelled to say something. "Ask Younce again. If he has not offered the position to someone else, I know Deracho is his favorite."

"You should have Tresh ask him," Cielle said. "He always blushes when she's not looking. I think he likes her."

Tresh let it pass, the Williwaw gryphon not knowing her history with Younce, but Thenca was a little shrewder.

"Are you two back together for this season?" the wingtorn asked. "You seemed so happy last year. I remember at the Blue-eyed Festival, you two—"

Tresh cut her off. "Not in front of the fledglings."

Cielle and Pumpkin both glared at her.

"Fine." The gryphmint had taken hold of Tresh's beak. "Yes, I invited him to the shore this winter. Last year, I overheard Thenca telling him that Urious killed my family. I did not want him to have to lie to me or betray Thenca's trust, so I left. And I saw the way he was with teaching the new taiga gryphlets, and when I see that, I see my brother with his chicks." Her paw touched the story beads on her harness. "I do not want to have gryphlets in this world. I do not want to *lose* gryphlets in this world."

Thenca's surprise caught Tresh off guard. She'd assumed Thenca knew or that Younce had figured out the reasons. It hadn't occurred to her that she'd been holding onto all of that without anyone else knowing.

The wingtorn's kind words always sounded a little angry. "Okay, yes, I can be a bit of a capybara's backside, but if you'd waited around until morning, I would have told you myself. I *knew* I was putting Younce into an impossible position, but you just left before I could make it right!"

"Well, you... you..." Tresh paused. "I lost my thought. You are right, this gryphmint is far too strong. I need to sleep if I am going to be able to fly tomorrow."

Despite Thenca being the last person Tresh wanted to be around right now, she was the only one who knew where Tresh was sleeping, so the wingtorn guided her past the celebration to the nesting grounds.

Tresh had found her makeshift nest and was just dozing off when Thenca prompted her.

"Tresh?" Thenca said, waiting for a drowsy confirmation of awakeness. "Thank you for getting my brother out of the bog. I said a lot of things to Rorin two days ago, and while most of them were true, they weren't the whole picture. I don't think it's common knowledge that Urious was the target of Vitra's assassination attempt. But I know how much you and Blinky did to make sure he came home alive. He's an idiot, but I don't know what I'd do without him."

Tresh had already set four paws firmly in the land of sleep, so she didn't know if she responded or not. In her dreams, she was back at the dig site, near the border of the Emerald Jungle. Biski and Henders were scraping moss off rocks—Biski to put in her medicine bag, Henders to reveal the carvings underneath.

Jer and Xalt were talking to Urious, playing some sort of game. There were friendly shouts followed by laughter. Tresh padded over to the pond, where Erlock stared down at a reflection. The small podium that had once contained a mummified seraph was now a block of ice, a pristine rainbow of feathers shone through it.

Tresh looked down at the water. In Erlock's reflection, her fore- and hind-legs were both feathered. Tresh's reflection remained unchanged, except that it wore a bloody shark mask.

She looked up at the seraph in the ice, except the ice was long gone. Vibrant and ephemeral, the seraph was staring at Tresh.

Tresh reached up to touch it, but her legs were now chained down. Erlock wrapped her in thin strips of stormcloth, blackened in the fires they'd used to burn the infected, as the seraph rose into the sky and flew northeast.

Tresh tried to speak, but her beak was already wrapped, then her eyes. Just before her ears were covered, she heard the chittering of a million starlings.

She awoke with a start. In the distance, she could still hear the celebration, but Thenca was long gone.

I am never drinking anything a bog witch offers me again.

IONY MADE sure his pride members were being taken care of before slipping away from Bogwash and towards the raftworks. He didn't have a good pretense for doing so, but it would be easy to claim he'd gotten lost.

Cielle, a gryphon he found it hard to be mad at considering his heroics the past few days, had used up all of the spare feathers. The strange taiga-fisherfolk was now a rainbow of flight feathers, but that put Iony in a predicament. He needed to get word north to Rybalt, but he wasn't about to walk there—especially not after finding out that the Seraph King's forces were attacking the Crackling Sea.

A chance comment had offered him an opportunity to solve both of those dilemmas. One of the rangers left watching the raftworks during the rescue operation commented that a goliath bird wagon had arrived just before everyone left, and a particularly bossy Redwood Valley merchant had demanded to be treated like a reeve in their absence.

The merchant, a blue bird with a splotchy pattern, had fled the Crackling Sea with all of her wares.

Iony had always felt himself in possession of a large amount of luck, and he was happy for a chance to cash it in. Between the evacuation of his gryphlets and his rescue at sea, he'd used up a good portion. But it seemed he had a bit left.

He snuck up behind a merchant stuffing her face. She'd stolen several eel steaks from the celebration and was packaging them away to eat—or perhaps sell —later.

"Hello, Didi," he drolled.

She screamed and hit him with a fillet. "What are you doing here?!"

"I was rescued by your hosts." He licked lemon-orange sauce off his whiskers. "From the Seraph King's flagship, no less."

Seeing that she wasn't moments away from being killed by Iony's associate, Didi relaxed the slightest bit. "Well, they should have left you there. It'd certainly make *my* life easier if you'd jump head-first into the Emerald Jungle and get—"

"It's always such a pleasure talking to you," he growled. "I need you to pack up your wagon and bring us north. They're out of imping feathers here, and I need to check on my gryphlets."

Didi sat on only her hindpaws, an opinicus trick that put her eyes above his, though his ears still towered above her. "Oh no, I know what this is about, and there's no way in the depths I'm going back to the Crackling Sea! Even if I wanted to, they're evacuating the place. *They* don't want *me* there."

Iony wasn't one to be intimidated by any opinicus, let alone one of the squeaky ones. "Fine, you're a merchant. Let's strike a bargain. I need to get north. You give me a few of the feathers off your wings. If I get imped tonight, I can fly tomorrow. I'll head up to

Poisonmaw. Then you take my pride north on your wagon. Surely, an eyrie has enough feathers to spare. Once they're taken care of, I'll tell Rybalt what a good spy you were, staying on the front lines until the last moment, while you take your wagon and hide in the weald."

"No deal!" Didi spat. "You can take my feathers and shove them up your nose or another hole for all I care, but I don't answer to you. Only Headmaster Neider got to order me around."

Iony was sympathetic to Didi, he really was, but that sympathy was running thin. "Didi, I am not asking nor ordering you. I am *threatening* you."

"Pfffft," Didi scoffed. "Look, there are things I need that Rybalt won't let me have. He's afraid of me running off."

"Which he should, because you probably will." Iony knew how hard it was to get spies in the southern eyries, let alone retain them.

She rolled her eyes. "Details! My feathers are too pretty for your ugly butt, however, I have found myself in possession of a large number of discount taiga feathers I'm willing to sell you for a small markup. I'll make a list of my other demands. And I'm not going within a frog's hop of the Crackling Sea, but I'll take your gryphons as far north as the kjarr nesting grounds. Deal?"

"You have a large number of taiga feathers?" Iony's ears went back in distrust, but his main concern was the safety of his children. "Enough to imp me tonight and the rest of my pride on the trail tomorrow? If that's true, you have a deal."

Didi chirped and held out a talon. Iony sighed and

held out a paw so she could shake it. Redwood Valley merchants were particular about how they concluded trade deals.

"Excellent!" She led him to her wagon, parked outside the goliath bird stable. "I hope you like pink."

27

CAVE GRYPHON SEARCH

Cielle disentangled himself from Pumpkin and crawled out of the bog nests to find breakfast. Some of the other witches were stirring, so Cielle didn't think he'd be alone for long, but Pumpkin had expanded to fill up the nest and was snoring loudly.

He'd just washed up and finished his grooming when Tresh and Rorin appeared with a bowl of cold eel strips and a small keg of pumpkin water.

"Best eat up." Rorin sat down beside him. "You've pushed yourself these past few days. Once you get to Sandpiper's Dune, I'd like you to take a few days to rest, then help the ship find its way out to wherever Crane's Nest is hiding these days, then to your home."

It seemed the shipwright would finally get his wish, to see The Wrecks. Despite the access to lumber, old ship parts, and stolen stormcloth, Cielle didn't think they'd be able to make more of their own ships without access to a working metalworks.

The Williwaw gryphon looked up from stuffing his beak. "But won't you need me at the Crackling Sea?"

"A battle is not the same as a rescue." Tresh went around to his other side. "The water of the Crackling Sea is dangerous. I can see your ribs and skeleton. By the time you have recovered enough to be useful, it will be over, one way or the other."

On the docks, a crab and gull fought over scraps from the previous night's celebration. Despite the comments on Cielle's appearance, he couldn't help but notice that his companions had also seen better days. He could count every one of Tresh's ribs, and there were scratches anywhere her harness and mask hadn't covered. Rorin had so many stitches that it was inconceivable the medicine gryphons had given him permission to fly later today. While most of his beak had been wiped clean, there was still dry blood crusted around his nares and cere, and his left talons shook when he tried to lift a bowl.

Of the three of them, Cielle was probably in the best shape, give-or-take his fragile ear. Diving down to pick off opinici hadn't put him in much danger. And while his tail looked like he'd sat on a rainbow, the imped feathers were holding their own.

With that in mind, and because Cielle didn't like being left out, he pushed back. "I've always wanted to see the Crackling Sea. I hear it's full of lightning."

"Jellies," Rorin corrected. "Maybe islanders call them jellyfish. Anyways, they light up like lightning during storms. You'll get your chance to see it. But not this time."

"Getting to Sandpiper's Dune is more important. We need Quess to meet us up north," Tresh reassured him. When he bristled, she continued, "I have spoken to Thenca. She says you fell out of the sky from exhaustion, lucky to hit water instead of a stone. Then you were nearly eaten by sailfins. That kind of overwork stays with you. It requires a full season to recover from. You must trust me on this, I have seen it from everyone we saved from the bog."

He wasn't convinced, but he held little sway over such titans of the fisherfolk as Rorin and Tresh. Inside, a guilty part of him was relieved. Having permission to step away from the fight meant he'd be safe. Even if things went horribly wrong, The Wrecks were deep in the ocean. It was possible the war would never reach them. He'd have time with his family and Pumpkin.

And yet, he hated leaving things unfinished. He liked helping, and he wanted to do more. Wanted to see more of the world. The thing about living on an island was he knew everyone who resided there and every nook and cranny. He even knew the coral reefs and shipwrecks by heart from helping the fishers so often. It was why he volunteered to fly to shore and back, despite how taxing it was.

Still, with a ship, there's a lot we can do. Trading is limited by what I can carry now, or what the most adventurous of rafters are willing to gamble with. But this opens new opportunities.

"Okay," he finally agreed. "I promise I'll take the ship home when it reaches Sandpiper's Dune."

Rorin and Tresh shared a look, and Rorin was the one to speak. "If you want to learn more about the world, there are two salt traders you may wish to speak to. Do you know Ashfoot Isle?"

"Of course," Cielle said. "My ancestors' dirty paws gave it that name. Gold clover and mint grows all over."

"That is it," Tresh said. "Ask for Piprik and Lei. Pip

has taught Lei much about the mainland. I am certain he would not mind saying a little more."

Cielle nodded. "I'll do that. I just need to check in with Pumpkin, then I'll hurry to the dunes."

"Not so fast." Thenca came up from behind him. "With everything going on, there are three cave explorers who don't know about the danger. I need you to go and seek them out."

Tresh looked intrigued. "Anyone I know? I am somewhat of a cave explorer myself."

"Yes, yes, we know about your exploits," Thenca said. "I think you'll recognize at least two of the explorers, they spent several seasons helping you out."

"Zeph and Kia, from Hatzel's pride?" Rorin asked. "Is that where they've run off to? I've missed Kia's guidance and Zeph's... Zephiness."

"Who is the third?" Tresh asked.

Thenca finished chewing her eel before speaking. "You remember the trial in the weald at the start of spring? Cherine Metalbeak is here with them, too."

"I heard he was pardoned," Rorin said. "Must be an interesting opinicus."

"How will I know them when I find them?" Cielle asked.

Thenca used a claw to trace the mountains. "I assume you know Hoarfrost and Williwaw, yes? They're searching these caves here. They started north of the falls, so they should be south of it by now. And you'll know them. Zeph is unassuming but loud, Kia is bright green, red, and blue."

"And Cherine has metal on the tip of his beak," Rorin added. "Really, just shout and see who shouts back."

"If you hear a chittering sound, fly away fast as you can," Tresh added, earning a laugh from Thenca.

"Most of the parasite has been cleared from the Flower to the taiga, so you shouldn't see any starlings," the wingtorn assured him. "Mind the red-spined sail-fins, though. They can carry the parasite without turning rabid. They're too important for the ecosystem to kill, so we've been leaving out bowls of pumpkin-and-meat soup. But after your run-in with them on the way here, have Pumpkin check your eyes each morning."

"Sounds easy enough." Cielle grabbed his bowl in his beak and carried it back to where a ranger was washing them. Now that the sun's rays were hitting the shore, it was a good time for him to take a short flight, testing to see which feathers needed more preening. He'd broken a few on the woodpecker sailor, but nothing important.

The dishwasher called up to him, so he practiced a hard landing next to her.

"Oi, not so rough inside the nesting grounds," she said. "The bog gryphons are particular about that, especially with the wingtorn around."

Cielle bowed his head. "I'm sorry, I didn't even think about that. I-I've never been around wingtorn before."

"If you're up early doing some fancy flying, can you take these up to the raftworks?" She produced a small package of lumber.

He'd seen several like it by the stables. There were talks of trying to secure the raftworks as best they could for the rangers remaining there, so supplies were being shifted. At the first sign of trouble, the bog gryphons would flee to a hundred small burrows hidden north of the mangroves.

"Yeah, I'd be happy to." It was a little heavier than he'd like for a morning flight, but the raftworks was close. He climbed the stable to get a little extra boost, then took off to the west.

Down below, mangroves hid a treasure trove of interesting, edible animals. On land, red crabs waved their claws angrily at him as he flew by. Something fuzzy, perhaps an escaped capybara, disappeared into the neighboring palm fronds.

Next to the loch and lake, an opinicus waved him down. He landed next to her, carefully this time, and she took the lumber from him to where several rangers were securing the windows closed. There also seemed to be a pawful of wingtorn digging an escape tunnel for their ranger friends. Based on the chatter, it sounded like the raftworks was one of several locations with a reputation for being indefensible.

North of the main building, several wagons had been strapped to goliath birds, and a small blue opinicus appeared to be in charge. She was arguing about something with Iony. It looked like he was booking passage north for the rest of his pride.

Cielle chirped a hello. While he understood that the long-eared, short-tailed gryphons from up north were on a different side than the weald gryphons and opinici he sometimes chatted with at Sandpiper's Dune, that didn't mean much to an islander.

"Well, if it isn't the Williwaw gryphon," Iony said. "This here's Didi, a merchant who charges a tail and a leg for the most basic services."

The merchant pulled out a large notebook full of loose pieces of paper and tossed it on the ground in front of Iony. "Here's the *receipts* for your boss. Make sure I'm paid in full."

Iony grumbled but managed to secure them to his harness.

Didi's grim demeanor softened, and she curtsied, feathers spread, to Cielle. "Williwaw, you say? I hear they're in the market for sealant, warm-weather bedding, and cold-resistant foodstuffs. I don't suppose you're headed there now?"

"Ah, no, sorry." Cielle held up a paw. "I'm afraid my family hasn't lived there since the Connixation. I keep meaning to take a look, but I live out on the islands."

"Islands still need things," Didi pushed. "In fact, islands often need common things and can trade rare things for them. Next time you're in Sandpiper's Dune, come find me. I'm sure we can strike a deal."

Whatever bad deal Iony had made with Didi, he was clearly unhappy with her. "I wouldn't think an opinicus from a merchant family as prominent as yours would want to be so far from the action. Such a small songbird in such a salty place. It might not be *safe*. I think you should stay north."

"I can make a profit anywhere." Didi poked Iony in the ribs, which were protected by the strange ledger. "As long as your boss remembers to pay his bills. Now, I think it's time to get going. The paths aren't going to stay safe for long once the army pushes east. It was nice to meet you, 'Williwaw gryphon.' Maybe don't spend so much time around gryphons like Iony."

The glacier pride leader made a *harrumph* sound but let the caravan go. "Are you headed north? Want to fly together?"

"Can you fly so soon?" Cielle asked, then he noticed

all of the pink feathers. "Oh, Younce feathers. I have a few of those myself. Molting must be hell for Didi to have stockpiles of his feathers."

Iony shook his head. "I doubt they're his. They have the feel of Snowfall about them, but any gryphon or opinicus with white feathers can turn a profit dyeing them pink. A few even smell of bleach."

"Oh," Cielle said. "That makes sense. But no, I'm heading east. It's time for me to go home. It was interesting meeting other taiga gryphons, though. I didn't know any mainlander settlements other than Snowfall had survived."

"You're starting to sound like Younce." Iony shook his head. "Alright, keep your tail on straight. With any luck, you won't see me again. But if you find yourself needing a favor—*a small favor*—feel free to ask. Just not around the opinici."

Cielle watched Iony fly. He wasn't particularly graceful, but his feathers were quiet, owl-like. Combined with so much muscle, he was probably a good forest hunter.

What am I going to do with a favor from a glacier gryphon? Cielle wondered. Well, that was a question for another day. It was time to check on Pumpkin and head east.

ZEPH CRAWLED through another cave on his adventures with Kia and Cherine. The tall, metal-beaked opinicus scholar was certain there were cave gryphon dens somewhere in the weald or taiga, but due to his habit of getting kidnapped or captured when he went anywhere alone, Zeph and Kia weren't letting him out of their sight.

The first two caves had proven fruitless. As best any of them could tell without echolocation, they stopped twenty feet into the ground. They were usually empty, though the last one had the remains of several dead starlings. Kia wrote down the location so the medicine gryphons could return and dispose of the bodies.

This latest cave, however, was starting to look up.

Zeph pulled himself on top of a rock and pointed to the ceiling. "Looks like we have some glyphs here."

Cherine put down his lantern—a gift from the sand gryphons out of their stores of stolen glassworks items—and adjusted it so it illuminated the wall.

"Are these cave gryphon glyphs?" Kia asked. She'd voiced her reservations about the existence of cave gryphons after the battle at the ruins of Crestfall, but several months of the sand gryphons insisting cave gryphons were real had softened her stance.

While Zeph had grown up with stories about cave gryphons as monsters and myths from his taiga mother, he'd been easier to convince. The sand gryphon's *guest cave* smelled like it had been full of a new type of gryphon. Kind of warm and oily.

"I'm not sure," Cherine said. "The glyphs in the guest cave were from the sand gryphons. I never saw how the cave gryphons marked their territory."

"Looks like taiga glyphs to me. We could ask Younce." Zeph stood on top of Cherine to get a better look. "They look a little like grave markers. Maybe some gryphlets from Hoarfrost or Williwaw died in here? It smells sour, like sailfins or monitors."

Opinici had no sense of smell. Their hard beak and

nares were woefully underdeveloped compared to the softer beak and sensitive nares of a gryphon. That wasn't to say gryphon didn't have a nasty bite. Their beaks may have more flex to them, but they were often lined with a serrated edge just inside called tomia.

"Strange to see the taiga islanders starting to revisit the mainland," Kia mused. "The term *taiga pride* is becoming a bit of a misnomer now that the Williwaw Pride has been found among the fisherfolk and we know about the glacier pride up north."

"Younce is good at bringing gryphons together." Zeph peered at the back of the cave. He could smell sour water in the air but couldn't see what lay past the darkness. His eyes had yet to begin their change to blue.

Cherine finished sketching the glyphs. "There are just too many small caves out here. Maybe it'd be better to have Zeph sniff them out than explore each one."

"We might find new dens for gryphon prides to live in," Zeph mused. Hatzel and Ninox's prides both competed for territory north of the Redwood Valley. They'd created a no gryphon zone between Poisonmaw and Iony's giant, frozen mountain.

"Or saltpeter." Kia looked up from her notes. "What? Both the Blackwing Eyrie reeve and the Seraph King have access to it. It's more dangerous to be without."

While there were still free prides and Ashen Weald prides, Satra had reached some sort of agreement with everyone both south of the Crackling Sea and east of the Emerald Jungle. The threat from the north was too big to stand divided, at least for now. The only exception was the last of the bog crones, hiding near the Heart of the Bog.

The trio made their way deeper into the cave. Zeph

stepped in a tiny stream making its way out of the cave and shook his paw.

"So, Zeph, how's mating season going?" Cherine asked.

Zeph blinked with surprise.

Kia rolled her eyes. "That's a rude question."

"Oh!" Cherine said. "I didn't mean it like that. I just meant, y'know, have you found anyone special? A gryphon or opinicus?"

Zeph poked at a lost mangrove crab before deciding to eat it. "I'm not having much luck. Everyone I like is intimidated by the Reeve's Bane thing. And everyone who likes the Reeve's Bane thing isn't really interested in me for who I am."

With the two cultures coming together, Zeph had gotten used to opinicus questions about mating season. While it was rude to pry, there had been a lot of broken hearts between opinicus-gryphon couples who met in the first autumn after the fire, fell in love, and then spring came, and the gryphons assumed the relationship would end.

"I heard about the troubles at Poisonmaw," Kia said. "The opinicus refugees who joined Hatzel's pride say the gryphons are really needy over the winter and distant in the summer."

"I guess." Zeph could hear water up ahead. The cave grew warm the louder it became. "The gryphons say the opinici are distant in the winter and clingy in the summer."

"Would you settle down with an opinicus?" Kia asked.

Zeph reared up on his back paws like an opinicus and put his paws over his heart. "Are you propositioning me? Oh Kia, I didn't know you cared! Of course, I'll settle down with you."

He made a purring noise, eliciting a laugh from her.

"Oh no. I've learned my lesson from watching Cherine pine over Ninox," Kia said. "You want to marry me, you're going to have to go full fisherfolk wedding ceremony. None of this cuddly in the winter, distant in the summer."

"I'm afraid that's not in my nature," Zeph intoned the old saying, "said the monitor to the parrot. Say, how are things going with you, Cherine? Aren't you supposed to be an honorary sand gryphon now?"

Cherine the Metalbeak looked up from putting water from a hot spring into his vial. "Er, well, it's just a formality. And not so great. Sponge and Ninox are fighting."

Zeph and Kia looked at each other.

"Over *you?*" Kia asked.

"No, not really." Cherine stopped the glass container and put it in his harness. "They're just fighting with each other. I don't think I want to go through another gryphon mating season again. I told Ninox that I don't mind the summer distance, but if she's interested in me, she has to at least commit to us spending every mating season together."

Kia smirked. "She seems like the kind of gryphon who likes having ultimatums."

"She seems like the kind of gryphon who wants to have the smartest hatchlings possible," Zeph said. "I hear she kidnapped a ton of scholars, and she has a secret harem now."

"That's not true," Kia laughed.

"Well, it's half true," Cherine added, surprising them

both. "She's set up a university in the Owlfeather High-lands to attract the scholars who didn't turn out to be spies. It's not like a secret harem. She just wanted to find a way to put a lot of smart scholars next to a lot of Strix Pride gryphons right before mating season."

"I guess that's one way of going about it," Kia said. "Though if the scholars are there for her pridemates, maybe she's considering your proposal."

"Well, she didn't say anything before we came south," Cherine continued. "So I assumed we were over. But then Sponge keeps showing up, and now those two are fighting every day."

Kia shook her head.

"Gryphons are prone to jealousy and pride some-times," Zeph said playfully. "I knew two gryphons, a magpie and a copper hawk, who both fell in love with a fantail one mating season. They spent all autumn fighting over her."

Cherine looked down from his perch where he was poking the cave walls to make sure they weren't secretly cave gryphon feathers. "What happened to them? Who got the fantail?"

"Neither of them." Zeph's tail twitched with amuse-ment. "They enjoyed fighting each other so much, they ended up together. The fantail had a lonely winter all alone, but the couple had like twelve gryphlets together."

"Xavi and Pink Paw?" Kia guessed.

Zeph nodded. "Xavi and Pink Paw."

"There's a hole here." Cherine shone his light into the ceiling, revealing a passage that had been covered up with leaves. "None of these leaves look native, either. This might be one of their hideaways when they travel."

He pulled out a turquoise bead, one of his old feathers, and a salted fish bar. He set them just inside and restored the leaf barrier.

"Still seems farfetched." Zeph sniffed at the pools. This would make a good bathing hot spring, but the water wasn't safe for drinking.

Kia examined a leaf. "Unless I miss my mark, it's maple. You might be onto something. If Piprik and Lei are right, these don't grow east of Whitebeak."

"Whose land is this?" Cherine asked. "The cave entrance was just over the kjarr border, but this goes back a ways. I'll bet it's taiga above us before the end."

"Depends on the tree line, but Younce'll know," Zeph replied. "He's figuring out what to do with the old Williwaw and Hoarfrost hunting grounds. Last I heard, he's up near Poisonmaw, trying to reach out to the glacier pride to share stories of the Connixation. Might be back at Snowfall by now."

The sound of scratching came from the cave entrance. Zeph tensed. There was still the scent of sailfins in the cave, but it was old, so he'd felt safe.

Cherine turned the lantern to see their guest and nearly dropped it. Standing in the entrance to the cave was a tall, thin taiga gryphon with long wings and a feathered tail.

"Relax," Kia said. "That's not a ghost. It's a fisherfolk. Remember the one who flies into Sandpiper's Dune once a season? I forget what Naya said his name was."

"Cielle?" Zeph prompted.

"Oh!" the taiga-fantail said, noticing them for the first time. "Sorry, it's just these glyphs by the entrance are Williwaw. This is where Tielle's brother, Cici, died. I'm named after the two of them."

Cherine got out his notebook and guided everyone into the light. "You'll have to tell me the story."

Cielle shook his head. "There's no time. You three are needed at Poisonmaw. I was sent to find you on my way east. There's been trouble."

Zeph didn't wait to hear what the trouble was about. He got a head start flying north. A williwaw gryphon and two opinici would beat him there, but he didn't want to lag too far behind.

Behind him, he could just hear Kia asking for the details while Cherine packed up their camp-nest.

28

HINTS OF RED

Zeph made it as far as Snowfall before he needed to take a break. Kia had long ago passed him and was already so far ahead that she was out of sight, but she'd filled him in on the basic details of what was going on before leaving him behind.

Cherine arrived at Snowfall before Zeph, filled them in on what had transpired with the ships and the seraph king, then departed as Zeph arrived.

"Where's Younce?" Zeph asked. One of his old pridemates directed him to Deracho, who stood next to Naya and Orlea, all huddled around a large hide map of the weald. Several other hide maps of the bog, kjarr, Crackling Sea, Poisonmaw, and the desert had been stitched together. Much was missing, but Zeph was surprised to see he'd visited many of the locations. His world had grown larger than just the small stretch of weald by the Summer Falls.

"Zeph!" Deracho hooted. "Cherine said you'd be by. I forgot you three were searching for cave gryphons, or

I'd have sent someone to fetch you. I'm glad Thenca remembered."

Zeph bowed his head a little. "I'm sure Cherine and Kia will fill me in later, but what's the general idea here? How're things holding together?"

"Not well," Orlea said. "We've been expecting an attack from the Blackwing Eyrie. Those snakes would have had to come via boats—without anywhere easy to land—or the long way around the mountains. Either way, we'd have time to stop their supply chain."

Naya pointed to polished white stones going from New Eyrie up to the Argent Heights, Whitebeak, and Reevesport. "We didn't have a good way to watch the strip of shoreline north of the Crackling Sea. There's a lot of food, supplies, and fresh troops moving that way. New Eyrie has already fallen. We've evacuated most of the Crackling Sea Eyrie. All of those caves Younce found will serve as hideaways, and the Fantail and Feathermane Prides have opened up their homes."

"Do you think they're cutting around the desert to get to the blackwings?" Zeph asked. "Or are they coming into the weald?"

Deracho shook his head. "Nobody knows. For now, the best we can do is make the Crackling Sea Eyrie a tough target."

War, logistics, keeping everyone fed. Zeph had been around a lot of gryphons and opinici who understood those things. That had never been his way. He liked small goals. Hiding. Helping. He'd go mad if he kept staring at the map, but he could go and see what Hatzel needed help with.

"What about Poisonmaw?" he asked. "Are they evacuating or staying?"

Orlea shrugged. "That's up to Hatzel. We're certain the Blackwing Eyrie knows about Poisonmaw and The Crawl, but it's anyone's guess as to if the Seraph King does."

"When Cherine ran into Rybalt at the palace, he said Mally the Nighthaunt had killed Headmaster Neider in The Crawl," Zeph explained. "So probably."

Deracho frowned, something easy to miss with his small beak. The key was to watch the feathers around his eyes. "You're all welcome here at Snowfall, of course, but I don't know how Hatzel will feel about that. Tell your pride leader that whatever she wants, we'll make it happen. Our prides have always been close."

"Thank you," Zeph said. "Now I need a nap before I continue. Where are Younce's quarters? If he's not here, then no one is using them."

Naya laughed. "Down past the hot springs. Second cave on the right. Vosk's old quarters."

Zeph shook his head. It made sense as Younce was the pride leader, but his old friend had kept the same drafty nest up high for nearly a year. Zeph wouldn't want to live in Vosk's old quarters *or* next to Mignet's room. As he made his way into the dark, past the humidity, he paused by Mignet's room. There was a hide barrier providing privacy. He reached a paw out to push it aside, but he heard the sound of laughter.

Redwood Valley opinici chicks?

He supposed everyone needed a place to stay. There was no sense keeping the room shut up as a shrine, especially not with so many in need. He kept going, entering Vosk's old room. The colorful stones had been cleared out, and there were several goliath bird hides piled in the corner. It needed a cleaning, but Zeph couldn't afford to be picky.

He curled up, put his paws over his beak to keep it warm, and took a quick nap.

DESPITE THE CIRCUMSTANCES, Kia was glad to be back at Hatzel's nesting grounds. While Poisonmaw wasn't the same nesting grounds she'd recovered in after Reeve Brevin's death, it had all of Kia's favorite faces: Pink Paw bringing in a new kill, Xavi attempting to keep the saberbeak gryphlets from biting the glacier gryphlets, and the stable, strong presence of Hatzel.

"Stop moving," the once-last saberbeak grumbled. "It's hard to groom you when you move so much. I'm almost done."

Kia allowed herself to be groomed and fed. She didn't even mind how much spit the gryphon grooming her used. She was starting to feel like herself again, and she was going to ask for Cherine's help in inspecting the glacier gryphons for injuries, but he'd been waylaid by Ninox upon landing. What they were arguing about, Kia didn't know. It wasn't like they were together again. She scooted closer to listen in, earning Hatzel's good-natured ire a second time.

"I want to spend more time with them, but every time I come up here, you try to jump me," Cherine was saying. "You need to decide what you want."

"I know what I want." Ninox spoke softly and was harder to hear from so far away. "I just need you to want that."

Cherine sighed. "I don't. I would love to have a

million cute little gryphlets with you, to teach at the Darkfeather University, but I need a commitment. And I need you not to get angry if someone else likes me."

Their argument was mobile as Ninox led him into the woods where Grax waited with Marshmallow, Squirrelbane, and Sound of Snow.

Kia looked up at Hatzel. "Is it always like that?"

"It is," Hatzel said. "And Cherine insists on meeting Ninox here, so we get to hear it every time. If they stay long enough, you get to hear Sponge's name, too."

Kia laughed, and when Hatzel gave her a funny look, Kia shrugged. "I like Sponge. She understands thirty languages. She is, for lack of a better word, refreshing. I don't think Cherine would be any happier with her than Ninox, though. In a way, they're too much alike."

"You should say that loudly around Ninox, see if it changes her mind about Cherine," Hatzel said. "There, you're groomed. Let's find the glacier gryphlets. They're little monsters without their den mother."

Xavi ran by with a saberbeak gryphlet attached to his tail.

"Speaking of den mothers." Hatzel detached the small saberbeak from Xavi's rear end and held it up in a giant paw. "No biting, you hear me? We're all friends here."

The little saberbeak, still mostly down and sabers, hissed at her. Hatzel sighed, then tossed it twelve feet in the air, alarming Kia, but caught it on the way down.

The gryphlet laughed loudly, then managed a slightly trilled, "Yes, pride leader!" before running off again.

"Keep hoping an eagle will carry them away when I

do that, but I think they're getting too big for that to be a realistic dream." Hatzel led Kia to where the glacier gryphons had been corralled into a small hut full of nesting material.

Kia approached the closest one, which hissed at her. She tried making cooing noises at him, but his ears were down, and his tiny nub-tail shook back and forth.

Hatzel put her head down to eye-level with the gryphlet, or as close as her saberbeak allowed her to get, and let out a tiny roar.

The gryphlet squeaked, then laughed and allowed Kia to inspect him. He had energy, his ears and tail were working fine—both important parts of socializing any gryphon children. But when she held his paw pads and extended his claws, they were translucent.

Is it my mind playing tricks on me, or is there a hint of red?

She picked up a chew toy and put it in the gryphlet's beak to hold it open. She hadn't noticed it at first, but his beak was also paler than usual, and there were specks of dark red that didn't wipe away.

The glacier pride could have its own disorders and diseases to watch out for. There was no reason to think this was bloodbeak. But she needed to be sure.

She inspected several others, then the fledglings, who had the same thing. What she really needed was an adult glacier gryphon to compare them to, but they were all in the bog, according to Cielle. Iony was on his way up, but she needed to know now.

"You said Cherine and Ninox argue here all the time?" Kia asked. "I need him to look at this. Can you show me where they're at?"

Hatzel sighed but guided Kia out of Poisonmaw to a

small clearing. Grax cooed at them as they came close, ever the bodyguard, and they found Cherine and Ninox playing happily with their offspring.

"Aunt Kia!" Sound of Snow shouted. She bound over, still a bundle of fluff, and Kia picked her up happily.

"Rawr!" Squirrelbane said to Hatzel. "Rawr, rawr!"

Hatzel lowered her head. "What are we today? Another monitor lizard?"

He shook his head. "I'm the reeve's pet! I've climbed out of the water to attack Poisonmaw. Defend yourself or be eaten!"

Kia handed Sound of Snow to Grax, then pulled Cherine aside while Ninox tried to stop Marshmallow from eating some flowers. "I need you to look at something. It's important."

Cherine frowned. "Of course. Are you going to tell me what I'm looking for?"

She shook her head. They returned to the Poisonmaw nesting grounds, and Cherine confirmed her findings.

"This is just like it looks in the textbooks," he said. "The only way to be sure is to check an adult."

As luck would have it, Iony and Zeph appeared in the skies above.

"I caught him trying to sneak back to Poisonmaw," Zeph said.

Iony scoffed. "You didn't catch me, you daft wealder, I was already on my way here. And I didn't sneak here the first time, it was abandoned."

Kia tried to remember if she'd told Zeph about the glacier pride's kidnapping and rescue. She couldn't remember if she had.

"Open up, Iony," Cherine commanded. Iony looked confused but obeyed.

Kia took his paw, pushed on the main pad, and watched his claws extend. "They're a lot darker."

"Same with his beak," Cherine confirmed. "Seeing what a glacier beak is supposed to look like, it's easy to see where the pigment is gone."

Iony pulled his paw back. "What are you two talking about?"

Kia frowned. "It's the gryphlets. They're not harmed, but all of them are showing signs of bloodbeak. Every single one."

"That's impossible." Iony's ear twitched. "We treated them all as eggs. And even if we hadn't, it's unheard of for an entire year's clutch to have it. You must be wrong."

"The signs are obvious. I'm sorry," Cherine said.

Kia looked around at the magpie and copper hawk gryphons preparing to move into the cave system or go aid the Ashen Weald. She couldn't help with the war, but something was very wrong here.

She looked at Iony's pink replacement feathers. "How sturdy are those at high altitudes?"

"Sturdy enough. Why?" Iony asked.

"You said you treated the eggs," Kia began. "I need you to show us what you treated them with. It's possible someone did this deliberately. You're right, it's too strange for an entire hatch-year to get it."

Iony tensed. "It's not possible. Impir himself delivered the medicine."

Cherine and Kia both stared at him, and he conceded.

"Okay, I know. Better safe than sorry." He looked at

the pen where the glacier gryphlets were playing. "It's just... there's no cure. If there was, Mally would have disappeared long ago."

Zeph looked up from where he was panting. "Just how high up is the glacier peak?"

"Stay down here with your pride, Reevesbane," Iony said. "The fewer of you who go up there, the better. The Blackwing reeve will have figured out what happened by now. I might have to sneak these two in."

"Oh, thank goodness," Zeph managed. "I'm going to go sleep for a week. Tell me what I missed when you come back."

Kia rolled her eyes. "Can you fly now, Iony? The sooner we find out, the better. There's not a lot we can do for bloodbeak, but the things we can do, we need to do immediately for them to help."

The glacier pride leader didn't answer. He just looked at the gryphlets, then got a running start and leapt into the air.

Kia flew after them, leaving Cherine to grab one of the egg kits from Poisonmaw to compare it to and catch up.

29

CROWN OF THE WORLD

At the highest point on the continent, a storm threatened snow. Kia led the way, but as they neared, Iony ordered her and Cherine to get behind him.

She'd never seen a pride that lived so high off the ground. *Those are sheer cliff faces. One gust of wind and the gryphlets would go flying. Though I suppose we're so high up, there'd be plenty of time for someone to catch them before they hit the trees.*

The foliage was also interesting. There were some redwoods at the base of the mountain range, then a layer of aneda, which preferred the higher altitude. Before the peak, however, even the anedas gave way. She had no idea what the final stretch of trees were. Something evergreen. Maybe Iony would let her take samples. If they needed this kind of altitude to grow, she didn't know of anywhere else they could exist on the continent.

From the southwest, the mountain looked like any other. But as they flew around the eastern face, a small village took form along the coast. A talonful of wrecked fishing boats still floated in the harbor, and several of the buildings had collapsed. There were large footprints in the snow, perhaps feral goliath birds. A wide trail wound its way up towards the peak, though Kia couldn't imagine coaxing a goliath up so high.

Even the new type of trees gave way before reaching the heights of the glacier pride's nesting grounds. Carved out of the top of the mountain was the long-eared gryphons' home. It was a bit of a mess. Blood stained the ice. There was a large hole where the frozen seraph had been removed. Several of the caves carved into the ice had collapsed from the explosion.

Iony landed effortlessly, his large paws walking on ice as easily as if it were stone. Cherine landed next and slid fourteen feet, hitting a wall before stopping.

Kia slowed to a glide, backbeat her wings, and tried to land without any forward momentum. It was close, but she managed to stay upright.

"Not bad for a talon-foot," Iony said. "We'll need to remove a little rubble to get to the medical supplies. Figures Mally would leave a mess. Only consolation is we did a much bigger number on his Crestfall workshop."

Kia and Cherine started pulling out the rocks, and Iony would push them to the edge of the mountain and drop them down below. At least once, an angry goliath bird *mronked* up angrily at them.

"You're lunch, you treacherous bird!" Iony shouted down at it.

Kia laughed, but something changed in the air pressure, and her hackles raised. Amidst the grey skies and ever-present flakes of snow hanging in the air, several colorful shapes descended upon them.

"Stay frosty," Iony said. When neither opinicus knew what that meant, he clarified. "Be calm, let me do the talking. Stripes there likes me. We're basically family."

'Stripes' was a hooded pitohui opinicus. Unlike Rybalt, her armor was thin, immaculate, and free of leather straps and shackles. Her back half was as orange as her front half, with a stripe pattern Kia had never seen before. She was flanked by eight gryphons. They resembled fantails on a superficial level, with a thick beak, but their tails had two long feathers on either side that ended in fans.

"Motmot pride," Iony whispered. "Live around Rybalt's eyrie. Immune to pitohui poison. Most of the opinici were up by Blacktalon, thinking the king's new flagship meant he'd be attacking from that direction. Like us, they stayed behind to avoid the algae blooms."

"Iony!" Stripes shouted. "The Blackwing reeve demands an explanation for what happened here. Why have you abandoned our most crucial port town?"

The glacier leader walked out to greet the opinicus and motmots. "Stripes! I've missed you so much. I just knew you couldn't stay away when you heard I was in trouble."

He wrapped his large paws around her and pulled her close, then twisted, sending her sliding across the ice.

"Damnit, Iony, don't you dare break one of my feathers!" Stripes struggled to keep her paws under her, but surprisingly, she pulled it off. "Stop messing around. I'm here under orders of the reeve."

Her sliding took her past the blood stains and scorch marks, and her severe demeanor softened a little. "What happened here? Where's your pride? Iony... what's going on?"

Iony walked between the motmots, nudging them to see if they could keep their footing. They glared at him. Kia wasn't sure if there was a rivalry between the two gryphon prides in the Blackwing Alliance, or if they just disliked Iony. Both seemed plausible.

Don't we have more important things to worry about? What's Iony's game?

"The Seraph King himself showed up, Mally and Hikun in tow, and they blew up my home to get their seraph icicle," he said. "Then they took me and the rest hostage. Meanwhile, their armies from Whitebeak and Reevesport are marching on the Crackling Sea Eyrie as we speak."

Stripes took a few tentative steps towards Kia and Cherine, noticing their harnesses and plumage for the first time. "Wait, is that...? That's not the Pink Reeve's Daughter, is it? Did you take him hostage?"

Kia covered her beak to muffle her laughter. Cherine seemed to be developing a reputation as someone only to be detained at high risk.

"I'm not daft, Stripes," Iony said. "The Ashen Weald attacked the king's flagship, rescued me and my pride."

The pitohui looked from Kia to Cherine to Iony. She seemed to note the wild look in the glacier gryphon's eyes. "You can't help them. You'll get locked up. They're the enemy. You should let me take them prisoner now before you do something stupid."

Iony pointed a large paw and a long ear towards Cherine. "By all means, lock him up. See if that ends any better for you than it did for the Ashen Weald, Merin, or Crestfall."

"I'm not superstitious," Stripes said, though she didn't make any moves towards Cherine, and when he shifted to scratch his back paw, even the motmots stepped back with a hiss. "Look, leave with me now. They can get back on their own. You're going to get in trouble, and Rybalt's not here to save you."

Iony grinned. "But Stripes! I'm like a brother to you. I just have a few things to pick up here, then I need to retrieve my pride, and I'll be right back. It might take a few days."

"Big, dumb, self-absorbed, and a terrible liar," Stripes said. "Yep, you could definitely be my brother. I'm leaving. You do what you want, but I'm reporting back to the black reeve."

"Hold up," Iony said. "Can you wait an hour? There's something we need to check first. Something I need to know, and something I need you to tell your actual brother."

She paused. Despite their banter, she did seem to hold some affection for Iony. "Fine. Motmots, head into one of the spare caves, re-preen yourselves, and warm up. We're going to hit snow on the way back. Now, what do you have to show me?"

Iony caught her with a paw when she stepped towards the cavemouth where Kia and Cherine were waiting patiently. "Hold on there, little sister. They haven't spent years building up an immunity to pitohui poison. You've been on the island too long. You forget you're death with wings."

"Death with wings?" She laughed. "Are you flirting with me, Iony? I thought I was your little sister."

"More like a distant cousin?" Iony nodded to Kia and Cherine. "Go on, find what you're looking for. I'll hold Death here at bay until you finish.

KIA AND CHERINE entered the ice cave while Iony and Stripes bickered at the entrance. For all of the theatrics they put on in front of the motmots and Redwood Valley opinici, Kia was surprised to hear both relax once they thought everyone else was out of earshot. Kia picked up sincere worry in Stripe's tone before the stacks of crates muffled the sound.

"You're becoming quite popular around the world," Kia mused to Cherine. "Wanted criminal in the weald, sought after by Crackling Sea rangers, Alabaster Eyrie prisoner, and then a sand gryphon. And it certainly seems as though the motmots, glacier gryphons, and pitohui know you."

"It's a little embarrassing," Cherine admitted. "Do you know the only thing I've ever wanted is to teach and do research, settle down with a little ranch of capybaras? I'd rather leave saving the world to you."

Kia laughed. "I'm not sure what you think I've been up to at the shore, but all of it was food and numbers. The fisherfolk aren't going to sing shanties about me."

"No, but I think that's just it." Cherine's tone turned serious. "Keeping gryphons and opinici fed, *safely* fed, is crucial. How many wars die on the vine if everyone has enough to eat? Even diseases are less of an issue with proper nutrition. Famine, obviously. And sometimes, it's more about getting those with food to give it to those without. That way, when the situation has flipped, those they helped are willing to share with them."

"Mmm." Kia pried open a box marked for chick care, figuring it meant gryphlets in this case, and wasn't disappointed. She read through the ingredients list. "This looks like what we use to inoculate eggs against bloodbeak."

Cherine checked the medicine bags here against one he'd brought from Poisonmaw. "It makes sense. Mally discovered the test, brought it north to the Black-wing Eyrie to get funding for his Emerald Jungle expedition. And Iony said Impir the Mad, the Nighthaunt's old apprentice, is handling things. The mad peafowl probably had as much to do with finding a cure as his master did. The only thing that looks off is the testing packet. This one is damaged."

"That's strange." Kia looked closer. "How'd that goo get mixed in with it? Looks like someone deliberately broke it. I guess this is a common enough egg treatment that you'd just assume it's probably safe, even if the test had broken. Remind me, we use this on the blood?"

Cherine found the testing kit from his Redwood Valley supplies, which hadn't been tampered with. "Right. It'll turn blue if the blood came from someone with bloodbeak. Well, and a few other disorders, but overall, anything that makes it unfit for use on eggs."

The cure involved soaking eggs in a weird mineral bath, one of the main ingredients of which was blood from certain opinicus bloodlines that had never had bloodbeak. If they bred with those who were suscep-tible to it, their offspring could still get it. But their blood on its own could be used to protect the egg.

To illustrate his point, Cherine put a drop of the test

packet into the blood the glacier gryphons had used. She could smell the preservative used to keep the blood fresh from here. The test turned a bright blue.

"That's... not the color I thought we'd get. Is the reaction normally so vibrant?" she asked.

He shook his head. "This blood came from someone whose body was riddled with the disorder, near death."

"It could be a problem with the kit you brought." Kia went through her packs and found a vial of blood she'd found next to the kits at Poisonmaw, presumably from one of Hatzel's pride. "Test it out on this."

Cherine put a drop in, but the blood remained a dark red color. There was no change. The two scholars both cut their forelegs, letting some blood drip into a spare vial, then added a drop from the testing kit. Nothing.

"So it was deliberate. Why would someone infect a bunch of gryphlets?" Kia asked. "And in such a remote location. I don't understand what the point would be. It feels... spiteful."

Cherine packed up the kit. He took the vial of tainted blood with him to dispose of. "Unless it's not just the glacier pride."

They made their way out front. The long-tailed motmot pride, tropical birds that they were, stayed hidden from the cold, but Stripes remained outside, pressed against Iony's thick fur coat.

She stepped aside when Kia and Cherine reappeared. "About time! What were you two doing in there?"

Iony looked at their faces and tensed, expecting bad news.

"The blood's tainted," Kia said. "For the last year and

change, someone has made sure that every glacier gryphlet was infected with bloodbeak in the egg."

Stripes drew back as though struck. "That's... not possible. Impir tested and delivered these himself. There hasn't been a problem anywhere else."

Cherine sighed. "It won't turn fatal until adulthood. Gryphlets mature faster than chicks, so it's already starting to show. Since there's a preventative, nobody really checks for it anymore. We just assumed it wouldn't be a problem going forwards, and we do what we can to help those already suffering with their fate."

Iony stared out at the oncoming storm. "Mally refused his 'fate.' A year and change, that's when Impir escaped his prison and came north with Bario and Neider."

Stripes put a talon on Iony's shoulder. "It has to be a mistake. There's no proof Impir is a traitor. He's not trusted, exactly, but he's the blackwing reeve's prize. A famous scholar, assistant to the Nighthaunt himself, turned plume to our side."

"Two generations," Iony muttered. "Two generations of my pride will die early. That's your proof."

"Sorry to interrupt, but it could be worse than that." Kia motioned to Cherine to hand over the Redwood Valley testing kit. "Your testing kit was broken. You need to check... well, you need to check everywhere. Until you do, you have no idea the extent of how wide-spread this is."

"Are you saying pitohui and motmot offspring could have it, too?" Stripes asked.

Cherine shook his head. "No, I'm saying that if you put Impir in charge of this, every egg he inoculated in the Blackwing Alliance could have it. Rumors say that

Mally's workshop at Whitebeak had stalls full of opinici he'd given the disorder to, and he was collecting large amounts of their blood. He could have been sending that blood to his old apprentice. The gryphlets, chicks, and fledglings aren't going to be easy to test this early. You need to check their talons and beak."

"That's an unbearable number to imagine," Stripes whispered.

"But it could just be us?" Iony asked. "Just my pride? Rybalt and I have been after Mally a dozen times, nearly killed him twice now. It could be personal."

Cherine was quiet.

Kia didn't answer, instead offering that they'd bring more safe testing kits. If the tainted blood had come from Whitebeak, there was the possibility that her brother's blood had played a part in this. She'd just assumed Mally was using the blood for some sort of test, not that he'd weaponized it.

"Stripes, I owe the Ashen Weald a debt," Iony began. "I'm going south to pay it. But there's another debt here, and I need you to be my claws in this matter."

"Wait, you want to *murder* Impir? You have to run this through the Blackwing Eyrie first." She looked at Iony with panic in her eyes, but he was stalwart. "I'll... I'll get word to my brother on the front lines, okay? But you can't just murder a prominent scholar in the greatest eyrie in all of Belamuria."

"You can murder anyone, anywhere, if you're fast enough," Iony growled. "Did your brother not teach you that? But you're not flying out to Blacktalon. The moment one of Impir's agents sees something awry, like a gryphon on the red coast, he's going to get out of here as fast as he can. No, you need to kill him *now*."

"I'm not... I'm not like you two. I can't just *kill* some-one. I'm not trained for it," she protested. "I have more in common with these scholars than an assassin."

Iony swatted her so hard she slid towards Kia and Cherine, both of whom dove for safety. "You're poison. You're death. You were born to it. It's the family business."

"I can't!" Stripes shouted. "And it makes no sense! Why would anyone do this?"

Kia sympathized with the pitohui, but she had to disagree with that assessment. "It makes a certain kind of sense. Cherine said the world had given up on finding a treatment for the older patients now that a cure had been found for eggs. If you couldn't find a cure on your own, there's only one way to get the universities of an entire continent to start looking for you."

"Mally the Nighthaunt is holding two generations of your children hostage," Cherine added. "You find a cure, or they start dying. A cure he needs to save himself."

"What if I capture Impir alive?" Stripes offered. "Won't he have some valuable information to help?"

Iony angrily preened his flight feathers, mindful of the pink ones. "Didn't you hear the reds? If he knew how to cure it, he wouldn't have done something so drastic. When you reach the Blackwing Eyrie, head to the docks, third supply warehouse from the waterfall. Look for the crate marked with a scarab. She won't talk to you on your own, so you're going to have to convince her that your brother sent you. Since you're planning to murder someone, she'll probably believe you. She can get you into the university undetected. Don't bring your motmots. Lose them on the way. And stuff your beak with as many scarabs as you can find. I barely felt a tingle when you cuddled up to me a moment ago. It was so mild I thought it might be love and not poison. You need to be dripping by the time you get to him. He'll have antivenom on his harness somewhere, so while he's twitching, you need to remove his head."

Stripes didn't respond until Iony shouted at her to leave. She called for the motmots, and they disappeared north.

"She's a sweet opinicus, but she's too kind," Iony explained, as though there was any explanation for plotting a beheading in front of Kia and Cherine. "What I don't get is why the Nighthaunt would bring my pride into this and not try to convince his new Alabaster Eyrie allies to help him instead? If we find the cure, I'm sure as hell going to do everything in my power to make sure he dies before he gets it."

The glacier leader leapt off the mountain, leaving Kia and Cherine to catch up. As they flew back south towards Poisonmaw, Kia had a strange, terrible thought. In a sense, Iony was right. If she were in Mally's position, if she had his morals, it would be better to have both the king's universities and the Blackwing Alliance universities working on a cure.

How many opinicus chicks are born north of the Crackling Sea in a year? Two years?

The gamble was terrible, but it also made sense. The only way to save two generations of offspring would be to cure Mally the Nighthaunt. He had found a way to hold most of the world hostage. Only the Ashen Weald and most of the starlings would be unaffected, though her first step upon getting back would be to test *everything* in the Ashen Weald medicinal stockpiles.

She looked to Cherine, but he already had that same

look of determination on his face. Ninox had a small army of scholars in the depths of the Darkfeather Highlands. They'd need to convince those scholars to work hard to find a cure before the first of the new generation of bloodbeak offspring began dying from the iron disorder, despite none of the opinicus chicks or weald gryphlets suffering from it.

She remained quiet on the flight home, but just before she reached Poisonmaw, she had her own terrible thought. Her brother, Olan, had been inflicted with a slow-acting variation of the iron disorder by the Nighthaunt. If the entire world was working on a cure, it wasn't just the Nighthaunt who would benefit.

She'd be able to cure Olan, too.

30

COBRA

Henders perched atop a wagon, listening for the sounds of starlings. When no chittering came, he raised his wing to let the others know it was safe to continue, dislodging some hanging moss from a cypress tree.

Coming from the Flower outpost, he should have reached the Clover Ranch yesterday, but the rangers had insisted on staying off the main path, figuring it was the most likely place to run into bandits or enemy forces. After a few attempts to cross the lowlands had ended with goliath birds and wagons stuck in the mud, they'd decided to cut towards the Jadebeak River, follow it until it curved towards the mountains, and head north from there to bypass the flooding. It wasn't the ideal path, but it was the only one Henders knew well and was pretty sure would be dry this time of year.

Unfortunately, this put the wagons in a precarious position. The rogue bog pride still held the area on the other side of the Jadebeak River, and if any starlings had been trapped when the glyphs went up, they'd be somewhere around here. Despite the burning of the mummy, the wildlife in this stretch had been exposed to the parasite for longest, and there were constantly new flare-ups of infection.

Henders's eyes and ears were sharp, but they were also easily distracted. All around them were the ruins of stone walls with six-winged carvings. He kept his eyes out, yes, but he kept them out for signs of structures buried under vines and vegetation.

The path narrowed, stone on either side, forcing the goliath bird wagons single file. He didn't think much of it until the canopy overhead grew thick with hanging moss, too thick to fly through. And then an opinicus stepped onto the path ahead of them, causing the domesticated goliath to balk.

The opinicus planted a banner in the road, black and with two red circles on either side. She hunched down, concealing her size. She looked to be a peafowl of some sort, feathers a dyed black color that nature rarely produced. One foreleg looked normal, but on the other, she seemed to be walking on her knuckles, her talons turned back.

When Henders called out to her, asking if she was hurt or needed help, she reared up, spreading her tail-feathers. They held the same red circles as her banner. At her full height, her right talons were now visible— she had on some sort of long blades attached to each, so long they must have made walking difficult.

She rushed the goliath bird, cutting it down with her metal weapon before it had a chance to defend itself. In its death throes, it pulled the wagon over, sending Henders into rocky ruins and trapping him under a crate of wingtorn armor.

While he struggled to free himself, a dozen flamingo opinici attacked from the back of the caravan and several more peafowl, blue and less dramatic than their leader, came from the front.

Two rangers made for the skies, one hitting the moss and becoming tangled, the second breaking through the hole created by the first. In the air, several silver shapes began their dives to catch the ranger.

Henders's heart ached at the cries of several goliath birds being put down. Then the black cobra opinicus came back and found him struggling to free himself.

"Hello, little bird." She hissed her words. "I have a few questions for you before you join your friends."

He gulped. Across from him, scraped off by the toppled wagon, he saw part of a mural showing the body of a seraph being wrapped in strips of cloth. It might be the find of the year if he survived to come back and catalogue it. He might not be a scholar, but he sure loved pictures on rocks.

BLINKY WANDERED among the wounded at the Clover Ranch. Foultner had escorted Satra to the Crackling Sea and returned just as New Eyrie was lost, and her injury —a wing sprain—had actually come from trying to help the wounded escape. She'd be fine, but she was complaining loudly while Blinky ignored her.

"Blinky!" Foultner shouted, waiting for her friend to look at her. "Will you go check on Henders for me?"

"He is fine," Blinky said. "He is only a little late. There are many reasons for that. He often gets lost."

Foultner sighed. "I know you're right, it's just... I

worry about him. And the wingtorn are going to need
that armor if we're going to retake New Eyrie. I don't
want him getting yelled at if he's late. And, well, I trust
you to keep him out of trouble."

Blinky had reached the kjarr nests only to discover
that the armor hadn't arrived yet. She'd given them
orders to evacuate the young and send the fighters up to
the Crackling Sea Eyrie to defend it. Then she'd swung
back by to see if she should head down to the Flower,
only to come across the wounded fleeing New Eyrie and
word that Henders had gone south already to fetch the
armor.

"He is good at trouble." The owl gryphon thought
back to the incident with the electric knife fish. And the
incident with the leafcutter ants. And the incident
where two capybaras trapped him in a burrow. And
several more incidents after that. This could also be a
good opportunity to get word to Black Mask that she
wouldn't be able to go south for a while. Black Mask did
worry about her, almost as much as Foultner worried
about Henders.

Blinky allowed Foultner to continue trying to
convince her, pretending she wasn't listening until the
magic words were spoken.

"Fine. I have four salted fish bars hidden near my
nest upstairs," Foultner said at last. "They're yours if you
bring him back safely."

Blinky perked up. "No, I will eat them on the way. I
will need the salt in the bog. You know how it is."

Foultner did not know how it was, but she always
liked to act like she did, so she finally conceded and told
Blinky about her food hiding place.

The owl gryphon retrieved the snacks, startling the

wounded opinicus who was under the nest in question, and then ate all of the fish bars back-to-back so she didn't have to carry them.

A snack eaten now is better than a snack you might lose before you eat it later.

She drank enough water to make up for the salt, then headed south. While the infected starlings had been cleared enough to make flying relatively safer than it had been during her first journey out here, there was still the matter of the enemy.

Nobody knew what they were doing at New Eyrie. The whale had been spotted several times nearby, but it had stopped its rampage partway through and seemed unconcerned with finishing off the fishing village. But Silver's argent hawks now controlled the skies around the fishing village, and it was possible they were watching the bog, too.

Blinky flew as far as she felt safe, watching to see if anyone was using the trail from the Flower. Not seeing anyone on the boardwalk, she slipped down and disappeared under the brush. She'd been out here enough that she had a certain path she took when she visited Black Mask so she wouldn't be seen. Some of it required crawling, but mostly, she'd taken a page from Hatzel's flyway and cleared out certain branches so she could glide for long stretches without getting tangled in moss.

It was a good system. Though the moss always grew back. Still, that meant that if she were gone for a while, her path would disappear entirely. There were benefits to that, too.

She was nearly to the Jadebeak River when she smelled blood. She slowed, locating some moss. It was possible Vitra's insurgents had crossed the river to attack the goliath birds. The no-gryphon-zone was more of an agreement than anything concrete, since the two factions weren't talking in an official capacity. But it was possible it was someone else.

The smell of blood often drowned out all other scents for gryphons, so Blinky used the moss and vines to mask her scent. Black Mask's warnings that the vine scent would stand out now were well-received, but at the same time, she believed the blood would keep any wingtorn from thinking hard about crushed vines.

She glided from tree to tree, playing lookout. She poked her moss-covered head above the canopy once, spotting several argent hawks in the skies above.

That is not good.

She'd known that Mally the Nighthaunt and Reeve Silver were aware of this section of the bog, having attempted to steal the mummified seraph from it in the past. But it hadn't occurred to Blinky they might have a reason to return. Perhaps they were just checking to make sure there were no wingtorn hiding out here.

Blinky reached a point where the canopy was too dense, and she crawled along the forest floor like a megapede. She heard someone talking in the distance. There was an opinicus trill to the voice, feminine, but with the sort of detachment she'd seen from opinici who were career rangers or soldiers.

Blinky crawled closer, recognizing a single hostage among the dead.

Henders!

Foultner had been right. Blinky should have come out earlier. She could have stopped this from happening. Around a campfire, the goliath birds were being eaten by the Seraph King's soldiers. There was only one of the smoky-eyed, white-plumed opinici of the Alabaster Eyrie itself. Instead, the forces were made up of several peafowl with hen-colored plumage, not always an indicator of gender in an opinicus, a dozen grizzled pink Crestfall soldiers lacking their glass trinkets, and two silver hawks who were reporting to the leader.

The black peafowl was something new. Blinky had never understood the Redwood Valley's obsession with giant snakes, but it was clearly something they'd brought with them from Reevesport. This strange assassin, or perhaps warrior was a better word, listened to the reports while dining on goliath. Every so often, she'd stuff a little piece of food in Henders beak like he was a pet.

That was the moment when Blinky knew Foultner would require this cobra-opinicus to be killed. But there were too many for Blinky to take alone, especially while they controlled the skies.

She had an idea, though. It would require someone else to serve as her muscle. When the leader moved away, Blinky prowled as close to Henders as she dared, quietly hooting to get his attention. When he turned in her direction, she whispered directions to him.

"When you hear my sign, I need you to talk about what is in the wagons," she whispered. "I need you to say those words. But then I need you to get the leader to speak a name."

Henders shook his head, confused. He beaked the words "What name?", or at least it looked like that's what he was trying to say. Opinicus beaks were so hard and unexpressive, it was a wonder they had learned speech at all.

"She must say the name 'Jonas.'" Blinky disappeared back into the brush, making her way south. She'd not only memorized when Black Mask's schedule gave him alone time, but she'd also made a note of when he was leading a large war band to clear out the Jadebeaks trying to sneak across the mountains.

Unless that schedule had changed, he should be just across the river from her now.

BLACK MASK LED MOST of the remaining rogue wingtorn through the foliage. Behind him, he could hear their confusion at the lack of starlings. The jadebeaks *always* came through this section of the bog because it had the most pumpkins. In fact, the bog wingtorn had been cultivating several colorful, golden pumpkins out here. While their natural immunity meant they didn't require them for their own purposes, they lured starlings and Ashen Weald alike, at least before Satra had ordered the Ashen Weald not to cross the Jadebeak River.

Today, however, the bog was empty. No starlings, suggesting Satra's glyphs had worked, and no Ashen Weald. They'd heard some goliaths *mronk*, a tasty snack if caught, but the birds seemed to know not to cross the river, and their sounds remained in the distance.

While the wingtorn complained, their bog witch escort padded ahead to catch up to Black Mask.

"So, how did it go?" she asked. Her eye was wide, and her tail swished back and forth. "Did she agree to be your mate? Did she like the flowers? She did, right?"

"Yes, the flowers worked wonderfully. Thank you." Black Mask didn't tell Thistle that Blinky had eaten them. "And yes, we'll still have to do a bit of sneaking, but we'll spend the winter together as best we can."

Thistle purred, happy her gift had been well-received. "Maybe there'll be peace by then. You never know."

You never know had become a mantra among the rogue pride. It was true, nobody knew what would happen next. But peace and reconciliation weren't things that happened by chance, like a heavy storm coming off the ocean and flooding their burrows. They needed to be worked at.

Black Mask's patrol had nearly reached the bend in the river, Thistle continuing to try to figure out what sort of gryphon Black Mask's secret mate was when he heard a hooting sound. At first, he dismissed it as an actual owl. They did sound similar to owl gryphons, if you didn't know the nuances. Blinky wouldn't dare try to reach him while he was leading a raiding party.

Yet when it continued, he heard a few owlish words mixed into the hooting. He needed to listen to their third or fourth repetition before he caught on, but it sounded like Blinky was trying to get him to cross the Jadebeak River.

He looked back at the troops with him. Thistle was practical, careful to a fault. But the wingtorn here had been itching for a starling fight since the day began. While they may worry about killing an uninfected Ashen Weald member, if he could convince them it was just some starlings...

"Wait, harken!" he said, wishing he'd chosen a word that sounded more natural. "I hear chittering, and I saw a flash of orange just across the river."

Thistle bristled. "We can't cross the river. You know the rules."

"I hear the sound of someone throwing up after eating too much pumpkin," he added. One of the wing-torn nodded along, claiming to hear the same thing. "They must be infected starlings, just starting to turn. Surely, that knifefish of a gryphon Urious and his mata-mata-faced master, Satra, wouldn't begrudge us killing a few silver-eyed ghouls."

The wingtorn agreed. Thistle started to protest, but Black Mask leapt halfway across the river, landing on a small island in the center. The large, mossy turtle bobbed up and down, but before it could snap at him, he'd already reached the far shore. The others joined him, finding actual islands, rocks, or sleeping turtles to use as steppingstones.

Thistle sighed, then fluttered after them.

31

RETURN OF THE BOG MONSTER

Blinky waited until she heard rustling from the direction of the river, then hooted at Henders to begin talking. The problem with chatty opinici was that they were very easy to kill, but Blinky hoped these particular ones would want information from Henders.

"I don't know why you attacked *my* wagons," Henders said. "There's nothing in here for you. What did you want? Food? Medicine? Well, that's already safely at the Clover Ranch."

The leader ignored him, prying open a crate and pulling out a set of armor. She poked it with her left, organic talon a few times. She pulled back with her long, metal talons and stabbed it, but they didn't break through. Her fancy dye job and designs were apparently too important for her to try it on herself, so she handed it to a silver hawk.

The Argent Heights opinicus tried to put it on but couldn't find the holes for the wings. She was slim and squeezed in with her forelegs at her sides, a tight fit, but she looked more like an eel wrap than anything ready to fight.

"They're designed for wingtorn," Henders said louder than Blinky wanted. She'd hoped he'd be subtle, but he did not appear to have that capability. "You can weave spikes into them to ward off flying attackers, and they're reinforced with blackwing steel, stolen from the north, so flechettes can't puncture them."

The leader stared at him. "I don't need your information. I figured that out on my own. I'm not an idiot."

Next to her, the silver hawk was begging anyone for help getting out of the jacket. The Crestfall opinici laughed at her, but nobody rushed to her aid.

"What're you going to do with armor like that? It's useless for you," Henders continued. "This has been a waste of time."

"Has it?" the leader asked. "Depriving our enemies of a weapon is just as valuable as having it ourselves."

Across the way, Blinky saw a spiral of bright green foliage next to a half-oval of bog blossoms. She'd seen that same shape follow Black Mask from time to time, trying to figure out where he disappeared to. It was one of the bog witches.

The owl gryphon cooed to Henders, letting him know it was time.

"Will your leader feel the same way when you come back with a bunch of armor he can't use?" Henders shouted, again far too loud. He lacked subtlety. "You can't think your leader will be happy when you return to New Eyrie with *metal wingtorn armor that protects them from airborne opponents* and nothing else to show."

The cobra hissed. "I do not care with Jonas thinks. If

he could win this war on his own, he would not have pledged his loyalty to the Seraph King."

No one said anything, but they all looked at Henders like he'd gone crazy.

He is very bad at this, Blinky thought. *I forgot how unsneaky he is with his words.*

Still, he had done all she'd asked of him. The silence stretched long until the argent hawk said, "Okay, but I'm really stuck, and I need someone to help me."

Then the swamp erupted with bog wingtorn, descending upon their unsuspecting prey with a precision that came from months of hiding from Ashen Weald patrols.

Blinky chewed at the rope holding Henders in place. It was just goliath bird rope, but the thing about goliath bird rope was that it had been made to resist goliath bird beaks. She tried to use her paws to work the knot loose, which seemed to have more success.

A flamingo was the first to fall. Blinky had heard tales of how the Crestfall opinici shattered into a million pieces upon death, but she was disheartened to see they died just like everyone else.

Not even a jingling sound. Disappointing.

The lone Alabaster Eyrie opinicus fought hard, but he was outnumbered. The second argent hawk, the one not currently wrapped in wingtorn armor, made a dash for the clearing, but the bog witch caught his back paws and pulled him down to the wingtorn.

Blinky managed to free Henders, but instead of running away, he tied the rope into a lasso and threw it around the restrained argent hawk, then yanked her into the forest with him.

"Help!" she screamed until Blinky knocked her

unconscious. As Henders pulled the dead weight after him, Blinky returned to the fight to make sure Black Mask was okay.

The other wingtorn were dealing with the rest of the flamingos and some newly-arrived argent hawks who attacked from above but were afraid to go under the canopy. Black Mask and the bog witch faced off against the leader.

"Watch her talons, Thistle," Black Mask said. The little witch seemed terrified, young.

She will never find a match for the mating season if she cannot murder an opinicus or two.

Black Mask's armor, once White Stripe's armor, wasn't as strong as what was in the boxes. When the long-nailed peafowl struck with her right talons, she pulled away with a spike going through her palm. She switched to using her long, metal talons on the other side, rearing back to give her a height advantage.

Thistle flew up towards the opinicus's face, but the cobra moved with supernatural speed, knocking the witch back and into the dying flames of the cooking fire. Thistle swore and put out the smoldering ashes but was afraid to approach again.

Even for one so young, she is bad at this, Blinky thought. *She would not make a good owl gryphons. What do they teach the young bog gryphons? Not the correct things, that is certain.*

Black Mask struck out with a feint, shifting the opinicus off balance, then bit into her back leg. She shrieked, both from the bite and the spikes when she tried to push him off, then she stabbed with the metal talons, piercing the spikes and armor and catching him in the side.

Blinky knew he'd have a lot to explain if she left her hiding place to aid him, but he may not be alive to do that explaining if she didn't help. His stupid bog witch was still worried about ash and fire. Her eye was not even on the fight.

Unlike the bouncy wingtorn or shouty opinici, Blinky was silent. Her cobra-patterned prey had used her metal talons to flip Black Mask over and pin him to the ground. Blinky waited for her opponent to stretch her neck long, then struck right where the neck attached to the skull.

Owl gryphons, as the peacock found out, may have small beaks, but they had exceptional biting strength. She went limp, and Blinky slipped back into the foliage after a quick blink to Black Mask.

She watched as he stood up, the dumb witch finally coming to her senses. Thankfully, she was better with bandages than she was with fighting, if barely, and with shaking paws she managed to stop Black Mask's bleeding and leafcutter him up.

Blinky longed to go out and comfort him, but she had no idea where Henders had wandered off to, and there was a fifty-fifty chance he was now lying unconscious in a puddle of knife fish. The wingtorn were on high alert now, so she didn't dare hoot. She stuck around just long enough to make sure Black Mask had started stealing the crates off the wagons and figuring out who fit into what armor.

While she searched the lowlands for Henders, she considered what she'd done. On the one paw, she'd just armed the enemies of the Ashen Weald with the best wingtorn armor money and craftsman could produce.

This was armor intended for Urious's elite forces in particular.

On the other paw—which was her favorite paw because it was her killing paw, though she was also fond of her back left paw—she knew how Black Mask would use it.

Better it be in the possession of someone who will use it against our enemies than let it go wasted.

She hoped that was true.

"Blinky!" a cry came from above. "Help, it's those same capybaras again!"

She zeroed in on the sound and quickened her pace, afraid to see what Henders had come across.

THERE WAS MORE armor here than Black Mask could carry. Not that he, personally, could carry any of it. While his wingtorn and Thistle hadn't noticed a Redwood Valley hostage and an argent hawk disappear during the fight, he had. He recognized the names of all the opinici he had just fought from Blinky's stories, but he was very careful to keep words like *Crestfall* or *Argent Heights* or *Alabaster Eyrie* off his tomia lest the others ask him where he learned them.

The new armor looked impressive. His armor, once his friend's armor, was just a set of stolen Crackling Sea harnesses sewn together with palm spikes attached. These were much more secure, and they covered both the head and the tail—useful, as unlike his peers, he now knew the enemy had flechettes.

Where possible, each wingtorn draped an extra pair over them. There'd still be a few crates left here if the

Ashen Weald wanted to retrieve them, but every rogue bog gryphon would have a set of armor. He even thought that his mother, as adept with spikes and stolen harnesses as she was, might be able to figure a way to create wing holes for her beloved witches.

The wingtorn with him wanted to come back and take the rest of the crates with them, but Thistle's anxiety won out.

"The Ashen Weald will be here at any minute," she scolded. "They're going to think we're responsible for killing their stupid birds if they catch us. But if we leave now, they're going to have no idea we've stolen their precious armor. This is a major victory, but only if we're not caught."

Black Mask pretended to be disgruntled, then bowed to her superior wisdom. Bog gryphons in general trusted the witches and were used to obeying them. It was a handy trait in situations like this.

Because it had been easiest to open the crates from the front and back of the caravan, he'd discovered two particular sets of armor he knew the crone would be fond of—they had the names *Thenca* and *Urious* embroidered into them. When Thistle offered him the Urious armor, he declined. He made it sound like his issue was that he refused to wear armor belonging to such a traitor, but really, he just didn't want to see that name. Maybe one day soon, he'd get to return that armor to Urious.

When they reached the Heart of the Bog and the nearby spike nest, the crone waited for them. When she asked what they were wearing, he let Thistle answer.

"We stole these from an Ashen Weald caravan,"

Thistle said. "It's fancy armor intended for Urious himself! But it's ours now."

Concern was etched around the crone's eyes. "The Ashen Weald brought a caravan through our home?"

"N-no, sorry, that's not what I meant," Thistle stuttered. "We were along the edge of the river patrolling, and, um, an opportunity arose."

The wingtorn had the good sense to look embarrassed. They knew the crone's rules.

Black Mask, though, had no such concerns. "It was my fault, Mother. I was chasing a starling, and it fled over the river. Thistle told me to stay back, but I had the taste of its blood in my beak, and I couldn't stop. When I reached the other side, I found a caravan under attack. Thistle heard the fighting and thought I was in trouble, so she came to rescue me."

"R, right," Thistle confirmed. "But the Ashen Weald was fighting another army, and they were losing. But we defeated both armies and stole their armor!"

"I saw a bog monster, too!" one of the wingtorn said.

Black Mask tensed up, but everyone laughed, assuming that wingtorn was just seeing things again, so he relaxed.

Bog monster, indeed. That's my mate you're talking about.

Blinky was still a bit of a legend after the incident at the Flower outpost. While a few had guessed she was an owl gryphon, there were still rumors of a creature of vines and moss that could materialize anywhere in the bog if you spoke her true name.

Interestingly, everyone referred to the bog monster as *she*. He didn't know where that had started, but it persisted even now.

The crone was already picking at Thenca's armor, pulling at the stitches and looking for a place to remove some of the metal to make room for a pair of wings. As much as these were stolen vests, the design itself had been stolen from the White Stripe's old armor—it had been designed to make it easy to add palm spines through it to add an extra layer of protection.

Black Mask had seen his mother pleased before, though it had been years upon years. There was a time, long before the salting of the fields, when she'd loved teaching the young bog witches. Not about stories, war, death, or the spirits. No, long ago, she used to teach them how to weave fronds together and paint them. Back then, she loved nothing more than to design new glyphs.

There was the barest glimmer of that enjoyment in her eyes now. He hated to ruin it, but he knew why the Redwood Valley opinicus who had been tied up had said that name so loudly. While the crone's one true hatred would always be the kjarr pride, the wingtorn here shared a different hatred.

"The other army said they reported back to Jonas," he said.

The wingtorn hissed. They hadn't been close enough to hear the conversation, but Thistle had, and she confirmed it.

"I don't know Jonas," she said. "Who is he?"

The wingtorn paced and hissed, moving around her. Black Mask stood on a rock at the center of the bog nests, mindful of the spiked ceiling, and told his tale.

"Jonas is every scar you see around you," he began, and he didn't need to go further because the other wingtorn told the tale for him, their voices bleeding together like one."

"Jonas spat in my face as he sawed off my wings."

"Jonas kicked my wings to the sailfins to eat."

"Jonas came down, decided who got medicine or not, and watched the others die of infection."

"When my sister leapt off the cliffs, he laughed as she fell to her death."

"Jonas is every opinicus who has ever wronged you."

And then, as one, when their tales ended, they had the same final verse: "Jonas must die."

The crone listened, not happy, but not particularly surprised, either. She listened to their sorrow. Perhaps she thought she could use it.

"You say the Ashen Weald is no longer able to hold the bog north and east of the Jadebeak River?" she asked.

"That's not exactly—" Black Mask began, but Thistle interrupted him.

"Yes, that's true, crone mother," she said. "We can reclaim the rest of the bog. Now is our chance."

The crone considered her next move carefully. Black Mask weighed his options. With the wingtorn riled up, he needed to be the one to direct their ire. And he needed their wrath to cut a path to New Eyrie.

Finally, the crone spoke. "Black Mask, extend the border north. Mark and control every tree from here to the grasslands. I want to know if anyone is trying to live here. Now is our chance. With the Ashen Weald on its knees, we can reclaim our home."

"Only if Jonas doesn't win," Black Mask cautioned. "When the blue reeve died, Jonas rallied the opinici, befriended the other eyries. So long as he lives, we will always be in danger."

Thistle nodded. "There were opinici I had never seen before. Pink, white, shiny, and black with large red circles."

The crone considered her son for a long time. "Yes, if it pleases my wingtorn children. We will make our vengeance absolute."

Black Mask breathed easier, but then the crone turned to Thistle.

"Fetch your sisters," she rasped. "Tell them to fly down into the Heart of the Bog, into the sunken eyrie ruins, and meet me in the high place."

He frowned. Surrounded by wingtorn, there was only one place the crone could hide things—in places that required flight to reach. He didn't know what she had squirreled away, but it couldn't be good.

But if I get my revenge on Jonas, the nightmares will stop.

"What're the rest of you waiting for, dinner?" he shouted. "Go fetch the longest, most poisonous spines you can get your paws on, and let's turn this Ashen Weald mating garment into something fit for war!

As he carefully chewed off spikes from neighboring spike palms, he tried to allow his hatred of Jonas to overcome him. And yet, it wasn't Jonas that lived in his thoughts right now.

He was worried about what the war would mean for Blinky.

32

SILVER AND BLUE

Reeve Silver soared over the misty skies of the Crackling Sea. She didn't dare get too close to the Crackling Sea Eyrie, but she wanted to remind them who was on their border—and to get a glimpse at the dark shape patrolling the island fortress. It was dilapidated, but she didn't want to find out an army was hiding in its depths waiting to flank her, so she'd had several of her night flyers set up scent lures along its shore.

These weren't filled with the old reeve's blood, so they wouldn't drive the creature into a frenzy. But they were specifically designed to keep it curious and in that general vicinity. Anything to keep their enemy ill at ease.

As she approached the island, she saw the long-tailed shape of several fantails launching themselves from the eyrie's cliffs, and she changed course. She had too much of a head start for them to catch her before she reached New Eyrie, but if they wanted to try their paws at it, she never had fewer than a dozen of her patrols waiting in the clouds above her new home.

The fantails backed off, and she smirked. One fantail scout may have caught them unawares on their march south, but it wouldn't happen again. Anyone could get lucky once. The key was making sure your enemies were never lucky the same way twice.

She circled New Eyrie's crispy towers once, checking to see how repairs were going.

The Ashen Weald sure likes burning things. I'm glad I live in a stone eyrie.

Though the fires left by the retreating force had been more about smoke, the reeve's pet had done a number on most of the large buildings. That helped confirm rumors that the southerners were out of explosives.

The last intelligence report Silver read said they were still trying to replicate Bario's flameworks without much success. Not that the Alabaster Eyrie had replicated his formula, either, though that was to Silver's favor. Her mountains had several working saltpeter mines. Once the Seraph King could create his own saltpeter without mining it, her value to him would diminish.

She landed atop the main building, jokingly named reeve's nest, and preened her feathers. She enjoyed flying, had started life as a messenger before becoming a guard, and then reeve, but the Argent Heights were dry. Flying here left a sheen of salt over her fur and feathers that never washed off.

I wonder what it would take to install freshwater pools for rinsing in. Maybe we can get some hot and salty ones for the pinks.

Several flamingo guards watched the gates to the city, checking to make sure no spies were attempting to slip in. Espionage was a tricky affair when so many cities had only a few breeds of opinicus available. In fact, Silver had practically begged Hi-kun to take the peafowl with him on his journey and let her have the woodpeckers.

"The Imperial Guard was created to guard the king," Hi-kun had parroted to her. "Besides, Reevesport has yet to earn its keep in recent years. They need an opportunity to prove their loyalty."

Silver had scoffed. As much as they'd come to serve as a royal guard, the woodpeckers had been 'created' for another reason. Mally the Nighthaunt had invented a brand new opinicus species to prove he could. Back when the purple salts seemed limitless, he'd proven his value to the king by finding a bird species with no matching gryphon or opinicus, then creating one of each.

The king had volunteered his guards for the experiment, and they were loyal to him. All had deformities, injuries, or conditions that had taken them away from their duties. In addition to their new, strong-beaked appearance, the Nighthaunt's machinations had cured many of them.

Instead, she'd been asked to siege the south with a set of troops who resembled the enemy. That was bad for war. It allowed the possibility of spies, provided opportunities for empathy. She'd mitigated the damage as best she could, bringing only their craziest, most blood-thirsty warriors. The Reevesport berserkers had a reputation for violence and theatrics.

Much like my last two mates, may they rest in pieces.

Most importantly for her was the *theatrics*. Their strange black dyes and snake patterns would make it hard for any Redwood Valley opinici to imitate them.

Not that any of these troops were her first choice, except for her own. She was waging a war with table scraps. When she retreated up to her tower perch where the other messengers and scouts resided, her argent hawks complained night and day about who they were fighting beside.

Some of that was just politics. They certainly had a lot to say about Hi-kun's forces from Whitebeak, and the one time they'd been ordered to help defend Duckbill against the abyss gryphons, there'd been a string of very unusual incidents leading to the apprehension of a serial killer.

Flamingos, Whitebeak rejects, and apple merchants —she was scraping the bottom of the cider barrel. Even the Crackling Sea opinici still loyal to Jonas felt more like religious zealots than warriors, though she was grateful for their inside information.

Thankfully, she didn't need to win this war. *Jonas* did. Her orders were to keep a supply line going. If Jonas won, great. She knew what he'd been promised, the same thing as the woodpeckers, essentially, plus his eyrie back. And if he failed, her orders were to hold back the blackwing and ashen tides long enough for the king to finish with his...

She couldn't bring herself to think the word. It was absurd. The thing about having a mad opinicus in charge was if you lived in the eyries neighboring his, you started to believe his lies. That was the real reason Crestfall, Reevesport, and the Argent Heights had been sent on this mission. None of them held the faith.

She took a deep breath, braced herself, and entered the reeve's nest building. Technically, *she* was the only reeve here, but she couldn't tell that from the way Jonas held himself.

Long-necked, yet duck-billed, the blue reeve's consort wore his mate's old adornments, stolen from the Crackling Sea in the spring. The tentacles of the necklaces didn't quite reach, so they'd been fixed at a flameworks over the summer. A matching metal half-mask covered his facial burns, but the ones on his neck and body he left bare.

She'd been there when his half-dead corpse had been recovered from the fire. *Corpse* because she'd thought he was dead. Mally the Nighthaunt spent months at the Argent Heights, fixing him up, getting him healthy again. Jonas had barely been able to speak without rasping. His voice was still a little rough now, but once the conversation had moved past pleasantries, it was easy to forget.

"Reeve Silver." He stood and managed a slight bow, his mask never slipping. "It's good to see you made it back unscathed. You need be mindful of the weald gryphons. They're a much more vicious lot than you've ever faced."

She didn't correct him. She'd faced many gryphon prides over the years, the starlings and cave gryphons both being particularly nasty. Ever since the gryphons of the abyss discovered what Mally was doing to them at his first workshop, rumors of opinici disappearing near caves across the kingdom had sprouted up, though bodies were rarely found. And her previous venture to New Eyrie had nearly been her last, thanks to the arrival of the glacier gryphons that never seemed to leave Rybalt Reevesbane's side.

I was nearly another name crossed off his list. I wonder, does he count it if he kills more than one Argent Heights reeve? Or is he just out to collect one of each of us?

The real question was whether or not that list included the Blackwing Eyrie's reeve. The Seraph King had spent a lot of beads trying to turn Rybalt without success. Silver had protested the entire time. He was one face that never left her nightmares. He represented her greatest failure, the death of the previous reeve. In a sense, her promotion to reeve had been a punishment.

She curtsied her tailfeathers, then settled onto a cushion across from the would-be Crackling Sea reeve. "How's your health this morning?"

"My health?" He laughed, a cough or two mixed in for good measure. "It's never been better. Do you know I built this fishing village? Not that I commissioned it to be built, like some pomp-and-puff peafowl. Those docks along the shore? I drove the nails in myself, helped cut the wood. I did that myself."

Silver had heard these stories before. They were of a certain type that all so-called 'self-made reeves' professed. Unlike those born to wealth and privilege, these had worked hard to get there. Often, it was reeves attempting to curry favor with her. They thought of her as being someone who worked her way from messenger up to reeve.

If only they knew that I was promoted as punishment for letting the previous reeve die.

No one expected her to live so long on a border eyrie. Back then, Rybalt and Iony had been ever-present, their poisons and explosions and ambushes a constant threat. No one was more surprised than her when the king finally convinced Crestfall to end its neutrality and the attacks on the Argent Heights dried up.

"And did you carve the Crackling Sea Eyrie from the cliffs yourself, too, and will the stormcloth into being?" she asked with a smile. "I appreciate your past accomplishments, but what the king needs isn't a well-made dock, as pleasant as those are. He requires a fortress along the southern coast of the sea to hold the Blackwing Alliance at bay, to launch his own attacks. I don't need the best craftsopinicus in the land. That individual does not get someone as valuable as me protecting his back. What I need is a reeve."

Jonas puffed up a little. "Do I not look the part?"

"Looking and acting the part aren't the problem," she began. "I want to know why you've ordered a small army to leave New Eyrie before it's secure to take a goliath bird ranch. Not just a goliath bird ranch, a poor excuse for one, too! I'm still coddling the last fifteen goliath birds I bought from there, and they won't do an honest day's labor. They're more pets than beasts of burden."

She was surprised to see real anger in his eyes. She didn't know anyone felt that strongly about goliath birds.

"Silver." His tone was cold like the seas, and it held a charge to it. "I know you don't trust merchants or craftsopinici, and I've been both. I know you're tired of the stories. I'll make this simple for you. Clover Ranch is mine. Before I was married, before I lived behind the throne room in an eyrie, before I had a dozen stepchildren, before they were all taken from me: I built the

Clover Ranch. It's where I met my friends. It's where I met my future mate. It's where he proposed to me.

"And I will not. Do you hear me? *I will not* have a bunch of mud-stained bog wingtorn wretches running *my* ranch into the ground. I would rather see it burned to ash."

She bowed her head the slightest amount. One of her orders had been not to upset Jonas too much. "I understand that. But it's a lot easier to take and hold the ranch after we're secure here. Or, better yet, after we control the Crackling Sea Eyrie."

He stuffed another cooked crab into his beak and glared at her. "There's a lumber mill south of the ranch. You need wood to reinforce New Eyrie, don't you? You're getting what you want."

What I want is to be up in the Argent Heights, out of the king's gaze, minding my own eyrie.

"Yes, a ranch in the middle of the plains, surrounded by sawgrass taller than you," she drolled. "And a lumber mill next to a bog famous for being full of hordes of silver-eyed starlings, evil wisps, and monsters. That is exactly where I feel most secure. If you'll wait, they'll bring lumber down from the heights in a few days."

He stood, his sign that he was done with both a meal and a conversation. "Which one of us is in charge here?"

She also stood, making sure her eyrie badge with its reeve crown was visible. Since she never wore her crown, she used the badge as a stand-in. "Do not mistake my aid for subservience. You may boss around the troops inside the walls, but I control your supply lines. You'll get your eyrie, you'll get your face fixed, but only with me at your back."

"Silver, Silver, let's not fight." The softening of his

tone was another of his tricks, one she'd grown tired of. "You don't know these gryphons the way I do. You came out here on your own once and what? Some fantail knocked you down, took your beads, kicked dirt on your pretty beak? I lived here. The army of wingtorn you're so afraid of in the tall grass? I forged them out of wild beasts. Their leader, Satra the Kjarr? I raised her like a daughter. I made her what she is. Of course, you haven't been able to defeat her. That would be like defeating me."

Silver didn't respond. She'd spent her own time among the weald gryphons, however briefly, and she knew they weren't to be treated as pets or children. She even genuinely liked Satra, had tried to warn her of this very invasion. If he hadn't learned that from the loss of the Redwood Valley and Crackling Sea, he wasn't going to learn it from Silver.

"Now, my dear reeve neighbor, I could use some scouts while I retake my home." He led her out of the reeve's nest and towards her tower. "Why don't you pick out some of your best to send with me?"

Whomever Silver chose, she'd hear about it from them later. Already, they were terrified of the long grass after watching several of their friends get pulled out of the air by wingtorn in small hideaways invisible from above. Hideaways the war goliaths were still rooting out.

Instead, she picked the first opinici to exit the tower. "You're in luck. Those four are the best I have. They'll keep the skies clear from anything smaller than an army."

"Excellent," Jonas grinned. "That wasn't so bad, now was it? Just think of all the trade that will open up once I've tamed my home again. If you help me reclaim it, the first thing I'll do is send you the best mating pair of goliath birds I can find. It won't do to have *gryphons* sully the good name of my ranch by selling you weak stock. We'll get that fixed right up."

Silver counted to ten before responding. "Of course. If you need anything else, send a messenger. I need to go over the accounts before we visit this ancestral home of yours. There are rumors of padfeet striking south of Whitebeak which require my attention."

He grinned and bowed, leaving her to her books.

CLOVER

The wingtorn armor presented one small problem for Blinky's current predicament: it made their argent hawk prisoner too heavy to fly with. While she and Henders had gone back and forth, they'd ultimately decided it was better to tie her beak shut and return to the ranch by paw.

The argent hawk, supposedly a marvel in the mountain skies of her home, was not particularly good at walking. And wherever Henders went, he was shadowed by two capybaras. He'd spent enough evenings trawling the edge of the grasslands trying to get escaped capybaras back in their pen that they recognized him, though they were confused as to why he'd tied up another opinicus and not them this time.

Curious as they were, they trailed behind the trio, making snuffling noises from time to time. Blinky didn't know if they'd follow him back to the ranch or not. They might be safer in the bog, the way things were now. Capybaras, however, were not her concern.

Henders's safety was, followed by getting her prisoner to the Crackling Sea to be questioned.

The argent hawk started shouting the moment the bog gave way to sawgrass, forcing Henders to tighten her beak restraint.

"If you stay quiet, I will take the vest off you when we reach the Crackling Sea," Blinky promised. "If not, I will see to it you are buried wearing it."

It was unclear whether the argent hawk was persuaded more by Blinky's words or by the peacock blood on her beak, but she didn't attempt to shout the rest of the way.

As they approached the ranch, Blinky could tell something was off. There were no goliath birds nor wagons. It had rained lightly all day, and wagon wheel tracks went south, towards the lumber mill. The usual set of fantail guards weren't overhead.

"Wait here," she told Henders and the capybaras. "I will check things first."

Sawgrass was unpleasant to walk through, but she stepped off the old ranch trail and made her way through the scrub, trying to ignore when it cut her paws or face. She kept her eyes pointed down and half-closed.

There were too many scents for her to tell much of anything, the effect of so many gryphons and opinici coming through. She was forced to stop a few times and fend off a grass snake or two who were riled up by the noise of the previous day.

Yet when Blinky reached the ranch, it didn't seem in trouble, just empty. She sat and listened, waiting until she heard a familiar sound—Foultner's grumbling.

"And now Blinky and Henders are both lost, so I'm

going to have to walk through the bog to find them both," the ex-poacher was saying.

Blinky rolled her eyes but hooted a greeting. Then she exited the round ranch building and gave Henders the sign that it was safe.

"You found him!" Foultner wrapped her talons around Blinky's neck, a sign of affection the owl gryphon could have done without. "I knew if I shared half my fish bars with you, you'd pull it off."

Only half? Blinky stored that information away for later. Next time, she would ask for more in return for a favor.

"Who's your friend?" Foultner asked Henders, pointing to the wrapped-up argent hawk. "And how'd you get her in that?"

The prisoner glared.

"She kind of did it herself," Henders admitted. "I just lassoed her. Where is everyone? This place looks abandoned."

The two capybaras, upon seeing Foultner, beat a hasty retreat back to the bog.

"Come on, I'll show you around." Foultner led them through the ground floor of the ranch. There were mostly wounded here, those whose injuries had prevented them from flying or walking east. Up top in the observation area were four healthy fantails, but only one kept watch while the other three rested. They nodded down to Blinky when she came in, recognizing her facial scars.

Foultner put a talon on one of the wounded, mindful of his bandages. "Xalt and Jer were supposed to take the wagons and grab whatever lumber they could find down south, and then swing back up to get us. We haven't heard anything yet, and there's a real cracking storm coming south."

"Crackling?" Blinky suggested.

"Cracking," Foultner insisted. "It's rancher talk."

The owl gryphon shook her head. "I do not think it is. I think you are hearing it wrong."

"Henders?" Foultner prompted.

He shrugged. "I've heard it both ways."

That wasn't the response Foultner wanted, but thankfully, she seemed pleased to have him back and let it go. "Once the wagon returns, we can make a break with the rest of them. The fantails are more here to send word back if anything bad happens. They were expecting to have left by now, too."

Blinky looked at the four gryphons, their long tails draped over the balcony. The chances they'd stop anyone was slim. They might slow them down a little, but the wounded here were the ones who couldn't escape anyways.

She flew up to the closest fantail. She had a hard time telling them apart, even though their old weald territories had bordered Strix's. If she looked closely, she could recognize Erlock by the small white stars in her pattern, but these fantails were a plain brown and green.

Down below, Foultner and Henders were arguing affectionately. Blinky sighed. She hated to leave them undefended, but she had her priorities.

"Fantails," she addressed the lookouts. "We need to get this prisoner to the Crackling Sea soon. She will know what is going on."

The fantails looked at each other. One of the males

spoke. "Our orders are to stay here until the ranch is evacuated."

"Who gave you the order? Is my order more important?" she asked.

The male spoke up again. "It came from Ranger Lord Mia herself. Her last words to us before she flew off."

Lightning sounded off the sea, and the water below it lit up in response. There was a dark shape moving along the coast. When the next flash of lightning came, it had gone out to the deep water again.

"You do not know if anyone is coming, but you know this prisoner needs to be moved," Blinky said. "I think you will help anyways. I am friends with Mia. I saved her once. She will trust me."

A gust of wind brought cool air through the opening the fantails were looking out of. They shivered, and one of the others spoke up. "Look, I think we're going to have to leave sooner or later. There's not much we can do anyways, right? Why don't we leave before it starts raining?"

The fantails argued amongst themselves, then decided that Blinky was right. They found some cloth to cover the argent hawk's head with, grabbed an old fishing net so two at a time could carry her, and they began their flight east.

"I must go to tell Satra what I saw," Blinky told Foultner. "I will come back to find your wagon after we are safely there. Good?"

"Sure," Foultner said. "Why wouldn't we be?"

Blinky could think of a few reasons, but she didn't say them out loud. Instead, she nuzzled her two friends, then raced after the fantails. Even with their extra baggage, they were excellent at flying.

DESPITE IT BEING EARLY AFTERNOON, the skies over the Clover Ranch were black, and the only light came in bursts from the sky, and then from the water north of them.

Foultner climbed down from the observation area, resisting the urge to glide. She'd been told not to tax her wing unless they came under attack. She could easily have Henders fly up top and look out the windows, but she liked to see that the rest of the world was still out there.

At least, that's what she *wanted* to see. Really, she could only make out wind and rain. They were still in the storm season, albeit near the end of it, and she'd forgotten how bad things could get. Thankfully, a ranch so close to the sea wouldn't have lasted long if it didn't take precautions. Which was to say there was a wide moat to direct the water away from the bottom story living quarters, though things were still getting a little damp.

"Do you think Xalt and Jer are still coming?" Henders asked. His question was echoed by the wounded.

Foultner had done her best to tend to their bandages, but none of the medicine gryphons had stayed behind. They'd gone with an earlier wagon carrying those in critical condition. "Look, I don't know. Wagons don't do well in mud. They're probably stuck."

"What if the lumber mill was taken?" Henders

asked. "I was attacked in the bog. Maybe they're starting to take it over."

She shrugged. "So what if they do? These opinici aren't like starlings. The moment the parasite takes hold, they'll start killing each other. Let 'em try to go through the bog."

Thunder shook the ranch so hard that one of the doors flew open. She walked over to close it, taking a moment to feel the cool water on her face and look out at the stalks of sawgrass moving like waves in the heavy winds.

Hearty stuff, sawgrass. Impossible to uproot.

Just before she latched the door closed, she thought she saw a pair of eyes in the grass. She shook her head, figuring it was just the capybaras come to steal what they could before disappearing into the distance. But the more she thought about it, the less confident she felt.

"I'm going back up top to keep look out," she said.

"Again?" Henders was working on a stew for the wounded. Once it became clear the storm was going to be a long one, he made it his mission to keep everyone fed.

Foultner found the closest wingtorn ramp and made her way up the floors towards the surface, calling down the open center. "Yup."

With all of this walking, I should have just gone east with the wingtorn.

That wasn't the real reason she'd stayed. She'd been worried about Henders. But seeing who was left behind, she felt glad she could provide them with some comfort.

The walk up top took a while, giving her an appreciation for what wingtorn went through every day, but she finally hit the top bunks and climbed up into the observation area. It still smelled of fantail.

She looked north, watching the water light up. It was beautiful, in its own way. Of course, the same thing that made it beautiful made it dangerous. *Isn't that always the way of things?*

She sighed and lazily turned to look east. The Crackling Sea Eyrie wasn't visible. Nor were the paths, absorbed in the undulations of the tall grass. She looked south, hoping to see some sign of the wagons despite the weather. She could make out the start of the trail, the first pieces of the boardwalk, but the lumber mill was too far.

If I'd been smarter, I could have sent Henders there first. At least then, we'd know what was going on. There's nothing I hate more than not knowing. That, and boredom.

She finally looked northwest, in the direction of New Eyrie, and she wished she'd looked that way first.

Shapes came through the grass. Her first thought was some Ashen Weald rangers had waited until cover of the storm to sneak away from New Eyrie, but when the lightning flashed again, she could see that they weren't wearing the black and gold of the Ashen Weald. They were wearing the old Crackling Sea harnesses from the era of the previous reeve.

She looked past the blue herons, seeing many more shapes behind them. For the most part, these were the so-called Jonas loyalists Merin had locked up, who had then disappeared after being released.

Merin really missed his chance to say, 'I told you so.'

She saw two shapes at the back, however, that worried her. One was duck-shaped with old burns and ornamented armor, and the other was her old friend Reeve Silver.

Foultner swore. In the next flash of lightning, she caught sight of two silver hawks headed straight for her.

She dove down the ranch as one window shattered, letting in the wind and rain. Her wing cried out at being forced to glide, but it held.

She looked at the door facing east, then at the wounded. There was no way they would make it in time.

But Henders might.

"Hends!" she shouted. "You need to fly now and tell the Crackling Sea what's happened!"

Her warning came too late. The doors from all directions opened, revealing the strike force from New Eyrie.

They were clearly expecting a fight, so when they crashed in, they were disappointed no one had so much as a weapon. One of the herons honked back at the sawgrass, and the ornamented opinicus walked in.

"Ah, home at last," Jonas said.

SILVER SHOOK water out of her feathers. She'd planned to spend tonight warming her talons at a fire, eating something delicious, and going over the books. Instead, she learned that two of her scouts had gone missing, and she didn't trust Jonas not to put them in danger if he found them.

The ranch didn't seem to be anything special. She'd been in quite a few goliath bird ranches in her time, and none particularly impressed her. Really, the more ostentatious an opinicus tried to make their stables, the sillier it became. By that metric, this ranch was acceptable. At least there was no mother-of-pearl or jewels like at some of the Alabaster Eyrie stables she'd come across.

The small strike force had been more than adequate to take the ranch. A swift breeze could have taken it. She looked down at the wounded, recognizing one of the wingtorn with a long stomach wound by her bright red plumage.

"Muzzle that one," Silver ordered. "Even wounded, she's got a nasty attitude."

Nobody put up much of a fight, and there wasn't much need to move everyone together as they were all side-by-side and wrapped in bandages.

"See? It was simple." Jonas walked the length of the ranch, judging each aspect as good or bad based on how gryphonic it smelled or some internal system she was unaware of.

"You got lucky," she said. "They'd already left. Now, let's get out of here."

Jonas looked surprised. "Leave? This is my home. I'm staying. You can go if you want. Just take care of the prisoners before you leave."

"Take care of them?" She looked at the wounded. While some were soldiers, at least two looked like ranchers who were in the wrong place at the wrong time. "What do you mean?"

"Kill them. We have no need of them." Jonas hung up his tentacled talons and necklace on a hook. The name over it had been scratched out, but it had once read *Jonas*.

Silver thought quickly, even when surprised. "I have orders to interrogate them. We need to know what their situation is with the Blackwing Eyrie. Crestfall seems to think they were working together, but we've never been able to find any evidence to back up the pink reeve."

"Fine," Jonas sighed. "Take them down to the lumber mill, put them in cages, and let the Reevesport peacocks pull the answers out of them. Then have them killed. I just don't want them in my home."

The troops had been trained to listen to Silver over Jonas, and their training held. She wasn't sure if she could order the captives kept alive without Jonas finding out. Maybe if there were other prisoners, she could mix them in. At best, she'd given them a stay of execution of a few days.

There were two, however, she could save. Two whom she owed her life. And also the price of fifteen goliath birds who had been kept and not returned at the end of their rental period, no matter how pampered the birds turned out to be.

"Wrap their bandages as best you can to keep them dry, and take the prisoners down to the lumber mill," Silver ordered. "I'll take my informants with me to debrief them back at New Eyrie. Those two on the end, the ones who are obviously ranchers and not soldiers. We'll escort you safely to your new quarters."

The male peregrine falcon opinicus looked at his house sparrow mate and said, "You know, we met and fell in love at New Eyrie."

"Shut up, Henders," she responded.

Silver's argent hawks led them out into the storm. She hadn't seen these two in a long time, not since she'd come here with Mally the Nighthaunt, but they looked to be doing as well as expected. If they were smart and kept their beaks shut, they should get out of this alive.

"Can you fly?" she asked Foultner, seeing the wing brace.

Foultner, as grumpy as Silver remembered, shrugged. "What's my other option, stay back inside and get beheaded at a lumber mill? I'll figure it out."

Silver ordered her hawks to keep a very close guard on the two 'informants.' They'd handled real informants and spies in the past who had a change of heart when the Seraph King's forces arrived at their doorstep and the consequences of their information came to fruition, so they understood they were to make sure Foultner and Henders arrived at New Eyrie okay and were assigned rooms without windows.

34

THE NIGHT PARROT

The storm caught Blinky before she hit the Crackling Sea, and she spent most of the night curled up in front of a fire while the prisoner was questioned. She'd only intended to sleep until the storm ended, then go back for Foultner, but by the time she woke it was already light out.

Grenkin arrived with a plate of food, a mix of cooked and raw meat, some fish and eel, and then a variety of rimu olives and other delicacies. "You look terrible. Did you sleep okay?"

"I do not like waking up with the light." Blinky groomed her feathers before eating. "When did the storm let up?"

Grenkin speared a fish with his beak and ate it raw. "Just after dawn. It's still drizzling a bit outside."

"What did you find out from the scout?" she asked.

Rorin stoked the fire to get it going again. "She was pretty resilient until we brought in Soft Paws. She seems terrified of bog wisps, so she became much more talkative when she saw the skull paint. We didn't learn much that Erlock's fly-over hadn't already told us, except that the supply lines are much more extensive than we thought. This is a serious invasion."

Blinky stood and stretched her cold paws. "I should make sure Foultner is taking care of herself before I go out again. Where are the wounded?"

"I'm sorry, you were our last arrival," Grenkin explained. "Sometime in the night, the ranch and lumber mill were lost. We think the caravan from the lumber mill escaped into the bog, but where they're at now is anyone's guess. Someone's flying the old Crackling Sea banner over the ranch, though."

Blinky leapt over the plate of food and made her way out of her room, dropping down from a balcony at the end of the hall into the amphitheater, then she flew up a few levels, scrambling past a startled wingtorn, and made her way into the throne chamber.

The stone throne was long gone, chiseled away by Grenkin's sculptors, but several places to sit had been set up along with a row of tables. It served as a war room, and the leaders who hadn't been evacuated to the weald remained here.

Blinky saw Satra talking with Younce, who had brought a few taiga gryphons with him. She only caught bits of what he was saying, but it was about what she expected—the taiga gryphons hadn't stood by the kjarr pride last time and things went poorly, so Younce was here personally to remedy that.

Mia and Olan were looking over complicated maps of the hidden rooms and escape tunnels out of the Crackling Sea, explaining to a collection of opinici wearing flameworks harnesses how the stormcloth curtains worked. Saltpeter was in low supply, but they weren't planning to blow up an eyrie this time—just fuse all the pieces that controlled the foot-thick layer of stormcloth that served as a barrier against invaders if they had to escape.

It was a plan that suggested they knew they could not hold the eyrie, so they wished to take away its greatest defense when it fell. That did not reassure Blinky. She did not want to see Jonas step foot into this eyrie again without paying for it with his blood.

The strangest addition to the war room were two dozen parrotface gryphons, moving between the different tables and factions with information and food, keeping things clear and tidy. Blinky's eyes missed them the first time, but she was hooting quietly to reassure herself, and that sound bounced off their feathers in a strange way. It was like a living carpet of green moss in a room of stone.

From one of the side chambers, Erlock stepped in with some feathermanes and began issuing orders about what troops were in charge of each area. Blinky decided her old friend was now her best bet.

"Erlock," Blinky said. "When are you saving Foultner and Henders?"

Erlock stopped, causing a parrotface who was anticipating her tail to keep moving to trip over it. "They were okay last time I saw them. What happened?"

Blinky explained about the ranch and the lumber mill. Grenkin had followed her up here, but he was waved down by Satra before he could confirm her story.

"I see." Erlock paused, and in Blinky's experience, pauses were not good when action was required. "I'm sorry, they're reinforcing that tiny ranch as fast as they can. They outnumber us greatly, and this is a war we're only going to win so long as we bleed them for every inch of this eyrie they take. Once we leave the eyrie, they have the advantage. I could spend a hundred of my fastest fantails, fifty of my strongest feathermanes, and they'd all die getting back one poacher. I like Foultner, and I'm a big fan of Henders, but I can't advise the ranger lord to make that decision."

Blinky thought of trying to argue her point, but that didn't seem like it would work. She looked around the room to see who could help her, and she came up blank. Everyone was busy worrying about saving the Ashen Weald, saving the largest number of gryphons and opinici possible. Nobody was worried about saving her best friend.

Except there was one pair of eyes staring at her. It was the parrotface who had fallen over Erlock's tail. He backed up a pace when he saw Blinky was now staring back at him, but she stepped forwards and caught him with a pounce before he could escape.

"Why did you pounce me?" he asked.

She stared into his eyes. "You looked like you were going to run away."

"I was. Because you looked like you were going to pounce me." When she didn't say anything else but kept looking at him, he spoke more. "I heard about your friend. You probably don't remember me, but I was one of the gryphons who helped find the cure last time we were stationed here staring out at New Eyrie. Remember the poisoned carrots? The monitor you said was your pet?"

She blinked.

"Well, I know the feathermanes and fantails are saving themselves for the big battle," he continued, "but us parrotfaces have been out in the grasslands every day finding things to eat and herbs for the medicine gryphons. And doing a bit of spying."

She continued staring.

He gulped. "I guess I'm saying that I could get a dozen of us from here to the lumber mill. If they don't have anyone with night vision, I'll bet we could get your friend out of there, as long as we don't have to do the fighting. We're impossible to spot in the grass."

"Hmmm." This wasn't the strike force she wanted. It wasn't even the terrible one she'd had in the bog. But it wasn't nothing, either. "What do they call you?"

He puffed up his chest feathers. "The Night Parrot."

"No," Blinky said. "What is your name?"

"Oh, it's Veron," he replied, deflating a little.

"You would be more valuable to me if you could fight, but I think I can find someone to do the fighting for us." Blinky hoped she wasn't asking too much of Black Mask. Mates from different prides sometimes felt pulled in both directions, but mates from opposing prides had their own issues. "You will need to sneak and extricate my friends during the chaos. Will that work?"

"Of course!" Veron *skraarked*. "I'll head out now. We have a hidden path through the bog. Give us a little time after dark to get into position, and we'll be ready and waiting."

Before she dismissed him, Blinky tried to memorize the features of 'The Night Parrot.' Other than their pride leader, it was hard for her to tell the ground parrot gryphons apart. But when she looked closely, she noticed that most of them used some sort of starberry-based pigment somewhere on their body. For Veron, that was around his eyes. For others, they tipped their ears or paws with it.

Purple eyes is Veron. I can remember that.

Now that she had her team in place, she'd need to see if Black Mask was ready for a fight. It was time for her to go back to the bog.

First I save Henders, now I must save Foultner and Henders. I am good at saving opinici. I wish they were not so good at getting captured.

But first, she slipped down to the kitchen to steal food. Fortunately, Biski had already had a similar plan and was being scolded by the chefs. While their backs were turned, Blinky ate her fill, stuffing her cheeks, and then slipped up through the throne room, through the royal bedchamber, adding a few tasty treasures to her hidden stockpile in the consort chamber, and out the secret passage by the reeve's old quarters and into the air.

35

BROKEN

B lack Mask listened to Blinky's plan without comment. He appreciated the new armor and the possibilities it unlocked for his rogue pride, but he also didn't appreciate being manipulated into helping the Ashen Weald.

"This is not helping the Ashen Weald," Blinky insisted. "It is helping me save a friend. Satra and the others are inside the Crackling Sea Eyrie and cannot afford to leave. This is for me."

His side still ached from where the peacock had stabbed through his old armor. He was quickly becoming a collection of old scar tissue and wounds healing into new scar tissue. And he didn't like where things were going.

"You want me to attack an Ashen Weald lumber mill, full of Ashen Weald prisoners, but I'm not supposed to hurt any of them." He waited for her to nod. "So we're supposed to... what, attack the lumber? Or the mill? What's the point in that?"

Blinky made a quiet hissing sound, her sign that she was unhappy. "You know why."

"Yeah, I know why, but my pride doesn't." He stood and paced their hideaway along the Jadebeak River. "How am I supposed to convince them to go through with this?"

Blinky tried to pace with him, but she gave his new palm spikes a wide berth. "You lie to them. Tell them Jonas would be there."

He stopped. "Would you lie to your friends?"

"To make them save each other? Of course," she replied.

"What about me?" he asked. "Would you lie to me?"

She nodded. "Yes."

"Have you lied to me?" he asked.

"No. Not yet." She seemed to understand why the truth was important to him. It was to many gryphons. But she didn't seem willing to stake her friends' lives on it. "I promise I will not lie to you while we are mates. Will that work?"

He shook his head. "Will it work? I don't know. Help me understand why this is so important. Not to you, not to your friends, not even to me. Help me understand why this is going to help my pride."

She considered her words carefully before speaking. "I told you when Jonas was near. And he was seen at New Eyrie. Clover Ranch was his home, once, and he will go there at some point. But he is going after the Crackling Sea."

"What're you doing?" Black Mask asked. This was a strange response to his question.

She tilted her head to the side. "Telling you things that help the pride. You are helping me, I am helping you. I do not know where Jonas is right now, just nearby. But it is clear that for so many wingtorn, his death is what you want most. I promise I will do all I can to make sure someone gets to him."

An end to the nightmares for so many of us. That is something of value.

He finally conceded. "Okay, I'll take a small patrol out. You said they're stretched thin and worried about the ranch? If that's not true when we reach the mill, we're leaving. But if it checks out, I'll go for it."

She blinked at him.

"Don't thank me yet," he hastened to add. "I can't promise no one will get hurt in the cages. Everyone here holds a grudge against the Ashen Weald. You're going to have to be ready to open the cages and take back your prisoners. I'm not going to be able to do you any favors there."

Blinky purred and very carefully nuzzled his neck. "That will work. Thank you. Foultner and Henders are my best friends. They are not able to take care of themselves, but I will miss them when they die."

"Night songs carry word of all good deeds," he said in the language of the owls. Or, at least, that's what he thought he said. He mixed up some of the words sometimes because the sounds were hard for him to hear. It was possible he'd said something much less suited for polite company.

She repeated it back to him, correcting his pronunciation. "I must go. I have very few who could help me, but they're the best at what they do."

"I hope they're owls," he said. "At least they can hide in the dark and kill things in the sky. You should really make more friends in your own pride."

He wasn't sure why she seemed to have so few owl friends. He knew from his brief time as a spy in the Ashen Weald there was some sort of split between the dark-plumed owls and that many of Blinky's friends had left to form their own pride, something that caused a rift. But he didn't know why she didn't have more friends from the owls who had stayed.

When she didn't confirm who was coming, he tried another. "Maybe a feathermane or two?"

"Have you heard of... The Night Parrot?" she asked.

"No," he replied.

"Me neither." She licked his face, careful of the new spikes, and walked towards the exit to listen for eavesdroppers.

He hated to see her go, so he offered up a little hope. "After we save your friends tonight, I'd like to meet them properly. If they're your friends, I assume they're trustworthy. Why don't we meet them to go fishing? I know a place that neither side seems to be aware of. It's buried under the ruins, but there's light that slips in from above, and the cavefish are good."

She looked back at him and blinked, then she slipped out into the night.

Nothing left to do but see if I can get the others on board with this.

He sighed and left his hideaway. If they were going to get up there by night in this heavy armor, they'd need to get going.

BLACK MASK HAD BEEN FORCED to pull in some favors with Thistle to convince the pride to go along with his night raid plan. Normally, that wouldn't be a problem, but she'd been acting extra strange ever since meeting with the crone.

"Are you worried because you don't have armor?" he asked as they jogged north, following the hidden paths beneath the palms. "I'm sure the crone will figure it out before we get back."

Thistle frowned. She walked with a lighter, steadier step than usual and kept checking her pouch as though she had an egg inside she didn't want to crack.

"I'm fine," was the best she offered. She didn't ask him about his secret mate, leaving him to wonder if she'd figured it out. That wasn't necessarily a problem, exactly. With the split in the weald owls, he could claim that Blinky was from a free pride, not the Ashen Weald. Clearly, Blinky had no problem lying now and then.

Of course, I spent months plotting the death of Satra and Urious while in the Ashen Weald. I have no moral heights to fly upon, could I even fly.

Thistle normally liked to be in charge, but the closer they got to the lumber mill, the more nervous she became. In fact, several of the wingtorn who had escaped before Satra's liberation also looked nervous, and he realized most of them never spent much time away from the Heart of the Bog. Seeing that the cypress trees had an end that wasn't the Jadebeak Mountains, seeing that a new world existed beyond them, must be upsetting.

"Hey, gather up," he said when they reached drinking water. "I want to go over the nearby hiding places in case we need to flee. This isn't that different from down south. There're no mangroves to worry about. Sure, there's a lot more snakes than usual so check your burrows as you enter them, but you're going to do just fine."

He'd met Vitra several times in this section of the highlands, and as they paused to rest, he took it upon himself to check each burrow and make sure they were all fine.

Fine in this case meant there was no matamata in them. Snakes and bog crawlers were a given but considering where he and the others had been living, he didn't think anyone would complain.

Once they were rested, he brought them to the edge of the bog and looked out upon the sea of sawgrass, much of it flooded from the previous night's storm. There were dark clouds in the sky above, blocking the last of the day's light, but no lightning. They'd probably still get a little wet, but nothing dangerous.

I'm not looking forward to carrying this armor all the way home while soaking wet.

Still, the things he had done for love—and hate, in the case of Jonas. He hadn't lied to his wingtorn, precisely. He hadn't told them Jonas was here. Instead, he said he'd caught sight of Jonas moving from the ranch to New Eyrie. Supposedly, Blinky's spies had seen him there. What he proposed about the attack on the lumber mill was a chance to see who their enemy was and cause chaos. Make Jonas think that the Ashen Weald was causing the problems.

They took turns napping and watching the lumber mill until the light was entirely gone. There weren't many opies stationed there, fewer than there had been at the armor caravan. These were more peacocks, one black and five blue, and then the cages of prisoners like Blinky had warned him would be here. The enemy didn't appear to have any green peafowl, or if they did, they were even rarer than at the Redwood Valley Eyrie.

Before the light had gone, he'd tried to get eyes on the two his mate was after. He was surprised to learn he knew both of them. Foultner, he'd met in the depths of the Crackling Sea Eyrie. She'd opened the cell door to let the bog wingtorn out. Henders had been with him as part of the expedition, though Black Mask had little memory of that particular opinicus. His part had been to lead them astray, then set up Urious for an ambush. As such, he hadn't spent time with the others once they entered the bog proper.

Still, he didn't see anyone who looked like a Reeve's Guard or a poacher. Most of the prisoners were wingtorn, and the others had a Crackling Sea look to them. He hoped Blinky's friends weren't already dead.

Once the darkness took over, the peacocks lit a fire. That was good, because it meant their night vision would be poor. He didn't know how to keep his wingtorn from killing the prisoners, so instead, he offered a little helpful advice.

"Don't forget the peafowl can fly," he said. "They'll go for help if we let them get away. The ones in the cages can wait. They're not going anywhere, and we should make sure none of the wingtorn are ours."

The bog gryphons nodded, their beaks chattering with anticipating, their tails swishing back and forth. It was a wonder the new spikes on the wave of tails didn't impale anyone.

Thistle sat to the side, looking nervous. He went over to her.

"What's wrong? Is this about the caravan?" he asked.

She shook her head. "No, it's just... witch stuff. Sorry.

I know I did a terrible job last time. I have no idea how you killed that cobra-opinicus all on your own. I'll do better this time, I promise."

She put her paw over his and squeezed it. It was a strange gesture, one she'd never made before, and he didn't know what to make of it.

"I know you'll do your best," he said, trying to offer her encouragement. "You're a good witch and an excellent gryphon. Fighting isn't for everyone, that's true. But most of any fight is about making good decisions, and nobody has a smarter head on their shoulders than you. Trust your instincts, do what's right."

Somehow, his words didn't reassure her at all. Enough time had passed since the fires had begun that it was time, so he gave the order and the wingtorn prowled towards the mill.

THE FIRST WINGTORN who pounced the camp fell short, forgetting how heavy his armor was. Black Mask had suggested not wearing the armor—it was night, and they were unlikely to run afoul of flechettes—but they'd all insisted. It was hard to say no to a shiny new toy. Black Mask decided not to test his jumping skills and just plowed through an opinicus, trusting the weight of the metal and the spikes to do his job for him.

He was successful, though his quarry let out a squeal of pain that could wake the dead. The other peacocks fought hard, slashing out with long talons, but the armor kept the wingtorn safe. This was a one-sided fight, and Black Mask was almost disappointed it was so easy. Rather than go for the black-and-red cobra opinicus himself, he let the other wingtorn handle this one and went to check on Thistle.

She'd disappeared when the conflict began, slipping towards the cages. While he wanted to make sure she was okay, he also wanted to make certain she didn't do anything rash.

Which, as it turned out, was what she was about to do. She unlatched one of her harness pouches. Most of the bog witches were using old medicine opinicus harnesses stolen from the Crackling Sea, so they included a lot of pockets, and hers was no exception.

When he saw what it held, however, he understood why she'd walked like she had eggs in her pockets. She sat on her back paws, and in her forepaws, she held a clay jar.

The design was unmistakable. It had come from the dig site. According to Blinky, Headmaster Neider had been filling the containers with parasites before he'd been forced out of the bog and back to the university with the disappearance of Cherine. What mattered wasn't so much whose clay jar it was so much as what it contained.

She took off the lid, and firelight reflected off the salts. For whatever reason, salt put the parasites into a kind of hibernation, allowing them to be transported. Similar clay jars had been destroyed and burned by the Ashen Weald, but the crone kept a few, burying them in case they were ever necessary.

They were a weapon too terrible to use, or so Black Mask thought. But a terrible, opinicus-weaponized tool like the parasite sounded different when spoken of from the crone's beak. She considered the bog pride's immunity a kind of blessing, a mark of the chosen. Never mind that the kjarr gryphons shared it, and she'd never call them *holy*.

With a trembling paw, the green-painted bog witch moved towards the prisoners.

"Thistle!" he shouted, and she nearly dropped the jar. "Don't you dare."

"Black Mask," she squeaked. "You need to go. Once the parasites take hold, they're going to attack everyone. I can fly away, but you need to leave now. If we can get a few of them spreading the parasite, they'll take care of the Ashen Weald *and* Jonas for us! We'll be safe in the bog, ready to reclaim these lands, too!"

The parasite didn't work that fast, but he didn't tell her that. He'd listened to the gruesome details several times now, the tiny bugs laying eggs in the blood stream, the strange rabies-like effect caused by the eggs or the bite or perhaps some disease the parasites carried. Nobody was sure, though they'd cut up a lot of dead starlings trying to find answers.

He decided to put the fear of death into her. With one pounce, he knocked her down, watching as the clay jar shattered and the salt spilled out across the mill floor. The weight of Black Mask plus the heavy armor pinned her down, and he ripped out several of her flight feathers, a painful but necessary process so she couldn't fly away from the consequences of her actions.

"No!" she shouted. "NO! We won't be able to get away in time!"

He let her go, and she watched as the black flecks in the sand stirred now that they were exposed to the moisture in the air. "No, Thistle. You don't get to leave these prisoners here to tear themselves apart while you watch from a distance. You don't go and turn the wounded into a weapon."

She cowered, and he knew he was saying too much, but he continued.

"You need to decide what kind of gryphon you are right here and right now. Are you the sort of gryphon who steals eggs and raises them to be assassins? The sort of gryphon who would kill thousands, steal their minds from them and watch them feed upon their loved ones? Because what happens if you get your wish. What if the infection did spread from here, like you seem to want it to, and it wiped away all life south of the Crackling Sea. You know who would be left? Murderers. Monsters. You."

His speech was running long, but he grabbed the back of Thistle's scruff in his beak and shoved her towards the prisoners. "Open the cages and take back your soul, if the crone doesn't own it in a clay jar under her nest."

By now, the wingtorn had finished off the peacock and were watching the events unfolding. While they'd all been brainwashed by Vitra and her crones to some degree or another, the remaining bog witches had been through the worst of it.

When the wingtorn saw the clay jar and salts, disgust went across most of their faces. The thing about being traumatized was that it tended to have one of two effects on a gryphon. Either they went on to traumatize others, or they devoted themselves to making sure others weren't hurt. And it was entirely possible for the first group to become the second, given enough time and the right nudge.

While Thistle, shivering and with blood dripping

from her wings, used a shaking paw to try to unlock the first cage, one of the other wingtorn stuck his face *into* the bonfire to grab out a log, then used the fire to try to box in the squirming parasites.

Black Mask had been worried his speech would get him torn apart by his pride, but the other wingtorn risked their own conflagration to pull out flaming branches, to ring in the parasites, to put more fire on top of them and let them burn.

He was proud of them. Maybe it was the smoke from the fire, or some ash stirred up by their efforts, but the black patches under his eyes were wet with tears.

None of the wingtorn helped Thistle, however. They all stared at her, waiting to see what she did. Her wings twitched, a common occurrence when a gryphon had lost feathers and wanted to fly but couldn't. But she stayed on the ground. Her paw wasn't listening to her, but she used her beak and managed to work the cage door open.

The first prisoner pushed past Thistle and dashed into the tall grass. Black Mask couldn't hear anything from where he stood, but he watched the Ashen Weald gryphon suddenly stop moving in one direction, listen, then head off in another. He hoped that was the legendary Night Parrot at work.

The next cage had a kjarr wingtorn, her cardinal plumage playing against the light from the fire. When Thistle got the door open, the cardinal didn't leave immediately. She put a paw on Thistle, then she lifted her beak and whispered something to the witch.

Whatever the kjarr wingtorn said seemed to have worked, because Thistle's paw had stopped shaking enough that she opened the next cage in half the time.

Black Mask and the bog wingtorn behind him stood by and watched Thistle open every cage on her own. When she was done, Black Mask approached her, and he felt a pang in his heart when she flinched away.

"We're not going to hurt you," he said without apologizing for his actions. "Thistle, you're an adult now, and you need to see what the difference between right and wrong is. You needed to look into the eyes of every gryphon and opinicus you were about to kill so they could see how sorry you were."

She trembled for a long time. Most of the wingtorn gave her that time, but several went to chew down one of the cobra banners near the dead peafowl.

When Thistle finally spoke, she said, "I think I understand now. This... isn't just about here. This is waiting for us back home, isn't it?"

Black Mask nodded. "We came out here to kill Jonas, and we're going to get that slimy bastard one way or the other. But I don't think he's the one that's been slowly killing us. It's time to confront the rest of our pride. It's time we let go of Vitra's hatred and moved on with our lives."

Two of the wingtorn went to either side of Thistle and helped lick her feather wounds to stop the blood from running, then they escorted her towards the exit.

Black Mask waited until they were gone, then hooted into the sawgrass. He didn't hear back a response, but he hoped Blinky had found who she was looking for.

By the time he caught up to his pride, he overheard one of the wingtorn asking her what the cardinal had whispered to her.

Thistle stumbled over the words a little before

getting them out. "She called me sister, told me that she loved me, and told me all of us were welcome in Bogwash when we were ready."

As they went back, Black Mask considered the wingtorn he had here. He'd chosen this group because they were the most likely to stay loyal to him. But that meant only those already inclined to follow him had been there to witness the jar of parasites. The three witches back home, the number of wingtorn equal to his own, were loyal to the crone.

I could leave. Take these wingtorn, go to Bogwash, turn ourselves in. That would halve the number of insurgents the Ashen Weald has to deal with down here.

It was true, but he also thought back to a strange face the night the Heart of the Bog had gone to hell. It was young bog witches, the ones who would later found Bogwash together, and they were pulling their friends out of the water, rescuing them, and telling them that there was a better future ahead if they fled east but that they could flee west if they wished.

He thought the wingtorn still at the nesting grounds deserved that same chance. They deserved an opportunity to be better than who they'd been the last few months, and he'd give it to them.

But not the crone.

Not his mother.

The only thing waiting for her after she tried to turn a child into a mass murderer was death.

36

FRIENDSHIP

The journey through the sawgrass took most of the night. Blinky assumed the parrotfaces were going to sneak through the bog to return, but apparently, they'd run into some trouble on their way here and decided the best option would be to navigate the tall grass around the Clover Ranch and make their way back via the shoreline.

Veron led the way, and he didn't allow any talking. The most Blinky had managed to get out of Cardinal before being hushed by parrotfaces was that Silver had taken Foultner and Henders away to New Eyrie to interrogate personally.

Blinky had a healthy trust in her abilities, but New Eyrie buzzed with argent hawks in the skies, armored goliath birds patrolling the ground, and constant construction of new fortifications to keep wingtorn out. She didn't see a way to get close to it, let alone to escape out of it with two opinici in tow.

Something was happening on the south side of the Clover Ranch, so they were forced to go north along the western side, which put them in a difficult position. A line of goliath birds moving between New Eyrie and the ranch had created a road where the grass was stomped down. Caravans moved back and forth. It was too risky for all of them to cross at once, so teams of two went, one wounded and one healthy, when Blinky's night vision said it was clear.

It was slow going, made even more dangerous when a team from New Eyrie started putting up glass-covered lights along the path. Had they moved any faster, they would have caught up with the parrotfaces. Thankfully, they'd heard of the fire danger posed by the sawgrass, and they were setting up sturdy enclosures to keep the fire from escaping.

As it was, Blinky nearly stumbled into a Crestfall opinicus relieving herself far from the trail and had to stop herself from murdering the flamingo out of habit.

Every so often, Veron would pause and watch the skies. The argent hawks seemed hesitant to fly too far from the ranch, which meant that once Veron spotted the fantail patrols overhead, they were safe to speed up.

The Night Parrot fluttered into the sky, startling both Blinky and the cardinal wingtorn, neither of whom had ever seen one fly before. A small team with a wagon came out to meet them, and Blinky was ordered up top.

"Satra and Erlock are expecting you," was all the medicine gryphon said. His tone did not inspire confidence, but Blinky wasn't one to shy from danger.

She considered flying out over the sea, but she shared Foultner's perennial worry about being spit out of the sky by the whale. Instead, she flew around to the cliffside, slipping back through the passage under the trees, though the royal chambers—with a short detour to retrieve a few snacks from the consort's quarters—and into the throne room.

Erlock was there when she came through the passage, already shaking her head. "I don't envy you getting shouted at. At least tell me that you got our mutual friends out of there?"

Blinky shook her head. "The silver reeve picked them out and said they were her informants. She is holding them at New Eyrie."

The fantail pride leader was hard to read. She pointed a wing towards the library. "I think they wanted to speak to you in private."

Once Erlock had gone back to whatever important things she was doing, Blinky skulked through the throne room and into the library doors, closing them behind her.

"Ah, my wayward bodyguard arrives at last! I hope it was worth nearly getting killed." When Satra saw the look on Blinky's face, she softened. "Are they still alive?"

The owl nodded and explained what had happened with Silver.

"Better they be at Silver's whims than Jonas's," Grenkin said. He'd taken off his eye patch and prosthetics and sat in front of the fire. The prospect of losing the Crackling Sea Eyrie seemed to have aged him ten years.

"Had they been with the other prisoners, they would be safe now," Blinky said. "I do not think I can get them out of New Eyrie. Its walls have grown high, and the forces there increase every day."

Satra joined Grenkin by the fire. If Grenkin looked old, she looked young again, inexperienced. "The sand gryphons are hitting every caravan left unguarded coming down from Whitebeak. I'll ask them to keep an eye out. But if Silver takes them straight to the Argent Heights, we're not going to get an opportunity to retrieve them."

"It is also possible this is Foultner's intent." When neither of them knew what Blinky meant, she clarified. "Foultner is a spy. *Informant* was a strange word to use. She may have intended to get close to Reeve Silver. We should see if she finds a way to send us a message."

Satra slicked back her crest with worry. She'd done this enough that the black dye meant to hide her from assassins had come out, and her tongue was black. "You're right, of course. I hadn't considered that because, well, who brings Henders along for spycraft? But in a sense, it's the perfect cover. She mentioned that Silver was indebted to her, though I never got the details. I suppose we just have to trust this is all part of her plan."

Blinky could not tell if these were hollow words non gryphons used to make each other feel better or if there was truth to them. "Then, for the moment, I will stop trying to rescue her. What do you need done here at the eyrie?"

Satra sighed. "As best we can tell, Jonas is unaware we found his secret passages. Well, at least most of them. We've done our best to trap the most useful ones or barricade them up. Our thinking is this: if he doesn't know which ones are safe and which aren't, he won't feel safe using any of them."

"The next generation of phoenixes has set explosives around the stormcloth curtain fasteners," Grenkin continued. "When we lose the eyrie, we can at least prevent them from raising the barrier and using it in the future. And good luck fetching the curtains out of the water; that took us months the last time. It's not just about making it hard to defend. The storm season is still raging, and it's going to get very wet and very cold without the barrier."

To Blinky's knowledge, *summer storm season* and *winter storm season* took up almost the entirety of the year with a pawful of days on either side, so the distinction wasn't meaningful.

"Right now, the eyrie seems like the safest place. We want to make it close to uninhabitable," Satra concluded.

Blinky couldn't help but notice the use of *when the eyrie fell* instead of *if the eyrie fell.* "You think we will lose it? Then why defend it at all?"

"Pride," Grenkin said. "Maybe shame. Perhaps I just can't stand to think of Jonas walking these halls again. We need time to regroup. I think they're going to find taking the eyrie is easy, but holding it is hard. They're surrounded by enemies on all sides. The autumn harvest has been moved to the weald, and the scribes have deliberately left false documents suggesting the game in the kjarr never recovered from the parasite. Right now, their supplies from up north are flowing freely. When those dry up, we can plan our next move."

Satra stared at her claws. They'd been sharpened with one of the medicine gryphon's stones. "I think the bigger the fight we put up here, the less likely they are to chase us into the taiga and weald. I think every twenty Alabaster Eyrie opinici we kill today saves one of ours tomorrow. But I'd need a larger army to have any hope of defending this place. And I'd need a miracle to hold it if they still have that giant whale on their side."

The door to the library opened, and Erlock led in several visitors. "Actually, I might be able to help with both of those problems. I hope you're decent for guests?"

Grenkin grumbled but put on his eye patch and metal talons. "Who's come so late?"

The first gryphon to step through was Younce, followed by several of the taiga pride. "Satra's already heard this, but I thought I should make this official and let the rest of the Ashen Weald know. The last time the kjarr and weald gryphons asked for our help, we stood back and watched you die, watched your homes burn. This time, we'll stand by your side. We've uncovered dozens of old dens in the taiga, and we've stocked them with supplies for the refugees. And everyone who could be spared is here to fight."

Blinky tended to think ill of Younce but only because of his associations with Ninox. Had he not handed Strix's daughter the Owlfeather—now Dark-feather—Highlands she would have been forced to keep the owl pride together.

Still, Tresh and Thenca both spoke highly of him, and Blinky trusted Sharkbeak's judgement. She had been trying to learn not to fault gryphons for being kind, and access to warm homes in the frozen taiga might be the most valuable contribution to the war effort.

The next gryphon to walk in was particularly surprising, and he was shadowed by several of the Ashen Weald rangers who looked ready to stab him in the back.

"Quite the welcome party you've got going here," Iony rumbled. He had more pink feathers than Blinky remembered, and he looked like he'd been through hell. "Officially, the Blackwing Alliance thinks you brought this on yourself by not joining us. You're bloody idiots for standing alone against the Seraph King, and you're a pain in our southern border, too, if you catch my drift."

Blinky did not.

"But I'd be in a prison right now if not for the Ashen Weald and your free prides." Iony took on a sarcastic tone when he said both. "I don't like being in debt. And when I was told I could either let Younce come bore us to tears with his stories or I could kill a couple of alabaster scum, well, I knew which one I wanted."

Grenkin watched Iony closely. "You didn't bring your unusual nestfellow with you, did you?"

"Rybalt?" The glacier gryphon laughed, his ears wobbling. "No, no. He's not around. This time of year he vacations up north."

"It is a shame," Blinky said, earning her a dirty look from every heron opinicus in the room. "A reeve is holding my friends. I could use an opinicus who assassinates them."

Iony shrugged. "If the opportunity presents itself, I'll do what I can. As it stands, I think you're probably screwed. I've never seen the inside of this place before, I left the sneaky stuff to Rybalt. This eyrie is a trash heap. I've seen gryphlet nests better defended."

Satra started to scold him, but he interrupted her. "But we'll do our best. Now, if you'll excuse me, I need to check on my pride."

From the other room, Blinky caught sight of a large number of long-eared grey gryphons with pink flight feathers. She wondered if that was a fashion thing or if it was their natural plumage.

"Well, that gives us a little more of a fighting edge," Satra said. "That solves all of our problems except one."

Erlock winked at Blinky, then opened the door a final time. In walked Rorin, Tresh, Quess, and a dune fisherfolk. Rorin wore a harness filled to the brim with spears of all shapes and sizes. It seemed unlikely he could fly without them spilling out.

Blinky could only guess that she was seeing Tresh because the petrel's face was covered in a wooden mask with a shark teeth design on the beak. Blinky already knew Tresh had trouble not biting things, and the mask was a nice way to keep her from hurting herself. Next to her was Quess, whom the owl also nearly missed because of how healthy she looked. The penultimate time Blinky had saved her, she'd had silver eyes and was near death. The time after that, she was stabbing Urious through the shoulder.

Blinky wasn't familiar with the blue heron standing with them. She looked Crackling Sea, but her harness was of a fisherfolk design.

Grenkin spat out the water he was drinking. "Gressle? I thought you said you'd never come back."

The heron fisherfolk put on a glare that would freeze even a glacier gryphon in place, but it softened quickly. "I did say that. But times change. What's more, you changed. I heard your speech on the shore, but I wasn't convinced. Then Xalt and Jer came back and said you'd done right by those rangers, and you were doing right by the fisherfolk, and... it's been a long time to hold onto my anger. Besides, you seemed like you could use some help."

"More specifically, you seem like you could use some monster hunters," Tresh said from beneath her mask. "We have a plan to kill the reeve's pet."

Grenkin and Satra looked at Rorin, but he shook his head and pointed down to Quess.

"You're not going swimming with it, are you?" Satra asked. "You can't stand flipper-to-tooth against something so big. The jellies will kill you before you even get the opportunity."

Quess and Tresh looked at each other, but it was Gressle who spoke. "You find where the whale is located tonight, then leave it up to us in the morning. We've got something special planned."

37

MONSTER HUNTERS

Tresh stood in the workshop amidst the red metal cracks and wished she'd chosen a better place for her demonstration. When she'd heard *workshop*, she had been thinking something like the raftworks hangar. She had no idea the strange history of the place.

While they waited for the leaders of the Ashen Weald to assemble, she sat by Urious and looked up at a pair of metal wings.

"Jun the Kjarr's," he explained. "Grenkin didn't gild them, Jonas did. I wish we could bring them home, but where would we put them? Jun's body is lost to sea. His soul can't rest without both pieces."

Tresh thought back to Swan's Rest. That was Rorin's village, his decision, but she resolved herself to seeing Jun's body returned if they survived this.

Satra, Grenkin, a red owl with black underfeathers, and several more important gryphons and opinici gathered in the workshop. Tresh tried not to look at Younce. She knew he would come, that was the sort of gryphon he was, but she hated the thought that one or both of them would die here.

"So what's this weapon you have?" Grenkin asked. "I heard rumors that it was meant to be used against *us,* is that true?"

Rorin laughed, a sound that echoed in the small room, then said a simple, "Yes."

Gressle was dressed as a Crackling Sea ranger. In fact, supposedly they found her old uniform in a storeroom, complete with her favorite pair of metal talons. They shone with jelly toxin in the brazier light.

"Originally," Quess began, "we were working on a way to counteract your greatest weapon, the toxin. A lot of fisherfolk drowned at Sandpiper's Dune because we had no way to fight it. Thankfully, Gressle used to be a ranger, and she had access to all of the medical information of how rangers were treated when they accidentally knocked themselves out cold."

Gressle pretended to slash at Rorin, who played unconscious. "But it didn't really work. Not the way we wanted to. We couldn't prevent the initial loss of consciousness. We tried everything, and the treatments only work to wake up the unconscious. That had limited use if we found ourselves fighting the Crackling Sea a second time."

"Except we ran the tests a few times with different fisherfolk, and we noticed something strange." Quess walked up to Gressle. This time, Gressle actually cut Quess, and the petrel fell unconscious. Younce gasped, but there were already cushions on the ground for just this purpose, so she was unharmed.

Tresh nearly missed her cue but stumbled forwards and went through her pack to find one of the strange containers of ointment. She put it in the wound and along Quess's nares.

Quess stood up again. "How long was I out? Not long?"

Grenkin shook his head. "That's a fast recovery, but I don't see the point of this or how it helps us with the whale."

Quess grinned. "That's what I'm getting at. See, all of this felt fairly useless. But then something happened."

"Actually, I happened." Thankfully the masked covered Tresh's embarrassment. "I woke up from the ointment, then I sat down on the blade we were using to test with."

Quess pointed to a small white scar on Tresh's hindquarters.

"Thing is, I did not fall unconscious again," Tresh said, moving her hindquarters out of view from the gathered group of individuals who had all been staring at her scar.

To illustrate their point, Gressle scratched Quess again, but she just stood there. She even licked the jelly toxin off the talon. "You probably don't know this, but the jelly tastes a little tangy, like craneberry."

Rorin stopped playing dead and stood up again. "Only the petrels have this reaction. It doesn't work for the sandy terns or the cranes. But the immunity lasts a good, long while."

"The reeve's pet, for all of its weird tricks, large size, and bad attitude, is just a whale," Tresh said. "We kill serpentine whales all the time."

"What makes it unique is that it's encased in a swarm of jellies and doesn't like to surface," Quess continued. "Tresh and I can dive down with it, get its attention, and bring it up top where Rorin will be waiting with two flights of sentries."

Rorin nodded at Grenkin. "What's even better is that we can lure it to the island ruins or near the coast here and attach ropes to the javelins. If we get enough into it, we should be able to stop it from diving."

"Even if we fail," Gressle said, carefully removing her toxic weapon, "we can still wound it enough to make it think twice about coming to this side of the sea again. It's an animal. One with limited training, sure, but at the end of the day, it's something we can kill."

"Or make fear us," Tresh added.

The leader of the Crackling Sea looked over the group with pleasant surprise etched on his face and posture. "Word is, our enemy is still trying to fortify the Clover Ranch. They don't seem motivated to come after us for a few days. Erlock's fantails tracked down your whale nearby. I think we can get your ropes and javelins set up within the hour."

"One more thing," Satra said. "This whale loves to spit. I don't know if that's something your ocean whales do, too, but it has enough force to knock a gryphon out of the sky."

"No worries," Rorin said. "We've faced some weird things in our day. You get us set up, and we'll take care of it. Just make sure we don't come under attack before the whale dies."

TRESH AND QUESS waited on the island until everything was ready. The rangers gathered as many ropes and chains as they could locate. With help from the fisherfolk, they were in the process of attaching them to javelins, fishing spears, and Rorin's secret weapon: a thick, metal-tipped harpoon stolen from the abandoned Alabaster Eyrie ship.

The tower ruins rose from the tiny village at the center of the island, reminding Tresh of her last visit here to check on Piprik. Erlock had flown her over, and with rumors of golden pumpkins circulating, Biski had joined them at the last moment. None of them knew what awaited them in the bog.

A light, misty rain began fell. To the north, there were already hints of lightning. That would make weapons slippery and vision a bit blurry, but if the jellies started pulsing, that would help Tresh and Quess navigate underwater.

When Rorin gave the sign, Tresh and Quess both lay down on a cushion and let Gressle cut them with a small toxin-laced knife. The world turned woozy, then grey, then black for Tresh. To the audience last night, the time from cut to regaining consciousness took only seconds. Yet Quess's question about how much time had passed wasn't rhetorical. In actuality, the time under seemed to stretch long enough for dreams—or nightmares.

In this case, it was a bit of both for Tresh. She saw herself and Younce living on an island. Somehow, she knew the mainland was gone now, that even Swan's Rest and Sandpiper's Dune had been razed by the Seraph King's forces. The worst part of it was that they were happy without the Ashen Weald, without eyries, without redwood trees. They were living on the deep islands together.

Then, in the distance, she saw the mast of the

Seraph King's dreadnaught. More sails came into view, hundreds of them.

And then she was conscious again.

"You two doing okay? Nothing feels numb or wrong?" Gressle asked.

Quess stood, then cut herself with the knife a second time. "Still standing. Guess we're good. Tresh?"

Tresh held out her paw to be cut. She wouldn't say she felt okay, but she felt as good as she'd expected to. They'd run a few trial runs in shallow water, but this would be their first time testing the limits of the immunity.

There was one more thing they hadn't taken into account. The jelly toxin the rangers used was diluted, but Tresh and Quess were about to leap into an entire swarm. They walked to the shoreline and waited for lightning. The skies were only grey, not black, but the water still lit up in response.

Tresh stuck her forelegs in the water and pulled out a jelly, holding it in her paws. It sparkled angrily in defiance at being lifted from its watery habitat.

"Okay, that's one way to do it. Now, give it a big kiss and toss it back," Gressle said.

Tresh did not oblige with the first part, but she returned it to the sea. The plan was for her to go in first so Quess could pull her out if she got light-headed. It'd be dangerous, but most things were.

"The beast should be somewhere in this swarm," Rorin shouted from overhead. "The fantails say it spat at them and dove down west of here, moving in our direction. Just follow the jellies, and you'll run into it eventually."

Tresh nodded and waited for the next lightning

strike. All along the shore of the island ruins were small mounds of sand. It was strange, she hadn't seen them here on her last visit. She wondered what caused them.

Probably something that bites. Perhaps leafcutter ants have taken over the island.

The sky flashed blue-green, electricity charging the air around her, and a moment later the entire sea pulsed in response.

She'd heard that with the reeve's pet running wild, the jelly swarms had spawned out of control. What she didn't expect was to see the entire bay from the Crackling Sea Eyrie out to the island light up. She felt like she was standing on the moon.

She didn't have time for stargazing, however, and she took a plunge into the bright water. Below the surface, she could make out the rocky coastline and a few features. The jelly light faded before she found the monster, so she contented herself with testing the potency of the pure toxins and getting a feel for the water.

Something that always surprised her about the Crackling Sea was that the water was salty. It wasn't the same salinity as the ocean, but it still made her cuts burn. The inland body of water felt like an oversized lake here on its southern tip, but it stretched far north. Now that she had a workaround for the jelly toxin, she hoped to someday swim around the entire thing with Quess.

Quess, who is still bragging about getting to swim Glacial Run. As if I did not fall in and do the same thing as a gryphlet!

Brief flashes gave her more glimpses of the aquatic world around the eyrie, a side of it no blue heron had likely ever seen. Long strands of seaweed made visibility hard even with the bioluminescence. She wove between them, finding some had been nibbled on. As was her fate since gryphlethood, she kept an eye for crabs of unusual size. She'd done her best to talk to the fishers in the area, but they didn't think with the bottom of the sea in mind.

The floor had barren areas, cleared out by lobsters, it seemed, but several types of mussels had taken root, and below Tresh was a carpet of sharp shells. She made her way up for air, signaled to Quess that everything was okay, and then descended again, bumping into a shell of another type.

The sea turtle was different than the ones Tresh was used to. Ocean sea turtles sometimes grew even larger than the matamata, though they lacked their bog cousin's bad attitude. This one was much smaller, perhaps the size of Quess, though on the next flash of lightning she saw several that were a little bigger than her weaving through the weeds.

To her surprise, they weren't chewing on the seaweed, lobsters, or even the small fish darting between them. Instead, they fed on the crackling jellies.

She followed them for a few minutes, trying to keep track of where she was in relation to Rorin and Gressle. The swarm moved past the seaweed, past the sharp-shelled mussels. All she saw beneath her was a dark form, perhaps a rock formation or some other type of shell or coral.

When the lightning next hit, she recognized something was wrong with the shape below her. Part of it had moved. As a series of fast strikes lit up the water in succession, she watched as the *ground* rose, catching one of the large sea turtles in its mouth and swimming towards the surface with it.

Of course! The reeve's pet stays with the jelly swarms to catch the turtles that feed on them. Which is why the swarms have grown so much.

She followed after it, Quess coming in from the other direction, and watched the whale breach and toss the turtle into the air.

It landed back on the water with a crack, its soft shell unable to handle the impact. The whale took only a few minutes to chew on its meal before going under, but that was enough time for Quess to let out an *oo-awk* to signal Rorin.

Quess stayed behind and just above the whale, mindful of its tail. Serpentine whales were a little tricky, as their body shape tended to writhe through the water instead of depending only on the up-and-down motion of their tails. Indeed, they seemed to use their side flippers for steering or crawling on land to chase prey more than for locomotion.

Tresh took a different approach from her brother's mate. When the sea next lit up, she located a large, older turtle that was having trouble swimming. The perfect bait. The whale slowly wove through the reeds, starting to circle back. Unbeknownst to it, a diving petrel, nimble even underwater, doubled back and found an intercept course.

Sea turtles weren't the speediest of prey, and the whale took its time. Tresh swam up below it, building speed. Just as the reeve's pet opened its mouth to grab its snack and fling it at the surface, Tresh crashed into its nose and began slashing with her claws.

The whale let out a pitiful sound, then an angry

sound, and rose to the surface with incredible speed for its size. When it breached this time, it flung Tresh off, likely think it was done with her.

Tresh, however, was ready. She used the momentum to circle back around, and this time she flung herself at its eyes.

It closed them and went underwater again, but Tresh held on tight. Whenever she found an opportunity, she harassed the whale, trying to convince it that it wasn't safe underwater.

The serpentine whale wove back the other way, towards the island, and Quess waited. She'd taken several fishing spears, tied to ropes up top, and loosely wedged them between the mussels for easy access.

As the whale came by the first time, she stabbed one into its stomach. It writhed and let out a stream of bubbles, giving Quess time to put two more spears into it before it decided it was safer at the water's surface.

For the moment, the opinici on the shore let the rope run loose. A serpentine whale could easily pull out one spear and the hook it was connected to. The time to try to rein it in was when it had a dozen spears sticking out of it.

Tresh held on tight as the whale splashed out of the water a third time, not wanting to get flung. But when she crashed onto the surface, she saw a javelin coming right for her, and she leapt off lest she be impaled to the beast.

"Sorry!" Rorin shouted after Tresh. He wasn't expecting her to be on the serpentine whale's nose when it surfaced, and he'd nearly skewered his best friend.

The mounts on the eyrie side were sturdier than those on the island, but very rarely did monster hunting go as he wanted. He'd learned to make the most of it.

His first spear had gone wide, clipping the monster's forehead, but his next spear caught it by the left flipper. Overhead, his sentries did their best to keep up, landing several more. Rangers flew the ropes to the island and secured them to stone ruins.

In the rain, one of the cranes next to Rorin was starting to lose the red paint splashed on her chest. She'd scored three of her javelins in the creature, but she'd forgotten about Satra's warning.

The whale wheeled around, spitting a stream of high-powered water at the sentries, knocking four of them out of the sky. Rorin caught the one next to him by the harness before she landed in the waves. The rangers, already aware of the danger, swooped down to catch the others.

"How're you holding up?" he asked the fisherfolk in his grasp.

She shook her head. "Packs a strong punch. I wasn't expecting that. You can let go now. I need some time to clear the water out of my brain, but I can help with the ropes until then."

He released his grip and watched her glide to the island. Already, teams of feathermanes pulled on the ropes, forcing the monster on land. The creature didn't seem to realize the danger this put it in. As Rorin knew from his past exploits, these creatures were happy to leave the water behind if you made them angry enough.

The trick was keeping them on land.

He pulled out three more harpoons, already prepared with a leather strap to give himself extra leverage, and tried to hit the creature's tail. He scored hits with two, and rangers swooped in to take the ropes and secure them to the island. Then he moved to the front and started shouting to get its attention.

The whale crawled onto the shore using its large, clawed flippers and chased Rorin to the ruined tower.

Mindful of what happened to his sentries, Rorin ducked behind a stone pillar before the next jet of water came. Quess and Tresh were both back on land now, and they took turns dashing in to scratch at it with sharpened claws, dancing out again when it swung its tail at them.

Rorin tossed two more spears, flimsy bamboo things, nearly catching it in the eye. It turned and focused its watery stream at him again, but he was on top of the tower ruins now. The scorch marks up top had been cleared near where the Ashen Weald had transformed it into a place to hold rabid starlings, and he used the stairwell to protect himself.

When the whale ran out of water and the spitting stopped, it crawled to the tower, curling around it and pulling it down with its massive flippers.

This was the moment he had been waiting for. More harpoons hit it from all sides, and the rangers began securing the ropes to every edge of the island, effectively trapping it in the very center.

Finally realizing the danger, the whale tried to untangle itself and move back to sea, but the spears attached to the other side of the island held. Several rangers and sentries working together brought in a large, sharp harpoon they'd salvaged off the Seraph King's escort ship.

They flew towards the monster, and on the count of three, they let go. The harpoon caught the whale on the back of the neck, killing it quickly. If there was one thing Rorin hated, it was to see an animal suffer.

Once they were fairly sure it was dead, he flew back down to look it over. He'd seen serpentine whales before. The smaller ones enjoyed the waters off the ocean side of Luminaire. This beast, however, had grown large without any competition.

Its indigo skin matched the rocks and water of the sea. Whether it had been born immune to the jellies or developed immunity over time, Rorin didn't know how to find out without tossing a new baby whale in to see what happened.

A crust had formed over most of the beast, giving it an outer layer of sharp-shelled mussels. Fully half of the harpoons his sentries had thrown at it had bounced off the mussels. It was an unusual kind of living armor.

Tresh flew up next to him, and Grenkin joined them.

"It's strange to think of it as gone," he said. "The reeve's pet has been living in the sea for longer than I've been a ranger."

One of the blue opinici touched the body of the whale, not realizing it had spent its life swimming through swarms of jellies, and collapsed on the ground, causing Tresh to snort.

Rorin shot her a glance. They were here to help, not aggravate.

"What?" Tresh said. "It is funny when it happens to them. You cannot tell me it is not funny, pride leader."

Grenkin sighed. "I think you've earned your laughter. Maybe we can see about having your petrels clear the body while we keep watch for the Seraph King's forces. I can't help but notice the design of the large spear. Where did it come from?"

"We pulled it from one of their ships," Rorin said. "I'm not sure how it's supposed to be used, but I thought we could figure something out."

Now that the danger was over, or at least this particular danger, the skies outside the Crackling Sea were full of blue herons shouting their approval.

Rorin started to reach a talon towards the whale's face, then remembered the slime and thought better of it. "I'm glad we could help. I wish the battle that lies ahead were similarly easy."

"Easy?" Tresh shook her mask. "I was almost sucked up its nostril! Not to mention the spears raining down from above. You were not down in the water with it, Rorin Fish-dropper. There was nothing easy about it."

Grenkin laughed. "Well, while we figure out what to do with a dead, toxic whale, may I recommend a bath and some food? Anything you'd like, just tell the chef, and if we have it, we'll make it happen."

Tresh perked up. Swimming always took a lot out of her, but Rorin already understood why Grenkin had a smirk on his face.

"I'm going to assume all of the good food has already been moved to the weald?" he asked.

Grenkin grinned. "Oh, I don't know. Fish jerky has always been a favorite of mine. Based on how much of it gets stolen by Blinky, I'm not alone in that assessment. Now, go and rest. We'll figure the rest of this out. And tell Quess and my cousin that they did a good job here.

"I already know that!" Gressle shouted from down the whale. "I don't need you to tell me."

Grenkin and Gressle went off to chat about old times, and Rorin settled down next to Tresh.

"It's been a strange journey, hasn't it?" he asked.

She nodded. "Are you staying or going? It is not sea monsters we next face."

He looked to the eyrie. He couldn't tell if he was seeing Younce or not, but several taiga gryphons flew around the cliffs. "I'll stay. I assume you're staying for Younce, yes? I've seen how you two operate. One of you will summon sea monsters, the other can't swim. You need me to keep you out of trouble.

Tresh made a *tsk* sound from under her mask, but she nuzzled Rorin. "Speaking of Younce, I suppose now is as good an opportunity as any to spend time with him. There may not be a chance tomorrow."

Rorin nodded, but there was an extra layer of meaning behind those words. It wasn't just about time management. Any of them could die before this ended.

38

LOVERS ON THE SEA

Tresh dripped water through Mia's chambers—previously Grenkin's chambers—as she looked for the heated pool. Mia was busy with preparations, mostly trapping ways in and out of the eyrie, but had mentioned *hot* water as a good way to get the toxin out of Tresh's fur and feathers before the immunity wore out.

It was good thinking, and Tresh was glad she wouldn't randomly fall over from some poison trapped under her nails or such, but Mia kept hinting at something more.

"You know, so *Younce* doesn't fall over," Mia said with a sigh.

Tresh hadn't thought of that. She soaked until she no longer ached, using some of Biski's soap on her fur to be extra safe. At least, she thought it was soap. As with most things Biski had created that involved chemicals, there was always a chance Tresh could end up pink.

She didn't bother to dry off, instead walking through the corridors of the Crackling Sea sopping wet. She'd gone up a few stories before she realized she was lost. It was pretty easy to get from the main, open area with the balconies to a specific location, but the ranger lord's chambers were near the bottom of the eyrie, and she was so deep she started looking for a way out to fly to somewhere she recognized when she heard a familiar voice shouting for her.

"Hey Tresh!" Younce shouted. "I saw your fight with the whale. That was really impressive. You weren't hurt, were you?"

"Of course not," she replied. "How did you find me?"

He pointed at the trail of water forming a map of her wanderings. "I was just coming from the butchery with some food and happened to see it. So I went back for more food. Want to come back to my quarters for dinner?"

She nodded, sniffing at his harness to try to figure out what he had to eat, and followed him through a stairwell she hadn't even seen that went deep into the earth, then back again to just a small stone window she would barely have been able to squeeze through, then back into the earth, and then into the quarters where the taiga prides were stationed.

"How do you find your way around here?" she asked. "Without the sky or sea, I mean."

Younce shrugged, pushing open the door to the common area. Many rooms had some sort of barrier to keep water out. "I don't know. I guess I got used to sneaking around Snowfall's caverns with Zeph and Mignet, trying to hide from Deracho when we played games. It gave me a good head for these things."

When her old fluffy taiga mate had invited her back to his quarters, she'd been expecting something a little more intimate. Snowfall had been built to accommodate a large pride. Many of its caves were closed up or converted into storage, and every taiga gryphon had a very private room to themselves.

That wasn't the case in the Crackling Sea. They were sleeping two to a nest, and there weren't *rooms* plural. There was just one big, open area.

"I'm over here." He swished his tail, and she caught it in her beak lightly. It was how he'd used to show her through Snowfall's caverns so she didn't get lost. She hadn't realized how much she'd missed this.

While most of the nests were on the floor, one had been placed atop a large crate that smelled of salt. He climbed and settled in, trying to make room for her, but his thick coat filled up more than half the space.

She tossed his tail over the edge, kneaded against his stomach to push down the fur, and found her own space. Younce—and probably all taiga gryphons, though she didn't have experience there—seemed to take up a lot of space, but it was entirely fluff. If you were willing to push the fur and tail aside, the gryphon underneath was actually fairly small. In fact, as much as Younce looked larger than Tresh or his nestmate Zeph, Tresh wondered if that would hold true were he to let one of the rangers shave him.

Younce licked a paw, pushing the stray fur down around his ears, then tried to find his harness under all of the fluff.

Tresh laughed, a sound she hadn't made for days, and finally told him to stop. She placed her paws on one of the visible straps, then traced it to his side to find the pouch. Inside were several seaweed wraps.

"What is inside them?" she asked.

Younce shrugged. "I don't know. I just grabbed whatever I could get. Really, I arrived at the same time as Biski, and she started stuffing things in my harness when Soft Paws distracted the chef. Those two are becoming real padfeet the longer they stay here, it sounds like."

"I miss Biski. She does not return to the shore." Tresh poked a claw at one of the wraps, then stuffed the whole thing in her beak. The seaweed had a hint of salt, though it wasn't as bad as she was expecting. *They must soak it in freshwater first.* Inside, she tasted lobster, though it wasn't quite the same texture as she was used to. There was a little more spice on it, something she couldn't name.

Younce put one into his beak, then coughed when it hit his tongue. His eyes watered. "Maybe skip the ones that smell like radish."

Tresh laughed again, surprising herself. Curled up in a nest with just the two of them in a chamber full of other gryphons, she felt like...

A gryphon. This is what gryphons do.

Her mother and father had always been very keen on living in a nice bamboo home that didn't leak during the summer storms and stayed dry even in high tide. Tresh's mother often wove things with her talons, baskets or such, and later Quess filled that role with her woodcarving skills. Even Tresh's brother had been good with his talons. They loved their cushions, often purchased from Gressle at a hefty mark-up, and all the little trinkets they acquired from the eyrie.

That had never quite felt right to Tresh. Even with gryphons all around her, something about this nest in the corner felt private, intimate. She could still hear others talking, telling stories, sharing food.

"So I look down between my paws, and there's this eel the size of a megapede looking back up at me, and at first, I think I'm seeing..." Iony was saying in the distance.

Despite the chaos, it was nice. Pleasant. She curled up against Younce's warmth and closed her eyes. Everything she'd done as a gryphlet or fledgling, her father had insisted she use her beak, not her paws. She'd never given it much consideration. She'd thought then they were just trying to train her to reuse her beak after all the damage it had sustained.

Now, she realized that when they told her not to use her paws while they all used their talons, it felt like they wanted her to act more like an opinicus. To stop being a gryphon. At least, that's how she'd heard it.

"Are you okay?" Younce asked, putting a warm, dry wing over her still-wet form. "Sorry, I know this isn't the greatest place. But it's warm, and it has food. And I'm here."

"It is perfect," she said with a purr. "Can we spend the rest of the day here?"

Younce cautiously took a nibble out of another seaweed wrap, then made a face and put it aside before trying another. The next one seemed satisfactory, and he passed it along to Tresh to try.

"Of course," he said. "The day and the night, if you want."

She suspected Quess or Rorin would need her for something before the sky turned dark, but it was a nice thought. "Yes, I would like that."

Then she looked up at Younce's pretty green eyes, the first hints of blue ice upon them, and when he opened his beak and started to say, "I lov—" she shook as hard as she could, shaking off all of the hot water from the ranger lord's pool and transferring most of it to Younce.

"It is nice to be dry again." She reached up with her mouth took the last seaweed wrap out of Younce's stunned beak, and immediately her tongue started to burn.

Radish.

CIELLE SAT atop the crow's nest, looking out upon the ocean. Wind whisked past his ears, one covered in a small bandaged protector to keep him from chewing at his stitches. Every so often, he flew up, looked around, and made sure they were back on course. Usually, just being up high gave him enough of a view to see his usual long-distance sea flight markers, but a few times he'd had to fly off in different directions to see which islands were nearby, then return to report to the shipwright.

"Never knew anything was out here," the black crane grumbled. "I mean, I knew things were out here. Just not what they were."

The Williwaw gryphon grinned. "Wait until you see The Wrecks. They're amazing. There's crashed ships everywhere! You're going to love it."

The shipwright didn't look nearly as excited as Cielle had hoped he would, presumably because he'd spent his entire life attempting to keep ships afloat.

"Oh." Cielle blushed at the nares. "Don't worry, I

know how to get you in safely. Actually, we can put the anchor thing down outside of the atoll, then I'll have my moms guide you through."

The shipwright nodded and went back to captaining the ship, leaving Cielle to take a break for a bit. The ship had left Sandpiper's Dune full of fisherfolk, but they'd dropped most of them off on their island homes.

The Crane's Nest fisherfolk were having a bit of a crisis about their living arrangements, and it looked like the group might splinter further. Many of them were happy to live on their island again, in spite of their kidnapping. Some were ready to go back to shore. Others wanted to move islands, to try to set up a new village on Ashfoot Isle.

Cielle had done his best to dissuade that lot from their choice. It was a pretty island, it had fresh water, it was a great place to take a nap on the way to shore—yet it had little cover, and anything bigger than a thunderstorm would be dangerous to weather there. While one or two were going to set up a small building there and see what happened to it after a couple of storms hit it, others hopped back on the ship and set sail for The Wrecks.

There were two small oddities. Two salt traders happened to be searching the Crane's Nest homes for signs of their occupants when the ship rolled up. Once they saw it was fisherfolk, they happily climbed aboard. After a few questions, Cielle confirmed they were the same duo Rorin and Tresh had recommended he talk to: Pip and Lei.

Pip gave Cielle a fright with his pale plumage and dark circle patterns around his eyes, but the others reassured him that Pip was good.

"Don't you look familiar?" the shipwright had said, but he admitted his eyesight wasn't the best.

Pip had shrugged. "I used to do a brisk trade in apples up by Reevesport. Perhaps you've had some of my famous blue cider?"

The black crane had harrumphed and said he must have mistaken Pip with someone else.

Lei, however, was a bundle of energy and happiness. He liked to fly up with Cielle and try to keep pace when the Williwaw gryphon made his rounds. Peacocks weren't known for being the best flyers, but Lei took to it like he was making up for lost time.

As happy as the trip was for Cielle, there was one part that made him a little sad. Pumpkin, it turned out, got seasick while on a ship. The obvious solution, to take turns flying until it wore off, didn't seem to help. It was more about the motion of the choppy waves on the sea.

Cielle went below deck with a hug of water so Pumpkin could rinse out his beak. "We're just about there. Just a little longer."

Pumpkin looked miserable, but Cielle had to trust that when they reached The Wrecks, and he felt solid ground under his legs again, he'd perk up.

And, in fact, they should be reaching The Wrecks any time now. The first signs they were close were several Williwaw gryphons and opinici, their tails like streamers beneath them, in the sky. They were rightfully wary, so Cielle flew up and shouted a greeting. They still kept their distance, but not long after, Cielle's parents appeared in the sky, flying towards him.

"Moms!" he laughed. "It's so good to see you!"

They followed him down to the ship, where he

introduced everyone except Pumpkin. He would rather they wait and see his new mate in better form.

His moms had been worried when he was a little late getting home, worry that now transferred to his sail-fin-chewed ear, but they had never guessed the adventures he'd been on. They welcomed the Crane's Nest villagers. While his home's name suggested a small island with a bit of coral around it, The Wrecks was larger than Luminaire, as several of his new friends were experiencing for the first time.

Cielle's moms guided the ship. Getting to the island was generally easier, as they could build up a bit of speed, time it with a calm moment on the waves, and get through the small break in the reef. Getting out was going to be more difficult if the winds weren't in an obliging mood.

Only once they reached the island did Cielle go below decks to fetch Pumpkin, who had already perked up a bit when the ship stopped moving. Cielle helped him reapply his paint, and by the time the bog witch had stepped paw on the island, he was back to his happy, chipper self.

"Is that a volcano?" Lei asked. "How did a volcano get all the way out here?"

Pip dropped down with his medicine bag. "Lava plumes. Read that somewhere. Could happen to anyone, at any time. Can't be trusted."

"You said volcanic ash caused the Connixation," Lei pressed. "Is this the volcano that did it?"

Cielle laughed. "It can't be. Our ancestors were fleeing the Connixation when we arrived here. It must have come from the other direction."

The beach was beautiful, though the water was cold.

He was used to swimming in it even this chilly, but he suspected Pumpkin might prefer the hot springs. Though that would mean having to reapply the bog markings again after.

Hmmm. Perhaps I should ask my moms about pigments from the island. Pumpkin would like that. He might find some colors they don't have back at Bogwash.

The trees on the island were a mix of aneda, a few stray redwoods, blue cedar, and several different types of bamboo that fought for control over the north and west sides.

Cielle took everyone on a tour while his village prepared food. The southern section of the island, where the aneda and blue cedar had taken root, was frozen most of the year. Some of the heat from the volcano kept the west side pleasant, and as Cielle led them through the bamboo forests, roaming packs of capybaras passed them by.

"They're so tame," Pumpkin said. "They're not like the ones in the bog at all."

Lei petted one on the head. "Maybe they're a different type. Where do the capybaras come from, Pip?"

The medicine opinicus shrugged. "We'll have to discover that on our own one day. It might be easier if we knew what direction the ships from The Wrecks were going when they found this island."

Partway up the volcano on the northern side was Cielle's village. Well, calling it a village was misleading. No one knew how several boats had made it so high up the mountains, but they were frozen there, or so the story went. When Cielle was a gryphlet, he'd assumed Tielle and Golrin Goldpaw had pulled the ships out of the water and secured them to the side of the mountain to make nests and a living area.

It wasn't until after he'd fledged that he realized how silly that was. Instead, they'd been discovered in the snowy peaks, then secured in case they ever melted. Over time, several albino peafowl opinici had scavenged wood from the beach and used it to build boardwalks between the various wrecks.

A low mist came in from the sea, and Cielle grew excited. Mist was the best time to see his home. "Let's wait here with the capybaras for a few minutes. I want to make sure they have time up top to make food for everyone!"

In truth, he waited for the mists to fill the bottom of the island, but it gave Cielle and Pumpkin a chance to answer Pip and Lei's questions about what had happened at Bogwash.

"I'm glad Tresh and Rorin are safe," Lei said. "I miss both of them."

There was a strange edge, perhaps bitter sadness, to the young peacock's words, but Cielle didn't know enough to ask more. Pip was also a mystery, but now that Cielle had them both on his island, he was going to find out everything he could about them.

The mist was thick as soup when Cielle said it was time to fly and guided everyone out of the bamboo and up to his homes. The *oooooo* and *aaaaaa* reactions were well worth it. With the mist beneath the village, the repurposed buildings looked like ships floating on a sea of clouds.

While he hadn't been told to sell the Crane's Nest refugees on staying at the island, he was still pleased by the gleam in their eyes as they ate and looked out at the mist. Lei's excitement was enough for him and Pip, which also made Cielle happy.

Best of all, though, was Pumpkin—Cielle's moms were already stuffing him full of fish and berries and talking about the colors of the flowers in the spring.

Cielle landed next to them. He ate a little, but mostly he just watched. He was glad to be home, and he was glad to have someone with him. Poor Pumpkin would probably get more attention than he wanted for the first few weeks, but he'd settle in over time.

This was a happy place, a sanctuary, and having gone to the mainland, Cielle appreciated it so much more than he had growing up here.

And yet, he found himself looking north, in the direction he thought the Crackling Sea was located. There was still so much more out there, and he wanted to get a chance to see it.

Tomorrow, he thought. It was a word with two meanings out here. Tomorrow could mean the next day, but it could also mean someday after it. The first gryphons and opinici who had arrived here fleeing the Connixation had said they would return home *tomorrow*. And then they had stayed, that tomorrow reaching out into the infinite.

Cielle wouldn't wait as long. When the cold weather ended, he was going back to the mainland. And until then, he was going to cuddle Pumpkin and get as much information out of Pip and Lei as they were willing to share.

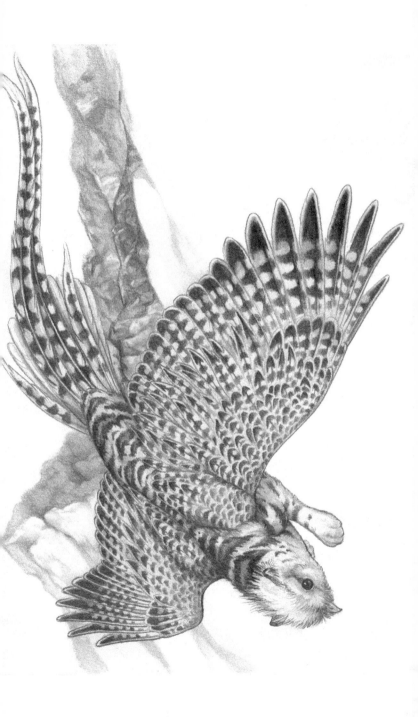

39

FRIENDS IN THE FOREST

Zeph wandered through Poisonmaw. While he thought of the old nesting grounds as his real home, he'd become fairly cozy up here, when he wasn't on the shore or taiga or getting into trouble with Kia and Cherine.

The copper hawk glided around, making sure everything had been picked up. The goal was that if any of the Seraph King's forces came through the valley, it wouldn't be obvious there was a pride living there. Currently, however, there were huts, nests, a dam, and a section for drinking water. Some of those would stay, their use disguised, like the dam. Others would be removed entirely.

Hatzel's pride had once been thirty gryphons strong, all magpies and copper hawks except for their leader. But with so many refugees, both gryphons who had protested the formation of the Ashen Weald and opinici fleeing the Redwood Valley's underbough, there were now around four times that number living here.

Living here—and now being moved into caves.

Poisonmaw had a few cave systems, many of which required monitor removal services first. There were probably more they hadn't located. It was said that the original saberbeak pride was able to fill the skies above the valley, then vanish without a trace. Unfortunately, while Hatzel had been born here, she didn't have more than a pawful of memories about it.

Which was exciting for Zeph. It meant he could feel productive while exploring. He'd already located one cave—full of snakes, Xavi's favorite—and he rushed back to tell Hatzel.

"Heya, copper hawk." The saberbeak beckoned him towards the entrance to The Crawl, a partially-underground passage that led from Poisonmaw to the weald, coming out at the Summer Falls. "We're trying to figure out our living quarters. Will you require an extra-large nest? Or is it just you this winter?"

He rolled his eyes at the question. While it was rude to ask a gryphon about their mate, most gryphons had subtle ways of finding out details that avoided coming out and just asking. "It's just me. How bad is the nesting situation?"

"Since we don't want anyone staying in a cave that's easy to stumble across, it's going to be tricky for a while," Hatzel said.

"I don't mind staying with you." When one of the saberbeak gryphlets ran by, he realized he was being presumptuous. "Assuming you don't need a, er, extra-large nest, too."

She raised an eyecrest. "I'm a little busy to go running off to visit someone in another pride this season. Sure, you can stay with me. It'll be like old times."

Old times meant *before the fire,* going back to when they were both young members of the pride. It was strange to think of all that had happened. For years, he'd felt immune to time's passing. Then the fire hit, and they all caught up to him.

"They're cleaning out the spiders from my cave as we speak. Just head down, first on the left," Hatzel said. "I'll tell them you're staying with me."

"Oh, how the opinici will talk." He dodged her large paw and padded away from The Crawl. "I'll go get my things."

ZEPH FLEW past several deconstructed huts and looked for the pile where he'd put his travelling harness. He didn't really hang onto any material goods anymore. He'd rather travel light. But Kia had given him a new harness with pockets for his hat, and he wanted to make sure he knew where his things were located if he was going to do more travel.

Oh right, the pile by the waterfall.

He flew over the bathing pools, waving to Xavi, Pink Paw, and Cherine, who were deep in conversation. They didn't see Zeph, which was fine. He'd catch up with everyone later.

He landed and searched for the packs. *I think mine was hanging from a tree.* His memory was correct, and under that tree was Kia.

"Hey Zeph, how's it hopping?" She put her journal down to try and searched her packs for an inkwell. "I wish I'd thought to stock up on ink when we were at Crestfall. Hoppy looted every bottle he could find and was emptying the ink to sell the glass. It was the good, archival-quality stuff, too. I told him to hang onto any more he found, and I'd pay him more than the glass was worth."

"I'm doing well," Zeph confirmed. "I'm just here to find my harness so I can move into my new quarters. I'm just inside The Crawl on the left."

"Right next to Hatzel?" Kia asked.

He nodded. "Yep. Right next to Hatzel."

Kia stood and stretched her talons. When she reached back for her journal, several wingless bugs hopped off it. "Wait, come back, I need to sketch you!"

Zeph laughed. "They're springtails. You can sketch them any time."

"How? I've never seen them before, and I've been here long enough to have named every tree and fern." Unlike Zeph, Kia had been splitting her time between the Crackling Sea and New Eyrie when she returned from the desert. She'd been reunited with her family, and she said she was trying to spend as much time as she could with Olan before bloodbeak made it too hard for him to speak.

Zeph understood but made sure she knew she was always welcome here. "Is your ink dry? Grab your journal and a pen and follow me. You're used to seeing the tops of the redwood trees or looking up at them from below, right?"

"Sure." Kia flipped a few pages back, showing off her sketches of lace monitors, ground parrots, capybaras, and even something called a slime monitor. "I've catalogued most of it by now. Pink Paw was nice enough to catch the flying squirrels and snakes for me, in addition to the usual grounded fare."

"The forests up here have more layers than just the ground and where the flying squirrels roost. Think of the redwood forest like Cherine's cooking." Zeph could never remember the names of foods, just how they tasted. "You know, when they're layered."

She laughed. "Yes, I got that."

Zeph beckoned for her to follow him. He could easily climb up with his paws, but it was tricky for Kia with only her wings once things became dense. The canopy of Poisonmaw was thicker than the Redwood Valley by virtue of having had long stretches of time without gryphons here to clear them out while hunting.

He had her land on a sturdy branch, big enough for a Hatzel to lie across its width, and then he pointed to the other side of the tree. "Keep quiet, and don't do any flapping unless you fall. Just climb up and look over the top. Here, I'll give you a steppingstone."

Zeph ascended halfway around the trunk, between the two branches, and held on tight with his claws and dewclaws. Kia reached out, catching his shoulder with her talons to judge the distance, then she stepped with her back paw and put it on his head, using his face as leverage to reach a higher branch, then swung herself around. She found an offshoot to hang onto.

He climbed up higher, then turned around and climbed down beak-first so he could watch her excitement. "Take a look. What do you see?"

She lifted her eyes above the top of the branch and gasped with delight.

He liked seeing her this way, as a scholar learning something new. The branches were so wide, so long, and so deep that they supported their own ecosystems. High altitude ferns took root, turned the redwood bark into soil, and then more plants and moss built up along them. Within that dirt, there were a lot of different animals. Gliding snakes and squirrels, sure, but there were also small, flightless bugs—springtails—and even more exciting creatures.

Kia pulled herself up and lodged herself between the branch and trunk so she could use her talons to draw. She nearly slipped off once, so he crawled down so she could lean on him. She'd sketched a dozen bugs before she noticed something was feeding on them.

"Is that a lizard?" she asked. The creature *was* lizard-shaped. It had long teeth and claws, but pale, wet skin.

"Nope, it's a newt," he explained. "Their long claws let them climb up here. You never see them on the ground."

She shook her head. "But they need water, right? Where do they find it up here? Is the moss enough?"

Zeph crawled over to the fern. Some of its leaves formed scoops that captured water, and he pulled one back, then let it spring back into place. Several angry frogs chirped at him, and when one tried to leap away, he caught it in his paws. "Here's another one for you to draw."

Kia spent the rest of the light sketching in her book, writing down Zeph's descriptions of each fauna and whether or not it could be found higher or lower in the forest. He was content to serve as her armrest and occasional table as she switched from creatures to the plants and ferns that only lived in the heights.

"We could spend a year doing this, and I'd never tire of it," she said as they lost the light. "That would be an incredible year."

Zeph carefully pulled just one paw off the tree and

stretched his claws before swapping to another leg. Once they were all done, he showed her how to glide back to the forest floor.

"We should definitely do that!" he said. "Maybe next year, if things settle down. Or maybe one day, we can visit the entire continent. Once the yolkbloom grows back, we should be able to get into the Emerald Jungle, if we can get invited. Can you imagine what interesting things are there to catch there?"

Catch and eat.

"Actually, I've been thinking, and I have an idea where we can find yolkbloom. The old botanical garden was full of both the vine and its seeds. We should search the ruins, see if we get lucky and some of them germinated after the fire." She tapped the tip of her beak, leaving a slight ink smear he didn't tell her about. "You know, a year together sounds a lot like my offer earlier."

It took Zeph a moment to remember her *offer* to spend a full year together, mating season and off-season, said in a joking manner. He was surprised to find himself blushing. "Well, I think this winter we're stopping an invasion. How about next year?"

"It's a promise." She held out her talons the way opinicus merchants did, and he took it with his paw. When he pulled it back, he saw that his paw pads were now stained with ink.

Kia looked down at her pen, which was dripping ink. "Oh, shoot. I think this quill pen has just about had it."

She tried wiping her talons off on the bark, and he reached up and wiped his paw, leaving two marks there. "Stay put! I have some oil that'll get the ink off."

While Kia flew off, Zeph stared up at the paw and talon print on the tree. *Was she just kidding? Or...?*

He shook his head. Those were thoughts for later. Right now, he needed to get his paws clean and his things moved into Hatzel's room.

CHERINE'S FACE WAS UNDERWATER, but his eyes were open, watching the clear depths for a sign of dinner. The light was almost gone, but there was a slight glint off his beak.

A large fish face appeared before him, attracted to the sparkle, and he lashed out with both talons, grabbing it and tossing it onto shore, where Pink Paw waited.

"See?" he told Xavi. "Nothing to it."

The magpie laughed, both at Cherine's unusual fishing method and Pink Paw groaning at how full her stomach was with fish. "Did they teach you that at Crestfall?"

Cherine shook his head. "They don't do much fishing in Crestfall except at the start of spring when the flood season starts. I'm not sure where I picked that one up. Probably washing my face one morning."

Pink Paw looked up at the dying light. "We need to check on Xin, our eldest. He's been spending a lot of time alone, and I don't want him to forget what it's like to be around other gryphons."

"And opinici," Xavi hastened to add. "We mean no offense, we're just getting used to all of the non gryphons in the pride."

Cherine dried off and put his harness back on. "No offense taken. Besides, I'm a sand gryphon now."

Pink Paw led the way. Her eldest son had lost most of his sight to the initial attack on the weald, and he preferred spending time in the medicine gryphon caves. Eventually, they'd found him a cave of his own along The Crawl. "You could have been part of Hatzel's pride. You certainly spent enough time here before Ninox whisked you off."

"Or a Strix gryphon. Er, opinicus," Xavi corrected. "Do they call you a sand gryphon or a sand opinicus? How does that work?"

Cherine tried to explain it as they entered The Crawl. "Sponge says sand gryphon, but every so often, Hoppy will shout something like '*And we have our own metal opinicus!*' at some random passerby."

This particular offshoot went a good distance back, giving Cherine flashbacks to his time in Merin's prison. He wished he'd brought a lantern with him. They could steal a few braziers out of the wreckage of the Redwood Valley, but that probably defeated the point of hiding. There was a small crack in the corridor that let a little light down, though judging by the pieces of wood and long leaves, the plan was to seal those up.

Several old taiga storm barriers covered in moss and painted like stones served to partition off the different caves the gryphons here were living in. Pink Paw tapped on one, waiting for permission to enter.

On the other side of the wood, Cherine thought he heard clicking. The sound was strange, slightly similar, but he couldn't place it.

Maybe something from university?

"It's your mother," Pink Paw shouted from the other side, pushing away the barrier. "We're coming in."

She didn't wait for her son but pushed open the

door. As dim as it was, Cherine could just make out a nest, some cooked, dried food, and a collection of trinkets. It was a fairly large cave for just one gryphon, but if it made him happy, Cherine wasn't going to complain.

Hanging on the wall were several drawings. *No, not drawings, rubbings? Engravings?* Kia had signed them. While she didn't talk much about the explosion and the medicine gryphon caves, she'd been there when Xin had been hit by the oil. Cherine didn't realize she'd been visiting him, too.

While Xavi and Pink Paw checked on their son, Cherine wandered the large room. Despite the nest, food, and textured drawings in the corner, it was fairly open. Pink Paw's voice carried and echoed.

The opinicus scholar stood in the spot with the least dust in the center of the room and tried to recreate the clicking sound he'd heard. Without anything to make the sound, it must have come from Xavi's son. Sure enough, the sound echoed all around him, earning him a few strange looks.

He apologized, but once their backs were turned, he rifled through his pack. Sponge had given him a cloth with her feathers tied to it. Mostly, the scent made Ninox mad, which was why Sponge had done it. But it also smelled like the desert, and he'd used it to wrap the last of the thunderbird jerky.

He held the cloth-wrapped jerky up to the ceiling and waved it around every corner of the room. By now, Xavi and Pink Paw both stared at him like he was crazy. Their son, however, clicked at Cherine, and he clicked back.

The walls didn't look fuzzy the way they had at the Padfoot Pride's guest cave, so he switched to the ceiling.

It appeared to be one single piece of rock, but when he reached the far corner of the room, he got his first bite.

Literally.

A fuzzy brown-and-grey face with long whiskers and black eyes seemed to come out of the rock face itself to nibble on the end of the jerky.

Xavi let out an *eep,* and Cherine calmed him down.

"It's okay, it's just a cave gryphon." Cherine turned to Xin, tapping his talons to make it clear he was walking towards him. "Are these your friends? Did they teach you to click?"

Xin nodded and held a paw up to feel Cherine's face, tapping the metal beak. "There's a small crack in the back of the medicine gryphon's cave, and they come in to trade for supplies sometimes. They found me there and helped me navigate the dark."

"The medicine gryphon knows about them?" Pink Paw asked.

"No, cave gryphons take what they want, and then leave equal value behind. That's what they mean by trade." Cherine pulled out some of his cave gryphon quill pens from his last interaction with them. Then he turned and went back to the invisible crack in the ceiling. "Hello! I'm Cherine, a sand gryphon, member of the Padfoot Pride. Sponge and Hoppy thank you for being their guests. I would like to trade this meat here for some answers if you speak my language and don't mind? I promise, we don't mean any harm. I left gifts at your other dens in the taiga."

A noise like bats rose in the distance, had bats not gone extinct, sounded from beyond the wall. Then the same face poked out and squeezed through, dropping down next to Cherine. He handed her the jerky.

She tried a few words, but he didn't understand them and shook his head. A second cave gryphon crawled out, offering up a new word, presumably for 'hello.' Cherine shook his head again. Soon, there were twenty cave gryphons in the small room. Pink Paw and Xavi were too surprised to say anything, but Cherine had heard that cave gryphons travelled in groups of fifteen to thirty when they left the Abyssal Naze. Or, as Hoppy kept calling it, the 'Abby Navel.'

Cherine tried again with his greeting, and this time one of the cave gryphons perked up.

"I speak opinicus," she said with an accent somewhere between Alabaster Eyrie and Reevesport trill. Her plumage was a lighter brown, and her whiskers were shorter than the others. She sniffed at Cherine. "You were in a weald cave. I remember your scent."

Cherine nodded. "That's right. I thought I heard cave gryphons, but I was worried it might have been Mally the Nighthaunt."

All twenty cave gryphons hissed, causing Xavi and Pink Paw to jump back. The light brown cave gryphon hadn't started the hiss, which gave Cherine an interesting insight.

"You said that you can speak opinicus, but they all seem to understand me." He looked at each of their eyes. While the black orbs were a little disconcerting, their big mouths, whiskers, and ears were expressive. It just took some adjusting as to what he was looking for. "So you all understand common, er, opinicus, but only one of you can speak it?"

There was a small chitter among the others, then light brown spoke for them. "It's hard to speak the opinicus language if you don't start at birth. It requires a trick of the beak and sounds we don't usually make. The gryphon languages are easier."

"Is there only one opinicus language? What about fisherfolk?" He was getting off-topic, but his curiosity was piqued.

More chitters, then their spokesgryphon said, "Fisherfolk have an argot, but the villages that started out as eyries all speak common. Most gryphons speak common now and their own language. It's safer that way. It's why I was taught. We thought we could deal with opinici. That it would be safer."

"Was it?" Cherine asked. The word *argot* wasn't lost on him. It was a strange word to know, suggesting they might have learned to speak from a linguist or scholar of some sort.

More chittering, but there were two distinct sounds being made this time. He thought he could pick out which were for yes and which were for no. They'd eaten through half of his jerky, so time was getting short.

"Sometimes," was all the spokesgryphon said. "Is this the information you wanted?"

Cherine shook his head. "The Seraph King is moving into this area. It's not safe for the local prides. I wanted to know the following: are there more caves or cave systems that are safe for non-cave gryphons to live in, how are you getting from one side of Belamuria to the other undetected, and is there a way I can reach out to talk to you? I searched all summer without luck."

More chittering. The light brown gryphon chittered back, including the words *sand gryphon* in common. Finally, there came a shrug and the answers to Cherine's questions out of order.

"There are cave systems across the continent, so we use those," she said.

Pink Paw chimed in from the corner where she and Xavi had been squeezed to by all the bodies. "Sorry, my son's bedroom goes all the way across the continent?"

More chittering, and a laugh. "No, no. The world isn't hollow. This cave system will take you to the other side of the taiga. Then we follow the forest north of the sea, and a canyon takes us to one side of Padfoot territory. Then the 'guest cave' takes us south of Reevesport, and there are several small caves we use until we reach home."

"Can I go there?" Xin asked. "Could my parents come?"

"Yes." More chittering. "Yes for you, no for your parents. Not... unless they learn to click. The caves require flight at points and are dangerous if you do not know what is ahead of you before you leap. And you should not go alone. There are voids where sound does not reflect."

"Sounds dangerous." Xavi looked at his son. "You're an adult, so you make your own decisions, but please don't get hurt."

Pink Paw felt differently. "You think he's in more danger down there than he would be up here? I think he should go now if they'll take him."

"The voids aren't dangerous, they just take practice," the spokesgryphon said. There was a lot more chittering, some laughter, and more chittering. The spokesgryphon didn't translate until pushed by the parents. "Sorry, I did not think you would want to know that. The voids are dangerous to one opinicus, the Nighthaunt. It is the only place he cannot hear us, so we guard those spots and wait, though he no longer travels under the earth."

Cherine watched the last of the thunderbird jerky go down the gullet of a cave gryphon. "What about the other questions?"

A barrage of chittering, and the cave gryphons started crawling back through the invisible crack in the wall. "There is a grove of trees northeast of here, off the main aneda forest, with a mossy cave. Most of us come through there at some point. You will need to leave your message with something tasty and fragrant that will not go bad if days pass without anyone finding it."

Nineteen of the cave gryphons had now left, leaving only the one who spoke common. She looked younger than the others. "They said you are not equipped to go into the deep places. I agree. However, many of the caves your friends are sleeping in were once connected. I can show you how to open up connections between those caves. But I have a price."

Pink Paw and Xavi looked at each other, then Pink Paw spoke. "I'll fetch our pride leader to make a deal."

The last cave gryphon kept looking back at the wall, then to Xavi's eldest, but she stayed until Hatzel arrived and explained her demands. The cave gryphon wanted to open up trade with the weald prides, but she wanted it opened the same way it worked with the medicine gryphons—essentially, she wanted a room where Hatzel would place valuable and edible things, and when cave gryphons came through, they'd steal them and leave payment. In exchange, this particular cave gryphon would stay behind while her friends went back north to provide word of the new trading post, and the next set of cave gryphons to come through would pick her up.

"It's a deal," Hatzel said. "How long do you think you'll need to stay to show us the tunnels?"

The cave gryphon tilted her head back and forth while she thought. "It depends on how fast you learn. Ten days?"

"I'll find a spare nest for you." Hatzel was taking the news of cave gryphons particularly well, Cherine thought, considering it had taken him months to try to convince Zeph and Kia, and, ultimately, he never had convinced Kia.

Of course, Kia still believes in bats, so maybe we'll never be on the same page there.

"She can stay with me," Xin said. The other gryphons looked at him like he'd offered to make Mally the Nighthaunt his guest. "I mean, I think she's already living on the other side of the wall."

The cave gryphon did her head tilt in both directions, then accepted the offer. "It is cold on the other side of the wall. You will need to find bedding materials and food for me. I will send what I have with my pride."

"Good job," Hatzel said to Xavi's eldest once the cave gryphon was getting settled. "Making friends with other prides is how you grow strong in this world. They can teach you things your pride can't. Also, I think she likes you."

He made a clicking sound, and Cherine made it back as best his metal beak would let him. He was about to go fetch Kia and Zeph, but the cave gryphon had already disappeared into the darkness.

Well, they'll find out tomorrow one way or another.

40

BARNACLE SCRAPER

The ground around New Eyrie had been flattened by the talons of large goliath birds with heavy armor. Rows of metal beak and claw guards emblazoned with the Alabaster Eyrie insignia hung on tacks in the stables.

Foultner's wings ached, and as much as she wanted to gather whatever intelligence she could, the birds down here weren't pets, and they'd already maimed several stabletalons, so she kept her distance. She'd been here a few days, and wherever she went, Silver's argent hawks followed.

They weren't unfriendly, exactly. They were polite to everyone. A sort of unfriendly politeness that they dished out to both Crestfall and Reevesport allies alike.

Or Redwood Valley prisoners.

Rather than annoy her captors, she went back to the tower, to her windowless room where Henders waited. They locked her in, though they'd let her out if she knocked, and she listened until they were gone.

"How're you holding up, Hends?" she asked.

He shrugged. "I wish they'd let us go back to the ranch. We can be useful there, at least. And I'm sure Blinky's looking for us."

One of the most frustrating things about the past few days was finding out secondpaw that their owl gryphon friend, or at least someone, had managed to stage a rescue. Getting sent to the lumber mill had seemed like a death sentence, but once they were tucked away in New Eyrie, it turned out that was the one thing that could have saved them.

"Yeah, I'm sure Blinky will come get us," Foultner said. "Though she may wait until we've left here to do so. It's pretty secure. You okay with that?"

Henders shrugged. "They're not hurting us. The food's fine. I kinda like apples."

If Foultner had a sweet beak, Hends had the exact opposite of that. He loved the taste of sour things. Which was good, considering the type of fare they were being fed. It was, as Foultner's grandmother would have said, sour enough to turn an opi's beak inside-out.

She curled up next to Henders and put her head on his shoulder. She'd brought him some strands of sawgrass, and he weaved them into a basket. Apparently, this was how the guards at the Redwood Valley botanical gardens used to pass the time. He had a real knack for it.

Foultner didn't like surprises. She didn't care for unknowns. A lot of her life, poaching and spying, included a bit of both. But she liked to have time to get her things together, get the lay of the land, and then dive in with a plan.

Two plans.

Twelve plans. Really, the moment something went

wrong, she already wanted to know what she was doing next, and this had thrown her off her game. There were opportunities here, sure, but she didn't know how they'd play out. And she didn't know what Reeve Silver knew, why she'd acted the way she had.

This could just be an enemy trying to save a few civilians, but it could also be something more. If Silver knew how important Foultner and Henders were to Satra, she may have decided to turn them in to the Seraph King herself to get all of the glory.

It wasn't unthinkable, but it was terrifying.

Foultner had fallen into a stress nap by the time knocking came at the door. She assumed it was just Henders knocking to go out and fetch more grass until she realized she was drooling on Henders. She sat up straight and wiped off his harness as a familiar face came in.

If Foultner always looked a little like she was wearing a stolen harness and hadn't taken enough time to preen—both true most of the time—Silver had that orderly look that somehow lasted in the heat, in the sky, and on the battlefield. Sure, a feather or two might be out of place, but it was that planned out-of-place look where the other feathers were still pristine. Like she'd deliberately forgotten to preen a feather to make everyone else feel better.

Is it feather oil? Does she have a team of argent hawks who groom her whenever I'm not looking?

Not that Foultner would want to look like that. Being too clean made an opinicus stand out. She just wanted to understand the trick of it. No one looked like that without something going on in the background.

"Reeve Silver," Foultner said. "Thank you for your help, but what happens to us now?"

Silver waved away her guards, which was a bad sign to Foultner's thinking. She probably didn't want them to know who Foultner and Henders really were.

"They don't know that you found me broken and dying after the Reevesbane's attack," the reeve explained. "Rybalt has ears everywhere, especially among the Reevesport peafowl, and I think if others knew, it would make you a target."

"I'm glad you're okay," Henders chimed in. "I was really worried about you. And I don't think your flying suffered an inch!"

Foultner didn't like having Henders around in dangerous situations, but his heartfelt charisma, one of the things she loved about him, also helped endear them to their captors. If she could just get him to say a little less sometimes, maybe they'd get through this okay.

Silver preened back a feather that wasn't even out of place, annoying Foultner. "Unfortunately, we have Mally to thank for that. Best in the business, if you don't think too hard about the cost of his knowledge."

Henders nodded, wide-eyed. He'd grown up like Foultner had, hearing underbough rumors about Mally. Not that Henders was underbough, really. He just lived in one of the poorer sections of the merchant quarter, in the back of a shop, before he'd made Reeve's Guard.

"Do you want to go back?" Silver asked Henders. He nodded. "Even knowing that the ranch is Jonas's now and that the Crackling Sea Eyrie will fall in a few days?"

"Our friends are there. I want to make sure they're okay," Henders said.

Foultner summoned up the most pragmatic tone she could muster. "Are you offering an alternative? I know you called us informants, but it doesn't seem like there's anyone for us to inform on."

"That was just to get you to safety," the reeve explained. "I'm offering you now what I offered you the last time we met. I could use two smart, capable opinici to take care of my goliath birds."

"*My* goliath birds," Henders began, but Foultner shook her head to tell him it wasn't the time.

Silver opened her harness, pulled out several metal beads, and handed them to each. When they looked surprised, she added, "Well, I'm not going to pay Jonas for them. Look, the Argent Heights is a dry, rocky place. It's not nearly so alive as the weald. There's rarely any rain. But we're no longer on the front lines there. I'm offering you a chance to do what you seem to enjoy doing, taking care of goliaths, in a place where you won't have to worry about when the next army rolls in and... well, orders everyone to the mill."

"Will we work with the same goliath birds?" Henders asked.

Silver nodded. "Them and more."

"We want living quarters in the eyrie," Foultner found herself saying. She wanted to be in a position to overhear conversations. "I never want to be stuck on a field of grass at night when an army comes through. I want walls between me and them."

The reeve reached a talon out, pulling back a quarter of the beads she'd given them. "Consider that my special rate. I never saw the Redwood Valley quarters, but I can find you something better than the Crackling Sea and *much* better than the torn-up tent you had the last time I saw you."

Foultner's home at the Redwood Valley Eyrie had been an old storage shed next to an abandoned gate with a nasty ant infestation, so she wasn't picky. What she needed to do was figure out how to get word back.

"Does this come with admission to your eyrie?" Foultner asked.

Henders nodded like he knew what she was asking. "So we're getting new harnesses and badges?"

Silver laughed. "I suppose if the reeve can't make that wish happen, no one can. Yes. And you're free, though I say that with caveats—you're under guard until we're away from the war zone. I don't want anyone executing you for your appearance. Henders, you're going to need a harness that's not so... colorful. Foultner, you can keep yours if you really want, but we'll get you a new eyrie badge."

'If you really want.' If it was good enough for me to steal, it's good enough for me to wear. Though I suppose a change wouldn't kill me.

"We're lucky you're not peacocks or herons," Silver continued. "Once you're in the eyrie proper, you won't stand out much. Especially not Henders. I'll have someone bring by your new clothing soon, then we're off."

Foultner didn't have to pretend to be surprised because the feeling was genuine. "You're not staying for the battle?"

Silver looked back from the open door. "This isn't my fight. Now that New Eyrie is fortified, my job is to make sure the supplies keep coming. I don't need to be down here for that."

Once she was gone, Foultner sat down with Henders. "Are you okay with this? If you want, I can find a way to get you lost in the forest and you can make your way back to Blinky."

"No, I'm fine," Henders replied. "We're not going to take care of birds, are we? We're going to spy?"

Foultner shook her head. "No, you're really going to take care of the birds. *I'm* going to spy. You just do what you do best and make friends. But this is dangerous, and it's going to be a long time before we can get home."

"If there's a home to return to," Henders said.

Foultner tapped her beak to his. "There will be. You've met our gryphon friends, right? You could burn down half the continent, and they'd find a way to survive."

Henders nodded and began unpacking his harness to get the new one.

Foultner considered what she had on her. She'd probably be better off taking the new harness. Really, it'd give them an opportunity to prove they weren't spies if they had all of their things lying out in the open.

"Hey Hends, block the door for me, okay?" she asked. Once he was in front of it, she took off her harness and looked for anything that might be suspicious. Would a poacher's knife be challenged? No, she'd just call it a ranching knife. A barnacle scraper was anyone's guess. She had some coins in the old currency, maybe she could trade for the metal beads Silver had given her. Foultner did have two things a normal rancher wouldn't have access to, two things she didn't want to leave behind. Not that they'd be less suspicious if they were found later in this room.

Two vials of red liquid, taken from Blackwing Eyrie

opinici at the start of the conflict with Rybalt, before he'd swapped out his so-called allies' antivenom with colored water.

She adjusted her wounded wing, trying to get the bandages close enough to examine. They didn't smell great, but if she could keep from changing them before they reached the Argent Heights, they'd make a good hiding place.

She untied the bandages, then retied them with the two vials in there, making sure they didn't clink together. Everything else she had on her seemed pretty innocuous. And Henders's collection of items was eccentric enough that hers looked utilitarian by comparison.

A few minutes later, an argent hawk appeared with two new harnesses and badges. "I didn't know your size, so I guessed. Once we get home, let me know if they're not the right fit. Also, welcome to the eyrie! Sounds like Silver is happy to have you. Those goliath birds have been running rampant. It'll be nice to have some real ranchtalons to help us out."

Foultner smiled and took the harness, making a show of putting her very normal things in it. It was a light leather, perhaps bleached white or grey, and the metal bits were silver-colored but too hard to be actual silver. The insignia was just crossed silver feathers that created a mountain, not exciting, but not every eyrie had electric jellies haunting its shore.

"Thanks!" Henders said as he took his. "It's great to be part of the team. So, what do you eat at the Argent Heights? Anywhere pretty we should visit?"

As they exited New Eyrie and made their way to the only wagon heading north instead of south, Foultner let

Henders do most of the talking. Instead, she pretended to worry at a talon while she kept track of who and what was coming into New Eyrie.

The number of troops seemed pretty light, but the amount of food and supplies suggested they were preparing to spend the season here—or feed an army based in the Crackling Sea. Whether that army was headed east to the weald or north to the Blackwing Eyrie, she supposed they'd find out in the next few days.

Now, if only I had a way to get this information to Blinky.

41

STRANGERS AT FATE'S WHIMS

For the seventh evening in a row, Nighteyes waited until her new stormtail mate drifted off, then slipped out of her burrow and fled east. She flew out of the Nightsky hunting grounds, past several sets of ruins whose origins had been lost to time, just past a set of wooden buildings that had once been an expedition from the Blackwing Eyrie, and then she felt forced to land. All she could do was look beyond her paw-marked tree to a gold and black symbol in the distance.

Her sight was strange on these border areas. She felt like she could see everything past the glyphs, but that was an illusion easily dispelled when she tried to pick out details. It was almost like looking into a fog bank. She could see maybe twenty yards away, but everything past that was mist.

If she flew up, she should be able to see for miles in every direction. And yet no matter where she stood, her vision was limited to no more than twenty yards east past the glyph.

Something waited for her there, beyond the fog. She

knew it was true, but she didn't know what it was or why it waited. When she tried to think about it, her brain turned as fuzzy as her vision, and she began forgetting words until she slowly remembered where she was and felt a strong need to return to her nest.

And there was nothing she could do about it. She felt this longing, this migratory instinct, yet she didn't know why. So she spent a few hours each night out here, staring off into space, hoping for something to happen.

For six nights, nothing happened. But here on the seventh, a voice came from behind her. A voice that snuck up on her, despite her always having a sense of where every starling in this section of the jungle was located.

"Hey, you look like you could use some company," Wendl said.

Once Nighteyes could see her, could smell her, the alarm went away. Wendl had always been a good friend, at least as far as Nighteyes could remember, so she tried to explain the feeling inside of her.

"You were given some elixir and spent a few months on the other side of the wall," Wendl said. "Maybe your nesting instinct is a little confused."

Nighteyes bristled. "I don't think that's it. I know there's something very important, something I have to do, and it's driving me batty that I can't do it."

"I know the feeling." Wendl watched the barrier.

Nighteyes kept a close look at her friend. Wendl's eyes were focusing on different objects in the distance, things Nighteyes couldn't see.

Why is she different? Is it because she was born else-where? Is it because she's an opinicus?

Wendl stood and started to walk away but seemed to

reconsider and looked back at Nighteyes. "If you really, *really* want to know, I can probably help you remember. Just follow me."

Nighteyes stared in disbelief, but even if it was some sort of joke, she had to try. She followed after Wendl, towards the ruined, wooden buildings. When they reached the entrance, Wendl went around back. Apparently, the building had an underground level beneath it.

"We used to store supplies down here," Wendl explained. "Basically, anything that had to be kept cool and we didn't want the squirrels to eat. I still come out here to think, sometimes. It's the closest I can get to home."

Small braziers lit the tunnel. Not just braziers, braziers with some sort of incense hanging off them. The smells were overwhelming, confusing. One smelled like lilacs, another like rotting squirrel. Nighteyes coughed a few times before getting past the corridors to the storage room.

It was fairly small, perhaps the size of Nighteyes's burrow. Several opinicus trinkets and drawings decorated the walls. Judging by the different pigment jars, Wendl had drawn some of these herself. She kept drawing this strange opinicus over and over again. A brown and black opinicus with dark eyes, next to two blackwings.

Friend? Lover? Family? Who is she?

Nighteyes didn't want to ask. The drawings almost bordered on obsession. Perhaps Wendl was looking for a way to leave the Emerald Jungle to be reunited with the stranger.

"How's your head feel?" Wendl asked.

To Nighteyes's surprise, it felt better. "It's like recovering from a sickness. I can think again."

"The jungle is full of scents. That's how you can tell where your pride is without seeing them," Wendl explained. "It's also how the pridelord sends information. It's a bit hard to explain. I kind of stumbled across it myself."

Nighteyes's memories slowly came back, and she remembered seeing Wendl with the pridelord, not forced to react the way the other starlings had. "You weren't under his control. How did you do that? Why do you do it?"

Wendl tensed. "I didn't think you'd remember that. It's not that I don't obey him. It's more like... here, feel my beak."

She pulled Nighteyes's paws onto her beak, which was much harder than a gryphon beak. "Hard, right? But I don't smell the same way you do. My brain seems to work the same, but the scents are fainter, and if they're not commands, I don't have to listen. Or I can wait to respond. I'm not sure how it works."

Nighteyes considered her friend. "Are there more like you?"

"Not... exactly. A few. I don't know how it is for them," Wendl said. "I don't think it's a coincidence the pridelord assigned us to different prides. We rarely get to talk, and I fear we've all grown distant."

Nighteyes watched Wendl. It was strange. She'd never believed Wendl's story about being transformed into a starling. Not that Wendl had repeated the story after the first few nights here. They'd all been found sick, rambling near the edge of the jungle. But Nighteyes was starting to realize she'd even forgotten that Wendl had ever told the story. Why did she remember it now?

"Do you want to live like this forever?" Wendl asked. "No longer tied so closely to other starlings, free to do what you want? I heard you had a hard time in the weald."

Nighteyes nodded, suddenly remembering the past few months. "At first, I loved it. I could do whatever I wanted. But over time, something felt wrong. I became depressed, and the mixture you gave me stopped working as well. The altruism kicked in, though I didn't realize it was altruism until later."

More of Nighteyes's memories returned, and she remembered seeing Wendl there at the border while the jadebeaks swarmed. "You don't have the altruism, either. I saw you, at the border. You just stood there, waiting until the jadebeaks returned to normal, and then you acted like nothing had happened. What... are you?"

Wendl looked over at the drawings. "A monster, I suppose, but that's what they'd call you where I came from. I'm trying to stop the altruism. I want to see my family again, but they're not starlings, and I can't do that if there's the tiniest risk I'm going to turn full-on monster and rip them apart at any moment. I need to be sure it's gone, but I think it's also the only reason the prides here can stick together. What I need to know is whether or not you'll help me. As a leader, you have access to the pridelord's temple. There's knowledge under there of how the Emerald Jungle was forged into one megapride, and I need to see it to fix things."

"Sure," Nighteyes started to say, but more memories were coming back now. "Wait, Erlock. There was an army marching on the Crackling Sea! My friends are there. I need to take my pride and save them! If we can just lure them to the border..."

She rushed outside, past the braziers and incense, and into the clearing. The cool sky was clearer than before, and when she looked east, she could see past the glyph markers, down to the world beyond her cage.

Then scents flooded her nares. She now knew there were two jadebeaks who had snuck away from home and were hunting squirrels in the night. The stormtail she'd thought was asleep was actually up and looking for her. The map of the jungle started falling into place again, and she had a general sense of where everyone was as each pride's scent reached her, relayed by other starlings.

Stormtails, Jadebeaks snapped into mental focus, then the Nightsky. When her own pride hit her, she started forgetting again. Forgetting what was so crucial to her moments ago. Nothing was more important than taking care of her pride. Her only friends were starlings, because only starlings could be friends. But something wasn't right. Something still pulled at her.

She wandered east, stopping at a paw print she had put up earlier that year. She could just make out a gold and black match to it a few trees away. Twenty yards past that, the world was enveloped in mist.

A twig cracked behind her, and she jerked around. "Oh, Wendl! I didn't know you were out here. Is everything okay?"

The starling opinicus looked sad, and Nighteyes came over and put a wing around her. "Hey, it's okay. We all have nights like this. Here, why don't I walk you back to the pridegrounds? I have some fish hanging out to dry. If a stormtail hasn't stolen them yet, they'll make a nice snack."

Wendl let herself be herded in the direction of Nightsky, but she stayed quiet for the first few steps. Finally, she said, "Yes, I think I'd like that. Thank you, Night. You're a good friend to me. I hope I can be as good a friend to you when the time comes."

They were strange words, but Wendl always said unusual things. Despite the tugging in her heart to go east, Nighteyes brought her friend west. The real night sky disappeared into the canopy, then the white flower blooms that marked her nesting grounds showed up above them. The water from the rivers played a pleasant sound as it split and recombined, navigating the rocky terrain.

The warm season was nearly over, and there was a chill in the air. Nighteyes shivered a little and pushed closer to Wendl. Soon, the different types of vines that provided the stars above her home would disappear to the first frost, and the skies above would turn black.

She hopped over the river and took one glance back east. What was there? What called to her? Her memory was gone, but there was a muffled voice inside her head. She just couldn't make out the words.

42

THISTLE

It was a long, slow walk back to the Heart of the Bog. The war band stopped to rest on the other side of the Jade-beak River, tending to any wounds, getting something to eat, and talking about the night's events. Once they reached the sunken eyrie, Black Mask realized they had a problem.

"There are more jars down there," Thistle said. "Twenty. Maybe more?"

In retrospect, Thistle's flight feathers would have come in handy here. As it was, the crone's hiding place was a pillar in the center of the water with no easy way to climb up to it or access it without flight.

A good place to hide things when most of your pride can't fly, but it raises some questions about why you'd want to hide something from your pride. What else is in there?

Black Mask stopped to consider his options. He could go straight home and confront the rest of his pride head-on. Violence was always an option but rarely a *good* option if there were alternatives. Even if they went down and retrieved the jars of parasites, while potentially damning to the wingtorn who knew how widespread the damage could be, it might not be enough to persuade the others. And it certainly wouldn't make the three other bog witches bat an eye.

But what if there is something else down there? Something I can use?

Black Mask stood above the sunken eyrie and pushed down a pebble. Several large, white cavefish dispersed in different directions. Not a problem. He'd dealt with cavefish before. But then what he'd taken to be part of the flooded stone flooring rose to inspect the ripples.

"Is that the matamata Tresh sent over the waterfall?" one of the other wingtorn asked. "It's still alive down there?"

"Sure is," Thistle said. "It's too big now, doesn't have a way out."

Water flowed down into the sinkhole through several old canals revealed in the flood, but the only way out was the small tunnels running through the eyrie or the river, currently blocked by pieces of the old stone bridge.

If this coup works, the first thing I'm going to do is see if the Ashen Weald can remove those for us. I want my home back.

Time was wasting, but he couldn't let go of the feeling that there must be more to the crone's hiding place. Once, it had contained eggs. With Thistle's help, he could see that there was a small entrance under the top of the pillar.

But an entrance to what?

"Who are our best weavers? I need a basket and

rope," he asked. The wingtorn looked at each other, then finally pointed to Thistle.

"I'm decent. How strong does the rope need to be? What does the basket need to carry?" she asked.

Black Mask dropped another pebble and watched the turtle snap it out of the air. "Me."

BLACK MASK CLUNG to the sides of a small basket hanging above a giant sinkhole full of carnivorous turtles and listened to Thistle overhead complaining about how bad an idea this was.

"Thistle, I'm glad you're feeling more like yourself," he shouted up, "but *yourself* whines a lot."

She hissed at him playfully. "I only whine when I'm worried. And I don't think this is going to hold. You need to treat, dry, and reinforce woven rope. You can't just grab reeds, put them together, and expect it all to work out!"

The other wingtorn hushed the two of them, pointing out that if they were overhead by the crone, it was all over.

Because of where the edges of the ground were located, they couldn't put Black Mask directly onto the old nesting pillar itself. Instead, they lowered him straight down until he was even with it, then began swinging him back and forth.

Turtles poked their heads out of tunnels, curious about this promising new snack, and came out of their hiding places, leaving Black Mask to wonder if the giant turtle had laid eggs or if more turtles had come down to feed on the dead starlings.

At first, the swinging was cautious, but it wasn't getting him close enough to the tower. He shouted up, and they increased it, but the basket got twisted, and Black Mask nearly lost his lunch. Once his stomach had settled, and he managed to right the basket, they got him going in the correct direction.

Unfortunately, on the upswing, he was a little too high. They were losing time, so rather than adjust, he just flung himself at the pillar.

Leaping after birds or sailfins was one thing. Jumping out of a moving basket proved much more difficult, and he nearly slid off his intended landing target, just managing to grab some thick vines mid-slide, allowing him to dangle off the other side of the pillar.

He looked down and saw the flat, diamond shape of a matamata head staring up at him. The large turtle's head stretched nearly halfway up the pillar.

How does it fit so much neck inside its shell?

Black Mask found some paw holds and climbed back up. Once he was on top, he located a small ledge on the other side that had once housed a gryphon nest. Mindful of the loose stones and sticks it was composed of, he climbed down.

From high above, Thistle shouted to check the pillar wall. Sure enough, some of the rocks were loose. He dislodged them, disturbing the turtles below and revealing the hollow center of the pillar.

This must have been a tower once.

Inside was a spiral staircase, worn down to more of a ramp in places. Clay jars were stacked along the perimeter, and it wasn't lost on him that all of them were probably full of parasitic bugs. While he seemed to be immune to their effects, he didn't know what would happen if an entire jar exploded on top of him. He carefully wove his way between them, descending further and further.

Despite its age, the tower was watertight. In fact, as he went down, he recognized the smell of different pastes that could be used to seal up cracks. Part of living in a sunken eyrie, back before the turtle infestation, had involved getting water out of old tunnels and keeping them dry. He'd wondered what had happened to all of that paste. It appeared the crones had turned this tower into their side project.

He climbed so far down that he was now certain he was beneath the water table. He reached up to poke at a paste-speckled crack, then thought better of it and continued his descent. He shivered, the air becoming much cooler the deeper he went. When he reached the tower's end, he found a door that had been covered in several layers of sealant.

He was disappointed. He turned to leave and happened to notice that one of the walls of the tower was thicker than the others. That wasn't unusual, who could say why opinici built things the way they did, but there was a single brick that wasn't slathered in sealant.

Curiosity got the better of him, and he reached out a paw, pulling the brick down. Behind it was a stolen, leather-bound journal. It looked like Crackling Sea make, designed to survive moist conditions. He had no idea what the inside was made of, but the old crone hadn't written in it so much as she'd used her claws to carve the words into the leathery pages.

Black Mask sniffed. The book contained scents other than his mother's. The other two crones, killed by the Ashen Weald, had a distinct smell he'd never forget. And even Vitra's flowery fragrance was detectable in the early pages.

He put the book, more of a tome, really, down on the stairs. He'd forgotten most of the bog language while he was locked up in the Crackling Sea dungeons, but he could recall a few words. It seemed to be a journal of the crimes of Satra's ancestors, ending with Jun salting the farmlands and killing all plant life there. Once that happened, each crone had left her personal glyph signing she agreed with the punishment.

There was something more about Vitra's mom, who seemed to have been a crone herself, and Vitra. Then there were pages and pages of circular etchings.

Black Mask traded his paw pad over them. They were... eggs. Eggs and dates according to the seasonal calendar. There were also several names in the kjarr language, up to four of them.

The parents', or at least the mother's, name.

The name they'd intended for their child.

And then the name the crones had given the gryphlet after the egg had been stolen and hatched here in the Heart of the Bog.

He was stunned. He'd assumed they'd taken the eggs and never gave a care about who the parents were, but that wasn't entirely correct. As he pawed through more pages, he realized they were trying to track down which eggs may have come from bog parents originally. They hadn't done this for the sake of the gryphlets, they'd been trying to track lineages.

Vitra's scent had disappeared from the book by now, and it took him a moment to realize what they were doing. Vitra's mother had been a crone, but her father was a Kjarr. Once Vitra was no longer using this book, the other crones were trying to track down someone of only bog descent with a better claim to lead the bog pride.

They were planning on betraying her all along.

He shook his head. That information was a formality at this point, but the eggs and the true names might just give him the leverage he needed.

He climbed back up the long ramp, careful not to hit any jars. If everything went well, he'd have some witches come back and burn it all. If not, well, he'd let slip to Blinky that they were here.

Once he was up top, he considered the weight of the book. Whatever it was made of was dense, heavy enough that the basket might snap from its line.

I should have taken my armor off before I came down. This stuff weighs as much as a small sailfin.

Thistle swung the basket back to him, and he caught it in his beak. They'd lowered it a little so on the upswing it reached the pillar just fine this time. He secured the book and had them lift it first without him.

While he waited for them to finish up top, several cave swifts, small darting birds with sharp beaks, dove at him. He was afraid they had a home on the pillar, but he didn't see any of their strange, silky nests about. Instead, it turned out they were after the little bugs he'd disturbed with his crawling and climbing. One of them nicked his ear chasing a mosquito, earning a hiss.

The basket lowered a second time, and he carefully put his forepaws on it. He gripped the woven sides and trying not to think about what could go wrong, then he hopped his back legs on and swung away.

"Whoa, whoa, too heavy!" Thistle shouted. "The reeds aren't going to hold!"

Black Mask's stomach was in his throat. He flew back and forth, slowing only marginally. The woven rope knocked loose cobwebs and bog crawlers, which rained down on him from above.

He let out a sound that did not evoke bravery, brushing them off. The little white-throated swifts came to his rescue, snapping up the spiders. He was just about to thank them when he noticed more crawlers moving up the line.

Black Mask made eye contact with a swift coming at him from the side. He opened his beak to shout "No!", even knowing that the bird couldn't understand him.

The bird's sharp beak caught the bog crawler and slashed the rope.

Black Mask froze in place, only water and turtles below him. Thistle stopped pulling, but the rope seemed to hold, so she started again.

Four more swifts came in, attacking the other bugs on the line, and with each miss, their beaks frayed it even more.

"Back to the pillar!" Black Mask shouted. "Lower me back! We'll make a new—"

The rope snapped, sending him into the depths of the sunken eyrie.

BLACK MASK narrowly avoided being caught out of the air by the large matamata, and the moment he landed, he swam beneath it and latched on to the bottom to keep from being pulled into the depths by his armor. He wasn't a fisherfolk, he couldn't hold his breath for more than a minute, but he needed a moment to figure out his next plan of action.

Unfortunately, breathable air was not his biggest problem. His biggest problem had a very long neck and a grudge against gryphonkind.

Hanging upside-down in the water from the bottom of a turtle shell, the reptile's neck stretched all the way around and looked him in the face.

It lashed out, catching his thick armor. Black Mask swore and kicked off the beast's face, trying to climb the turtle's tail and get on top of it. The head retracted, then came out again. He looked around him for dry land, but all he saw were more turtles. He'd have to cross most of the water to reach the only tunnel he recognized as going up to the surface.

Between him and the exit were several turtles large enough to fit more than one gryphon on top. With sharp beaks and long necks.

And big shells.

The bite had broken the straps on his armor, and he wriggled out of it, shoving it towards the giant matamata's angry beak.

Chew on that instead of me, thanks.

Feeling much lighter, he leapt at the next turtle. It didn't anticipate a gryphon jumping towards it and missed its bite. By the time its neck had swung around, Black Mask was already four turtles closer to shore. He missed his last jump, splashing in the water, but crawled up the moss-covered stone and disappeared into the darkness.

While he felt safer on land—even muddy, slippery land—the scent of turtle hadn't faded, and he was getting worried. The largest turtle wouldn't fit through these passages, but the smaller ones might. And there was also the matter of the baby matamatas.

The large ones were ambush predators. They could afford to lie in wait, covered in grass and plants, and snap up anything that floated past them. The sunken eyrie gave them a particular advantage being at the bottom of a waterfall. Prey couldn't get away easily.

The babies, however, were something else entirely. An adult might kill a gryphon or take off a few toes, but the babies had a bad attitude and would chase anything that disturbed them. It had even given rise to the term *baby turtle angry* for when a bog gryphon was upset and couldn't let something go. When he'd had wings, the little beasts were amusing. But now that he was underground and forced to walk, well, they weren't as funny.

He hit a split in the tunnel that hadn't been there before. Erlock's explosive exit and the flooding had cleared out previously-unused paths in the lower levels. Left seemed to go up while right went down, so he started with left and immediately knew he'd made a mistake. There was standing water and the chuffing sound of angry sailfins in that direction. He slowly backtracked, careful not to make any loud sounds, and found the other path wasn't any better.

Old eggshells littered the ground, surrounded by pools with turtle-like shapes floating in them. He took a few steps between the wet spots, hoping to find an exit past them, and realized his mistake when the baby turtles leapt out of the pools and chased him.

Left it is!

He turned the corner going at full speed and found the passage with the sailfin monitors was more like a river filling an old canal. He knew it was a bad idea to get into the water with them, so he doubled his speed and leapt at the far wall, claws out, catching it and trying to grab onto the ceiling to keep running there.

In his head, it was a great plan. His claws would find traction, it'd be a story to tell Blinky and his gryphlets when they grew up. Sadly, it turned out that the top of this tunnel was dirt, and the dirt was looser than he expected.

He fell, upside-down, on top of a monitor. All of the sleeping sailfins woke up. It was a good day for sailfins, they so rarely had snacks come to them.

Black Mask hung onto the side of his monitor for dear life, trying to keep its chunky head pointed away from his face and its sail between him and the others.

One sailfin neutralized, twenty to go.

And then the turtles arrived. A swarm of tiny, bitey, angry turtles.

'Baby turtle angry,' indeed.

Sailfins always seemed so gruff, Black Mask had never considered that they might be scared of anything. The arrival of the baby turtles taught him better. Sailfins may not fear *gryphons*, but they certainly feared the flood of armored biters chasing them now.

The monitors stampeded up the tunnel, through some loose dirt into a hidden hallway, and kept going as the turtles pursued them to the ends of the continent.

Black Mask, still hanging on, burst into the daylight and knew where he was at. He leapt off the sailfin and ran off in a different direction than the turtle-sailfin parade, though four turtles changed direction and kept chasing him. They followed him to the other wingtorn, who were attempting to construct a new, bird-proof basket.

Thankfully, his army of wingtorn was enough to kill four baby turtles. Though there were a few yelps in there.

"Is the book okay? Did you get it?" he asked.

Thistle nodded. "I haven't had a chance to read it. Is it important?"

Black Mask shook his fur, throwing mud everywhere, and looked for one of the turtle-free pools to rinse off in. "Yes, we need to hide it somewhere new so we can retrieve it later, but before we do, I need you to memorize three names."

Four, really. One of which is your own.

Thistle's reading skills in bog glyph were better than his own, and by the time he was clean, she'd located the information he was after.

With a nod, they moved past the Heart of the Bog and sought out the spine-laden nesting grounds to confront his mother.

43

SPIKE PALM

When having an emotionally charged confrontation with abusive family members, it's best to find a safe, neutral place to begin the conversation.

Unfortunately, that wasn't an option for Black Mask. He was talking to his mom, more of a cult leader than a parental figure, in the middle of a dome made out of poisonous spines. The edges of the area were full of wingtorn, and the last three flighted bog witches were there, looking horrified at Thistle's feathers and reassuring her that they'd imp in a new set after they healed.

Black Mask had intended to have a calm, rational conversation where he respectfully asked his mother to step down as leader of the pride because they were all going to join the other bog gryphons at Bogwash. That had quickly devolved into a shouting match, mostly with her listing his 'crimes against the pride' such as not letting Urious fall to his death at New Eyrie.

Everything she condemned Black Mask for, she'd

forgiven and even praised White Stripe for, so her words fell on deaf ears. When that didn't work, she tried to turn the conversation to the Crackling Sea opinici and the past Kjarrs, listing everything they'd done wrong, claiming he was on their side.

"No," he said at last. "I'm not going to try to convince you they're good. I'm not here about them. I'm here about you. Look around you? These gryphons? You've stolen their future, their happiness, their hope, their names. You've driven them to this small corner of the bog because of your hate, and you need to let them go."

The crone hissed back at him, and tensions were running high on both sides until Thistle stepped in.

"Milun," she said to the only male bog witch. Then she listed off his parents' names. "You have four other siblings older than you that are still living, three others who died. Your parents are both kjarr gryphons. When they had your egg, they put a little moon trinket on top of it."

He looked confused, so Thistle moved on to the next one. "Sirelena. Your father was a bog gryphon, and your mother was a kjarr gryphon. Before they were taken away to the Crackling Sea, they built you a nest using the bones of dugongs."

She moved on to the third bog witch. "I can't pronounce your name in kjarr, so I've written it down here in the dirt. Isn't it pretty? One of your parents is Ari, the kjarr den mother. That means you have a lot of half-siblings. It's not clear who your father was, I'm sorry. You're going to have to ask her. All I can tell is that you're listed as full kjarr."

Then she stood in front of the crone. "My name is Thileen. My mother was a bog gryphon. My father was a bog gryphon. They're both dead, so all that remains of them is their names, which you hid from me. Which you *stole* from me. Every gryphon here probably has family on the other side, and you've set them at odds. You've kept them here as part of a lie. Even your bog witches are lies, most of them aren't born from the witches buried by Jun the Kjarr. They're just eggs you stole out of someone else's nest. But they're not yours to keep, and it's time for you to let them go."

The crone made a strangled cry and leapt at Thistle, aiming for her good eye. Black Mask managed to pull his mom off the younger witch, but the crone was all gristle, and she got onto his back. With his armor on the bottom of the sunken eyrie, his neck was open for attack. She reached her claws around to tear out his throat, and he did the unthinkable.

He used all of his strength to leap straight up into the long palm spines.

His mother's body took the brunt of it, impaling her a hundred times over. Many made it through her and into him, but luckily his eyes and nose were spared. It took Sirelena and Milun flying up to pull him free.

The poison of so many spikes killed the crone quickly, and it took a large dose of the antidote to keep Black Mask from suffering a similar fate. They got the bleeding under control, but the wounds ached like snakes bites.

The wingtorn loyal to the crone were stunned, but they didn't fight. Thistle and the witches took them aside while Black Mask was led to a clean nest. He'd felt terrible many times in his life, but this was a new feeling as the spines' toxins worked through his system, making his limbs burn and twitch. He entered a kind of fever dream, and it was the next day before he awoke to find the nesting grounds abandoned.

BLACK MASK SHOOK off the sweat. For as terrible as he felt, someone had been tending to his wounds in the night. He slipped out of the grove and into the world again, where the pride was packing up.

"How do you feel?" Thistle asked. "That much palm poison is always a tricky thing. You're going to feel some intense joint pain."

He thought back to the grove, to his mother impaled on its ceiling. "Not great. But... at least it's over. Who's in charge now? Please don't say it's me."

"I don't know how to tell you this," Thistle said, "but you've got a bad attitude, and you're a terrible leader."

He laughed.

"Nobody's in charge," she continued. "But I'm going to lead everyone to Bogwash. I don't know if they've been hit yet, but if not, it'll give us a place to start looking. Do you want me to take the book with us?"

Black Mask raised an eyecrest. "Am I being kicked out of the pride? What's all this 'us' talk?"

"I know what an owl gryphon smells like," Thistle said. "I don't know which owl gryphon you're sleeping with, but the den you had us stay in on the return trip *definitely* smelled like an owl."

She whistled for one of the other bog witches to come by, holding the tome. "We'll send some rangers back to burn the clay jars, stop the parasite for good. But I thought you might want to take this with you. It might persuade them of your good intentions."

Getting a new heavy, armored harness back on felt like hell where he'd been pierced by the palms, but in between his groaning, he thanked Thistle for tending to his wounds while he slept. This was Urious's armor that they'd set aside initially. In its pouch, they found several claw weapons designed to give weapons back to the wingtorn declawed at New Eyrie. That led to everyone checking their armor's pouches, and those who had claws in them handed them out to those in need. They'd take a little practice, but the effect on the declaweds' mood was immediate and profound.

Even with the boost in spirits, he didn't expect that his pride would have any fight left in them. He thought the witches in particular would want to get reunited with their newfound parents. But when he turned to go, it turned out that wasn't entirely right.

"Is it true you're going to kill Jonas?" a wingtorn asked, a pair of metal claws glistening at her feet. When he nodded, she continued, "Then we're coming with you."

He knew their nightmares, so he didn't protest the wingtorn. When the bog witches wanted to come along, especially Thistle, who couldn't fly, he tried to stop them.

"This isn't your fight," he said. "You didn't see what we went through. I'd feel better if you just... lived your lives."

But Thistle wasn't hearing it. "Our job is to take care of the wounded. There'll be wounded wingtorn up north, and you're all going to need someone to take care of you. We've packed up the crone's supplies and notes. If the fighting is at the sea, then... well, Bogwash can wait. If things go poorly, this is the last chance for some of us to meet our family members who might be fighting there."

He hesitated, then finally agreed. "Okay, let's do it. But we have to assume the bog is occupied by more of those flamingos and peacocks. So we go slow, and we clear out any we find. Good?"

"Good," Thistle nodded. While some of the other bog witches now seemed to be going by the names written on their eggs, Thistle held firm to hers, and her thorn-design face paint remained unchanged. The full-kjarr witch, Milun, no longer wore any of his old paint.

Black Mask let out a small cry, waited for his pride to echo it back to him, and began the trek north.

44

KEYTHONG

Black Mask and Thistle came across several groups of the Seraph King's forces on their journey, catching them in ambushes and killing them one at a time the way they'd done with Crackling Sea rangers in the past, but that was to be expected.

What Black Mask didn't expect to see on this trip were two familiar faces, their wagons full of lumber and stuck in the mud. He called for a stop and crawled forwards, careful not to spook them.

"Xalt, Jer," he called out to two of the Ashen Weald rangers from his hiding spot. He tried using a voice that wasn't his but also wasn't any other wingtorn they may already know.

The two rangers had come with him in the now-infamous murder bog expedition, and it was a miracle they'd survived the affair. In fact, by the look of things, it was a miracle they were surviving their current affair, either. Black Mask had assumed they'd died off. Only Xalt's pink sheen to his blue feathers let Black Mask tell that it was them at all.

"Who's there?" Jer asked. "Why are you hiding?"

Black Mask stuck just his beak out of the moss pile he was speaking from. "A wingtorn that would like to help you, but I think you're going to try to kill me when I step out. And if you do that, my friends here will probably kill you to get revenge. So I'm hoping we can be civil."

"Ain't never had a problem with a wingtorn," Xalt replied. "Show yourself."

Black Mask revealed himself, and both rangers scrambled to grab their metal talons and nets. He waited until they felt secure with their weapons before speaking. "I mean you no harm. We've come north hunting Jonas. We bring a gift for the Ashen Weald."

"Sure," Jer said. "Let's just follow you into the deep bog a *second* time and see if you don't try to murder us again."

Xalt's comments were much more profane and creative, but he had some interesting ideas with what Black Mask could do with his 'help' and where that help should be placed.

Black Mask hadn't realized how much he'd missed ranger talk. It was certainly colorful. "You're surrounded by bog gryphons right now. If I wanted to attack, I would have just done it. But you seem stuck, and this whole place is oozing with flamingos. Are you sure you won't let us escort you?"

When they hesitated, Black Mask whistled, and several bog wingtorn showed their flame patterns while the witches' skulls peeked out from above.

"Blimey, it's all of them," Jer muttered. "Okay, yes, we could use help. We had a bunch of lumber and decided to cut through the south to bring it around so we didn't get spotted from above. Then we heard the attacks, so we tried to go off-trail. It worked for a bit, then we hit the mud."

Black Mask investigated the small caravan of goliath birds. They looked hungry. Several of the wagons were empty, having lost their lumber in their flight, but that provided a new opportunity.

"I can't help but notice that you have room in the back," he said.

Xalt shrugged. "We can carry you so you don't have to walk if you can get us unstuck."

"Oh, we'll get you unstuck," Black Mask said. "Thing is, another of your caravans fell to the west, near the old swamp tower. You remember the one."

"You mean the one you filled with water and sailfins and infected rangers and tried to kill us with?" Jer asked.

"You all ended up fine." Black Mask shrugged. "I'm not sure why you're mad. But yes. The rest of the wing-torn armor is there. Do you want to reach the eyrie with a bit of lumber or with armor? Are you willing to take a small detour?"

Jer shook his head. "Last detour took a month off my life, and I still have to spread bitterweed across my gape to keep the beakrot at bay."

Thistle looked at Black Mask in confusion, so he translated. "That's how rangers say yes."

"Kashow root would fix beakrot without the itchiness," Thistle shouted to Jer. "Bitterweed is nasty stuff to put near your nares or beak, let alone risk getting it in your eyes."

She was still hesitant to be near the opinici, as were many of the wingtorn, so Black Mask set the example. He let the rangers tie a rope to his harness, then he began pulling the wheel unstuck. The goliath birds didn't like having him there, but when they bit at him, they got a spike to the face, and they ended up leaving him behind as long as he stayed away from their legs.

Black Mask helped move a few wagons to dry land, then left half the wingtorn to guard them. Xalt and Jer went with him back the other way, keeping a close watch on the trails.

"You'll be fine," Black Mask assured them. "We cleared everyone out on our way up. We'll have to be careful crossing the boardwalk, but that shouldn't be an issue."

Their hesitancy persisted through the lowlands, best known as a mire of mud, but he showed them the path through where the submerged boardwalk still existed. The two empty wagons only got stuck once before they made it to the armor.

"Remember that time I lured you into here right as the flooding hit?" Black Mask asked. "That was hilarious."

"No, it really wasn't," Xalt said.

Jer just shook his head.

"Tough audience." While Black Mask wouldn't say the rangers he'd once tried to kill warmed up to him, they were less chilly once he'd helped them retrieve the kjarr wingtorn's armor and made it far enough east that the Crackling Sea Eyrie was in sight.

Which was just before things went wrong again.

BLACK MASK STOOD on the edge of the bog, looking into the grasslands between him and the Crackling Sea

Eyrie. Thistle shouted the all-clear, and in her defense, it looked pretty clear. A fantail had come by not long ago, but she hadn't spotted them in the foliage. The skies seemed fairly clear. It was only once they were in the tall grass that things fell apart.

Domesticated goliath birds were, relative to feral goliath birds, often fairly small. They were larger than a gryphon, but no opinicus wanted to be around an animal that could kick them to death in one or two blows. So there was a give and take between 'useful beast of burden' and 'would hunt you through the frozen taiga.'

The goliath birds Jonas had brought from the Alabaster Eyrie were firmly on the wrong side of that line. By the time the caravan stumbled upon one feeding on the carrion hidden beneath the sawgrass, it was too late to retreat.

The giant beast rose, letting out an angry *mronk* sound that seemed ferocious where the domesticated versions seemed cute. The tiny wagon birds spooked, chewing out of their harnesses and fleeing back into the bog, leaving the wingtorn to defend the carts.

There must have been a small team of scouts nearby, because when the animal *mronked*, opinici appeared in the skies.

"Go, fly!" Black Mask shouted to his ranger friends.

The herons had just gotten into the air to leave when one shouted back, "Flechettes!"

The wingtorn echoed the command back. Xalt and Jer dove under a wagon, but the wingtorn just tucked their paws under their armor and braced for impact.

The bog witches, unable to fit their wings into the

special armor and thus not wearing theirs, froze in place, not understanding what was about to happen.

Black Mask shouted, "Get the witches!" as he threw Thistle under himself, telling her to "tuck her pride."

She grabbed her tail and pulled it under her as the ground around them was filled with sharp points of metal. Several hit Black Mask, and the impact of his armor pressing against the palm spike wounds he'd suffered earlier was incredibly painful but not incapacitating.

"All clear!" Xalt shouted, and the wingtorn rushed towards the goliath bird. This was something Black Mask hadn't considered. That they'd armored their goliaths so they could fling flechettes down around them.

A few wingtorn took metal to the paws while running, and the bog witches mended wounds and got them on their feet again. The others surrounded the goliath, which stomped the ground in anger, then charged.

Black Mask was used to being much lighter on his paws, and only Thistle pulling him to the side got him out of the way in time—though she suffered several pricks from the spikes. The goliath crashed into a wagon, destroying one of its wheels, then turned back to them. The wingtorn hissed and scratched, avoiding its feet, keeping it pinned to the vehicle. From overhead, three of the bog witches flew up and slashed at its eyes, staying out of range of its beak.

While they kept it busy, Xalt and Jer grabbed rope from the wagon next to the bird. They tied one side to a wheel, then threw the other over the goliath's neck and pulled back, giving Black Mask his opportunity—which he missed because overhead, the Ashen Weald's flyers had finally arrived, and the familiar tones of Erlock Chartail shouted down "Flechettes!"

The wingtorn instinctively ducked, pulling the nearest bog witch underneath them.

Black Mask got Thistle again and used the opportunity to chat. "Do you have any of that beakrot powder?"

"Bitterweed? For the ranger? I don't think now's the time," she replied.

"For the goliath bird," he corrected her. "That stuff stings like hell if it gets in your eyes, right?"

The next round of flechettes hit the ground. This time, several slipped through the goliath bird's armor plates as the rangers held onto their rope even under the wagon.

Black Mask stood up, and Thistle grabbed a bag from her pouch and flung it at the face of the goliath bird, filling the air with a cloud of white powder that drove the bird mad once it inhaled.

Xalt and Jer were back from under the wagon and yanked the rope. Black Mask leapt towards the goliath, catching it by the throat, thinking he was about to end its life.

Instead, he found out just how leathery and tough a goliath bird's neck was. The creature ran off with him still attached. The three flighted bog witches flew after him, shouting something he couldn't hear. His eyes stung from the powder.

The fleeing bird took him twenty yards before two bog witches landed and tried to hold a rope between them to trip the goliath bird. It worked—sort of. The goliath bird kept walking, but the bog witches, still biting the rope, were pulled together, and their combined weight on the line brought it down. It took the rest of the wingtorn to kill the goliath, then they all retreated to the wagons.

The Ashen Weald's ground forces had arrived, along with several medicine gryphons. While Urious was surprised to find Black Mask there, Soft Paws nodded to him and called for one of the opinici to use their water to clean out his eyes.

"Sorry, I borrowed your armor," Black Mask told Urious. "It's a little sweaty. And bloody."

Urious shook his head. "I wish I could say it's good to see you. Actually, I will say it, and I am glad. It's good to have you back."

The other wingtorn came up behind Black Mask, and the witches landed. Jer stood by them to make sure there were no understandings, and Xalt poured water into Black Mask's teary eyes.

He nudged Thistle with a paw, mindful of his spikes, and she stepped forwards.

"Pride Leader Soft Paws," the green bog witch said. "We've come to ask to combine our pride with yours, a single, unified bog pride. And in exchange, we've brought a gift."

Soft Paws had always been unreadable, even to her old pride, but she sat stoically and listened, a floating skull in a field of sawgrass and bones. "Thank you for the wingtorn armor. It will save many lives in the days to come."

"Oh no," Black Mask said. "That's not the gift. Tell her, Thistle."

She unhooked the book from Black Mask's harness, pulled it out, and read aloud. "Your birth name is Kharalos. Your parents were Ari and..."

Thistle was cut off by the sound of goliath birds honking. "Well, we can finish inside. But I think we have the names and families of every stolen egg. Both the bog name and the original name, so it'll be easy to match up."

Several fantails provided cover by harassing the incoming goliaths from the air, Urious and the kjarr wingtorn guarded two opinici while they fixed the wheel, and Soft Paws led Black Mask and the others into the Crackling Sea Eyrie.

Never thought I'd come back here voluntarily.

It was a cold thought, but there was an even colder one. He was here because Jonas had returned. He'd saved the last of the bog pride. All that was left of him was vengeance. Whatever it took, he would kill the opinicus who had taken his wings.

Yet as he was led around to a long tunnel lined with crates leading into the eyrie depths, he caught a glimpse of several owl gryphons flying out to help defend the caravan, and he realized that wasn't all there was to it. Once he was inside and his wounds were treated, he needed to find Blinky.

"Are you okay being in charge for a bit?" he asked Thistle.

To her credit, she'd had her feathers torn out—by him—she'd been attacked, threatened, stomped on, flattened beneath an armored gryphon to avoid flechettes, and a dozen other things, but she seemed at peace with the decision to join up with the other bog pride.

"Of course," she said with a smile. Her eye was on the other side, so he found himself looking at her spiral of thorns design on one side of her face. "You go find your owl. Do I get to know her name now?"

He hooted her name in owlish first, then repeated it in common. "But you can call her Blinky."

The wingtorn in front of Black Mask skidded to a halt, nearly sending Black Mask's face into his spiky back. "Wait, you're mated to the *bog monster*?!"

45

HOME AT LAST

The sun shone through the observatory window and onto Jonas's face. He slipped a new piece of silk over the burned section, then attached the metal half-mask the Seraph King had given him. If everything went well, Mally would fix his wounds. If everything went well, Jonas would finally become the Crackling Sea reeve to honor his mate's memory.

Still, it felt good just to be home again. He'd had his allies scrubbing the scent of gryphon from his ranch day and night, and it'd finally faded. They'd lit scented candles from Duckbill to help change the smell further. It was pleasant.

He found an open door and exited into the morning light, stretching and looking out on the ranch land he'd developed. The stables were packed, though they were full of Alabaster Eyrie goliath birds. Nasty things, foul-tempered, but he supposed that's what you wanted during a war. They'd certainly turned out to be an effective way of digging up wingtorn burrows in the sawgrass marsh. He missed Tilly, the hatchling he'd raised from an egg. He wondered if she was among those at the Argent Heights stable. He'd have to find out.

He perched atop the main ranch building, soaking in the sun. He always woke up early. It was in his personality. His mate had been the same way, and he'd actually proposed to Jonas atop this very spire.

He was already blue reeve by then, though it was still the early days. The previous reeve had passed away without any clear successor, leading to some infighting. Only rumors of the Blackwing Eyrie possibly invading —rumors that turned out to be true—had allowed Jonas's mate to pressure the others into supporting him.

Times were simpler back then. The blue reeve knew he wanted a male mate, but he also saw the chaos caused by not having a successor, heir or otherwise. So he waited until after he and Jonas were married before finding opinici to have chicks with. Jonas was there before them, he helped raise them, and, sadly, he was still here after them.

He sighed. Every good memory was tainted with the bad. What would his fate have been if he'd stayed a lowly merchant? Would it have changed anything?

Rybalt would have killed them all either way.

Rybalt Reevesbane. The Seraph King's goal may be the Blackwing Eyrie, but Jonas's sights were set a little farther out to sea. Without the backing of the mainland eyries in the alliance, the Pitohui Eyrie would be defenseless. It was a day he looked forward to.

A grey-plumed messenger landed nearby and waited for him to acknowledge her. He took in a little more of the morning light, then motioned for her to join him inside, where food was already waiting.

"What word on my pet project, my wayward gryphon daughter?" he asked.

The messenger flinched. They were uncomfortable with Jonas referring to Satra that way. "The Kjarr remains out of sight. We still have loyalists inside the eyrie, but it's difficult for them to get around. All of the paths in and out are being guarded. The only one we've had a good look at is the passage that goes from the eyrie towards the Redwood Valley, the one they've been evacuating civilians through."

"Did she flee so soon? Have you searched the kjarr nesting grounds?" Jonas often had to explain where these locations were to his new allies. To them, the land south of the Crackling Sea was a blank spot on the map. They knew there were starlings in there somewhere, and they'd heard there was a small group of other gryphons in the southeast, but many of them didn't know the Redwood Valley had once housed an eyrie.

Reeve Brevin, my old friend who had the courage to save her opinici. What happened to you that night? How did you meet your fate? Where are your children?

He'd asked after them, but Mally the Nighthaunt had dismissed his concerns. "None of them took up the mantle of reeve after the blackwings murdered Ivess. If any survived, they're being smart and not telling us about the fact."

Jonas remembered eating dinner with Brevin's family, listening to them recite their snake stories. He could tell that she loved her children just as much as he had loved his. It was one reason she'd indulged him with Satra, giving the kjarr fledgling access to the university, although under guard.

"She's a hostage, not a child," Brevin said one night when it was just the two of them alone. "If they learn to be opinici, great. But never forget where their value lies."

Jonas had disagreed. "She just needs guidance. They all do. The bog and kjarr gryphons were at each other's throats when I stepped in to save them. Now, I can fix what's wrong with them, make them civilized. We have fifty hostages down there. What does Satra matter?"

"She will always be her father's daughter," Brevin said, emphasizing the word 'father.' "It's Jun we need to keep under control."

Jonas missed his chats with Brevin. Sometimes, when he talked about the lengths he was willing to go to protect his eyrie, other opinici looked at him askance. But she knew. Brevin knew that sometimes, you had to strike first and kill your enemies while they were still asleep. That was the only way to be certain they didn't kill you in the morning.

"Reeve?" the messenger said, pulling Jonas out of his memories. "Are you okay?"

Jonas smiled, or did his best imitation of one. "Sorry, at my age, sometimes memories are all you have left. Is it true that Mally's... process... also makes one younger?"

The messenger shook her head. "I'm sorry, I don't know. I don't spend much time in the capital. I said we've confirmed that Satra was there yesterday. She's been seen around the throne room from time to time."

"Mmmm." It made sense his adopted daughter would want to be near the throne. She probably missed him and had fond memories of it. Or perhaps she was now calling herself reeve and had taken over his old quarters. That had made sense when she thought he was dead, but it wouldn't do now. She'd need to be punished.

He stood up to stretch his legs, leaving from the large doors facing the path south. There were ambushes along the road now in case the Ashen Weald had forces hiding in the bog, but for the most part, they seemed to be in the clear.

He looked out at the land around the ranch. There were camps and camps of troops. With his permission, the Reevesport contingent had torn down an Ashen Weald banner and replaced it with their snake insignia. The Crestfall flamingos had formed their own little wading pool where the capybaras used to live. The single contingent of Alabaster Eyrie troops who had been charged with keeping him safe was to the north, fishing. And a constant stream of recruits, war goliaths, and supplies streamed in from New Eyrie.

"Where is Reeve Silver? Why is she not giving me these reports?" he asked the messenger.

The argent hawk bowed her head. "I apologize for my reeve's absence, but the padfeet attacks have grown more severe, and she was forced to go deal with them herself."

He grumbled a little, but he understood the need to make sure everything was right on one's own. It was a trait he admired in Reeve Silver. That, and she was the one reeve he could boss around.

Though, once I have my eyrie back up and running, an eyrie crucial to the conquest in the west, I'll have better standing than both Silver and the Crestfall reeve.

Which would make him a target for Rybalt again.

Jonas shook his head. No need thinking about such

things now. First, he needed his eyrie. Then he'd worry about Rybalt. By tomorrow, he'd have all the forces he needed at his command. While he felt sad he wouldn't be there in person to lead his troops, well, safety first. He'd enjoy the view from the ranch.

He had taken the last of the scraps of cloth stained with his mate's blood and put them in vials. He'd give one to each of a team of argent hawks and let them spill the contents. If Satra and Grenkin thought the storm curtains could hold back his pet, they were sadly mistaken. He'd watch their greatest barrier get torn down around them.

He'd just calmed himself down when a second argent hawk appeared in the sky.

"Reeve Jonas!" the new hawk shouted. "It's... you need to see this!"

He yawned but beat his wings to get back into the sky. The underlings were in a tizzy, as usual. No sense feeding into their desire for attention.

His Alabaster guard flew up to meet him, watching the skies for weald gryphons. He could never remember the actual names of the prides, so he'd made up names, calling them streamer-tails.

His facade of calm boredom lasted until he caught sight of his old island fortress on the Crackling Sea. It wasn't seeing it in ruins that upset him so, it was the sight of what lay dead on top of it, a creature he'd helped raise.

Jonas's anger hit its flashpoint, and he felt so hot all over it was like he was back in the Redwood Valley conflagration. As his mind churned and boiled, his beak stayed calm.

"Order all of the troops to prepare for war," he told

the nearest Alabaster opinicus. "We march on the eyrie at midday, and we liberate it before dusk."

46

MASKS AND BLINKS

This morning, Blinky had developed a second shadow. As she patrolled the halls of the Crackling Sea Eyrie, making sure there was no way to get in, several parrotfaces followed along behind her in case she needed something.

It was frustrating because it interfered with her ability to sneak. When she'd finally had enough, she turned a corner and waited for them to follow. Six ground parrot gryphons stared up at her.

"You, you, you, you, and you may go," she ordered. "You can stay, but only for now."

Veron slow blinked at her, but she didn't return it. He'd earned some goodwill, but she was still annoyed at being followed. Owl gryphons did not need bodyguards. Owl gryphons *were* bodyguards.

Because everyone who wasn't part of the war effort had been evacuated to the Redwood Valley, the Ashen Weald had taken a different strategy in defending the eyrie than when they were last here attacking it. Back then, Grenkin's plan had been to limit the wingtorn's ability to move from floor to floor, so barriers had been constructed, blocking off each section. This time around, they wanted the wingtorn mobile. So long as the curtains were up, the wingtorn could fight in the small corridors better than their opponents.

And, unlike out in the sawgrass marsh, the large, armored goliath birds shouldn't be able to get into the eyrie. Or so they hoped.

Blinky's ears were attuned to her friends, and she found herself tracking them down. Tresh and Younce were sleeping in the taiga quarters—Blinky had memorized the sounds of all of her friends while they were sleeping, just in case. Many friends spent a quarter to two-thirds of the day asleep or napping, so if she'd only memorized their awake sounds, she'd have been at a disadvantage when she needed to locate them.

Foultner would have said that was weird, but if Foultner wanted an opinion on these things, she should not have allowed herself to be captured.

Blinky leapt off the balcony, then glided back around to the lowest story, where the stormcloth barrier didn't quite reach the bottom anymore. Veron flew after her, nearly missing his landing on the wet stone.

Quess waved from the shore's edge. "Hey Blinks. What's the word from the dry sector? And who's your friend?"

"Nothing yet," the owl gryphon responded. "This is Veron. He helped me not save Foultner."

The ground parrot shook his head. He seemed shy and didn't introduce himself to Quess.

"Do not be rude," Blinky said. "I will not have a rude shadow."

"Sorry!" Veron *skraarked*. "Hello, Fisherfolk Quess. I

saw what you did to the reeve's pet. You're an incredible swimmer!"

"Don't let Blinky bully you," Quess countered. "She can be bossy if you don't take a stand early."

Blinky rolled her eyes but let Quess walk them along the bottom reaches. About twenty feet down were a mixture of sharp and dull rocks, usually inhabited by sailfin monitors. Somehow, they knew when the jellies were coming and returned to land. But they enjoyed eating the scraps that fell from the eyrie.

There were several petrels here, a stockpile of the jelly toxin, a smaller supply of the antidote, and some sentries checking the harnesses. Quess was no longer unique among the petrel fisherfolk as the only opinicus, she'd found a few on the islands who were willing to come and learn how to swim.

The waves were starting to reach up to the bottom level, so Blinky and Veron said their goodbyes and flew higher. The fantails and feathermanes, they skipped over. Both prides were always ready for a fight. Instead, Blinky followed two more voices into the medicine gryphon quarters.

"Hey Blinky!" Biski shouted. The room was empty. There were nests, aneda wraps, and a lot of boiled water ready to go. "Everyone is being extra careful today, so there's no one to see to. Just a bunch of wingtorn we patched up and sent to take a nap."

Wingtorn were getting wounded all the time, usually snake and bug bites, so Blinky didn't think anything of it. Urious and Thenca kept the wingtorn in top shape, so there was no need for the owl gryphon to check on them.

From the back, with her tail curled around her leg

and her wings spread, Soft Paws looked like a painting of a field of flowers. When she turned around, however, she was all skulls and blue claws.

"Blinky!" the young witch said, startling Veron. "It's good to see you. I stole you something from the kitchen. I like how the chef makes things for us to steal."

She handed Blinky some fish jerky. It wasn't easy to dry strips of jerky on the sea, so it had to happen near open flames. Blinky ate most of it. She offered a little to the ground parrot, but he declined.

Do the parrotface pride eat meat? I have not noticed.

"I do not think the chef intends for his creations to be stolen," Blinky said. "Make sure Biski does not get you into trouble."

"You sound like Erlock." Biski stuck her tongue out at Blinky, then went back to preparing everything for the upcoming battle.

Soft Paws followed them out of the infirmary and to the stairs, stating she was going to check in with Urious and the new wingtorn. Technically, she was in charge of the bog pride. There were few enough of them up north, but she wanted to make sure they were all okay following his orders.

Blinky trusted Urious to be one of the few in the eyrie who wouldn't need extra help. The term *new wingtorn* was a little alarming. Had someone been injured? Perhaps more wingtorn had come back from the kjarr nesting grounds. Blinky continued up to the top of the eyrie, where Satra and Grenkin were situated.

It took the owl gryphon a little searching to find them. She heard them talking, but they weren't in the throne room. Nor were they in the library. When she finally followed their voices, she was surprised to see they were securing the workshop.

"What do you think about the old secret passage?" Satra traced her paw over the stones. Many had fused together after Bario's explosive exit. Later, they were turned into a shrine for Merin's pridemates who were buried beneath.

Grenkin looked them over. "If he's going to get through here, he's going to need some explosives, which are just as likely to bring down the roof on his head. Still, I had them seal up the entrance to that path, just in case. We have to assume he'll try it. It leads to the top floor, and that's too convenient to pass up."

Several Crackling Sea builders were hard at work inside the room. They kept looking over at Satra and Grenkin, possibly in awe of being in the same room as such important figures. The rangers were often more professional.

Blinky hooted a greeting to the leaders. "Why protect this room?"

"It's the last place Jonas would think to find Satra," Grenkin explained. "We think he'll try to get to her, either because of their past connection or because she's in charge. So we're putting her in a place that's both hard to get to and he's unlikely to search."

That made sense to Blinky. She sniffed around the room, trying to catch any sign of a second secret passage, but if there was one, the explosion had collapsed it. She did get the slightest hint of air between the rocks, but not enough for someone to get through.

She let Veron follow her as far as the library, then she told him to get lost. "I must now check my snack-hiding places. Go spend time with your mate or something."

"Never was one for mates," Veron said. "But you can be alone if you want to. Just let one of us know if you need something."

Blinky hadn't considered that the parrotfaces might stay. "You are not leaving for the weald? It would be safer."

"When things go wrong, you'll want us here," he countered. "There's always something to fix or move, and the medicine gryphons need us to carry the wounded and clean up."

That made sense, so Blinky let him leave. War wasn't like hunting. There were a lot of things going on, a lot of gryphons and opinici around who weren't here to fight but who could die all the same.

Blinky didn't care much for that. Not at all.

She went through the throne room and waited. Without Erlock or Satra here, it wasn't as busy as it had been in previous days. She waited for a break, then snuck away to go check on her hidden snacks.

She was just about to slip into the royal chambers when she saw a familiar face looking at her from across the room.

It was Black Mask: not as a prisoner, not as an attacker, just walking with several kjarr wingtorn. When they saw Blinky looking over at him, they disappeared.

He hooted her name from across the room.

She hooted his back to him.

And then the cry came from the fantails outside, a cry taken up by every gryphon inside the eyrie, echoing all around them as the storm curtains fell.

The Ashen Weald was under attack.

47

BY LAND, SEA, AND AIR

Of all the things Quess owned, she hadn't expected the water-sealed bag to be the most valuable for war. She only had one, but it'd been filled with flint and tinder fungus.

"Everything they don't know about us is a spear in our quiver," Rorin explained to the small team of petrel opinici. "They'll have heard about Tresh. Or, if they haven't, they're going to figure her out when she leaps out of the water and starts pulling them under."

Tresh nodded with her mask on. It made Quess happy to see Tresh wearing it, and it took away her greatest worry—of Tresh breaking her beak for good. "They do not know two important things. They do not know we are immune to the jelly swarms, though they may figure it out when the afternoon storms roll in. And they do not know that we have petrel opinici."

Quess turned to the few recruits around her. "In a moment, we'll scratch each of you, knocking you unconscious. After that, we'll wake you up. You've probably seen us do this before, right? Well, just be aware that the mind will play tricks on you when you're under. It'll feel like hours. It's only been seconds."

"They're thinking of this as a fight over land and air," Rorin continued. "They're not thinking about the sea. And they're not watching their docks."

"We are not asking you to take New Eyrie by yourselves, but we are asking you to make it look like you could," Tresh said.

Quess held up her pouch. "We're going to swim into the raftworks. Last report, it's still in disrepair. Then we'll split up and light as many fires as we can in a short period of time, then slip back into the waves. Don't be a hero. Don't take any risks. If they don't know what's causing the fire, they won't know what they need to defend against it. Be sure to grab a bag of flechettes, courtesy of the Padfoot Pride. If there's time, hit the supply lines north of town before you return to the water."

"What about those of us staying here? What're we doing?" one of the petrel gryphons asked.

Tresh's ears perked up. "Chaos."

"Rescuing any of the Ashen Weald members who fall into the water," Rorin corrected. "Especially if the jellies swarm along the coast again."

Tresh shrugged. "And before that, chaos. We can get behind the enemy, come up from below. Kill as many as you can. Confuse them."

"Remember that your non-petrels allies aren't immune to the jelly toxin," Rorin added.

Tresh continued. "And that means our non-petrel enemies are vulnerable to it, also."

"Don't forget this effect wears off," Quess said. "You don't want to drown out there. So we're going to have two shifts. After about an hour, come back in and the next one will go out. You'll stay in here, with a medicine gryphon watching over you, until we can put you under again and bring you out."

Soft Paws raised a skeletal wing. "Hello! I am handling the wounded at the bottom of the eyrie. Look for me or someone like me."

Her skeletal paint stood up surprisingly well, Quess thought, considering how wet it was down here. The color was a little different, so perhaps she'd found a more water-resilient paste to use.

In the skies above, feathermanes and fantails held back the first of Jonas's forces. They were playing it careful, being cautious, retreating. The goal was to split the forces in half. Already, one of Merin's children had killed someone important and was being pursued by peacocks towards the large escape tunnel the last wagons departed from.

In the other direction, Erlock Fantail used her sharp tongue to say something so offensive to flamingos that they split off from the main group and came out over the water.

"That is my cue," Tresh said. "Team Shark, to me. Let us see how flamingos taste."

Quess held up a warning talon, and Tresh slow-blinked at her before being put under with a scratch, then brought back to consciousness.

"A joke, a joke! I will claw and lick. No biting." Tresh slipped down into the water, avoiding the rocks. Water-resistant paint had been used to mark the safe places for diving. And, if Quess wasn't mistaken, it was the same shade of blue as Soft Paws.

Quess rolled her eyes. "Hold up a few moments. Let

Tresh begin her assault, then we're going to swim for it after our enemies are occupied. Remember that diving under stress takes more air, so swim out to the other side of the island fortress first, then come up and breathe. Get calm. We'll regroup, then start swimming out to New Eyrie. We're separating from the Ashen Weald, but we're not on our own. We have each other. Got it?"

Several small cheers. Then unconsciousness. And when they woke back up, Quess saw a shark-like form rise from beneath one of the flamingos skimming the water and pull it under.

"Okay, let's go!" she said as she dove off the cliffs and into the water.

RORIN SLOWLY ROSE above the battlefield, watchful for any enemies above. Below him, fantails and flamingos battled for the skies as petrels pulled them into the depths from below. He caught sight of one of Quess's team surfacing for air past the island fortress, then disappearing beneath the waves. It was a long swim to New Eyrie, but if anyone could do it, it would be them.

High in the sky, Ranger Lord Mia served as a spotter for both Rorin and the fantails. What she was trying to spot was one very specific thing.

"Saltpeter!" Mia shouted. "Ranch side, coast side, and eyrie side!"

Rorin's sentries split into groups. Rorin himself went after the one coming from the south, over land.

The argent hawks were hard to spot but carrying such a large crate of saltpeter slowed them down.

Erlock, green tail streaming behind her, harried the hawk, forcing her to slow, distracting her from looking up, and then let out a screech and dove away.

That was Rorin's sign to take over. The sentry next to him struck flint and tinder fungus, lighting an oil-soaked javelin on fire, and Rorin tossed it at the argent hawk.

The hawk's face was one of relief when the javelin hit the crate instead of her. There wasn't time for her to register that the spear was on fire before it exploded.

Another loud explosion came from the north. The last argent hawk nearly slipped through, but a second flaming spear hit her crate, and she dropped it over the workshop, causing it to land on the old secret entrance and blow the top open.

I hope Satra's okay down there. I'll bet she's dealing with falling rocks.

Rorin caught the wind and rose again, getting into place. That had been close, and it was just the start of the day. He'd only just caught his breath when Mia shouted again. "Argent hawks! Four of them! Land, land, ranch, and sea side!"

Four hawks were too many, and this set brought defenders with them. The flamingos were easy to outmaneuver, but several silver hawks kept the fantails at bay.

Hitting a fast target was harder than a slow one, but he waited for the wind to be in his favor and tossed his spear. The first went off without a problem. The fire on the second javelin went out before it hit the crate, startling the hawk holding it but not causing an explosion.

The winds picked up, and his sentry had a hard time lighting the third spear on fire. By then, the hawk hit the ground above one of the entrances, lit the fuse, and didn't quite get away before it went off, reducing her and the ground beneath it to dust.

I wonder if she knew the fuse was so short.

He'd suspected a few would get through. Already, some of the Seraph King's forces headed for the entrance on the weald-side had changed direction and attempted to clear the rubble and descend into the eyrie.

I hope you're ready, Urious.

MOST OF THE explosions overhead were loud, but only one shook Urious's hiding place. The cardinal wing-torn next to him hissed in response. She still wore her armor, minus the spikes the bog wingtorn were so fond of using, but Urious's plan required him to be naked.

"If I still had my wings, I'd take care of those hawks," Cardinal grumbled.

Urious grinned. "Pshaw, *if you had your wings.* Look at you now! You're a killing machine. You've fallen off the walls of more eyries than most gryphons siege in a lifetime."

"And now I find myself defending one!" She sighed. "Hardly seems fair."

Several of Merin's old pride flew down through the tunnel and into the eyrie, followed by a dozen of their new feathermane pridemates. Urious and Cardinal remained hidden in the empty boxes piled along the route. There was a reason they'd evacuated everyone through the same tunnel and kept wagons leaving through it every day. Urious *wanted* Jonas to invade from this angle. It made their lives a lot easier.

It didn't take long before the first goliath bird crashed through, its armor shining in the sun until it stepped into the shadows. It sniffed around, noticing the heavy crates secured with netting above it, and Urious thought the game might be over before it began, but a white-tailed hawk opinicus drove it forwards, sending it charging down the hallway.

Urious counted the opinici who ran by. These were mostly peacocks. A few wore the strange black dye, but most looked like they'd been farmers conscripted to play soldier.

All of the wingtorn remained silent, waiting for Urious's order. He continued counting. The enemy had a lot of forces, but the key was to divide them into small, bite-sized chunks.

Once a hundred had passed, Urious nudged Cardinal. While she chewed through the ropes holding up heavy crates, Urious gave the signal, a resounding cry in Jun's voice.

Large crates fell, blocking the entryway, and several smaller ones crashed at set intervals, killing and driving the Seraph King's forces into disarray. The wingtorn launched themselves out of their hiding spots and began killing as fast as they could. Outside, he could hear someone shouting to use the goliath birds to clear out the rubble.

The wingtorn had just finished up when the first of the crate barricades fell. They grabbed their wounded and retreated deeper into the Crackling Sea Eyrie. Anyone who needed a medicine gryphon was redirected down a path that was more like a slide, opening into the throne room, then it was sealed up and hidden. The rest moved to new hiding places. The enemy would be more cautious now, warier. But they'd be looking for wingtorn or crates to fall from above. Maybe something from the front.

Urious pushed himself behind a stone statue, then found his burrow hole. It was a tight fit, which was why he was slightly oiled and not wearing even a harness or his leather bracers. He could only just squeeze in here, which should mean anyone with wings was out of luck even if they discovered the hole.

The rest of his forces had gone down below, careful not to step on the center of the ramps and staircase leading into the eyrie proper. Urious crawled behind the stone wall until he reached the aqueduct system that brought water down from the rain barrels and cistern where it was stored. As part of the restoration, Triddle had made some modifications. Grenkin had protested, but Triddle pushed back, claiming there would always be a time when you needed to drain the entire freshwater system with one rope. Last night's planning session had reminded Urious of its existence, and it was one he planned to make good use of.

I hope Askel and Triddle are safe at Crestfall. We never stopped to consider they might be hitting several places at once.

The next set of troops stalked into the long tunnel to the eyrie. A goliath bird sniffed at the statue but couldn't find a way behind it, nor would it realize that Urious had crawled above them now. These forces had wizened up, and they sent the birds in front, letting them investigate.

Goliaths were designed to smell for living enemies,

however, and when the first one slipped on the oiled stairs, the same oil Urious had rolled in earlier, it went sliding down, and then out a stone balcony with the railings removed and a flap cut into the stormcloth.

A peacock laughed at the bird's misfortune. He found his flint and struck it against the rocks, but the oil didn't catch fire. It was a straight shot to the balcony from here, but they had figured out that the sides of the ramps weren't slick.

While it would have been nice if more of them had slipped on the oiled stairs, that wasn't actually Urious's plan. He just wanted the staircase filled with slow-moving targets.

His enemies were about halfway down when he yanked the rope to pull out the single stone holding together the sabotaged cistern. The 'Triddle Stone,' as they called it.

A deluge of water spilled down into the tunnel from behind the peacocks, flinging them down the slick ramp and off the balcony and into the sea, where Urious wished them many, many jelly stings.

This isn't so bad.

He slipped down from his hiding spot—literally, slipped and slid, barely squeezing out from behind the statue. Another set of opinici was working its way through the tunnel, but Urious pulled himself from between the statue and the wall and tried to run for the stairs. Unfortunately, his view from above hadn't been perfect, and a single black peafowl stood at the top of the ramp, a set of long claws dug into the wall to keep him from flying off.

The peafowl hissed, shaking away the water, and fanned his tail, showing off his cobra-like markings. It was all very impressive, but the Reevesport opinicus had failed to anticipate what Urious would do next.

With an earsplitting-shout, the lead wingtorn flung himself into the peacock, sending them both down the oiled ramp, out the balcony, and into the skies.

The wingtorn slashed at his opponent's wings on the way down, then kicked off from the peacock long before the rocky spires rose to meet them.

A fantail appeared out of nowhere, summoned by the screaming, and latched onto Urious's naked body after several tries to find an un-oiled location, then pulled him up into the sky.

"Please tell me that was your plan going wrong," Erlock Fantail chided. "Because if that's what happens when everything goes right, I don't want to see the alternative."

Urious grinned up at his savior. "Hey, I've killed about a hundred opinici today. How many are you up to?"

She rolled her eyes and dove down, tossing Urious into the fisherfolk staging area at the bottom of the eyrie before flying back up.

Soft Paws was there with a blanket waiting to catch Urious from sliding and remove the oil. "Weren't you at the top of the eyrie? How did you get down here so fast?"

"Practice," Urious said, then he wiped his paws off on the wall and dashed back up top for the next stage of his plan.

48

NEW EYRIE, REVISITED

Quess paced herself on the trek across the southern tip of the sea. It wasn't as much for her muscles, which were used to swimming incredibly long distances for fun, but the petrel opinici with her hadn't devoted a large percentage of their lives chasing after Tresh in her adolescent years.

Spending so much time with her sister-in-law always made Quess miss her mate and children. It was a bittersweet feeling. She'd met Tresh's brother before Tresh was born, so they'd been in each other's lives a long time. For Tresh, that was her entire existence, though Quess had always felt a little like an outsider.

It was still painful to think back to those days. When she did, she found herself becoming angry, inconsolable, the way she had been right after it happened. She could still feel the anger rising in her, overwhelming in its ferocity. At the battle for Sandpiper's Dune, she'd been terrified. The seas were full of sharks, her friends were dying left and right. She didn't have it in her to give in to the anger. But when the rangers fled, when she sat on the sand of the dunes and cried, she'd lost herself to the grief.

Part of her soul had been gone the entire time she traversed the bog. She'd volunteered to track the rangers past the raftworks, into the depths. And it had cost her another friend, Beaky. For a while, it had cost her mind, too, when the parasite took over.

It was strange to think of her time spent infected. Most of it was a blur of talking to Soft Paws while being treated, her sight turning grey, lost time. New anger took hold, one that didn't need memories of her dead children to fuel it.

Then Blinky had come, rescued her. For days, Quess had sat in the back of a cave, shivering, drinking strange elixirs, unsure what was real. She'd had nightmares that felt real, and reality felt like a dream. When she'd come out of it, all that remained was her anger, and she'd honed it to a blade she used to kill Vitra and nearly kill Urious.

Anger was alive in her now. Indignation. She was missing the one thing that had helped keep her sane— having someone to talk to who had never known her as a mother or sister. Bruen, a simple ranger, once an enemy, someone she could have killed if they'd met under other circumstances, had served as a sounding board.

He often joked that anyone could do what he did: sit there and listen to Quess speak. Maybe he was right, she didn't know. But getting to talk to someone who knew the bog, knew what had happened, but didn't judge her for it was...

Stabilizing.

She wished he were here now. While Grenkin's

pardon had helped many of the rangers from the bog transition back to life with their families, she wasn't willing to risk Bruen's life on it, so he'd stayed behind. She'd seen how he bristled, but she needed him to be safe. They'd fought side-by-side in the past, she didn't doubt his prowess with talon and net, but one of his greatest traits could also serve as his downfall this far north: he was second in command to ex-Ranger Lord Ellore.

The crime of loyalty.

They were nearing New Eyrie now, and Quess gave the sign to group up. The others came close, but not close enough to draw attention if any patrols flew overhead, and waited for Quess to poke her head above water. The skies were dark and clear of argent hawks. The rest came up to breathe, to relax. There was no more talking to do. They all knew the plan. Quess just pointed to each of the buildings, and the fisherfolk with her nodded.

They dove deep, into the long reeds, and through the turtles. The old raft hangar was still falling apart, so that would give them a chance to re-do their jelly immunity in case a fast escape was needed.

They approached from beneath the water, slow and spread out so no one would notice them. Though the enemies' eyes were on the sky, there was something watching the water.

Several sailfins, lazing below the docks or on driftwood, took note of the meals coming up from below. Quess paused, the petrels behind her doing the same. One of the larger sailfins swam towards her, wiggling back and forth. That was good, as it gave them an opportunity to kill it.

She gave the sign, and the petrels went in different directions. Quess kept the big sailfin's attention, causing it to focus in on just her. It was two meters away when petrels on either side caught it in the ribs, leaving long gashes on it.

It exhaled bubbles angrily, but Quess and the others disappeared into the depths. Sailfins tended to prefer the shore and easy meals. They didn't swim too deep, and the sea still had enough of a drop-off to dissuade them from chasing too far.

The large sailfin turned to swim back to shore to recover, trails of blood behind it, when it realized the danger it was in. The disappearance of the petrels into the weeds hadn't slowed the smaller sailfins coming up behind it. Instead, they were now looking at it as their next meal.

Quess waited until the frenzy had begun, then she led her team to the remains of the hangar to dry off and prepare for part two of her plan.

QUESS WOKE up from the toxin's dreams to one of her team giving her the antidote in the burned-out hangar. She'd let too much time pass since the last time at the Crackling Sea Eyrie, and this dose hit her harder than she was expecting.

We're lucky we didn't run into jellies on the way over. I wonder when our immunity ran out?

Once everyone was awake again, they got to whispering. The hangar was partially flooded, but the rafters were still clear and gave them a bit of breathing room from sailfins. There were also enough gaps in the roof to let them get a good look at New Eyrie. Really, New New New Eyrie after the number of times it had been rebuilt. It no longer resembled a fishing village at all, which was too bad, as Quess loved fishing villages.

The Seraph King's forces had rebuilt Reeve's Nest. If Silver were still there, it'd make a tempting target. As it was, no one knew where the only full reeve in the enemy's forces had disappeared to. She didn't seem to be directing anyone, and the teams of ground parrots who spied from the sawgrass at night hadn't caught sight of her in a few days.

In fact, it almost appeared as if no one was leading New Eyrie at the moment, which might work even better. Once flint and tinder fungus had been handed out, Quess managed to sneak near enough to the gates to overhear what was going on there. The guards seemed confused about where to put all of the traders. The stables and garrison were both full. They wanted to direct everyone to continue to the Clover Ranch, but the traders were pushing back, saying they'd just ridden through the desert, and they wanted nothing more than to rest.

Excellent.

Quess used the confusion to slip deeper into the city with two petrels in tow. She didn't know how bustling New Eyrie had been in the past, but right now, it was full of opinici and supplies, two things that reacted poorly to being near fire.

It took some timing to get past the heated flamingo pools to the large, fancy tower at the western edge of the walls. Once she was in position, however, she found herself with too much waiting time. She'd told everyone to start their fires when the seventh lightning strike hit, but the brewing storm seemed content to sit on the sixth rumbling thunder and not provide her with the sign she needed.

Her mind drifted back to a different shore, the home she'd made there, and then back to Tresh. Quess was just starting to go back to the dark place again, a place filled with chittering and silver, when lightning struck and the entire camp shook with thunder.

She crawled up and over a balcony, to the edge of a very large pantry, and found the dry goods. Then she started a fire and slunk back beneath the building, past the pools of sleeping flamingos, and past Reeve's Nest, a building that already smelled of smoke. She made it to the raftworks to wait for her friends.

When the fire hit the flour and the bottom of the tower exploded, they were still missing a fisherfolk. Quess ordered the rest to hit the water and get into position with their flechettes, but she remained. She wouldn't leave anyone behind.

When the last team member crawled into the raftworks, she was bleeding profusely. "I wanted to open the gates before I lit the stable fire so none of the birds were hurt, but they weren't very appreciative of my efforts."

Quess patched up her friend as best she could. She knew this scout, had learned to weave next to her in the early days at Crane's Nest. "The water isn't going to be safe for you. But it's not safe to stay here on land, either. I want you to count to a hundred, dive, swim as far out as you can, and then take to the sky and head east, got it? We have no idea what sorts of creatures your blood will draw out of the depths."

The scout nodded, and Quess waited until she was

sure her friend wasn't going to pass out before taking her flechettes and getting into position.

While New Eyrie was now buzzing like a wasp's nest, the road of goliath-pulled wagons seemed unfazed by the fire. They carried on as they always had. Quess watched from the water, staying far enough out that the sailfins weren't willing to risk coming for her. And what she saw was a road that wove through the dry parts of the sawgrass marsh, with small railings to deter the predators.

A tiny fence would work to herd the sailfins if there was no food on the other side. It was what fisherfolk called a visual barrier: it worked to keep salamanders out of the garden so long as they weren't hungry or chasing something. But a side effect of the small strip of dry ground making up the road was that it gave Quess a great target for her metal spikes. Enough dead goliaths or opinici would lure the monitors onto the road, adding to the chaos.

She counted the lightning strikes, musing this might be the only place in the world where they served as an accurate timing mechanism, and on the twentieth, she flew out of the water, rounded on the road, and emptied both her bag and her wounded friend's bag on the wagons below.

All along the path, her petrels attacked with flechettes. It was grisly work, goliaths and opinici screamed and died, but her petrels hit the water and swam out to sea again to escape.

They were into the depths before Quess noticed her wounded friend was nowhere to be found. She called out an *ooo-awk* to the others, and they backtracked. Her missing fisherfolk struggled to get out of the water, so they wove back around, grabbed her harness, and helped lift her into the air. Once she was out of the sea and the water had slipped off her oiled feathers, she was strong enough to stay airborne as they flew home.

I hope this was what you wanted, Rorin.

49

CROWNS OF BLUE AND GOLD

The greatest lesson Satra had ever learned was to trust her friends, her pride, and the other prides that made up the Ashen Weald. She'd even come to trust the free prides, now that she better understood them.

Which wasn't to say she wasn't anxious. She'd agreed to let Ranger Lord Mia run the defenses. Mia had Olan running back to Satra with reports every so often, but overall, it was Satra's delegates who were handling the tactics while Mia managed the strategy.

Olan, out of breath from running up to the workshop and bleeding slightly from his nares, shouted another report at her before disappearing again. He didn't look like he'd seen combat, just that his condition was starting to worsen. Satra felt for him. His sisters had moved sky and mountain to save him from Mally the Nighthaunt, yet it was unclear if he'd last another four years, let alone two.

The Kjarr of the Ashen Weald sat in front of the window. The sky was dark, but the rains hadn't reached her yet, just a light mist that clung to the stormcloth and made it hard to tell what was going on outside.

She closed her eyes, pushed a paw against the strange material, and thought of Mignet. Her lover's greatest dream was to come to the Crackling Sea, to learn, to watch storms with her mother, Ellore. It was Mignet's love for this eyrie, the eyrie of her mother, that had influenced Satra's decision to spare its inhabitants. Since then, whenever Satra found herself here, she always took a night to listen to the rain and remember Mignet.

Satra's meditation was interrupted by a loud smack as a white, rosetted gryphon slammed the body of a flamingo opinicus into the barrier. She couldn't tell if it was Younce or not, but the gryphon flew off okay while the flamingo fell to the rocks, food for the same sailfins who had consumed the wings of her pride years ago.

Satra switched to pacing. Several crates of saltpeter crashed to earth, presumably courtesy of Rorin's spears, and the explosion wracked the small workshop she sat in. Rocks tumbled from the ceiling, and a pair of golden wings fell from the wall. She'd seen them several times, but she'd never bothered to give them a close look. She picked them up now, then dropped them when she saw her father's name on them, filled with disgust.

She moved away from the wall, closer to the storm-cloth, careful not to step on the lines of metallic blood filling in the cracks. She was halfway across when the biggest explosion yet landed atop the workshop, covering Satra in debris.

She pulled herself out, checked to make sure everything was okay, then looked to see if everyone through the corridor connecting her to the throne room was okay, but part of it had collapsed, trapping her in here.

She automatically checked the fuse on the explosives next to the control mechanism for the storm curtains to see if she could escape that way but stopped herself. She didn't have anything to light it with, and the longer the curtains held, the safer all of the Ashen Weald would be. This small corner had turned out to be pivotal in bringing them down last time. It might almost be better if she died here rather than give it up too early.

She walked back to the doorway, but she wasn't strong enough to move any of the large chunks. From the other side, she could just make out Olan.

"I'm okay!" she shouted. She couldn't tell if he was hearing her or not, but she was glad someone was working on the problem. All she had to do was what she had already been doing: sit here, remain calm, and let the gryphons and opinici she trusted solve the problems for her.

Calm. I can be calm.

A scream came, not from the direction of the corridor to the throne room but from the other direction. One of Grenkin's traps in the secret passage had sprung. Some of the dropped explosives must have opened up the entrance on the other side, something she knew would probably happen but had hoped wouldn't.

She braced herself, finding a place where rocks from overhead wouldn't hit her. The next trap should be an explosion. She sat and waited, but the loud bang never came.

One of the saltpeter crates must have knocked something loose.

From the shrine to Merin's pride came a scratching sound. She heard shouting, then she heard the *mronk* of a large goliath bird trying to dig her out.

She practiced breathing slowly. She'd hoped Grenkin's second trap would seal that tunnel shut. Now they'd need to defend the workshop, too. Still, there was nothing to do except wait and see which side reached her first.

I am calm. I will be calm. I am calming myself.

She thought of snowy peaks and hot springs and Mignet and sitting around a meal with her father and Thenca and Urious. She thought of the last Blue-eyed Festival. She thought of spending hours walking through the kjarr nesting grounds and chatting with Merin.

And then, the whispers started from the other side of the wall. She looked over, seeing an eye looking through a hole in the rubble blocking the secret passage.

"Satra, my dear little Satra." Jonas's voice. "Did you miss me? Is that what brought you to my workshop? There's still time for you to cast aside this foolishness. I've raised you better than this."

Her breathing turned rapid, and it was like she sat on the island in the sea while the reeve's pet wound around it again. She looked back at the rubble, but the sounds from the other side were a goliath bird again, pulling away at the rocks. She'd just calmed down when it started again.

"I treated you as a daughter," Jonas's voice came to her again. "I gave you an education and manners—which you were sorely lacking! I taught you how to live in the world of opinici. You were to be the first. I foresaw a world where gryphons lived in peace and harmony with opinici, and I see you've attempted to carry out my dream with your Ashen Weald."

She refused to look at the rubble. The goliath bird returned, scraping away at the rocks, then disappearing back up the secret passage.

"I woke up alone, burning, dying," his voice continued. "Even then, I knew what you had done. A saw, modified for gryphon use. A bonesaw, just like the one I used on your father. Satra, you were like a daughter to me. I offered you the world. How could you?"

She was shaking now and couldn't stop. Smelling him in the old royal quarters was hard enough. She'd had Grenkin there with her, she'd been drinking to Merin's death, and her nightmare was still just that—a dream. She'd both believed and hadn't believed Jonas was real at that point. She didn't know what it said about her moral character, but she'd secretly hoped Rybalt or the Blackwing Alliance would take care of him long before he reared his ugly head back here.

"There's still time. Surrender to me, my darling, kjarrling daughter, before I open the way back into my workshop, and you can live at my side again. Perhaps, were I not so kind with the gift I gave you, you would be easier to teach."

Satra knew what freedom he had gifted her. She looked at the metal wings, her father's gilded wings, now broken and crashed to the floor. The reflection looking back at her through them was a frightened child in trouble. Blood, tears, disheveled.

She licked a paw, slicking her golden crest into a semblance of normal. Then she cleaned everywhere she was bleeding until it clotted and ceased. The goliath bird gathered more stones, then left, and a bloodshot eye appeared at the crack in the shrine.

"I'm not your daughter, Jonas, and I'm not afraid of you." She stood and walked over, getting a small measure of happiness when the eye withdrew. "You tried to chop up gryphons to make them fit into your opinicus society, to take away our identity and culture. You wanted little opinici without talons to parade in front of other reeves. That's not what I've done here.

"The reason I succeeded and you failed is because I didn't bring together these prides and eyries by cutting away what made them different. Instead, I found the places where our sharp edges fit together and reinforce one another. I have never asked any gryphon or opinicus to give up what makes them who they are.

"That's why the free prides are here, too. Why the fisherfolk have come to my aid. These are all groups you tried to eradicate from the weald. They weren't some plague, some failure of civilization to burn out and replace with grass and ranches. They're my strength. They're my love. And they're beating you."

She looked down at the metallic blood in the cracks, down at the shrine to Merin's kin. Then she pushed her beak against the crack to shout.

"This is your last chance to surrender, Jonas. I can promise you a fair trial if you do. If you don't, my vengeance will find you, and it will not be quick. You'll bleed out on these cliffs you love so much, then your body will be tossed to the sailfins like so much refuse."

The secret passage turned silent. Had Jonas himself really come to the front lines to taunt her, or was it all in her head?

The shrine cracked, and what had once been a hole

big enough for an eye now fit the entire beak of a goliath bird.

Most of Satra wanted to scream and run to the far side of the room and pray. But that last, tiny bit of Satra that was pure anger and resilience was what she held onto, what had always guided her in times like this.

She let out a hiss to turn a monitor blue and slashed with her paws, slamming the tip of the goliath's beak into the rocks on the side. She ducked as an opinicus pushed a pole through to try to strike her, catching it in her beak and pulling it down. The goliath bird slammed its head against the shrine, and the wall gave way. The bones of the gryphons who died in the previous collapse tumbled past her.

She licked her paw, waiting to grab the next beak or paw or tool jammed through, when a familiar voice came from the other side of the room.

"Satra, to me!" Olan shouted.

She shook her head. "No! We can't let them in this room. I won't let them have it! They'll pull the storm-cloth down early."

While Olan retrieved her, some of the blood from his nares spilling on her shoulder, two opinici wearing Redwood Valley flameworks harnesses ran inside. They retrieved the explosive from the storm curtain mechanism, lit the fuse, and tossed it past the goliath bird's head and into the secret passage.

Satra latched onto her father's wings as several rangers and feathermanes pulled her down the opposite corridor. This time, when the explosion went off, the saltpeter from Grenkin's trap also detonated, collapsing the entire secret tunnel and the roof of the workshop down around it.

Satra, Olan, the two phoenixes, and a pawful of rangers and feathermanes sat in the throne room, covered in dust. Just as one of them started to speak, the corridor outside the workshop collapsed, sending another wave of dust at them.

"Satra," Olan coughed. "Satra, are you okay?"

The Kjarr of the Ashen Weald licked a paw and used it to clear the dust off her face and beak. "Perfectly fine. Now, I believe you're late in reporting. How are my wingtorn doing? What word from the skies?"

AN ENDLESS FLOOD of enemy forces spilled into the main tunnel leading to the Crackling Sea Eyrie. From there, they were forced to split into dozens of small side passages, some too small for goliath birds. Where the passages were large, they tended to lead to a series of increasingly elaborate traps and, ultimately, dead ends.

Where the corridors became narrower, they ended with small forces. Or, in the case of this particular passage decorated with desert rose petals, it ended in a small open space with a single angry bog wisp in it.

Black Mask stood in his full spiked armor. Thistle had painted ghostly wings onto his sides and a flower on the extra-long spiked piece covering his striped tail. The flower was twisted into the glyph for 'pride,' showing that she still had her sense of humor.

The opinici who came into the room found themselves in trouble quickly. They didn't want to touch Black Mask's long spines, but there wasn't space to use their weapons or get around him.

The bog wingtorn smacked the bottom of his tail

against a broken table, taunting the opinicus to come forwards. And when it did, he swung his tail, giving his enemy a beakful of spikes before finishing him off.

By then, two more were climbing over the rubble into the room. One of them pulled out a bag of flechettes and tried to fling them at Black Mask, but he ducked down, letting them hit against his armor. The darts worked best with a lot of room to fall and gain momentum, and these tickled more than hurt.

He charged, sending one opponent into the other, then tossed their bodies up the passage to slow down the next set who came down this road.

From behind him, there came a blast of heat on the stormcloth covering the balcony. "Got some saltpeter here!"

Immediately, several armored but un-spiked wing-torn appeared and hid throughout the room. The opposing force had more flyers than they did, and it was inevitable they would start using a combination of oil, saltpeter, and fire to try to burn through parts of the stormcloth.

Several Redwood Valley engineers also showed up with a contingent of parrotfaces in tow. Sometimes, the stormcloth could be repaired. Other times, it required a new barrier.

While Black Mask kept the room clear from one direction, Urious and his cardinal second-in-command attacked flamingos and peacocks who spilled through the hole in the stormcloth. A dozen made it in before a cry came from outside.

Twice their number in spears crashed down around the hole, impaling the opinici trying to pull themselves in. Urious shouted out a few kind words, or at least friendly banter, and the engineer and parrotfaces took some extra scraps from sails and began melting them in place to seal the breach.

"Saltpeter is here!" came some hooting from up top, and Black Mask recognized the hissing of his mate and her friends up one of the passages behind him. Several dead bodies fell down the ramp, tumbling near his feet.

"The peafowl is very meaty. In case you get hungry," Blinky shouted down, and Black Mask laughed, though the Redwood Valley opinici looked alarmed. There were rumors going around that Strix, the old ruler of the weald owl and Ninox's pride, would hunt and eat opinici. It was just goose tales and nonsense, but Blinky had played into it, sometimes muttering, "Just killing, not eating!" when he was close enough to hear.

The twin cries of Erlock and Younce pulling opinici off the stormcloth echoed through the break in the stormcloth, and the engineers and parrotfaces ran up to seal the new hole.

Black Mask finished off four small opinici who came down his corridor side-by-side, and Blinky appeared to help toss the bodies past the barricade.

She asked him how he was in owlish, he responded, she corrected his owlish, and then she carefully licked his beak before retreating to pull food out of one of the supply caches.

They had a few minutes together before the next wave came, and she backed up to give him room to be spiky. From down another ramp, he heard a group of Crackling Sea opinici, helpers and not rangers, come in. Blinky asked them what they were doing here, but they disappeared down another corridor.

"I am going to see who they were. You are on your own. Is this okay?" the owl gryphon asked.

He slapped the un-spiked bottom of his tail against the table to respond, then went back to killing and holding the line while Blinky disappeared into the depths of the eyrie again.

50

THE WOUND IN THE EARTH

B linky walked past bog witches, wingtorn, and a mix of all the weald and free prides. The smell of blood filled the eyrie with the curtains closed. And while Orlea herself wasn't here, Blinky appreciated the good a few flameworks engineers could do.

Yet something was wrong. She could smell it, in between the blood. There was a scent she couldn't place, and that bothered her. The strange herons who ignored her orders were part of it, but she hadn't pieced it together yet.

Whenever she thought she'd tracked down the herons, a new hole would form in the stormcloth, and she'd be forced to hold it until the engineers arrived. This was actually her favorite part, other than getting to fight alongside Black Mask.

It is good to see he can fight. I have only ever seen him lose before now, but that is because he was fighting me, so he was never capable of winning.

There was a moment when the opinici stopped coming through the hole in the stormcloth, when

Erlock or Younce or sometimes even Mia would slash down and clear the area, moments before the engineers arrived to close it up, when Blinky could talk to her friends on the other side of the wall.

This time, a peacock stuck its head through the hole, and before Blinky could kill it, a shark face appeared behind it and pulled it down.

"Blinky!" Tresh said. "How are things inside?"

Blinky blinked. "Good! I am killing many things. It is a nice feeling. They do not let me kill this many anymore. Not after the incident at the ranch."

Blinky headbutted Tresh's mask, and they separated. The owl gryphon knew there were a lot of things going on, and a lot of her friends were in danger, but she wished they could get together and spend more time bonding like this. It made her happy in a way she hadn't felt before. All she really missed was Foultner and Henders.

The engineers took over, and Blinky continued away from the hole in the stormcloth, but she suddenly knew what was wrong. Most of the holes were in the center trying to break through to the large amphitheater with balconies leading to all of the different floors. Yet when she walked away from the center, towards the outer areas where the stormcloth mechanisms were located, the smell of burning didn't get any weaker. She sniffed, following a trail left by a blue heron and the aroma of something sizzling.

She caught up to them near one of the stairwells that was supposed to have been sealed, but someone had re-opened it. They were far from the frontlines, which worried Blinky even more.

She shouted to the heron, and he turned around. In

his eyes, she saw fear—real fear, fear of her. Then she saw that he'd just lit the fuse on the saltpeter bomb placed next to the stormcloth mechanism on this floor, the ones that were only supposed to be detonated if all hope was lost.

"I've had enough of gryphons," the heron shouted.

She pounced, but she was forced to choose between killing the traitor, the *Jonas loyalist* as Merin would have called him, or stopping the bomb. She shoved her paw against the fuse, but it didn't go out. She took her sharpest talon and just managed to cut it before it went off.

That was too close.

She entered the corridor and chased the heron up the spiral stairwell, her claws scrabbling against the stone. She could hear more voices, more heron voices, above them. She'd just grabbed his back leg, pulled him down, shoved his spear-like beak aside, and could taste his throat when a series of explosions from inside the Crackling Sea Eyrie shook everyone off their paws.

SATRA, now marginally less dusty than she had been after the workshop, sat in the throne room and listened to reports from across the eyrie.

Things were going surprisingly well. Not just surprisingly well, reports had come in that New Eyrie was burning and the storm had moved east, towards them, so there wasn't any rain to put out the fires. The sea below crackled with excitement as the lightning started.

If the rains are hard enough, that might make it difficult for them to continue assaulting us from the air.

Against all of her greatest fears, the Ashen Weald was actually winning. The addition of the extra prides made a difference. Iony in particular had been given control of a huge cavern where goliath birds were usually stabled, and a lifetime of knowledge earned fighting the Seraph King had been employed there. She didn't know exactly what or how he was doing it, but the last reports said he'd killed a hundred opinici on his own.

When Mia had sent a messenger down to see what his tricks were so she could employ them elsewhere, the kakapo messenger had arrived back with a two-word reply from Iony: *Trade secrets.*

"Is it too soon to celebrate?" Mia asked. "This was an unwinnable fight, and we've just about won it. I don't care how good your supply line is. After a certain point, there are no bodies left to fight."

Grenkin and Satra shared a look, and the leader of the Crackling Sea suggested they not count their chicks before they hatch.

More reports came in. The series of tunnels had worked. The Ashen Weald never found itself in a fight where it wasn't in the winning position, except for outside.

But if the rains come...

A loud sound resonated off the Crackling Sea. Satra's first thought was thunder, or perhaps lightning had struck the eyrie. It was rare, especially with the curtains down, but it happened from time to time.

Seconds had passed before more explosions hit. This time, it was obvious what had happened. She rushed through the throne room to the balcony where the old reeve had given speeches to his opinici in the amphitheater, watching as the stormcloth barrier collapsed and sunk into the water.

Fantails shouted reports that echoed into the throne room. The enemy's retreat back to New Eyrie had halted. They'd turned back. The large entryway that had served so well to funnel the enemy into the tunnels where the wingtorn had an advantage was now seeing a reverse in the flow as flamingos and peacocks flowed out of it, then flew around to enter from the undefended cliffs.

"Give the order," Satra commanded Mia. "Give the order to retreat."

The ranger lord issued the command, echoing as the fantails relayed it across the skies.

Satra turned to the ground parrots and friends here in the center. It would only be moments before the enemy pushed in from the outside. "You've all done well. You did better than we could have dreamed. You stood up to the largest empire Belamuria has ever known, and you made them bleed. Your friends and loved ones who weren't here fighting beside you are all safe in the weald. Everyone you helped kill today is one fewer opinicus to chase us into the taiga and valley."

She nodded to Mia, who began opening the hidden passage behind the throne, courtesy of Grenkin's sculptors. "Now it's time for you to go. I don't know what awaits us, but I'm proud to have served the Ashen Weald with you. If you get lost, head up to Snowfall if you can fly, or the grove by the waystation if you can't. There are patrols and medicine gryphons there to help you find your new home. I'll send word once we have a new base of operations. Now go!"

Grenkin stayed behind to make sure the throne room was emptied, closing and binding the door from the balcony to the room itself, while Olan and Mia escorted Satra into the tunnel. It was small, dirty, and not particularly well-made even considering how little they'd had to work with, but it fit everyone.

Satra wasn't privy to where the tunnel let out. She didn't know if it would be safe, dangerous, or how far they'd have to go after that to reach safety. She hadn't succeeded in the sense of defending the eyrie or stopping Jonas, but she was at peace.

For once in her life, a bloody battle had been fought, and it wasn't the civilians who paid the price. That was the most she could ask for.

THE FIRST WAVES of rain hit Younce like a bad mood and refused to let up. He ached, he bled, he nearly fell out of the sky from exhaustion, but he fought on against an overwhelming force. The only thing that had kept the aerial forces of the Ashen Weald from succumbing to the enemy's superior numbers was their opponents' deep fear of the sea.

Lightning struck, jumping between three white-tailed hawks wearing metal armor on its way down, and as their corpses hit the water, the jellies lit up in response. The swarm seemed deeper this time, and Younce could see the bottom of the sea. More bodies than he cared to admit drifted there amongst the turtles and the seaweed.

He hated water. He hated jelly toxin. Fear of drowning was something that he hadn't known existed until he'd fought at Sandpiper's Dune. Only Tresh had saved him from dying that day, and even now, water that went above his head gave him a panic attack.

Erlock shouted, and Younce changed course, getting out of the way as a dozen bamboo javelins filled the air where he'd just been flying, catching several peacocks and Alabaster Eyrie forces.

The spears hadn't flown true, wounding more than killing, but the neon sea would do the rest of the work for Rorin.

Argent hawks had nearly been cleared from the skies, but an explosion on the storm curtains opened a new hole near the base, and a small team swarmed it. Younce was about to join in when petrels rose out of the water and attacked. Tresh, handicapped without her beak to bite things, slashed at the argent hawk, but he got away, trying to flutter up and out of range of her claws.

Younce flew after, hoping to help, but he was too far away. Tresh managed to force the hawk against the stormcloth near the very edge, catching a pawful of feathers and dropping her opponent down into the water.

Tresh latched onto the curtain to catch her breath. Younce breathed a premature sigh of relief, and then that section of the curtains exploded from the eyrie side.

Dozens more erupted, but he didn't see those. Instead, he saw Tresh, her mask hanging by a strap, go flying from the barrier, unconscious, and fall into the sea.

Lightning flashed seconds apart now. Tresh hit the water on her back, beak-up, but already the bodies around here were sinking into the luminescent depths. Only the thickness of the swarm where she'd hit kept her at the surface, and that wouldn't last.

Water. Jellies. Poison. Death.

Tresh.

Younce screamed at Rorin, and some carefully-aimed spears cut through the sky and gave the taiga pride leader the room he needed to dive down. If any of his body touched the jellyfish, he'd drown alongside her. But if he could just catch her harness, if he could just get enough lift...

He swooped down and only a last-minute pang of panic reminded him to lift his tail so it didn't hit the water. When he caught the top of her harness, he'd forgotten how hard it was to pull someone out of the water. He beat his wings, the tips of his primaries grazing the top of the water lightly but not touching any jellies, and just as his wings threatened to give out, he managed to pull her up.

He turned northeast, away from the conflict, away from the fighting. The only thing he could make out was the long rocks that formed Sailfin Point, but he saw several wounded there.

Some sort of green bog witch with partially-shredded wings flagged him down, and he lowered Tresh, stumbling his landing. When he rushed over to help move her on her side in case she had water in her beak, he had forgotten about her back, and he lost consciousness as his paw pad grazed a small jelly caught on her harness.

Younce had heard that for some types of poison, it was possible to build up an immunity to them. But with wasp stings, it seemed that each one made the next hurt more, and that was his experience with the jelly toxin.

Last time, he'd felt his mind floating above his body. This time, the world turned black. He thought he was flying, but the air was viscous and cold. He tried to swim up, but he couldn't find the top. When he looked down, he saw that his paws were made of stars.

He searched around, seeing more gryphons made of stars in the strange ocean in the sky. It was night, and the world was a dark blue. He swam down this time, and far below him, he could see the bog, taiga, and weald. He tried to reach them, but there was a thick film, like stormcloth, between him and the rest of the world. He slashed and bit at it, but it only wore down in small chunks. He shouted and raged, refusing to leave behind the world he loved, and the slightest break formed. He reached his paw through, lovingly caressing the cool night air, and woke up.

Zeph stood over him, Younce's Paw on his cheek. "Hey, I've missed you, too, buddy, but it looks like you've already made your choice for this season?"

Tresh was on the other side of him, mask gone, holding some of Gressle's anti-jelly toxin. "Would you like a moment alone? I could come back."

Younce withdrew his paw, coughed, then rolled onto his stomach and got up on all fours. His head was ringing. He looked up at the sky, at the fisherfolk's ocean of stars, but the storm was still raging, and the clouds blocked his view.

His brain began remembering what had happened, and he turned back to Tresh. "Are you okay? Did a medicine gryphon see to you?"

The bog witch from earlier padded over. "Hello, I am Thistle. I am glad to see you are okay. I'm headed south to take care of the wingtorn, but there are opinici at Poisonmaw who will see to both of you. Just follow the others."

Younce looked east, and there was a train of wounded walking or being carried into the aneda trees. The light was already fading from the sky, but he looked back at the Crackling Sea Eyrie.

"Satra abandoned it when the stormcloth fell," Tresh explained. "Everyone who could get out is now fleeing. At least so far, the Seraph King's forces do not follow."

Younce allowed Zeph and Tresh to guide him towards the mountains. Overhead, under cover of darkness, Ninox's pride flew out to retrieve anyone still calling for help.

"I can't believe it's gone," Younce muttered. "We were winning. What happened?"

All Tresh and Zeph had to offer were speculation. Once Younce's paws and wings both seemed to be working, Zeph went to find the rest, and an unusual escort flew down to help Younce and Tresh.

Hatzel landed away from the others and padded over, but the gust of her wings still dried Younce's fur. There was a look in her eyes, one that was sad. They hadn't exactly avoided each other since Vosk's death, but Younce knew that she had a hard time looking at any taiga gryphon and not thinking of her former lover and life-long friend.

"I hear you're both flightworthy," the saberbeak said. "I thought I'd keep you two safe. This batch is headed to my home, but I thought you might be more comfortable at Snowfall."

Younce allowed himself to be escorted south. He only wobbled in flight once, but by then they were deep over the taiga and there was no turning back. Hatzel flew beneath him and Tresh above, keeping him steady until they reached his home.

Snowfall's braziers burned brightly. Most of the wounded were going to caves throughout the mountain range, but different sets of medical supplies and food had been stored here and were being redistributed by Deracho, who hooted a greeting when they landed.

"I heard you two got shaken up a bit," the owl gryphon said. "Thanks to Naya and Orlea, I've got a handle on things here. We'll get everyone stored away fine. You two just relax."

Younce's head was still in the clouds, but he nodded and tried to look grateful. He allowed Tresh to guide him down to his home. They curled up together in his nest, but his entire body ached and wouldn't let up.

"Thank you for pulling me out of the water," she said. "Do you trust me?"

He always had, and he told her so. He let her guide him into the deepest hot springs, lighting the braziers so their flickering danced across the cavern. Then she showed him how to lie on his back and let the heat ease his pain.

He closed his eyes and just floated on the water, letting the aches and stress float away. Tresh playfully grabbed his tail with her beak and swam beneath the surface, pulling him in circles around the hot pool.

Younce didn't know when he'd dozed off. He just remembered waking up, draped over the side of the hot springs, as Tresh groomed his facial feathers.

"Deracho has placed food and a warm brazier in our room," she whispered to him. "Let us get you on your paws. It is a short distance. Do you think you can make it?"

He nodded, letting her help him out of the water. His tail dragged on the ground as he walked, but that was a tomorrow-grooming problem. Orlea showed up to re-do their bandages and check Tresh's head. She stayed until she'd seen Younce eat at least four different things from the bowl, then she left, closing the hide curtain behind her.

Tresh petted his head and groomed the water from his ears. She'd just started to say something that sounded a lot like *I love you* when sleep finally took Younce, and he began to snore.

51

REEVE OF THE CRACKLING SEA

Jonas flew through the storm despite the warnings of his bodyguards. They'd seen lightning claim many of their friends, but they didn't know the Crackling Sea the way he did. Their views were simple, superstitious.

This wasn't victory, this was *providence.* He had always been fated to claim the blue throne, and today was the day he seized his destiny.

A tear came to Jonas's eye when he entered the amphitheater. He used to come up here and play with his step-children on the balcony outside the throne room. Other opinici would fly by and chirp a greeting to him. He'd been popular, loved. The Crackling Sea had never had a reeve-consort with as much charisma as him, and he'd made sure everyone was happy.

Bodies were still being cleared from the corridors, but that was all a formality. It wasn't the Seraph King's forces who had won this battle. It was a talonful of blue opinici, fed up with having gryphons in their home, who had lit the fires that welcomed Jonas back again.

He would see to it that all were given titles, land, and power in his new government.

He stood on the balcony and breathed in the storm air. The bodyguards near him shivered in the cold, but he laughed. "Yes, let the storms wash away the blood. I'm home again. All is right in the world."

Little remained of his workshop, but he could make a new one. The library was still in good condition, though someone had walked through it with dirty paws. His portraits were all missing, the ones of him and his family, the ones of him and the blue reeve, but he could have new ones made—and there were always the ones hidden away in his consort chambers.

His victory was undermined further by finding that his old throne had been reduced to rubble. Still, he was in a kind mood. According to his agreement with the Seraph King, if he could stand in the throne room wearing the crown and trappings of his station, he was officially the Crackling Sea reeve. The throne may be gone, but promises were promises.

One of the Alabaster scribes opened a scroll protector and handed it over. By order of the king, Jonas was now a full reeve and a member of the kingdom.

And if that meant that he would have to house the Seraph King's forces? Well, that was no problem. They were marching to destroy the Blackwing Alliance and kill Jonas's enemies, after all. He was happy to help with that.

He ordered his bodyguards to clear out the throne room. Now that his dreams had come true, he wished to be alone. They protested when he walked back to the reeve's chambers, but he waved a talon to dismiss them.

He'd visited this room several times with Mally the

Nighthaunt once he'd recovered enough to travel. The straw and blood from his old mate were nearly gone, which saddened Jonas, but it was time to move on with his other plans.

Perhaps he'd chosen a bad gryphon pride to start with. The kjarrlings were barbaric, uncivilized. He could begin anew with fisherfolk gryphons, remove their wings, teach them how to live in eyries. He foresaw a future where gryphons were treated as equals. Well, if not equals, at least... members of opinicus society. Perhaps that was a better way of putting it.

He reached up to take off his crown and bracelets, their metal tentacles reaching across his body, then reconsidered. He'd wear them a little longer yet. He might be needed, and it wouldn't do for his allies to see him as anything other than regal.

He made a note to have some flamingos come in and redecorate the room, cleaning out the blood and spiders, then he twisted the pillar on the bed and listened for the click.

The wall shifted slightly, revealing the location of the hidden passage leading to his old consort chambers. They'd remain empty now. Jonas had no need of a mate. He'd loved and lost, and he refused to feel that sense of despondency ever again.

He hummed to himself as he strolled the passages of his old home in triumph. There were times when he'd lost faith, both in himself and his allies. But now he had a royal decree proving himself as a reeve. No one could deny it.

He exited the passage into his old quarters. Unlike the library, no one had removed the paintings of his old mate from this room. Perhaps no one had even found it.

A little light came from the reeve's quarters, through the passage, and into this side chamber. He looked around for another brazier to light, but there weren't any, which was strange.

He held the painting up to the dim light and stared into the eyes of the old reeve.

I love you. I am so sorry you are not here with me now. I will return the Crackling Sea to its former glory. I promise you.

He set down the painting in the corner but noticed something strange piled behind the door. It appeared to be... seaweed wraps? Fish jerky? Rimu olives? Eel skewers?

He shook his head. "Some squirrel must have moved in after I left."

He turned to leave and looked into the scarred face of death. The owl gryphon drove her claws into his stomach and stared him in the eye.

She spoke in the language of owls, a secret language, but the last two words she spoke were in common: "Black Mask."

The gryphon dropped Jonas's body, disappearing into the night. His blood pooled on the floor, and he screamed for help. His bodyguards rushed through the passages looking for him.

"I can't... die like this..." he coughed. "The king... promised..."

Someone shouted for a medic, who saw the deep wounds in his stomach and shook her head. "There's no fixing this. He's going to suffer incredible pain. I can patch him up, but this is out of my grasp."

Jonas gasped for air. "Mally... take me..."

The bodyguards looked at each other. Finally, one nodded to the medic. "Get him as stable as you can."

The other knelt to look at Jonas. "You're in the Nighthaunt's talons now. You'd better hope this is what you want."

Jonas managed to nod yes before the medic splashed his wounds with something that made them burn, and he screamed.

REEVESBANE

EPILOGUE

M onths later, Satra and her escort arrived at a secret location halfway between Poisonmaw and the glacier peak. Ninox's owls had secured the area and assured her that no one who wasn't supposed to be there had come.

Which didn't mean Satra was safe, just that she had a good idea of who might try to kill her.

She went through the long passage, smelling of bat guano, into a small room with cushions and crates. A single carefully-encased lamp sat on the center, no braziers.

Across from her were Rybalt Reevesbane, ex-Ranger Lord Ellore, and Bario. Three faces she had hoped to never see again. A branch covered in bright red rimu olives sat on the ground in front of them as an offering.

"How many other leaders did you kill after offering them the olive branch?" Satra quipped. She'd come alone because there was no one else's life she was willing to risk at this meeting.

It was difficult to read Rybalt under his tattered hood, but his tone came out amused. "Do you really want an answer to that? I could check my diary."

She hesitated, but there was no escape if they were after her life. She'd been in hiding for months now, dodging the patrols coming out from the Crackling Sea Eyrie. So far, they were content to march north. Every so often, they'd send a group through the bog to try to root out the Ashen Weald. Thus far, none had come close to their new, sunken home.

Finally, she sat down. "I'm listening."

"You have a bit of a problem." Rybalt's voice hadn't lost its amusement. "It's a situation we've all been in, trust me. So long as the Seraph King sends more troops and supplies through the Crackling Sea, you're never going to be free."

Satra pretended to examine her claws. "Let me guess. Your Blackwing reeve has a proposal for me."

"Oh, oh no," Rybalt smiled, "you misunderstand me. We're not here on behalf of *him.* This is just two reeves having a friendly chat. Now, I know the talons of the Seraph King are around your throat, and there is nothing in the world that would delight you more than to have someone else bite off that leg. But I need one simple thing in return. Reeve to reeve, as it were. No need to let the blackwings know we're doing this."

The Kjarr, or *gryphon reeve* as they insisted upon calling her, examined Rybalt. Both Bario and Ellore gave him a lot of space. She wished she knew what game he was playing.

"I can see your hesitancy," the Reevesbane said. "Allow my guests to offer you their gifts."

Ellore sighed. "I offer myself as a prisoner."

"What need have I of a prisoner?" Satra said. "Where would I even put you?"

"I want a cell with a view of the sea." Ellore's response surprised Satra. "If you give me Bruen and my pick of rangers, I can make the Alabaster Eyrie's life hell here. I just want a chance to do it."

Satra was skeptical, but she'd had letters from many of the rangers who had served with Ellore—including a salt merchant fisherfolk named Lei who had asked if Grenkin's visit to Sandpiper's Dune last year to pardon the rangers in the bog had included Ellore.

"And..." Ellore paused. "I need someone to remember Mignet with. You, Zeph, Younce, whoever is willing to speak with me. I thought I could live in the north, away from home, but I can't. I have too many memories. If I spend the rest of my life locked away in a Crackling Sea jail, it's worth it just to know that my home is free again."

"I don't speak for Mignet's other friends, but I'll see what I can do," Satra said.

Bario pulled out a map from his harness. "Officially, I do not have this map, and I am not giving it to you. You found it in the ruins of the Redwood Valley Eyrie on your own. The Blackwing Eyrie has decided that the Ashen Weald is as much a threat as the Seraph King, and we would never give you weapons like this. However, given our current... situation, I think you could make use of this against our common enemy."

"I've made no deal." Satra unrolled the map. On one side was a list of caves. Several had been crossed out, but a few had been circled and marked with a small bat icon, including the one they were currently in. Based on the signature at the bottom, this map had once belonged to Felicio the Phoenix.

"That's every saltpeter cave my father found but was unable to excavate," Bario explained. "On the back is my formula for creating your own without having to mine it. If the Seraph King believed you had access to a working flameworks, he would have destroyed you by now and taken it. Which means he is certain you don't. Just be aware the moment you use my saltpeter, that will change."

Satra folded up the map. She'd give it to Orlea. They'd need to talk about the risks involved. "What happened to Impir?"

"Escaped back to his master, presumably through Reevesport," Ellore said. "He was gone before our assassins arrived, but we'll catch up to him again."

Hooting came from outside. Ninox's weald owls seemed to be antagonizing Iony's glacier gryphons. Time was running short.

"Okay. I accept your *gifts*," she emphasized the word so they knew she wasn't giving anything in return. She looked at Bario. "Cherine and Kia send their regards and this notebook. It's everything they were able to find on bloodbeak from the Nighthaunt's personal copies of both the *Mal Grimoire* and the *Nachlass Mal*."

Bario took the notebooks with a bow.

Satra turned to the Reevesbane. "Now *you* tell me why you've really summoned me here."

"The seraph king believes himself beyond our reach because he controls the desert and the sea." The torn leather straps hanging from Rybalt's shredded mask moved as he spoke. "But that's not really true, is it? Our mutual, sandy friend controls the desert."

Satra tilted her head, seeing where this was going.

"You want the king's talons off your throat. If you convince the sand gryphons to allow me to bring an army across the desert *before* the king's forces reach Blacktalon, I will sever his supply lines and give you a fighting chance."

"Reeve Silver controls the supplies," Satra said. "You'd need to take out her, Whitebeak, and Reevesport to fulfill your promise."

Rybalt put a talon on the table between them and leaned forwards, his oily feathers glistening in the light. "I've killed argent reeves before her. If you make this deal, I can promise you an end to your occupation. All you need to do is trust me. Neither the Seraph King nor even my blackwing allies will need to know you were involved. Your sand gryphons run supply caches across the desert, one or two help guide my armies, and no one is any the wiser."

Satra rolled up the map and put it in her harness. She took a few steps before calling back, "We're leaving, Ellore."

The ex-ranger hesitated, but Rybalt waved her out. Satra exited into the light, and Ninox's owls flew down to form a barrier between her and the poisonous reeve.

Everything in Satra's soul shouted that making deals with the devil is what led to the downfall of so many prides and eyries. But this equation seemed so simple. Both she and Rybalt were at the mercy of the Seraph King. Both would benefit from this.

She sighed and turned back. "We'll send Ellore here with our answer on the next full moon. Between now and then, I'd better not see one pitohui or long-eared gryphon on my side of the border."

Rybalt bowed. "Always a pleasure, gryphon reeve. I look forward to our future partnership."

Satra turned back and disappeared into the redwood forests.

K. VALE NAGLE

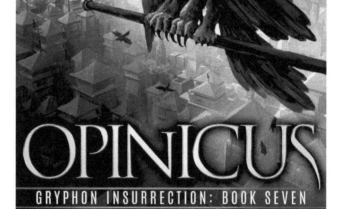

OPINICUS

GRYPHON INSURRECTION: BOOK SEVEN

KEYTHONGS AND GOD BIRDS
AUTHOR'S NOTE

First off, I'd like to apologize to everyone who read the last author's note and is getting increasingly worried by the oil in the Seraph King's lamps. I did warn you. But hey, isn't it nice to have more oilbird gryphons?

Over the last nine months, I've had a lot of fan mail, fan art, fan fiction, and people reaching out on social media. Thank you for all of your support. As exciting as it was to start IVIG treatments, they had to start at a very low dose, and I wasn't expecting to lose fifteen straight months in a row. Getting back into *Crackling Sea* was a little rough going there, but I'm approaching the dose they expect to work, and I've been feeling a lot better. I'd especially like to shout out authors Jess E. Owen and Chris Fox, both of whom did a lot to help me get back on my feet and writing well beyond my usual capabilities. And I'd like to thank Dustin Porta, who received his copy of this manuscript months later than expected but always stays in touch and works me into his editing schedule.

All-in-all, I'm doing well now. Catastrophic APS is a

tough one to treat, but as long as my body can handle the infusions, I could end this year feeling like a normal person again, which would be excellent.

Now, onto the actual gryphon-y information about *Crackling Sea!* When I proposed this series, there were several books that started out combined with other books or that I didn't realize I'd need. *Reevesbane* is one of the former. Originally, I was going to write one very large book called *Opinicus.* The more planning and work I did on it, however, the more it became apparent that the series would be better-served if I wrote a single book about everyone wronged by the *Crackling Sea* and split it off from *Opinicus.*

I'm always nervous when I do something like that. When there are conflicting themes, it works great. *Reevesbane* and *Starling* were just such a situation. But I thought to myself: Well, how long can a book about the *Crackling Sea* really be? Just how many characters have been wronged by the eyrie, the blue reeve, or Jonas?

Unless you skipped the novel to read the author's note first, you know the answer to that. For me, I had to read back through the other books to see the scope of the harm a single city had done. And as I read back through, I knew it was time to give Black Mask his first point of view scenes with Blinky tying him back to the others.

It was also refreshing to write Tresh and Younce again. It's been a long time since *Ashen Weald,* and they've always been a popular couple. It was nice to see them back together, with apologies to the people writing Rorin and Tresh fanfiction.

Speaking of Black Mask, do you know about the keythong or alce? Much like the opinicus, it isn't a gryphon type born out of mythology, rather it's a heraldic invention. The keythong came about in the fifteenth century as a flightless gryphon with its wings replaced by long spines of light. The name is a little silly, keythong more so than alce, but they were the motivation behind including the wingtorn.

(Savvy readers will remember that opinici sometimes serve a similar role in heraldry as a 'male' gryphon with no wings. I suppose the practical difference between that type of heraldic opinicus and a keythong would be if it has cat ears or not.)

White Stripe's armor from *Starling,* later the inspiration for Black Mask and Urious's armor, is a nod to the long spines of the heraldic keythong. I'm not sure if I'll reach every type of gryphon by the time the series ends, but I think I've hit most of the major beats, the ones I've always loved—including the microraptor-inspired seraphs.

Moving from mythology to ornithology, do you know of the imperial and ivory-billed woodpeckers? They're similar looking woodpeckers—black and white with red on the head. Both are (presumed) extinct now, but for the longest time, the ivory-billed woodpecker was called the god-bird because it was so rare and so often mixed-up with other woodpeckers in the area. White, black, and red are very common colors for North American woodpeckers.

The call of the imperial woodpecker was similar to a goose's honk. For the ivory-billed, it was more like a small horn in the style of a trumpet. As both birds are gone now, I had to ask an ornithologist about written descriptions of their calls. (Thank you, Oriana Pokorny!

This is definitely not the first author's note you will be thanked in.)

It's strange to me that the imperial woodpecker was mostly forgotten where I live, but the ivory-billed woodpecker became a kind of symbol of the rarest bird a bird watcher could find. What makes it special where the imperial woodpecker wasn't? What separates it from the *god bird*? Other than the location and width of its stripes, of course.

And here's where I leave you again, moving on to the next book and letting these words float between editors before reaching you months from now. A strange kind of time travel that exists even for the readers who pick this up from bookstores on launch day, an even stranger kind of time travel for those who read these words years from now, not having had to wait between *Crestfall* and *Crackling Sea*.

As always, thank you for coming along this gryphon-filled journey with me. If you're enjoying the series, leave a review, tell a gryphon-loving friend, or feel free to reach out. It was really the outpouring of fans that helped keep me going while I got back on my feet.

Keep your paws clean,
    Vale

ABOUT THE AUTHOR

K. Vale Nagle is alarmingly hard to kill.

While he's written his entire life, after surviving a pulmonary embolism and multiple organ failure, he began to take his writing more seriously and worked to get a degree in creative writing while recovering.

During that time another embolism struck and failed to kill him, at which point the doctors discovered an undiagnosed autoimmune disorder and patched him back up. Having used up two of his nine lives, he began publishing short stories and novels. When the doctors said that lung surgery was a 95% certainty, he dyed his hair dark blue, which is when he discovered that he was so unwell that his hair wasn't growing. A year later, and a switch from dark blue to teal, and his hair has finally started growing again (albeit silver instead of its pre-embolism black) and he's writing like a fiend.

Now, Vale writes feral fantasy—books with mythological creatures and nature-based settings, often involving gryphons and conflict.

He can be found online at kvalenagle.com, via his newsletter, or on Patreon.

- patreon.com/kvalenagle
- facebook.com/kvalenagle
- twitter.com/kvalenagle
- bookbub.com/authors/k-vale-nagle
- amazon.com/K-Vale-Nagle/e/B07ND33BHW

ALSO BY K. VALE NAGLE

THE GRYPHON INSURRECTION

Eyrie

Ashen Weald

Starling

Reevesbane

The Ruins of Crestfall

The Crackling Sea

Opinicus

Pridelord

SHORT STORY COLLECTIONS

Blue Eyes and Other Tales

ANTHOLOGIES

Tales of Feathers and Flames